Mark of the Raven

Books by Morgan Busse

THE RAVENWOOD SAGA

Mark of the Raven
Flight of the Raven

THE
RAVENWOOD
SAGA

BOOK ONE

MARK OF THE RAVEN

MORGAN L. BUSSE

BETHANYHOUSE
a division of Baker Publishing Group
Minneapolis, Minnesota

© 2018 by Morgan Busse

Published by Bethany House Publishers
11400 Hampshire Avenue South
Bloomington, Minnesota 55438
www.bethanyhouse.com

Bethany House Publishers is a division of
Baker Publishing Group, Grand Rapids, Michigan

Printed in the United States of America

Library of Congress Cataloging-in-Publication Data
Names: Busse, Morgan L., author
Title: Mark of the raven / Morgan L. Busse.
Description: Minneapolis, MN : Bethany House, 2018. | Series: The Ravenwood series
Identifiers: LCCN 2018019152| ISBN 9780764232220 (trade paper) | ISBN 9780764232824 (hardcover) | ISBN 9781493416165 (e-book)
Subjects: | GSAFD: Fantasy fiction.
Classification: LCC PS3602.U84496 M37 2018 | DDC 813/.6—dc23
LC record available at https://lccn.loc.gov/2018019152

Cover design by Kirk DouPonce, DogEared Design

Author is represented by The Steve Laube Agency.

19 20 21 22 23 24 25   8 7 6 5 4 3 2

To my son, Philip.
May you discover who God made you to be.

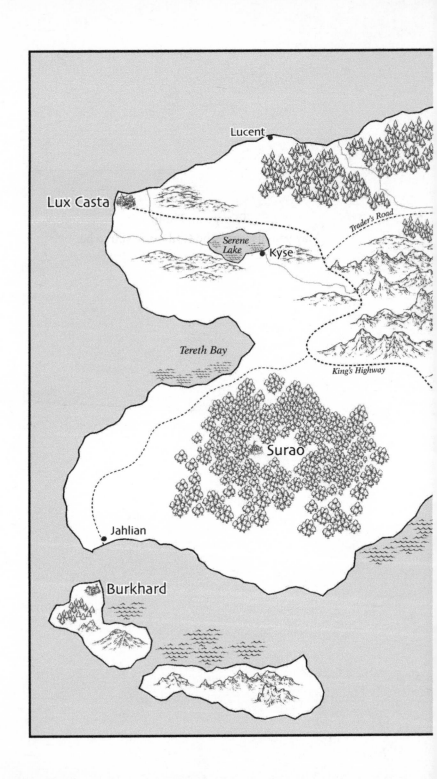

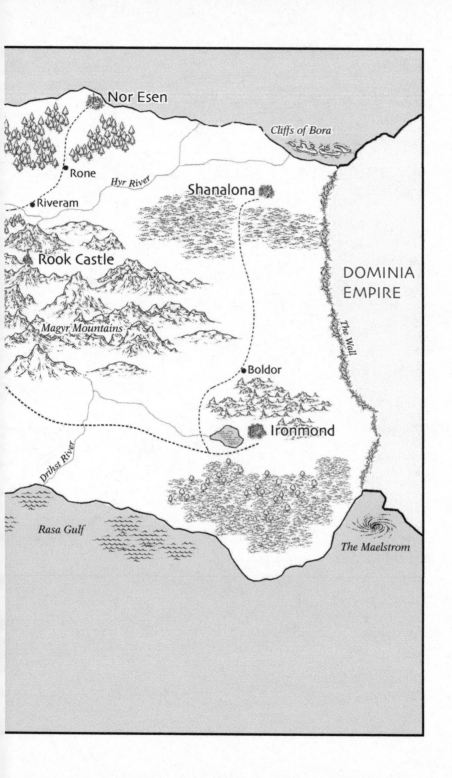

Character List

HOUSE RAVENWOOD
House of Dreamers

Grand Lady Ragna
Caiaphas (consort)
Selene
Amara
Opheliana

HOUSE MARIS
House of Waters

Grand Lord Damien
Grand Lord Remfrey (deceased)
Serawyn (consort, deceased)
Quinn (brother, deceased)

HOUSE FRIERE
House of Fire and Earth

Grand Lord Ivulf
Raoul

HOUSE VIVEK
House of Wisdom

Grand Lord Rune (brother)
Grand Lady Runa (sister)

HOUSE RAFEL
House of Healing

Grand Lord Haruk
Ayaka

HOUSE LUCERAS
House of Light

Grand Lord Warin
Leo
Tyrn
Elric
Adalyn

HOUSE MEREK
House of Courage

Grand Lord Malrin (deceased)
Grand Lady Bryren
Reidin (consort)
Terric (cousin of Bryren)

Cold.

So cold.

Every breath came out like a faint wisp, a lingering spirit within the sanctuary, only to evaporate into the frozen air.

Selene pulled her fur-lined cloak tighter around her shoulders as she knelt before the priest inside the sacred halls.

Mother knelt on her left, her head bowed and covered with her dark cloak. Amara, Selene's sister, knelt to her right. Behind them knelt a dozen other disciples, all garbed in black with hoods pulled over their heads. Wrought-iron chandeliers hung along the lofty sculpted ceiling, their braziers empty of light. Pale wintry sunlight shone across the stone floor from the tall narrow windows on either side of the sanctuary.

The priest spoke in the old tongue as he walked before the disciples. His dark robes swished along the stone floor, his boots a bare whisper. Incense rose from the golden burner that swung from his gnarled hand.

Selene's knees grew numb as they pressed into the stone floor. The incense filled her nostrils, the priest's words her mind. She did not understand the old tongue, only a few of the words. For as long as she could remember, the morning of every new moon was spent in the sanctuary, and prayers were raised to the Dark Lady.

The priest stopped in front of Selene.

She glanced up and blinked.

Pale, watery blue eyes stared down at her from sunken sockets rimmed in shadow. His head was covered with the mantle of his dark robes, but here and there tufts of woolly white hair stuck out. His nose was long and thin, with only slits for nostrils.

His eyes widened as he stared down at her in a trance. He began to speak fervently and swung the incense globe in front of Selene.

Heat rushed through her veins, burning away the chill inside her bones. She glanced at her mother, then her sister from the corners of her eyes. The priest had never done this before.

Her mother glanced back with the barest hint of surprise on her face. Amara appeared even more shocked under her otherwise cold veneer.

Selene glanced back at the priest. He suddenly stopped and went stiff. Slowly, he bent over and placed a finger on her forehead. His finger was like an icicle, and she suppressed the urge to shiver.

"The Dark Lady will be with you tonight," he said, speaking plainly for the first time. Then he moved his finger across her skin in the shape of a *T*. A sensation like ice water spread from his finger, across her face, then down her back. Selene shivered this time, and her heart thudded inside her chest. She wanted to stand and run away, but fear kept her in place. She tried to swallow, but her mouth was dry.

His finger left her forehead, and his eyes returned to their normal watery appearance. He straightened up and started chanting again in the old tongue as he turned around and headed back to the platform at the front of the sanctuary, seemingly oblivious to his trance from moments before.

Selene clasped her fingers together. She could still feel his cold finger sliding across her skin, marking her with some invisible sign. Did Mother know what it meant? She seemed as surprised as Selene at the priest's sudden gesture and words.

What did the priest mean by the Dark Lady being with her tonight?

The moment the priest finished the benediction, Selene got to her feet. Amara stood as well. Mother continued to kneel with her head bowed. For a moment, Selene wondered if she should wait, but then she turned and left. If Mother wanted to talk, she would come. Selene walked down the long corridor and past the other disciples, ignoring the hooded glances sent her way. Amara followed her toward the back of the sanctuary. The smell of incense continued to hang heavily in the air, filling her head with its overly sweet scent.

The two sisters exited through the tall double doors and entered the corridor that led toward the main rooms of Rook Castle.

Every few seconds, Amara glanced at her from beneath her hood, waiting for her to say something, but Selene remained silent. At the end of the hall, Amara grabbed her arm. "Wait!"

Selene stopped, her lips pressed together.

"What happened back there?"

Selene turned and faced her sister.

Amara pulled her hood back, releasing a cascade of dark auburn hair along her shoulders. Though she was loath to show it, there was a hint of curiosity on her otherwise sullen face. "Do you think . . . do you think he was referring to the gifting?"

If Amara's words had a physical form, it would be fire. Selene could feel the heat of her sister's jealousy and the stinging hurt in her question. If the priest's words were an indication that Selene was about to undergo the gifting, it was another log on the raging inferno between them.

"I don't know." Even those words were hard to form. It was as if the priest had silenced her and her mouth had forgotten how to speak.

Amara's face flushed and her hands clenched. "I will have my turn as well. I am also a Ravenwood. You'll see." She spun around and hurried to the left, disappearing around the far corner, leaving behind a wake of coldness.

Selene stood alone in the empty hallway, her throat tight, her gaze lingering where Amara had disappeared. She had always hoped they would serve House Ravenwood together as sisters when they came of age. If only the priest had marked Amara instead. If Amara received the gift first, perhaps it would have breached the chasm that existed between them.

Instead, a wall stood between them. Amara wanted more. She wanted power. She wanted the prestige of being a grand lady. She wanted what Selene had: the rights of the firstborn.

Instead, Selene had been born first. And . . . She lifted her hand and rubbed her shoulder. Only inches away, beneath her cloak, was the mark of the raven across her back. No other Ravenwood had borne such a distinct mark. Her mother saw it as a mark of power. To Selene, it was an eternal source of conflict between her and her sister.

Behind her, the muffled sound of voices and boots indicated the disciples were leaving the sanctuary.

Selene turned right and headed back toward Rook Castle. She had no desire to be a subject of the congregants' curious appraisals.

The farther she drew away from those hallowed halls, the more her feet felt like lead. Amara was right. The priest's cryptic words were a prophecy of her gifting. But never in the history of Ravenwood had a dark priest done such a thing. Why her? Her gift would come. It had come to every Ravenwood woman since before the time of Rabanna Ravenwood. It was not a surprise. So why the mark on her forehead? Why the utterance?

What made her gifting different than previous Ravenwood women?

Selene shuddered and folded her arms across her middle. A feeling of foreboding descended upon her with each second. She knew very little of House Ravenwood's gift, other than that it involved dreams. But whatever it was, the income it provided helped keep their people fed and clothed when the mines dried up.

That was good, right? So why the sudden alarm?

Selene pressed two fingers against the side of her head. Perhaps it was the fact that not only was she specially marked, but the Dark Lady herself would oversee her coming into her legacy.

"Why me?" she whispered. Her words echoed along the silent hallway, bouncing off the stone walls. No answer came back.

She let out a long breath and continued on. In her mind, she felt like she was standing on the edge of a cliff, about to jump into the misty emptiness below. And if she didn't jump, someone or something would push her. No matter what, there was no choice. She never had a choice. Tonight the gift of Ravenwood would come upon her. Tonight she would inherit her destiny.

The first pinpricks of pain came at dinner. Selene held still as faint flickers of light flashed across her vision like stars across a night sky, followed by prickles along her scalp. She waited for the lights to disappear as her heart beat faster and the hairs along the back of her neck stood. Through the haze of light, she watched her father as he raised his goblet to his lips. His silver hair was slicked back and his beard was perfectly trimmed, as always.

As an outsider from a lesser house of Vivek, did Father know how the Ravenwood gift came? Had Mother ever told him? Or was it another secret kept by the women of Ravenwood?

The lights passed, and Selene lifted her shaky hands and broke off a piece of bread from the platter nearby. It felt like gravel in her mouth as she slowly chewed.

Candlelight twinkled from the chandelier above, leaving the perimeter of the ancient room in shadows. Mother sat at the other end of the table, her face obscured by the golden candelabra placed in the middle. Amara sat across from her, occasionally glancing up with cold stares. Captain Stanton stood beside the door along with another guard, his dark eyes always on the Ravenwood family.

Family dinners were never warm or jovial, but tonight's dinner felt even more oppressive. Selene glanced at Father again. Did he notice?

The lights started flashing across her vision once more, followed by pricks of pain along her forehead. Were these the warning signs of things to come? How long before the gifting took hold of her body?

Perhaps she should leave now before things became worse.

Selene placed the half-eaten chunk of bread on her plate. Her soup lay untouched nearby. "Father, I'm not feeling well. May I be excused?"

Father placed his goblet down and looked at her. A frown covered his face. "Selene, you look very pale. Do you need me to call for a healer?"

Amara glanced up.

Selene brushed her fingers along her temple. "No, it's simply a headache. I wish to lie down."

He gave her an inquisitive stare, then nodded. "You may go."

Selene didn't bother to look at her mother. All she wanted to do was escape to her room before another spell took hold of—

A burst of light spread across her mind, followed by intense pain throughout her head. She almost cried out but clenched her teeth instead. She breathed through her nose. "Please excuse me," she mumbled and stood up from the long dining table.

Amara's eyes narrowed and her lips turned downward as recognition registered across her face. She had no idea how much Selene wished it was her at the moment.

Another burst of light flashed across Selene's eyes, followed by light-headedness. She needed to get to her bedchambers before the onslaught ensued.

She turned and headed for the side door, passing one of the servants carrying a wooden tray of roasted meat. The smell, rather than enticing her, only made her stomach churn.

Out in the dark corridor, the flashing lights inside her head changed to swirling colors. Selene stumbled down the long hall with her hand placed along the stone wall for guidance. The flickering candles on either side provided her only light.

She hurried toward the west wing. At the staircase, she gathered her gown and flew up the stairs, then down another cold hall until she reached the door to her bedchamber. Quickly, she entered as another round of lights and colors started across her vision, like those small, colorful explosives House Vivek would let off during the New Year celebrations.

A strange prickling sensation began on the right side of her temple as she shut the door, followed by a tingling across her back, the same place her mark was.

Selene stumbled toward her bed and fell across the thick furs and feather mattress. The tingling on her back changed to a burning. She panted as she twisted around and stared up at the heavy curtains around her bed.

The burn across her back deepened, like fire licking across her skin and leaving behind a line of singed, pulsating tissue. Sweat dripped down the sides of her face and dampened her dress and bedspread. Another round of fire came, seizing her body until it passed. Her head pounded with such intense throbs that she cried out.

The barest sliver of moon moved across the nearby window as night fell outside. The lights and colors across her vision were replaced by shadows.

Another convulsion ripped across her shoulders and mind. She curled up on her side and breathed her way through the pain. How long was this supposed to last? She tried to remember the last few months of training, but her thoughts were like moths dancing around a flame, unwilling to be caught. All she could remember was her mother saying the gifting would come with intensity, but never did she imagine it would feel like this.

Selene drifted in and out of consciousness, one moment completely submerged in darkness, the other watching the lives of those who lived here in Rook Castle unfold through muted color. All the while her body burned and an invisible ice pick was driven through her skull.

Minutes felt like hours, and hours felt like days. Sometimes she felt like she was walking through a deep mist, other times like she was watching from the outside of a window on a cold winter's night. On and on the images swirled by in the same way the courtyard looked when she danced around the spring pole on the day of the Festival of Flowers.

Slowly, the images were replaced by the softest of light. With that light, the raging pain inside her mind began to subside and every muscle in her body relaxed.

She heard a whisper inside her mind. Soft, yet powerful. Quiet, and yet like a shout for all to hear.

A dreamer has been born.

Then it was done.

Selene didn't know how long she lay in bed. She opened her eyes, half expecting to see the swirl of images again. But only the heavy bed canopy greeted her vision. She turned her head on her pillow and looked to the left. The rays of dawn trickled in through the window at the east end of her bedchamber.

The burning and aching sensation faded from her body, freeing her. But she had no desire to move. Instead, she closed her eyes. She never wanted to wake again. It was as if everything inside of her had been put through a furnace and come out as hard as steel. Her mind felt different. Her body felt different.

She was different.

"Is she awake yet?" said a low alto voice, vaguely like Mother's.

"N-Not yet." Another female voice. High-pitched and breathy.

"Then alert me when she is. I want to see her right away."

"Y-Yes, m-my lady."

There was movement, then the sound of a door shutting. Fatigue pulled Selene back under before she could open her eyes.

Full, bright sunlight filled Selene's vision. She groaned and pried her eyelids open. There was a small squeak near her bed and the loud thud of a chair hitting the stone floor. She slowly turned and looked.

A young woman no older than sixteen stumbled to her feet. A red flush filled her otherwise pale face. "M-my lady! You're a-awake!"

Selene let out a long breath and let her head sink back into the pillow. "Renata. What are you doing here?"

Renata wrung her hands in a nervous gesture and glanced at the door behind her. "L-Lady Ravenwood tasked me to watch you, and t-to let her know when you a-awoke."

"I see. How long have I been asleep?"

Renata stilled her hands and stared down at Selene. Her black hair was pulled back in a long braid and the grey dress she wore hung like a burlap sack across her thin frame. "Three days."

"Three days?" Selene sat up and instantly regretted it as stars popped across her eyes. For one moment, she feared the gifting was back, but the branding only happened once in a lifetime, and her gift was already imprinted inside of her.

"I-I must go and let Lady R-Ravenwood know you're awake." Selene brought her mind back. "Yes, go ahead, Renata. You are dismissed."

The maidservant gave her a small bow and quickly left.

Selene lay in bed, the furs pulled up across her lower half, and stared out the window. For as long as she could remember, her mother had drilled into her the responsibility she would have some day for the Ravenwood family, and the impending gift that would come. A gift that would allow her to enter the dreams of others. But no other details. Only hints that House Ravenwood and the mountain nation depended on that gift. Just training. Day in and day out.

Don't trust anyone.

You can only count on yourself.

You must be prepared for anything.

We will never be wiped out again.

Her mother's mantra, spoken every morning during training. Mother drove her and Amara hard, teaching them their secret family history and training them the moment they could lift a sword.

Someday when you have your gift, you will think you can rely solely on that. But you can't. You need to know how to protect yourself. Always. Because no one else will.

But never a reason why. Never an answer to all the questions that Selene longed to ask. Nothing to ease the yoke that had been upon her since birth.

"*Someday,*" her mother would say. "*When your gifting comes, I will reveal to you why. Until then, train. Train hard.*"

"Well, Mother. I am your heir now. And I am ready for answers," Selene whispered.

Almost in response, the door crashed open, and her mother flew in as if carried on wings. She came to the bedside and stared at Selene. Selene stared back. Her mother looked every inch like the matriarch of House Ravenwood. She possessed the thick dark hair of the Ravenwood women, along with high cheekbones and full lips. She was tall, but not too tall, elegant, and lean from years of secret training. She could move an assembly with her smooth alto voice and trap a man into doing anything for her. Sometimes Selene wondered if that was how Father came to marry her.

Her eyes bore fully into Selene and a glint entered those dark orbs. "Leave us," she said to Renata without turning to address the quivering servant girl.

Renata did not need to be told twice. She fled without the customary bow, the door thudding shut behind her.

Mother did not seem to care. "My dear, dear daughter," she said as she pulled the wooden chair to the side of the bed. "I had feared . . . but no. The Dark Lady has seen fit to bless our house with another dreamer." She let out her breath. "At last."

Her words felt like heavy stones placed upon Selene's chest. There it was again, that word. *Dreamer.*

"We will start your training tonight. Your gifting could not have come at a better time. There are things in motion, things I cannot do alone." Her mother's eyes went out of focus for a moment. "But all will be right again." She smiled and beamed down at Selene. "You will dreamwalk. Test out your gift. I'll be sure to prepare the servant you will use."

Servant? Selene blinked and clutched the furs between her fingers. What did a servant have to do with using her gift? Would she be walking inside the servant's dream?

"If your birthmark is any indication, your gift is powerful,

Selene. A gift we need if House Ravenwood is to survive. And survive we will. We will never fail again. And you will make sure of that."

Selene responded in the way she had been brought up. "Yes, Mother." But her insides clenched. What exactly did they do in dreams?

Her mother stopped and studied her. The sunlight cast a brilliant light across her mother's face, sharpening her features so that Selene could almost see the raven in her face. "There is no room for weakness. And you are not weak. You are my daughter and heir to House Ravenwood. Do you understand?"

An invisible hand clawed at Selene's throat, but she was still able to push out the rote words. "Yes, Mother."

"Good. You will be the one to elevate House Ravenwood back to its former glory. I believe you have the ability to surpass me. Perhaps even Rabanna herself." She stood and pressed her skirt down. "I will send your maidservant back in. Proceed with your training and other duties today. And then tonight we will begin your real training."

My l-lady?" a timid voice called out.

Selene glanced at the door, her mother's words still echoing inside her mind. *Tonight we will begin your real training.*

"Yes, Renata, you may come in." She flung the furs from her legs as Renata entered with a set of dark clothes hanging over her arm.

"L-Lady R-Ravenwood sent me b-back." Renata's voice was breathless, and she trembled at the mention of Mother's name. "Here." She thrust the clothes out, standing as far from Selene as she could.

Selene sighed as she stood and took the garments. No matter how gentle she was with the servant girl, Renata was as timid as ever. And Mother's authoritative way with the servants didn't help.

She crossed the room toward the changing screens in the corner. Images of House Ravenwood's past were embroidered across the screens, of elegant ladies and gallant men on horseback. Long ago, House Ravenwood had been one of the most renowned across the seven provinces. Now it was only a shadow of what it once was. And only select few knew that they still retained their gift.

Selene stripped off her stained dress and chemise and hung

both over the screen. Then she paused. Turning, she pushed her dark hair aside and glanced in the long mirror against the wall. In its reflection, she saw across her back a mark of light blue-grey, spread across from shoulder blade to shoulder blade like wings emerging from her spine.

Almost every Ravenwood woman carried such a mark, although one like hers had not been seen since her ancestor Rabanna. Mother believed it signified her gift would be exceptional. Selene wasn't sure if she wanted that.

She twisted, studying the mark from every angle in the mirror. Nothing had changed, despite the pain she went through during the gifting. It looked the same as ever. She let out a sigh of relief and let her hair fall back into place. Perhaps Mother was wrong.

Selene slipped into a fresh chemise and undergarments, then pulled a dark blue dress over her head and tightened the sash around her waist. When she emerged from the screens, Renata had pulled the wooden chair from the table over to the window and was waiting with a brush in hand.

Selene sat down without a word. Renata had been serving her for a year now, a refugee from a bandit attack and a quiet girl. Despite her shy demeanor and small stature, she was a hard worker and knew how to keep secrets, an absolute when serving House Ravenwood.

Renata started brushing Selene's thick, sleek hair. By the time she was done, there was a blue sheen to the black strands. With deft hands, Renata braided the hair into a long plait.

Selene glanced at Renata in the reflection of the window. "Thank you, Renata."

The girl blushed, bringing color to her pale cheeks, and bobbed her head.

Someday Selene would draw that shy girl out.

After Renata left, Selene stood and leaned against the side

of the window. A bright blue sky hung over the rugged Magyr Mountains that surrounded Rook Castle. There was no way in or out of the castle except by the wide stone bridge that connected Rook Castle to King's Highway, which ran through the mountain country. At least that was the only path most people knew about.

Selene leaned forward and looked down. Jagged rock teeth lay hundreds of feet below. Somewhere between those serrated edges were unseen paths inside the mountains, caverns and mines from the old days, now abandoned. Only the women of Ravenwood knew of those paths and the ins and outs of Rook Castle.

For a moment, she imagined what her life would be like if she headed down to one of the caverns and left this place. There was one that opened up on the far northern side of the Magyr Mountains, near one of the valley villages. Maybe she would make her way west toward the country of House Luceras. She had heard it was a land of lush green hills and cities made of beautiful alabaster stone. Or maybe she would go east and visit her father's country, House Vivek, where the ancient libraries were kept and people dedicated their lives to knowledge.

Selene laughed sadly to herself. "Maybe I'll spring wings from my back and fly away."

She dipped her head. If Mother knew her thoughts right now, of wanting to run away rather than embrace her heritage . . . Such cowardly thoughts unbefitting a woman of House Ravenwood.

Ravenwood women were strong. They were powerful. Selene was inheriting the might and legacy of the women who had gone before her.

Yet all she could feel was the weight of her house and people settle across her shoulders.

Selene left her bedchambers and headed for the training rooms below Rook Castle, located in a large cavern that had been carved out by Rabanna to instruct future generations of Ravenwood women. Here they trained, honing their physical abilities in secret.

Selene followed the stone halls deeper into Rook Castle, padding silently by the servants and other members of the family until she reached one of the rooms in the southern wing. It was implied that the Ravenwood women spent the morning doing needlework in this part of the castle and only Hagatha, her mother's maid, was allowed to disturb them. Only Hagatha knew of the secret passage beside the faux fireplace and the hidden training room below.

Selene entered the room and gently closed the door behind her. Wide windows graced the comfortable and tastefully decorated room. Tall wooden chairs with embroidered cushions were set in a half-circle around the fireplace, complete with baskets of colorful spools of thread and squares of linen for needlework. But needlework had never been done in this room. Briefly she wondered what it would be like to actually do the things noblewomen of other houses spent their time doing. Not that she was interested in the needlework itself, but perhaps the normality the other houses seemed to have. Then again, perhaps they had secrets of their own.

Selene crossed the room toward the right side of the fireplace. With precision and memorization, she placed her fingers in the three holes within a faint indented circle hardly noticeable in the stone wall and twisted clockwise. Gears groaned deep within. Seconds later, the wall slid to the left, revealing a narrow passage. Selene slipped in and used another hidden switch to close the opening behind her.

Down the dark stone tunnel she went until she reached a set of interlinked caverns, each one lit by torches hung along the walls. The *thumps* and *whacks* sounding across the cavern walls indicated Amara was already here.

Selene went into the nearest cavern, a small one, where black clothes were laid out on a slab of rock. Quickly, she changed out of her blue gown and into the loose-fitting clothes, then grabbed the set of swords that hung on the wall behind the slab of stone, one sword slightly longer than the other.

She headed for the larger room. The noise in the main cavern had stopped. As she approached, she spotted Amara standing in the archway that led into the training room, her sword hanging at her side, her face glistening with sweat.

"Selene," Amara said with a slight lift of her chin.

"Amara," Selene answered, preparing for the verbal barrage.

"So did it happen?" There was no excitement in Amara's voice, no congratulations. Instead, years of contention were vivid across her face.

As Selene stared at her younger sister, she wished at that moment they were closer, with the kind of relationship where she could share what the gifting had felt like, and her apprehension about this evening and what Mother was going to teach her. But Amara would not have it.

"Yes." Selene let a cold mask fall across her features, her defense mechanism against Amara's heated jealousy.

"And . . . what was it like?" A small flame of curiosity sparked in her eyes.

Selene readjusted her grip on her swords. "It was just as Mother said it would be: intense and painful."

Amara's lips curved upward as if savoring Selene's words. "Painful, was it?" Then her face went back to its hard features. "Will you start dreamwalking tonight?"

"Yes." Selene's stomach tightened at the thought.

Amara watched her with keen eyes, but Selene's face revealed no indication of her apprehension. After a moment, Amara's face turned sullen and she spun around and headed back into the main room.

Selene dropped her shoulders. She wished again that Amara's

gifting had come first; maybe then it would have brought them together instead of driving them further apart.

The cavern was set up much like the training grounds in the barracks. Torches cast an orange light across the stone walls. Straw-stuffed dummies were propped up, some showing more wear than others. A table sat in the back with leather whips, swords and knives of different sizes, and a set of brass knuckles her great-grandmother had wielded.

Selene preferred her own twin blades, employing the ancient dual-blade technique that Rabanna had brought back from the Dominia Empire and improved upon for House Ravenwood's own use.

Amara swung at one of the more worn dummies with her single blade, her hair swishing around her face. Selene watched her sister. Their fighting styles were different. Amara attacked with passion and ferocity, while Selene's own style was more of a calculated dance. For a brief moment, she wondered what their little sister Opheliana would be like when she grew older. The youngest Ravenwood had come as a surprise to her parents. And knowing how much they detested each other, Selene sometimes wondered how another daughter had come to be.

Selene headed across the room from Amara toward her own dummy and raised her blades to begin her exercises. Maybe she would drop by the nursery later to see Ophie. The nursemaid had said she was showing signs of talking soon. Selene hoped so. With each passing year, whispers were spreading around the castle that something was wrong with Opheliana, that the youngest Raven-wood female was cursed. Maybe Selene could coax some words out of her little sister. The thought brought a small smile to her lips.

Selene paused an hour later, her blades in the air, and glanced over at the stone archway nearby. Lady Ragna Ravenwood stood in the doorway, dressed in the same dark, loose-fitting clothing Selene and Amara wore. Her black hair was pulled back into a single braid, with only a sprinkling of grey amongst the dark strands.

Selene lowered her blades and walked over. "Mother," she said with a slight bow.

"Selene."

Mother turned around and started down the tunnel. "Walk with me, Selene."

Selene caught sight of Amara's hurt features before she turned and joined her mother. A sliver of pity entered her heart for her sister. Mother could have at least acknowledged Amara.

Their soft-skin boots barely whispered across the stone floor as the two ladies headed down the tunnel. "I had business with House Friere this morning, or else I would have been here earlier," her mother said, her voice echoing across the walls. "However, the news is in our favor. Someone within House Friere is interested in engaging our services."

Never had Mother spoken openly about the family business before. Unease spread through Selene.

"It is good that you will be dreamwalking tonight and testing out your gift. Soon I will be needing your abilities."

Mother's words echoed inside her mind and made her stomach churn. However, she answered in a clear voice. "Yes, Mother."

Her mother stopped and looked at her. "The coffers are running low and the silver mines in the south have not produced as much as we had hoped. Therefore, it falls on us again to provide for our people." Over and over again, as long as she could remember, it had been drilled into Selene that their people came first—by whatever means necessary. The torchlight along the walls sharpened her mother's features. Her ebony eyes bore into Selene. "You must learn quickly if you are to help our people."

Her throat tightened. "I understand."

Mother nodded. "I look forward to seeing what you are capable of."

What she was capable of? Selene hardly knew herself. Once again, the weight of who she was sank into her soul. Her family's future—and that of all the mountain people—rested on her gift. The very thought brought on a sudden wave of dizziness.

Mother didn't seem to notice. Instead, she glanced down the tunnel where the faint sounds of Amara's training echoed. "No more training today. You will need your rest for this evening. When the moon rises, meet me in the upper room. In the meantime, I will work with your sister."

Selene bowed once more, then left her mother standing in the tunnel. Amara would be pleased to have their mother to herself this morning. Selene might have the stronger gifting, but Amara had passion, something Mother did not seem to realize.

After sponging off the sweat from her workout and changing back into her gown, Selene made her way up the narrow passage and back into Rook Castle. In some ways, the split between castle and tunnels mirrored her own life: upstairs where she lived out her public life as Lady Selene Ravenwood, and down in the tunnels where privately she trained as the next heir to House Ravenwood.

What would it be like to just have one life? To simply be a lady of a Great House, where her only occupation would be an education in politics, the running of a household, and preparing for a future marriage alliance with another house?

Selene entered the small sitting room and pressed her fingers into the three indents, closing the secret door behind her. She looked around the sitting room, noting the thin layer of dust across the high-back chairs and the empty fireplace.

Was that what life was like for the ladies of the other Great

Houses? Did Lady Adalyn Luceras sit every morning and work on a tapestry? Did Lady Ayaka Rafel meet with the steward to go over that day's procedures?

Selene left the sitting room and headed to the library to continue her studies of the seven Great Houses, knowledge she would need to have when she took over House Ravenwood as grand lady someday.

Every house had their secrets—secrets bound by blood or by marriage. The only people who knew of the Ravenwood gift of dreamwalking were the Ravenwood women, their consorts, and whomever the grand lady of Ravenwood told. The rest of the family was bound to silence, willingly or unwillingly.

When she was young, she had tried to explain the gifting to her nursemaid, but instead of speaking, she had stood there with her mouth open and no sound. Later, Father had explained to her that only the head of a Great House could speak of the house secrets.

"But what about you, Father? Why can I speak to you about it? You're not a Ravenwood."

Father sighed and placed his book down on the small side table. "Because I am bound to your mother through marriage. When the words of bonding are spoken, all family secrets between the man and the woman are revealed. That is why many times those of a Great House choose to marry someone from a lesser house, to keep those secrets from the other Great Houses."

Selene wrinkled her face. "So, when you and Mother married, you found out about our gift?"

"Yes, the moment I spoke the words of rite while holding your mother's hands."

"And what did you think?"

Her father looked out the window nearby at the craggy peaks

of the Magyr Mountains. "I—like most people—had believed the gift of dreaming had died out. It was a shock to find out the gift of the dreamer still existed. The women of Ravenwood have hidden their gift well for many years."

"But you can never tell anyone."

"No, I cannot. It is not my secret to tell."

"And that's why Mother married you, because you were from a lesser house."

He turned back, his face impassive. "Yes."

"Will I be forced to marry someone from a lesser house someday?"

"Most likely. As heir of Ravenwood, someday the house secret will become yours."

"But what if I married someone from one of the Great Houses?"

Her father shook his head. "Your mother would never let that happen."

"But what if I did?"

"Then one of the Great Houses would know your secret."

"And I would know theirs."

Her father laughed. "Most of the Great House gifts are known, and most of them have grown weak over the centuries."

Selene cocked her head to the side. "Or so we think."

Her father sobered and nodded. "Yes, you are right. It was not supposed to be like this when the gifts were bestowed upon the seven Great Houses. The houses were given these gifts to help their people work together for the good of all. Sadly, greed, ambition, and pride fractured the unity between the houses."

"Do you think there could be unity again someday?"

He stood up from his chair. "I hope so, Selene. I hope so."

Selene opened the door to the library, the memory of that day fading away as she entered. Since then, Father no longer answered her questions, almost as if he had been silenced in the same way she could not speak of the family gift.

She sighed and closed the door behind her. Rows and rows of shelves lined either side of the long, narrow room. Leather-bound books and tomes dating from the first grand lady of Ravenwood lined the bookcases. The faint smell of dust, smoke from an old fire, and aging paper filled the room.

She glanced at the empty chair in the far corner, right next to the set of windows that looked out onto the Magyr Mountains. She missed those conversations with her father.

"Preparation must be done before you dreamwalk." Lady Ragna stood in the darkest corner of the hallway where the moonlight could not reach. "You must study the sleeper, use the skills you've developed to infiltrate his or her room, move in complete silence. But none of this matters if the sleeper awakens. That is why you must also be aware of your surroundings while inside the dream."

Selene stood beside her mother, dressed all in black, her long hair pulled back in a braid that hung down to her waist. "And how do I do that?"

"Being in the dreamscape is like being underwater. You are moving, hearing, feeling the water, but you are still aware of what is happening on the surface. Same with the dream world. You will be inside the dreamscape—hearing, feeling, experiencing the dream of the sleeper—but you must also be aware of your surroundings outside the dream. To make tonight's visit simple, I placed a sleeping draught inside Petur's drink. When on a mission, this isn't always possible, which is why you mustn't rely on sleeping herbs but rather be vigilant, both inside and outside the dream."

Her mother's explanation somewhat made sense. Hopefully

she would understand more once she was inside the dream. "We are entering the gardener's dreams? Why him?"

"He has a tragic past, one that will be easy to manipulate for your first dreamwalk."

Manipulate? Selene crossed her arms, an empty feeling expanding inside her stomach. What did that mean?

"And remember, do not dreamwalk in your human form."

"Yes, I remember." Although how exactly she was going to change form, she wasn't sure. Mother had explained the basics of dreamwalking when her training had first started, but hearing about it and actually doing it were two different things.

"One more thing. It can be difficult to enter a dream the first time."

Selene looked up.

"Dreamwalking is entering the river of consciousness inside another person. And much like a real river, entering and navigating a flowing stream can be difficult at first."

"Are some people's dreams more difficult to enter than others?"

"Yes."

Selene waited, but her mother did not elaborate, tapping her fingers across her forearms in unease. Minutes ticked by as the moonlight moved across the floor beneath a nearby window.

"It is time." Without waiting for Selene, her mother moved along the hallway like a shadowy apparition, blending in with the darkness of the night.

Selene followed, her footsteps as silent as her mother's. Down to the first floor they went, and then outside through the servants' courtyard. After checking for anyone about, they headed to the other end of the courtyard. At the corner, they turned left and went toward one of the doors that lined the square.

Her mother stopped at the farthest one. She glanced around, then quietly opened the door.

The door gave a small creak. Selene held her breath, but nothing moved. They both entered the small dwelling. The one-room home was barely half the size of one of the bedchambers inside the castle. A table sat against the wall, next to a small fireplace. There were no personal items, no handmade touches, no flowers or herbs hanging from the rafters, not even a rug on the floor. The place was as bare as a dungeon cell.

Next to the fireplace was a sleeping mat with a figure slumbering away beneath a threadbare blanket.

An ache filled Selene's throat. She had known Petur for as long as she could remember. The old, scarred man tended the herb and flower garden on the other side of Rook Castle. He had a gift for coaxing bright and colorful plants out of the cold, hard Magyr Mountains. Once he had given her one of the mountain daisies from the garden when he caught her watching him. She had kept that flower in her room long after it had wilted and died.

Selene approached his slumbering form and knelt down beside her mother. He looked so frail and small on his sleeping mat. And his room . . .

She looked around again and felt a pang in her heart. There was no warmth here, no love. Not even a flower. Why?

"You must make skin contact in order to enter his dreams," her mother whispered.

Selene turned her attention back to Petur.

"It doesn't matter where. You just need a point of contact between your skin and his." She nodded to herself. "His arm will do."

Selene spotted one of his arms sticking outside the blanket. He wore a loose tunic, leaving his wrist and forearm exposed.

"Are you ready?" There was an eager glint in her mother's dark eyes.

Selene forced her body to relax and took a breath. Now to see if she was truly as gifted as her mother believed her to be. She reached over and held her hand over Petur's arm. He slept on, oblivious to the two women at his side. Her fingers tingled, and her heart beat faster.

Then she clamped her fingers around his forearm.

M other said the first time would be the hardest.

She was wrong.

Selene slipped into the dreamscape the moment her fingers touched Petur's bare arm, as if she were submerging herself into one of the hot springs hidden beneath Rook Castle. As she passed into the dream world, she imagined one of the ravens used as couriers for House Ravenwood. In response, her body began to change. Her neck elongated while her back arched. Her arms and fingers grew longer as black feathers sprouted along her body. Her legs shortened and her head changed. Within seconds, she gave out a caw and flapped her wings.

She blinked her eyes. She felt the same and yet different. She tested her wings—such a strange sensation. And she knew what to do next, as if she had always been a raven. With a flap of her wings, she lifted up from the ground and rose above Petur's dreamscape.

Somewhere in the back of her mind, she could still sense the small one-room cabin, and where her fingers were wrapped around Petur's forearm, but it was just as Mother had said: like being underwater, barely aware of what was happening on the surface.

She looked around the dreamscape as she flew. She had expected some sort of color, perhaps faded like an old tapestry left in the sunlight, but color nevertheless. However, only a forest of black, grey, and white spread out beneath her. Tall, bare oak trees were scattered as far as the eye could see, save for one bare spot in the middle of the black forest.

Selene pumped her wings and glided along the wind toward the open area in the middle of the trees. As she drew closer, she spotted a cabin in the midst of the bare area. It was old and decrepit, with the thatched roof in disrepair and gaps between the hay.

She circled down and landed on one of the branches of a nearby oak tree and scanned the area until she spotted Petur. The old man stood silently beyond the tree line. At first he seemed surprised to find himself in this place. Then the surprised look morphed into shock as he took in the old cabin. He grabbed his chest with a clawlike grip and took a step back. "No," he moaned. "Not this . . ."

Selene looked around again, then watched Petur with a furrowed brow. Whatever Petur's past, it had to do with the decrepit cabin. Selene shifted her claws across the branch, her small body filling with unease.

A moment later, she left the bare branch and flew toward the cabin. She landed on the ground a few feet away and hopped toward the decaying structure. On closer inspection, she could see there had been a fire, though not recently. The wood around the windows was charred and black. More areas of charring pockmarked the walls.

Selene narrowed her eyes. Perhaps if she touched the cabin, she would understand what this place meant. She reached out her wingtip and brushed the side of the cabin. The dreamscape changed.

The monochromatic world transformed to a vivid red. Fire burst from the cabin, accompanied by screams and cries for help. The screams grew higher in pitch as the flames roared and smoke streamed toward the night sky.

The door opened, and a boy came flying out. He ran a couple of steps, then toppled to the ground. Seconds later, he pushed up on his knees and looked back. The skin across his right cheek was red and peeling, and his hair was singed around his face. His eyes watered and his face scrunched up. "No!" he screamed as he scrambled up and went back toward the cabin. "Mama! Papa!"

Selene's breath caught in her throat as she glanced back at the cabin. The screaming inside had stopped, and the smell of burnt flesh began to permeate the area.

"No!" The boy ran as close as he could to the cabin, then held back as the flames roared into an inferno. He dropped to his knees, his glassy gaze on the cabin. "No," he whispered. "You can't leave me!"

The fire continued to burn and parts of the roof crashed down, sending a wave of smoke and embers into the sky.

Selene yanked her wing back, and the fire, smoke, and burnt smell disappeared. She stood again in the empty area, the dreamscape devoid of color. Petur sniffled behind her.

Adrenaline coursed through her body, and her wings trembled at her sides. She slowly looked back at Petur. Now she understood where the scars across his face had come from. He wiped his eyes and stared at the cabin. "It was all my fault. I should have listened to you. I—I miss you both."

"It was Petur who burned his parents alive."

Selene jumped and glanced over to find her mother in raven form next to her.

"This event has been both his guilt and his fear for many years, and both are easily manipulated. Watch and learn."

Her mother spread out her wings, and then gave them a hard thrust. The dreamscape changed along the wind from her wings. Fire sprang up all around them, devouring the black-and-white images.

The adult Petur stood, his eyes wide. Her mother gave her wings another pump. The trees around the clearing caught fire as if they had been doused with oil.

"Can you feel his fear?"

Selene shivered and closed her eyes. Yes, somewhere deep inside of her where she was physically connected with Petur she could feel his fear growing by the second as the fire rushed forward, surrounding him.

"The mind is a powerful thing. And so are dreams. Once you know what a person fears, you can manipulate their dreams. Terrify them enough and you can kill them with it."

Petur cried out in fright as the fire consumed everything around him, leaving only a ten-foot circle of bare ground around him.

"But sometimes it is better to use guilt." With another sweep of her wings, her mother made the fire disappear. The scorched cabin came back, along with the bare trees. "Watch."

There was a rustling noise inside the cabin. Petur stood at a distance, his face even more pale in the black-and-white world. Two figures emerged from the cabin, shuffling across the open space. Their faces were burnt and only bits of hair dotted the head of the shorter figure. Singed clothing hung from their bodies like grey burial clothes.

"Why?" the shorter one rasped. "Why did you leave us?"

"I—I—" Petur sputtered as he took a step back, his eyes so wide the whites could be seen and his Adam's apple bobbing up and down.

"You did this to us," the taller one said in a broken whisper. "We know."

"But I—" A choked cry sounded from Petur, like a rabbit pierced by an arrow.

Selene turned away. She didn't want to watch anymore.

Her mother looked at her, then swished her wings and the dreamscape returned to its former gloomy appearance. Petur whimpered nearby, but Selene didn't look at him. Ever since she was a little girl, she had felt sorry for the old gardener with his scarred face and droopy appearance. Now she knew what had caused his disfigurement.

A sob filled her throat. He didn't deserve this. His dreamscape was already dark and lonely without his past horrors revisiting him.

Selene wanted to fly far away from this place, from Petur's heartbreaking cries, and from her mother's cold, callous look.

"Come, Selene," her mother said a moment later. "It is time we left this place."

"Yes, Mother," she said, barely holding back the choke inside her throat.

Selene followed her mother upward, away from the dark woods and lonely little scorched cabin, and away from the weeping man below. But she would never forget what she had seen here. It had torn a hole inside her heart.

Selene gasped as she drew back into her own body.

Her mother let go of Petur's arm and sat back, her eyes trained on Selene. "It's not easy the first time. The connections we make with the people we touch are powerful. It causes our hearts to open up to them, to feel for them. You must harden yourself to that, or else you will not be able to do what needs to be done."

"But why?"

"Why what?"

"Why did we visit that awful memory of Petur's?" Her lip began to tremble, so Selene bit down in order to stop it.

Her mother gave her a hard stare. "This is what we do. We discover people's greatest secrets and fears. This is our ability—our gift. It is how we have been able to take care of our people and keep House Ravenwood safe for hundreds of years. What good would it be if we only walked through good dreams? We cannot use those. Fear, however, we can use. And secrets. Those are what people are willing to pay for."

"People pay us for that?"

"Yes. We find information when we dreamwalk and we sell it."

This was how they used their gift? In a dark, twisted way, it made sense. And it made her stomach turn.

Selene put on her steely gaze and swallowed the bile filling her throat. "I understand." She didn't want her mother to see how shaken she was.

"It will take some time. Even I struggled at first." Her mother brushed her hands across her loose black pants and rose to her feet. "But with practice, you will learn to distance your feelings for people, and manipulating dreams will become easier."

Selene stood and joined her, gripping her hands together. "But if we are doing this for our own people, what prevents us from growing cold toward them?"

Her mother nodded. "That is a fine line we walk. It's about control, Selene. You must control yourself. Imagine locking your heart up in a chest. You only let it out when you need to. No more, no less. I've watched you over the years. You are excellent at restraining yourself, unlike your sister Amara. That is why our family line must fall to you."

Her stomach quivered inside her and once again the overbearing weight of the Ravenwood family settled across her shoulders. The future of her family—of her people—rested on her.

She swallowed. The future rested on her ability to manipulate the dreams of others.

Mother glanced out the small window on the other side of the cabin. Petur scrunched up his face and moaned.

Selene looked down at the old man. Was he still dreaming of his parents even though they had left his dreamscape? Mother didn't seem to care.

"Morning is coming. It is time we left."

Selene glanced up and noticed the first rays of light trickling through the dirty window.

Mother led the way out of Petur's small home. He moaned again as Selene walked through the doorway and closed the door softly behind her. The irony did not escape her that though her mother was teaching her to use the family gift in order to help their people, she had no qualms about hurting those same people.

When had her mother lost her heart?

4

Selene hit the dummy as hard as she could with her twin blades. *Thwack. Thwack.* Over and over she went through her routine until sweat poured across her body and her hair stuck to her face. But no matter how hard she tried, she could not run from the memories of the dreamscape from last night.

How do I—smack—*learn to*—smack—*control my heart?*

The darkness of the training cavern felt more stifling than comforting. Maybe she should have used the small outside area located in the inner bailey for her daily drills.

She gave one last lunge, then hung her hands at her sides, her fingers barely wrapped around the hilts.

Do I even want to control my heart? How do I help my people if I lock away my connection to them? Is this the only way to help our people?

Do I want to become like Mother?

"Selene."

Selene spun around. Amara stood in the archway, dressed in the dark training clothes, her sword at her side.

Selene's cheeks burned as she realized she had been so consumed with her thoughts and training that she never heard Amara enter the cavern. A first.

Amara sauntered across the room, reminding Selene of the cats that occupied the stables. She stopped near the wall and leaned against the stone in a casual manner. But her eyes gave her away. There was a feverish glint in her dark brown gaze similar to the one their mother wore the night before. "So what is it like?"

Selene turned back toward the dummy and slowly began her movements again.

"The dreamwalking," Amara said, a little more urgently.

"It is . . . different."

"Different? How?"

She paused, her swords held on either side of her body. How much should she tell her sister? Should she prepare Amara for what would happen when her own gifting came? Of what would be expected of her? Selene raised her right sword and swung hard at the dummy. She had a feeling Amara would have no problem manipulating dreams. She would do anything for Mother.

"Was it hard to enter the dreamscape?"

"No."

Amara scowled and looked away. "Are you really as gifted as Mother says you are?"

Selene stared at the dummy. "Apparently so. But I still have much to learn."

Amara looked back, the scowl replaced with a smirk. "Then you don't know everything."

"No, I don't." Selene raised her blades and with one swift movement, brought them together across the hay-stuffed canvas.

"Will you be going back again tonight?"

Selene stopped. Mother hadn't said so, but she had a feeling they would be visiting Petur again, and this time she would be the one manipulating the dream. Or at least trying. "Probably."

Lock your heart away, Selene. Control it.

Silence extended across the cavern.

"You won't tell me any more." It was a statement, not a question from Amara.

Selene glanced at her sister from the corner of her eye. They hardly looked alike. Selene had taken after their mother while Amara had taken after their father, back before his hair went grey. But out of the two girls, Amara was more like their mother than Selene was.

Mother had said Selene had the control it would take to manipulate the dreamscape without being caught up in the feelings of the dreamer. But Amara had the drive to become the next Lady Ravenwood. She would do anything Mother told her and would work hard until she had perfected manipulating the dreamscape.

Meanwhile, I'm questioning the very practice of our family dating back hundreds of years. Perhaps I am the weak link.

Amara huffed and turned away, her shoulders and back rigid.

Selene closed her eyes and sucked in a deep breath. Why didn't she tell Amara about the dreamscape, or about seeing Petur's horrible past, or how Mother could manipulate it all with a brush of her wing?

She swallowed and lifted up her swords and started her drills in earnest. As the answer came to her, she hit the dummy even harder until bits of hay came loose from the canvas fabric.

Because I'm ashamed of what I saw. And I'm ashamed of what I'll be asked to do next.

"Do it."

Selene lifted her wings. As she did so, she could feel her connection to Petur's dream, almost like strings on a marionette and she was the puppeteer. A tug here, a pull there, and she could manipulate everything around them.

"Set the forest on fire like I showed you."

Selene glanced at Petur's prone figure near the edge of the

clearing. His fear was already growing and not a single spark had fallen. A thought struck her. Just how many times had Mother come here and practiced her gift on the old man?

Selene clicked her beak together and swept her wings across the forest. An inferno rose with such speed and heat that her mother gave out a caw and sprang for the air.

Selene never wanted to come here again. Perhaps if she proved to her mother that she was more than capable of controlling the dreamscape, she would not have to come here anymore.

As the fire rose, so did Petur's fear. She wanted to stop, but it wasn't enough.

Lock your heart away. She clamped her beak shut, willing away all emotion until all she felt was cold. Just when she was sure Petur would go wild with terror, she swept her wings forward and the fire disappeared. Before her mother could say anything, she flew upward, higher and higher until she broke through the dreamscape.

Selene sat back and panted. A cold sweat had broken out across her body, seeping into her dark clothes. A shiver tore through her, and she wrapped her arms across her midsection.

Her mother came to a moment later, slightly short of breath. "That was excellent work, Selene. Never has a Ravenwood been able to manipulate a dreamscape so quickly after receiving the gift. You are truly as talented as Rabanna. But . . ." She stood and straightened her clothing. "You still need to practice. You need to learn how to find a person's fear within the dream. Sometimes it is hard to find. And you must avoid the soul when you are within the dreamscape."

"The soul?" Selene stood, her body chilled to the bone.

"Yes. What you see is only images of the person whose dream you enter. That wasn't really Petur we saw inside the dream, only his perceived image of himself. But dreams are a gateway into the mind and soul. If you see the person's soul, you must never touch it."

Her mother turned and headed for the door.

"What does the soul look like?" Selene asked quietly as they exited Petur's bare home. "How will I know?"

"They feel different than an image. Stronger, more powerful. Potent. Sometimes the soul looks like the person. Sometimes it looks like something else. The soul is the core essence of the person, who they really are. I've seen souls as dark as midnight, oozing and pulsating like a river of thick, black ink. I've seen others where it is a translucent image of the person bound in chains. And once I saw a soul so pure, so full of light, it was like gazing at the sun itself. Those are the most dangerous."

Most dangerous? How could something that sounded so beautiful be dangerous?

They entered the castle and moved along the hallway. "What would happen if I touched a soul?" Selene asked.

Her mother slowed down. "Then they would see you for who you are, and know you are there. We disguise ourselves as ravens within the dreamscape to hide our identity. We've been doing that for hundreds of years. You've heard the stories of the raven of Ravenwood, correct?"

"Yes."

"Those stories came about from our visits to the dream world. The stories have been passed down through the years, leaving people to wonder if the raven is real or not. These stories protect us so we can do our real work. But if someone were to discover who we are and what we can really do, we would be in danger." Her mother stopped and turned back. Half of her face was hidden in shadow, the other half illuminated by candlelight from a nearby sconce. "Ours is a powerful gift despite what the other Great Houses might once have thought. And it is our ability that caused our ancestors to be wiped out, save for Rabanna. We must never again let others know what we can do. Do you understand? You must never touch a soul."

Selene stared back, her face cold and impassive, but inside she shook at the intensity on her mother's face. "I understand."

"Good." Her mother relaxed and waved toward the corridor. "We will practice again in a fortnight." Her mother turned and left without saying another word, slipping into the shadows until only moonlight and silence filled the hallway.

Selene swallowed and headed toward her own bedchambers. Her mother's words stirred up questions deep inside of her, questions she'd had ever since she learned of the Great Houses and their gifts. Why were they given these gifts? Was there more to it than nightmares and secrets?

S elene slept later than she meant to. With blurry eyes and her gown haphazardly pulled on, she sat down and let Renata do her hair. The servant girl pulled back her long black strands, tugging and pulling here and there until every hair was captured in a complicated braid of sorts. Selene turned her head right and left, studying her reflection in the window. "When did you learn to do this?"

Renata gave her a shy smile. "I've been practicing. D-D-Do you l-like it?" The smile disappeared into a worried frown.

Selene smiled back. "I do. Thank you, Renata." Pity it would not last through her morning training.

After Renata left, Selene made her way to the faux sitting room, released the secret door, and headed to the training room down below. Silence filled the stone caverns. Amara wasn't here yet. Good. She wanted to go through her drills quickly so she could visit the library next.

Selene ended an hour later, her muscles sore but limber. *Vigilance. Constant vigilance.* Some of her mother's favorite words, and ones she used when reminding Selene and Amara of why they trained so intensely. Not only did the exercise help them control their muscles and allow them to move silently at night, but they also needed to be prepared should they ever be caught during a dreamwalk. *"Our family was almost wiped out once long ago. That will not happen again. You need to be prepared for anything."*

Mother never explained exactly what happened, other than House Ravenwood was handed over to the Dominia Empire during the razing. Maybe she didn't know. All they knew was that Rabanna was the only one to survive as a young woman and escape the empire, secretly making her way back to the mountains, where she married the new head of Ravenwood and kept her power a secret, a secret passed down for centuries.

But what was dreamwalking like before that, before we used it for uncovering secrets? Why were we given this gift? How was it used before Rabanna?

Selene pressed two fingers to her forehead. It seemed either no one knew, or no one wanted to tell her. She was tempted to use the hidden hot spring farther down the caverns to soothe her muscles, but even more she wanted to continue her research in the library. So she wet down one of the cloth strips on the table with a nearby pitcher of water, stripped off her training clothes, and wiped down her body. The beautiful hairstyle Renata had woven was loose, but still held. Selene tugged her gown back on, laced the sash, and pulled on her boots. There. A proper lady again.

But deep inside she knew she would never be a proper lady, not like the ladies of other Great Houses.

Selene made her way upstairs and through the sitting room, passing Amara as her sister headed down. The two exchanged glances but nothing more.

Selene spent the rest of the day in the library alone. Rain gently tapped against the window as a spring shower swept across the mountain peaks. She tucked her legs up beneath her dress and curled into a chair near the window, another book in hand. The library of House Ravenwood was not as big or spectacular as that of the other houses, notably House Vivek, but it did contain a couple of rare tomes, contributions from her father when he married her mother.

The book she held was smaller than most, bound up in leather and held closed by a long cord. She undid the cord and carefully opened it. It was a written account by a Vivek historian about the Great Houses. The people of the seven nations were once part of the Dominia Empire but migrated to these lands. It went on to describe the genealogy of each house before the razing of the empire. Fascinating, but not what she was looking for. Selene closed the book and headed for the long row of bookshelves. What she really wanted to know was what gifts were given to each house and for what purpose. But with many house secrets guarded so carefully, the chance of actually finding something about the houses was remote.

Still, she would look.

Dinner came and went, and Selene found herself slipping into her loose dark clothing and placing her twin swords in their sheaths around her waist, ready for another excursion with her mother. As the night deepened and the castle grew quiet, her stomach tightened more and more until she thought the little dinner she had managed to eat would come back up.

She placed a splayed hand across her middle and took some deep breaths while imagining locking away her heart in a cedar chest.

Don't think. Breathe in. *Don't feel.* Breathe out.

Selene closed her eyes and pictured the people around the castle: the servants, the guards, the families. They needed her to do this. If it wasn't for the money Ravenwood brought in, the entire mountain nation would be impoverished.

Everyone was counting on her. Her house. Her people.

But is this the only way?

She clenched her hand into a fist and pressed it against her middle and went back to breathing.

She kept up the mantra until the moon, half hidden by clouds, revealed it was time to go. She met her mother down on the first floor, and they made their way to the servants' quarters.

"Tonight we will be visiting my maidservant, Hagatha. This time you will enter the dreamscape alone and will search for Hagatha's fears. Some fears are easy to find, right there in the open. Others are hidden away within a person's dreams. Each time you go on a mission, the first night will be spent searching for that person's most intimate fear."

"What if you don't find it the first time?" Selene whispered.

"Then you go again. You cannot create a nightmare until you know what the person fears. As you become accustomed to the dreamscape, it will become easier for you to find out the sleeper's secrets."

"Have you ever encountered a person who had no fears?"

Her mother slowed. "Yes," she said quietly. "Once. Not so much that he had no fear, but that his fear did not control him. His is the only mission I failed."

Selene wanted to ask who it was but knew her mother would never tell. Each mission was held in sacred secrecy.

A light appeared at the end of the corridor. Her mother motioned toward the side hall, and Selene followed. They waited behind two pillars that divided the herb garden from the castle as the night watchman went by. When the light dimmed, her mother stepped away from the column and glanced around the corner, then waved toward Selene. They made their way to the servants' quarters and slipped into Hagatha's room.

Though as small as Petur's, the room was vastly different. A homemade rug graced the stone floor and a small quilt hung against the wall to the left. Fresh flowers stood in a clay vase set on a table beneath the single window. Embers glowed in the fireplace near the bed.

Her mother knelt down first beside the bed. "I will wait here for a time while you explore Hagatha's dreamscape," she whispered. "Then I will come find you and see what you discovered."

Selene gazed down at Hagatha. Wrinkles covered the old woman's face, and her white hair looked like sheep's wool. A snore escaped her thin lips, and her withered fingers twitched above the faded quilt.

Hagatha was a stern maidservant and more than once had turned her fierce gaze on Selene and Amara. But she loved their mother more than life itself.

The lump inside Selene's throat expanded until she could hardly breathe. Why would her mother do this to her loyal maidservant? There were dozens of other servants they could use. Or had she become so callous, her heart so locked away, that she didn't feel anymore?

Was this the kind of woman Selene herself was destined to become?

Selene ran a hand down the side of her face, her heart racing inside her chest.

I can't do this. I don't want to do this.

Remember your people. And if you don't do this, then Amara will. Or even Opheliana someday.

Selene dropped her hand and held it in a fist. She had no choice. *Lock away your heart. Feel nothing. Do the job.*

She reached for Hagatha's right hand and placed her palm over the translucent skin, then passed into the dreamscape.

Unlike Petur's dream, Hagatha's dream world held color, although faded. Her mind drifted in and out of different memories.

Selene spread her wings and took flight, watching the landscape change beneath her, watching Hagatha's recollections. The farther she flew, the younger Hagatha became. Most of the dreams were incoherent: laughing with the servants, brushing her mother's hair, quiet walks in the herb garden.

Now Hagatha was young. A chill flickered through Selene's subconscious, just a thread, but she felt it and moved toward that thought. Young Hagatha stood on a mountain path with a large stick in hand. Her fear grew, spreading across the dream.

Selene lit upon a cliff nearby and watched the scene unfold. Hagatha's subconscious tried to change it, but Selene closed her eyes and pressed against the command. Hagatha's fear was here, and she needed to find out what it was.

There was a snarl.

Selene opened her eyes. A timber wolf appeared, one of the largest ones she had ever seen. It stood eye to eye with Hagatha. It snarled again and bared its teeth. There was a crazed look in its yellow eyes and white foamy spittle formed around its mouth.

Hagatha brandished the stick, her heart beating like a galloping horse. Selene's own heart sped up to match it.

The wolf took a step forward.

"No, you don't." Hagatha swung the branch. "Not another step!"

"Hagatha, don't move!"

Selene looked back and spotted a man racing toward the young Hagatha. His copper hair and beard stood out from his dark clothes, and a sheen of sweat coated his pale face.

Hagatha turned her head halfway, keeping an eye on the approaching wolf. "Papa!"

The wolf snarled and stepped closer.

The man reached Hagatha. He grabbed her by the arm and pulled her back. "Run, Hagatha!"

She held the stick up. "But Papa—"

"Now!"

Hagatha dropped the stick and ran. The wolf ran too, right for the copper-haired man. He drew a dagger out just as the wolf leaped. The two went to the ground. The wolf latched onto the man's neck as the man plunged the blade into the wolf's chest. Fur and skin became coated in blood.

Selene turned away, sickened by the sight and sounds.

"Papa!" Hagatha screamed in the distance. "Papa!"

When the cries and snarling stopped, Selene glanced back. The wolf lay on top of the man, and the man's hand lay on the ground, the dagger dropped from his bloody fingers.

Hagatha screamed again and ran toward the bodies. Neither moved. "No, no! Papa!" She dropped to her knees beside his head. "Papa, wake up!"

Selene knew the man would never wake up.

An older feminine voice joined young Hagatha's voice. "Papa," the voice murmured. "Papa . . ."

"I see you found it." Her mother landed on the boulder next to Selene. "Hagatha hates and fears wolves. When she was young, a sick and savage wolf roamed the mountains. It found her one day, but her father intervened, giving up his own life to save his daughter. Now that you know what her fear is, I want you to use it."

"Use it?"

"Yes. Change the dreamscape. Use Hagatha's fear of wolves against her."

Selene thought she was going to retch. After what she had seen, how could she use that against Hagatha?

Her mother waited.

There was no getting out of this. Selene closed her eyes, burying her heart deep inside of her. *Don't feel. Don't feel.*

She focused on the wolf. With a powerful sweep of her wings, she changed the dreamscape. Hagatha stood alone on the path again.

"Now the wolves," her mother whispered.

"Wolves?"

"Yes. If one makes her afraid, then two will terrify her. But don't bring them all at once. Build up her fear. With practice, you will learn how much a person can take, and how slowly or fast you should bring on the nightmare."

Selene nodded, her mouth too dry for a verbal answer. She felt like she was about to jump off a cliff. *Don't feel.*

With another flick of her wings, she brought back the wolf. It stood where the path broadened. It took a moment for young Hagatha to register the wolf. At the same time, Selene felt sleeping Hagatha's heart begin to race.

She brought in a second wolf, this one on the other side of the path. Young Hagatha looked forward, then backward. She moved toward the side of the path and pressed her back against the rocks.

"Bring them closer," her mother whispered. There was a breathless eagerness to her voice.

Selene mentally urged the wolves forward, empowering them with Hagatha's memories. They snarled and growled with every step, and spittle formed around their muzzles.

"Have them lunge at her."

Selene hesitated. She could feel Hagatha's deep fear now and watched young Hagatha cower into a hunched position. *I can't do this! She's just a little gir—*

"Now, Selene!"

Selene severed the feelings inside of her.

With a flick of her wings, the wolves lunged at Hagatha, snapping at her, their spit flying from their jaws. Young Hagatha and sleeping Hagatha screamed at the same time. Hagatha's aged heart felt like it would burst at any moment.

"Feel that? Feel Hagatha's heart?"

Selene swallowed. "Yes."

"That is how you gauge how much fear the dreamer is experiencing. Push too far and you could kill her. Sometimes that's the goal. But not tonight. I simply wanted you to find Hagatha's fear and use it. Go ahead and stop."

Wait. Sometimes the goal is to kill? What did Mother mean?

Selene swept her wings back and with the rush of wind, the dream cleared. But she could still feel Hagatha's writhing body and hear her moans far off in the real world.

Selene's own emotions threatened to come back, but she held them at bay. If she let them loose, she would lose control in front of Mother.

Her mother narrowed her beady black eyes. "Come, Selene. Now that you've experienced the dreamscape, it is time to explain more of what goes on. Follow me."

Her mother flew up into the air. Selene followed, ready to escape this nightmare of her own making.

W ith a small gasp, Selene settled back into her body and let go of Hagatha's hand. Beads of sweat marred the old woman's face and trembles swept across her body.

"Hmm," her mother said beside her, looking down at the old woman. "You might have pushed Hagatha too much."

Selene glanced back at the maidservant, her eyes wide in horror.

"Not to worry, she'll recover. She's a tough woman. I practiced many times on Hagatha when my own mother was teaching me to control dreams."

Dinner threatened to come up, but Selene steeled herself against it. It was getting easier each time to turn off her emotions.

"Follow me to the caverns." Her mother stood and left without waiting for Selene.

Selene glanced down at Hagatha one more time. She wanted to tell the old servant she was sorry, but it would only make everything harder. So she turned and left instead.

Silently the two women made their way through the dark castle until they reached the less-inhabited part usually used only when there were guests. And there were rarely any guests at Rook Castle.

Her mother stopped before a wall inside one of the guest rooms and pressed on the hidden indents. A low groan sounded in the walls before the panel swung inward. Her mother reached for the oil lamp set on a small table beside one of the high-backed chairs near the fireplace and lit it. The two women entered the hidden hallway and shut the door behind them.

The light from the lamp cast a warm glow on the cool, jagged stone corridor, and the smell of dust and stone filled the small area.

"Now that you've experienced two dreamscapes, it will be easier to explain things to you," her mother said, her voice echoing along the passageway. "The jobs we receive come in many different forms. Sometimes our patron simply wants secrets for blackmail. So we search for those within the dreamscape. Other times, our patron wants revenge, such as making the dreamer relive his or her guilty past. And once in a while we receive a contract where the patron desires the ultimate of our abilities: death. Those are the most lucrative contracts. A contract like that can set up our family and nation for almost a year."

Selene's breath became lodged in her throat. "Death?"

"Yes."

Selene reached a hand over to the wall to hold herself up as icy cold adrenaline rushed through her body. So she had heard her mother correctly in the dreamscape. "We kill people?"

Her mother looked back, the lamplight dancing across her face. "It is our greatest ability."

"Our gift is to kill people?"

"It is one of our abilities. Fear is one of the most powerful human emotions. Once caught within the emotion, it is difficult for a person to escape. Even the mightiest of men eventually succumb to fear. And ultimate fear leads to death."

The tunnel began to spin around Selene. "So that's why we

search out a person's fear within the dream world. To manipulate it. To use it to . . . to . . ." She clamped her mouth shut and closed her eyes.

"To kill the sleeper." Her mother said the words with such casualness. "That is why you must learn to harden your heart, or you will find yourself unable to do what needs to be done."

Needs to be done? They were talking about lives here! She knew her family used the dreamwalking gift to support their people, but when had her ancestors crossed the line and become killers?

Did the ends justify the means?

Selene wiped her mouth and straightened up. She did not want to show her mother the raging conflict going on inside. She could be cold. She could suppress her emotions and lock them away.

She could harden her heart.

But for how long?

"How often do we receive such a contract?" Selene asked as she closed the gap between them, her voice even and controlled as she locked away the storm inside of her.

Her mother narrowed her eyes as if evaluating Selene.

Selene stared back.

Satisfied, her mother turned back around and continued along the tunnel. "Not very often. They are the most dangerous, both to us and to our patron, should the assassination be found out. However, our method makes it appear as though the person died in their sleep. Very convenient."

Her toes curled within her boots, but she kept her frozen veneer in place. "So nobody suspects that we use our dreamwalking abilities to kill?" Her voice didn't quaver or stumble over the word, but her heart gave a twinge.

"Oh, there might be a couple of people who suspect the dream gift still exists, and even fewer people who would consider that the gift is used in such a way. Because it is believed that our lineage died out during the razing by the Dominia Empire, hardly anyone knows. And thus our secret is safe."

It made sense. No one knew Rabanna was one of the original Ravenwoods, and thus carried the gift of dreaming when she came back from captivity. Selene continued to probe. As horrified as she was, she needed answers: why, how, and who. "How do we receive our contracts?"

"We work closely with House Friere. Grand Lord Ivulf has connections all over the great nations and even within the Dominia Empire itself. When he finds out there is a desire for what we do, his agents negotiate the contract. Then he sends word to me and I fulfill it. But soon that will be your job."

Selene's stomach tightened into a ball of lead as they neared the training rooms. It would be her job to fulfill those missions. Her job to kill.

She sucked in a quick breath and pressed on.

It was still too early in the morning for Amara to be here, and even if she were to arrive early, she would soon be privy to the Ravenwood secrets when her own gifting emerged. "You mentioned seeing souls inside the dreamscape."

"Yes." There was a cautionary note in her mother's voice. "The dream world is made from the dreamer's memories, mind, and subconscious. Because of that, there is always the chance of the soul appearing inside the dreamscape."

"You said it can come in different forms, but that I will know it by how it feels."

"Yes," her mother said again. They entered the training room. Mother walked along the perimeter, lighting the torches as she went. "Because the soul is the very essence of the dreamer, it will feel the most real, the most powerful, inside the dream."

Selene followed her. "You said never to touch the soul. Why?"

Mother lit another torch. The light inside the training room grew brighter. "We cannot control souls, only dreams. If you touch the dreamer's soul, he or she will wake up and stop the nightmare. But even more importantly, they will know your identity." Her mother turned around, the lamp still in her hand. Her eyes were wide, like black coals, her face serious. "You must never let anyone know who you are."

"But what about marriage? House secrets cannot be kept from a consort."

"Yes." Her mother's face darkened. "That is why we only marry those from lesser houses. That is how we have been able to keep our house secrets from those who would fear or abuse our ability."

"But House Friere knows our secret."

"Not quite. I think Lord Ivulf suspects, but he has never said anything. His cut on the contracts helps keep him quiet. He fears the rumors if they are true, because that would mean I could take him out if I so chose. Never underestimate the power of rumors and secrets, Selene. They are what have kept our family safe all of these years."

Mother finished lighting the last torch and placed the oil lamp down on the table. "There is one more group of people I must warn you about. I learned of them years ago, a coalition of sorts that has formed amongst the lesser houses and people. There are those who are jealous or feel threatened by the power possessed by the Great Houses. They wish to merge the Great Houses and do away with the gifts."

"But why? Our gifts help our people."

"Balance of power. Envy. We may be a small house, and exist in secrecy, but I will never unite with the other Great Houses. Never forget that it is the other houses that allowed our house to almost fall. We must stand on our own. Be wary of any group that wants to unite us all. In the end, they only want to take away our power. Our gift is what keeps us safe. We must guard that. Now, enough questions. I want to see how well you've been practicing."

They stopped in the middle of the training area.

"We do most of our work in the dream world, but there is always a chance that someone will find us while we are in the dream. We must always be prepared to fight and run."

"Were you found during a mission?"

"Yes. Twice. Once by a guard, once by the nobleman's wife. I was able to escape both without my identity being compromised."

"How?"

"I had to kill the guard. But I was able to escape the man's wife. That is why we wear black and cover our faces, and why you will take your swords with you on your missions."

"But didn't your appearance cause alarm? Didn't people become suspicious?"

"Yes, it did, and I had to let the rumors die before taking on more jobs."

"So there might be people out there who suspect what we do?"

"There might be. But the Ravenwood women have been very careful for hundreds of years. And we will continue to be, as long as you remain vigilant. You will spend your evenings practicing your gift of dreamwalking. You must learn how to enter the dreamer's room without waking your target, how long to spend in the dreamscape, and what to do if your dreamer ever awakens. These things you will carry out around the castle."

"On the servants?" Selene asked as Amara walked into the training room. Exhaustion hung across her body, making her thoughts and vision cloudy.

"Yes." Mother's eyes darted to Amara. "And don't forget to close off your heart. You cannot do what needs to be done until you've learned to do that."

"I understand."

Her mother turned. "Amara."

Amara looked up. "Yes?" she said with eagerness in her voice.

"I wish to see you and Selene spar. I want to see how far both of you have come in your training."

Amara raised her chin, her gaze set on Selene. "Yes, Mother."

Selene grit her teeth. She hated it when Mother pitted them against each other. It did nothing to help their relationship.

Amara grabbed her sword from the nearby table. Selene already had her twin blades with her, their weight becoming even more familiar each night as she learned to dreamwalk. Selene waited for her sister in the middle of the large cavern. Mother stood by one wall, her arms folded, her eyes dark with pinpricks of red from the torchlight.

Selene slid her swords from her sheaths. Why did Mother want them to fight now? Fatigue and the ebbing shock from her mother's revelation penetrated her muscles like a poison, making her feel sluggish, while Amara was fresh from a night of sleep.

Constant vigilance.

Mother's words rang inside her head as Selene wove her blades in preparation. Perhaps Mother wanted to see how well she could react after a long night if she were ever caught—

Selene barely had time to get her left sword in place as Amara's blade came in at a slant toward her chest. Selene deflected her sister's sword and answered with her right one. *Dart'an!* She usually wasn't this slow.

Amara left her little time to react as she came in on Selene's other side.

Again, Selene deflected as she jumped back to put some space between them. The single sword used a combination of strength and stamina, whereas her dual-sword technique required dexterity and speed. With her blades, she could continue to strike, beating an opponent back, or parry and thrust at the same time. However, time was against her and eventually she would wear out. Which was already happening.

Selene panted, then went in with a rush of strikes.

Amara blocked all but the last.

Selene grazed her sister's arm, then danced to the side and dodged Amara's swing. The tip caught her near the shoulder, a stinging nick through her tunic and skin.

"Enough."

Mother's voice echoed along the cavern walls. Selene dropped her arms and panted. Amara did the same.

"Very good, both of you."

Mother's words were like sunshine to Amara. Her face lit up with confidence and elation.

Although she was tired, a small smile slipped across Selene's face. It was good to see such joy in Amara's eyes. If only she could witness it more often.

"Selene, you are dismissed. You will continue dreamwalking tonight. Amara, we will train together this morning. I wish to see how you are progressing in other areas."

Amara straightened, her face beaming. "Yes, Mother."

Selene turned away, her mother's words casting a shadow over the bright moment. She would be dreamwalking again. And the next night. And the next. She lifted her hand and stared at her palm, a hollow feeling spreading across her chest.

This was her life now. Her burden.

But . . .

She glanced back. Amara still wore that look of confidence as she lifted her sword and prepared to spar with their mother. As long as she was the dreamwalker her mother desired, then perhaps Amara wouldn't have to experience the things she had to.

A spring rain sprinkled across the courtyard, filling the air with a gentle pattering and the smell of dirt and vegetation. Selene pulled her cloak closer around her shoulders and continued across the courtyard. Far off, the blacksmith's hammer rang and the clank of soldiers practicing their sword work echoed on the other side of the bailey.

Today was Opheliana's fourth spring, and Selene was determined to find the first violet in the herb garden for her little sister. Ever since Selene's gifting had arrived, a dark shadow lay over her heart, and the thought of visiting her little sister was a ray of light amongst the shadows.

"Morning, my lady." The guard who stood near the second gate gave her a short bow.

"Good morning, sir."

She passed under a stone archway and toward the gardens. She slowed. This path looked so different during the day compared to when her mother had brought her to Petur's humble home under a sliver of moonlight. Selene shivered and rubbed her arms. She passed under another archway and entered the garden.

It was as large as the inner bailey and bright green in the misty

67

rain. Trails of river stones wove through the patches of flowers, herbs, and trees. Although cultivated, the garden still retained its wildness. When she was young, Selene would pretend it was a fairy meadow deep within the Magyr Mountains and roam the garden with a flower wreath on her head.

Selene stopped beside a crooked apple tree, breathed in deeply, and sighed. The sound of a spade turning over fresh earth caught her ear. She could almost smell the dirt.

Quietly, she headed along the path to the right, drawn to the familiar sound. Just beyond the first bend and past a trellis full of ivy she spotted a man bent over, a floppy hat on his head, turning the dirt.

Petur glanced up at her approach. "My lady!" He pulled off his hat and bowed. "It has been some time since you visited the gardens."

Her eyes were drawn to the scars along the right side of his face and the way his hand trembled as he held the hat. Selene felt as if a millstone had replaced her heart. She clutched a hand to her chest and sucked in air.

"My lady?" The wrinkly smile vanished, replaced with concern. "Are you all right?"

"I am . . . fine." Mother was right. Selene could feel the deep connection she had made with Petur that night, so much so that the sight of him and his scars hit the very core of her being. All she could see was the fire and the old cabin in the woods, and she felt Petur's grief, fear, and regret. She glanced around and spotted a stone bench near a cluster of daisies. "I just need to rest for a moment."

Selene sank down onto the hard bench. The rainwater soaked her gown and cloak, but she didn't care. No wonder Mother said she needed to lock away her heart. She pressed a cold, wet hand to her cheek. She had thought she only had to do it during the mission, but she was wrong. The connection, once formed, was now there, linking her to Petur, to his deepest secrets and fears.

She closed her eyes and breathed in through her nostrils, willing her heart to disappear. She imagined a cedar chest inside of her, and taking all of these feelings for Petur and placing them inside, she closed the lid. Every time her heart beat, she pressed down on the imaginary lid again and again until—finally—she felt nothing but the cold condensation in the air.

Selene opened her eyes. Petur stood before her, his hat still in his hands, that same concerned look on his face. She only felt a hint of those feelings from moments earlier. *I am becoming better at this. I am growing stronger at controlling myself.*

Yet, that did not pacify her. Deep down, she grieved. She was sacrificing her heart for House Ravenwood.

Would she ever get it back?

Selene stood up and lifted her chin in the same way her mother would. "I'm looking for a violet for Lady Ophie—Opheliana. Have you seen one?"

Petur blinked at her. "Yes, my lady, I have."

"Then take me to it."

He visibly swallowed and placed the floppy hat back on his head. She wanted to take back her cold words, but it would only reopen her heart. Petur gave her one more glance, the scars across his face tightening, then turned around and headed for the eastern part of the garden.

The small smooth stones crunched under their boots. Raindrops clung to the slender new leaves and unopened buds along the path. There was such peace here in the gardens. A part of her wished she could just stay here and never go back to the main castle. But that was not her lot. No, hers was to sacrifice her heart so that House Ravenwood and the mountain nation could live.

She gripped her fingers tightly. *I must never forget that.*

"Here you go, my lady." Petur stopped and pointed at the small purple flower. It was the only one amidst the leafage. Selene bent down and plucked the tender shoot. It would not last long, only a day or two, then the flower would wilt and die. Her throat tightened at the thought.

Selene straightened up, the flower clutched within her hand. "Thank you, Petur. Lady Opheliana will love this."

Petur gave her a shy smile, and Selene felt like a dagger had been thrust into her heart. "My pleasure, my lady. Please visit the gardens anytime."

Selene merely bobbed her head and turned swiftly in the direction of the main castle. The gardens were a place of tranquility and calm. Because of that, she could never visit them again.

Selene pinched the flower between her thumb and finger as she made her way through the castle toward Opheliana's rooms. Would her sister speak to her today? Or would she give Selene her usual silent smile?

She looked down at the fragile bloom, her dress swishing between steps. The rain started again outside, lightly pattering against the windows that lined the long, shadowed corridor. Mother rarely visited Ophie anymore. She was dismayed when Ophie refused to talk—or maybe couldn't. The healer wasn't sure. Selene couldn't understand her mother's reaction. It was true that Ophie hadn't spoken a word since she was born and barely even cried. But she had the most wonderful smile and sparkling eyes. And there was a tenderness in her youngest sister that was lacking in herself and Amara. Perhaps that was what drew her to her sister the most. Ophie was everything she was not.

Selene reached the wooden door and turned the handle. Quietly, she opened the door and peeked inside. The main room was paneled in dark wood with a thick crimson rug on the stone floor, a fireplace to the right, and a set of high-backed chairs near the fireplace. She could hear a voice coming from the room beyond, crooning a soft lullaby.

Selene slipped in and shut the door behind her. She crossed the main room and looked into the bedroom. Two beds covered in furs and thick quilts were set on either side of the room, one larger than the other. A dark blue rug lay on the floor between them. Above, a long narrow window let in what natural light there was on this rainy day.

Ophie stood in front of the window, her face pressed to the glass, her head barely clearing the bottom rim. Her dark hair hung in curls down her back, with a red sheen to the strands. She wore a simple brown frock and soft-skinned boots. Nursemaid Maura sat on a stool next to her, singing in a low voice. She wore a white cap over her mousy brown hair and a matching apron over her woolen dress.

"Ophie," Selene said quietly.

Maura stopped singing and looked over. "Lady Selene!" She stood and gave Selene a short curtsy. "I did not hear you enter."

Opheliana turned around. Her dark eyes grew wide, revealing a hint of amber around the pupil, and a smile spread across her face with a dimple in each cheek. She dashed across the room and grabbed hold of Selene's dress, burying her face in the fabric.

Selene brushed the top of Opheliana's soft head. "I wanted to give Ophie a present."

At the word *present*, Opheliana looked up. Selene waited for her sister to say something, but her tiny mouth remained closed. However, her eyes darted across Selene's face, then toward her hand. At the sight of the flower, her smile grew even wider and her eyes sparkled.

Selene took a step back, then bent down until she was eye level with Opheliana. "Today is a special day. Four springs have passed since you were born. I brought you your favorite flower to celebrate."

Selene held out the delicate violet. With equal gentleness, Opheliana took the flower, cradling it between her small fingers. Selene waited, but Opheliana never said a word, just stared at the flower as if it were the greatest treasure in the world.

The emptiness and darkness from the last week disappeared from inside of Selene, replaced with a powerful feeling of warmth. Everything was simple with Opheliana. Every flower a treasure, every act of kindness cherished. Her throat tightened as love for her sister overflowed inside of her heart. Who cared if her sister didn't talk? She spoke volumes with her actions.

Opheliana looked back at her and placed a hand on Selene's cheek. Selene's eyes grew misty. Then a thought hit her.

She never wanted to see her sister become a dreamkiller. Never.

Such an occupation would shatter the sweet little girl. Instead, Selene wanted to see Opheliana grow up and remind the world that there were still good things, that there was still light and hope. The same went for Amara. Though they didn't get along, she didn't want to see either sister become a dreamkiller. Not if she could help it. That was why she needed to remain the heir to the Ravenwood dynasty. So that Amara and Ophie never had to.

Selene let out a long, shaky breath. "I have to go now."

Opheliana's face dimmed, and she cocked her head to the side.

"I have some very important things to do." The thought of going back into people's dreams and reliving their deepest nightmares made her stomach clench. It was like spending a moment in the sunshine, knowing she had to go back into the shadows.

But I will do it. For you.

"Opheliana!"

Selene stiffened and glanced back.

"Opheli—Selene." Amara stopped in the doorway, a small

wooden toy in her hands. At the sight of Selene, her face darkened. "I didn't know you were here."

Selene stood. "I was just leaving."

Amara stepped out of the way, as if to usher Selene out as fast as she could.

Selene patted Ophie one more time, then turned around and headed out.

"Thank you, Lady Selene," Maura said as she passed.

Selene gave her a small smile, then left the nursery. A lightness entered Amara's voice behind her as her sister babbled about the toy she had found for Opheliana.

Selene held her hand over the handle. Why couldn't she and Amara get along like they both did with Opheliana? Were they destined to always be rivals?

She opened the door, stepped out into the hall, then closed it, laying her head against the smooth wooden surface. The hallway was cold and silent. For the first time, she felt a twinge of feeling toward Amara, devoid of the recent aloofness and coldness she felt toward her sister recently. It wasn't much, but it was a spark.

Was there a way to change the future of Ravenwood? A brighter hope where she and Amara could use their gifts in a way other than hurting people, and in doing so, work together?

Selene straightened up and held a fist to her heart. "If there is any way that can happen, then I will find it, no matter what."

I t is time for the last of your training." Lady Ragna stood in a pool of moonlight cast by the nearby window weeks later. Every part of her was covered in black, save the upper part of her face. Her dark eyes stared out at Selene from below her cowl.

Selene stayed in the shadows, her own body wrapped in similar black loose-fitting clothes and head cover.

"As I shared before, our most lucrative contracts are those that require a life. Given how easily dreamwalking has come to you, I don't think you will experience any setbacks with dream-killing."

Selene folded her arms. She had spent all evening preparing for this mission, setting aside her emotions, fears, and trepidation. Every time she felt herself vacillating, she pictured Ophie. She would not let Ophie grow up to be a dreamkiller. That meant she had to take on the mantle. Or find a way out for both of them. For both of her sisters. "Whose dream will I be walking in tonight?" *Please don't let it be someone I know.*

"Your maidservant Renata."

Selene felt as though she had been punched in the gut. Renata? She was going to be forced to dreamkill her shy maidservant? Her insides clenched violently inside of her, but she did not show anything on the outside.

"You seem very calm about the matter."

Remember, lock away your heart. "I am ready." The lie slipped through her lips so easily it shocked her. Again, she never let it show on her face.

Her mother studied her for a moment, then nodded. "I'll lead the way."

They entered one of the more lavish guest rooms of Rook Castle. "There is a small entrance to the underground labyrinth beneath the balcony of this room."

"I know." Selene knew almost every tunnel and opening below the castle, the knowledge gained from years of exploring the underground maze as a child.

"You do?" That bit of information seemed to take her mother by surprise. Her mother glanced back as they crossed the wide bearskin rug that lay on the stone floor across from a large four-poster bed.

"Yes." Maybe Selene shouldn't have revealed how much she knew about the caverns.

Her mother turned back and exited out onto the balcony. At the stone balustrade, her mother gracefully maneuvered over the railing and disappeared. Selene followed.

A few feet below, a large boulder jutted out from the mountainside. Selene landed beside her mother in front of the entrance to a small cave. Without saying a word, her mother entered, Selene close behind.

Like most of the tunnels beneath Rook Castle, this one was narrow, dark, and rugged. A cold wind whipped through the passageway, whistling through hidden holes and crevices.

Selene shivered and rubbed her arms. *Just think about Ophie.* But instead of Ophie's face, all she could see was Renata's. She remembered the day she met the small, timid girl. Renata was so skinny that her arms and legs reminded Selene of a chicken. Her mousy brown hair hung over one shoulder in a stringy braid, and her eyes looked much too big for her pale face.

Renata was from one of the lower mountain villages that had been pillaged and burned by bandits. She was one of the few villagers to escape. After the survivors arrived at Rook Castle, her mother found placements for each of the people. Renata was assigned to Selene as a maid, despite her lack of experience. But the girl had proven a fast learner and hard worker who spoke little, traits of which her mother approved.

The tunnel began to ascend at a steady incline. They were almost to the servants' private quarters. Selene swallowed, her entire body cold and her throat tight.

The tunnel changed from an incline to stairs. At the top, her mother pressed an invisible indent in the wall and with a quiet groan, the stone door slid open, revealing the inside of a large fireplace. Her mother stepped over a pile of charred sticks and into the large common room used by the servants. A long wooden table took up most of the area, with doors on either side that led to small private rooms.

Selene brushed her hands as her mother shut the secret passage behind them. "This way," her mother whispered and headed toward the farthest room on the right. Selene followed, her heart growing heavy inside her chest. Her fingers were cold, like icicles hanging from a roof. Long, slender, frozen objects. She clenched her fists to get feeling back into her limbs, but they remained cold.

Her mother quietly opened the narrow door and slipped inside. The room was small, barely the size of a pantry, with a cot on the right and a single wooden chest beneath the window. Renata lay on the cot, curled up beneath a single quilt. Selene shivered.

She could almost see her breath in the air. How did Renata stay warm? She would make sure the girl received another quilt—

A sickening feeling washed over her. An extra blanket wouldn't matter, not after tonight.

Her mother shut the door and went right to work. She knelt down beside the servant girl and drew back the quilt. In the pale moonlight, Renata appeared even smaller and more pallid than usual.

How can I do this? Selene fought the urge to grip her own neck in a choking hold. *How can I hurt this girl?*

Her mother looked back up. "Are you ready?"

Dizziness washed over Selene, causing her vision to darken for a moment. *You can't stop now,* a voice whispered inside her head. *You've come too far. Finish it.*

With one last burst of will, Selene knelt down beside her mother. Her vision cleared, and her fingers stopped trembling.

Don't feel. Don't think. Just do the job.

Before she could form another thought, Selene placed her fingers across Renata's thin neck and closed her eyes.

She sunk into the dreamscape as if she were submerging herself in a pool of warm water. The moment she entered, she shifted her body, settling into the form of a raven. With a caw, Selene flapped her wings and hovered in the air. Renata's dreamscape was dark, save for a full moon that hung in the night sky. Down below, fog crept through a narrow valley between two mountain peaks.

Silence filled the air, save for the sound of her wings. Selene scanned the area below her. Somewhere within the swirling grey were Renata's fears and memories. Selene hovered a moment longer, then dove down into the misty banks.

The silence pressed in on her as she made her way through the fog. Every few seconds, the mist would lift, revealing a memory or long-lost thought. She caught a glimpse of Renata sitting on the floor beside a fire in a small cabin with an older couple. Then she spotted Renata in a field of wildflowers, weaving daisies into a wreath. The farther she flew, the darker the images became.

Selene flew by a hill covered in stones arranged in a burial mound. Renata sat, her face held between her hands. Then Renata packing the few things she owned into a small chest and closing the door to the empty cabin.

The fog grew even thicker, almost suffocating. Selene landed. She was close to Renata's greatest fear. She could feel it. The dreamscape mist swirled around her, leaving her cold and blind.

She looked back but could no longer see the other memories. She twisted and glanced forward. Nothing. She closed her eyes. Her connection with Renata was strong. Already, she could feel the girl's heart beating faster and a cold sweat breaking out along her skin.

Selene remembered her connection to Petur, and how lightheaded she felt when she saw him again after the dream experience. If her reaction was that strong with Petur, what would happen when she killed Renata?

Selene thought she was going to retch right there. It was more than just hiding her heart away.

She had to stop her own heart if she was to become a killer herself.

Coldness washed over her until she was numb inside. Selene lifted off the ground again and dove into the fog.

A road stretched out in front of her, hedged in by tall, dark trees. A caravan of wagons slowly made its way along the dirt path. Selene spotted Renata near the back, walking slowly with her head bent down.

Selene landed on the back of a wagon and watched the procession. Somewhere here was Renata's greatest fear. But what?

She watched the people trudge along, their garments much too thin for the mountain roads. Selene narrowed her eyes. Mother said she used contract money to help their people. Shouldn't they be dressed better?

A shout went up near the front of the caravan. Selene craned her neck to the side. More shouts erupted. Men dressed in dark clothing came pouring out from the surrounding forest. Some horses spooked and took off to the right, dragging a wagon behind them. Arrows rained down on the travelers. Screams and cries rent the air.

A man staggered past Selene, an arrow sticking out of his right shoulder. Bloody hands reached up and grabbed the side of the wagon. Startled, Selene flew up into the air. A fire burst from inside another wagon, spooking the rest of the horses. The wagon twisted from their sudden movement and fell to its side in a ball of flame.

A child lay nearby, his face lit up by the orange light, his hand clutching his chest, his breaths ragged. As a woman bent down to help him, she was grabbed from behind. Two men dragged her past the tree line and into the darkness. Seconds later, her scream filled the air.

Selene blinked. She felt as though she were going to topple over. Too much around her. Screams. Fire. Pain. Darkness.

A cry caught her ear, vaguely like Renata's. Selene shook her head, then lifted into the air and flew toward the sound. Renata stood with her back to a tree, her hands up, shielding herself from one of the bandits. The man grabbed her arm and pulled her toward himself. His face was covered in a dark, unkempt beard, and his eyes glittered red in the light from the burning wagon nearby. He smiled at her, then pulled her behind the tree.

A deep chill penetrated Selene's numbness, shaking her to her very core. She could see their legs and knew what Renata's most hateful memory was.

Selene could hold back no longer. She fell to the ground in her human form and retched. Behind her were the cries of a little girl, and the screams of people being ravaged.

No! No! She covered her ears. *I can't—I can't do thi—*

A torrential power welled up inside her, erupting from her chest and lifting her to her feet. Selene flung her arms out and yelled at the sky. "Noooo!"

The power burst from her and tore across the dreamscape like a fierce gale, devouring everything in its wake. Trees, wagons, horses, and people disappeared, leaving nothing but grey mist around her and an orb the size of a wagon wheel pulsating within the darkness.

Selene shook as she held a hand to her face. "I can't do it," she panted. "I can't—" She sobbed and held her hand over her mouth. Nearby, the black orb pulsed again. Within the swirling darkness were thin pewter chains rotating within the orb.

"Renata," Selene whispered, her eyes growing wide at the sight of the orb. She could feel Renata's essence within the sphere. This orb . . . It was Renata's soul.

She reached a hand out toward the soulsphere, but never touched it. Such darkness. Such . . . pain. She could feel it radiating out from the orb.

She drew her hand back. How could she take the life of a girl so bound in darkness that visible chains encircled her soul?

That same fiery rage from moments earlier returned, so strong it threatened to burst again from her body. But Selene held it back. Instead, she let it burn inside of her and wash away the shock and horror from earlier. There was no reason—absolutely no reason—to kill Renata.

Selene held up her hand, then clenched it into a fist. She knew her power now, and it was as strong as Mother had imagined. Even stronger. She did not have to kill an innocent girl to prove it.

A resounding crack sounded in the distance. Selene glanced up. The cracking continued, like the sound of a frozen lake breaking out of winter's embrace. Then a splinter appeared in the mist above her. Something was happening to the dreamscape. Almost as if . . .

Selene melted into her raven form and flew toward the sky where the barrier between the dream world and reality lay. The splinter spread into multiple fissures and the cracking sound grew closer. Just as she reached the top, the sky split and shattered like glass, falling into the mist below. Selene passed through the barrier. Behind her, Renata's dream world fell away like shattered bits of mirror, leaving behind a void of darkness.

With a gasp, Selene sank back into her body.

"What happened?" her mother whispered furiously.

Selene blinked, bringing her mind and body back into reality.

"The servant girl, she's not dead! Why are you back? Selene, I command you to go—"

"No." Selene twisted her head and glared at her mother.

Her mother grew very quiet, but her eyes burned. "What do you mean, no?"

Selene lifted up from the floor, her knees cold and numb. Renata looked pale in the moonlight, and there was a trickle of blood beneath her left nostril.

"What are you doing? You need to finish the job!"

"I said no," she said between clenched teeth.

Her mother slowly rose to her feet. "You would defy me?" she said in a low, cold voice.

"There is no reason to kill an innocent and hardworking servant girl."

"If you cannot kill a simple girl, then how will you ever kill a nobleman?"

Selene looked down at Renata. Something was . . . off. The blood looked almost black in the moonlight. Blood. Wait, there should be no blood. Her eyes widened. That shattering inside the dreamscape . . . had it done something to Renata?

Her mother glanced down as well. A moment later, she spoke. "I see. Perhaps you accomplished your mission after all."

"What do you mean?" Panic clutched at Selene.

"The girl. You did something to her."

The satisfaction in her mother's voice sent a chill through her body. "What do you mean?" she asked again.

Her mother studied Renata in detached curiosity. "What happened in the dreamscape?"

"I don't know. It's like the dream shattered."

Her mother's head shot up. "Shattered?"

"Yes." Selene held a trembling hand to her head, remembering. "There was a cracking sound, then a tear appeared in the sky. As I passed the dream barrier, the dreamscape shattered behind me, like glass."

Her mother slowly shook her head, her face deep in thought. "I've only heard of this happening once, by the first Ravenwood."

"By Rabanna?"

"No, the very first Ravenwood, when the gift of dreamwalking was given to our family. I thought it was simply a tale. It would take a great deal of power to shatter a dreamscape. But . . ." She looked up and there was a fire in her eyes. "Perhaps there was some truth in the tale." She looked down again at the servant girl. "I'm guessing that by shattering the girl's dream world, you shattered her mind as well."

"Shattered . . . her mind?" It couldn't be. Selene shook her head. She couldn't have done that. Not when all she had wanted to do was leave Renata's worst memory alone.

"I'll discreetly have a healer check out the girl in the morning." A smile spread across her mother's face. "This is even better than I had hoped for." The moonlight glinted off her dark eyes. "You are indeed powerful, Selene. So powerful."

Selene just stared down at Renata. Guilt clawed at her insides, leaving her feeling mauled from the inside out.

"Now"—her mother wiped her hands as if wiping away blood—"we need to get back to our rooms before the sun rises. If the girl's mind is indeed shattered, we will need to do away with her."

"What?" Selene's head snapped up.

"We have no room for a disabled servant in the castle, especially one bedridden and addled in the mind. It might have been better if you had outright killed her, but now we know what you are capable of."

Her mother turned and headed for the door. Selene stood there, the fire reigniting inside of her. Her mother paused and looked back. "Are you coming?"

Selene clenched her hands into tight fists. "No."

Her mother frowned. "No? You're not coming?"

"No, we will not do away with Renata."

"What are you talking about?"

She looked up and stared coldly at her mother. "I will not let you kill her."

Her mother sighed. "Be reasonable, Selene. There is no use for her here. In fact, she might prefer it that way."

"And I said no," she snapped. Her mind was already feverishly searching for a way she could help Renata. She had to! She couldn't leave her servant girl like this. If she possessed this kind of power, the kind that could shatter minds, couldn't she help them as well? There had to be a reason her ancestors were given this gift!

Selene glared at her mother. "If you do away with Renata, I will go after you."

Her mother's eyes hardened. "A Ravenwood has never killed another Ravenwood."

"I. Don't. Care." Selene seethed. She was done with this. "If you kill Renata, I will hunt you down in your own dream world." A small part of her was shocked. She was threatening her own mother! Another part of her didn't care. She would perform her duty for House Ravenwood and their people. But she would do it on her own terms, until she found out the real reason for their gift, and a way to free them from this accursed cycle of murder.

Her mother sniffed. "I have more experience than you."

Selene lifted her chin. "I have more power than you, and you know it. I would win in the end."

For the first time ever, Selene watched fear enter her mother's eyes. Good. Her threat was not idle.

Her mother looked down at the prone figure of Renata. "Fine, keep the girl. But she will be in your care, not mine." With that, her mother spun around and left the room.

The moment her mother was gone, Selene collapsed onto her knees. She pressed a cold hand to her forehead. "What am I doing?" she whispered. "What kind of person am I becoming?" Perhaps there was no escaping who she was. After all, she had just threatened to kill her own mother. *Maybe I am a murderer.*

But I don't want to be.

She looked up at the low ceiling. Some of the other nations believed in gods in some form. There were even whispers that a few of the houses still served the old god. House Ravenwood believed in neither, only in the Dark Lady, and even then Selene wasn't sure if she was real. But then where did their power come from?

"Please," she whispered. "If any of you are real, please show me what to do, and who I am. And . . ." She glanced back at Renata and her heart twisted. "Please heal Renata. Please."

9

Damien Maris smiled as he raised his sword and faced Taegis. The older man did the same. Without a second's pause, Damien advanced first.

Taegis blocked, then countered with his own move.

Damien sensed the movement a split second before his guardian lunged and deflected, then returned with a move of his own.

Thrust, parry, block.

The training room rang with the sounds of their swords and breathing. Sunlight streamed through the high windows on either side of the room, spreading light across the worn wooden floor. Practice swords and a jug of water sat on the table near the doorway. Although the training room was large enough to accommodate as many as ten men sparring, today only Damien and Taegis practiced.

Damien wiped the sweat from his face and brought his arms and sword back into a ready stance. Taegis did the same thing.

"Ready, or do you need a break?" Damien asked with a smirk.

Taegis grinned back, the scar along his right cheek more pronounced against his flushed face. "I'm not so old that I need to breathe between practices. Remember, I've been doing this since before you were born."

"All right, then." Damien lunged forward, going for the opening to Taegis's left. Taegis blocked, and they began sparring again.

Sweat soaked into Damien's tunic and down his back. He pushed himself until his muscles were stretched and limber. Although over twenty years his senior, Taegis could hold his own against Damien, something Damien admired.

"Message for Lord Damien."

Damien paused, his sword up, and glanced at the doorway at the other end of the training room. One of the couriers from the tower stood in the archway. Damien wiped his face and lowered his weapon. "Excuse me for a moment, Taegis."

Taegis nodded and lowered his own weapon.

Damien crossed the room and placed his sword on the table, then reached for the small rolled piece of parchment the courier held out.

"A raven from Rook Castle arrived minutes ago with this attached to its leg. Since we receive so little communication from House Ravenwood, I thought you would want to see it right away."

Damien took the small paper from the young man. "Yes, thank you."

The courier gave him a short bow before he left the same way he came. Damien continued to stand by the doorway, studying the paper. Instead of the usual insignia of Ravenwood stamped into the soft wax, there was no insignia. So it wasn't official news from House Ravenwood, which meant it was probably from Caiaphas, Lady Ragna Ravenwood's consort. Damien reached for the dagger at his side and slid the point through the slit and wax.

After a quick glance, he saw he was right.

Taegis came to stand beside him.

"Caiaphas wants to meet in person." He glanced over at his guardian. Taegis had served House Maris since Damien's father had first been named grand lord, and now served Damien in the same way. His honey-colored hair, streaked with grey, was pulled back in a short braid, and his beard was carefully trimmed.

His hazel eyes glanced at the paper in Damien's hand, then at Damien. "I'm still not sure if Caiaphas can be trusted. He has been with House Ravenwood for many years."

"But he's been part of the coalition for even longer. And was a good friend of Father's."

"I advise caution, Lord Damien, the same advice I gave your father years ago. Though Caiaphas is originally from one of the lesser houses of Vivek, he is now part of House Ravenwood. And Ravenwood is not to be trusted."

Damien rolled up the paper. "I will consider your words. But I also wish to meet with him. He may know something about the recent bout of murders within House Luceras and the rumors about the Dominia Empire. Perhaps he may have even discovered something within House Ravenwood."

Taegis crossed his arms. "You know Caiaphas cannot divulge any of House Ravenwood's secrets if Lady Ragna has silenced him."

"I know. But the whole reason he married into the Ravenwood family was to find out what he could. At least that's what Father said. Perhaps that is why he wants to meet."

Taegis shook his head. "I wish the leadership of the coalition had been placed on someone else. You are the last heir to House Maris. If something were to happen to you . . ."

"I know." Damien sighed. "But the houses are fracturing more and more as the years go by and secrets are keeping us apart. We barely survived the last razing by the Dominia Empire. We won't survive another one."

"And you really think the empire is on the move?"

"Yes." Damien crushed the paper in his fist. "The skirmishes along the eastern wall are simply a test by the empire to see how the Great Houses react. If the empire chose right now to invade, we would all be wiped out. It's only the wall—and the efforts of House Vivek and House Friere—that keep the empire at bay. The Great Houses need to unite, like we were when the nations first formed, even if we no longer possess one of the gifts the Light bestowed upon us."

"Your father thought the same way." Taegis smiled sadly. "I'm glad to see his will is strong in you."

Damien breathed in deeply and stared down at the crumpled paper in his hand. "It's not easy. I never thought I would become grand lord until I was much older."

Taegis reached over and placed a callused hand on Damien's shoulder. "You are strong in mind, body, and spirit. And you lead your people well."

"Thank you, Taegis. I think I'm going to end our sparring for today and—"

Another messenger from the tower burst into the training room. "Message for Lord Damien!" he panted and held out another rolled piece of parchment. "Urgent, from House Vivek."

Damien glanced at Taegis as he took the rolled piece of paper. Taegis looked as uneasy as Damien felt. Damien broke the official seal of House Vivek that was stamped into the wax and opened the letter.

A dozen ships have been spotted off the Cliffs of Bora with the insignia of the Dominia Empire. You and your people are in danger. You must raise the water boundary immediately before they reach your shores.

Lord Rune

Damien glanced at the date at the top. House Vivek used doves as their carriers, which meant the note was almost a day old. It would take the empire's fleet at least two days to reach a suitable beach to land on, if that was their plan, and two more to reach the city of Nor Esen and Northwind Castle.

Damien wrinkled his brow, his mind calculating the distance between Nor Esen, the speed of his ship, and the empire's fleet. If he left now, it would be close, but he could reach the area where he could raise the sea boundary and block the empire's fleet from landing. If not . . .

He shook his head. It would take too long to mobilize his own fleet. Raising the boundary was his only option.

"Lord Damien?" Taegis said quietly.

Damien looked up and realized he had been silent for a while. The messenger stood nearby, ready for orders.

"Lucas, I need you to run down to the port and tell Captain Stout that I need the *Ros Marinus* ready to sail immediately."

"Yes, my lord." Lucas bowed, then left.

Damien turned toward Taegis. "It is as we feared. The Dominia Empire is on the move. One of House Vivek's outposts along the Cliffs of Bora spotted a small fleet with the Dominia Empire's crest sailing our way."

"So the empire is going around the wall and coming by sea?"

"As far as we know, the empire does not have a large enough fleet to take all of us by water. I think Commander Orion is testing our defenses. A fleet that size could do little against all seven Great Houses. But it could hurt the Northern Shores if allowed to land." Damien placed a hand on the table where his sword lay. "That is how the empire almost won last time—not by facing all of us, but by picking off each house one by one."

Taegis pulled at the end of his beard. "Are you going to raise the sea boundary? Is that why you have Captain Stout preparing your ship?"

"Yes."

"Do you think you're ready?"

Damien turned and stared out of the window. It was one thing to move water or to raise a river—it was another thing to raise the entire sea boundary. His father had been able to do it, but his father had also had years of experience with their gift, whereas Damien had only been grand lord and sole heir of House Maris for less than two years. Those years had not been idle, though. He spent every day moving the sea and honing his gift. It was time to see if he could really protect his people. "I guess we'll find out."

A half hour later, the *Ros Marinus* sailed out of the harbor and into open sea. Damien stood at the bow and scanned the waters ahead. Grey clouds gathered above, snuffing out the sunlight from earlier.

"Clouds gather, but I don't foresee a storm at this point, my lord," Captain Stout said, coming to join him at the bow.

"That's good." A storm would complicate things. With this cloud coverage, all it would take was the wind picking up and a bit of rain to create turbulent weather. Hopefully they would be at the boundary by then. He didn't care what happened afterward, just as long as he had the boundary in place before the enemy fleet arrived.

Damien breathed in the sea air and closed his eyes. He listened as wave after wave crashed against the bow. He had only raised river boundaries, and those had been only for practice. This would be his first time raising the sea boundary.

"Worried?" Taegis said beside him.

Damien hesitated, then opened his eyes. "Perhaps a little."

Taegis leaned against the railing next to him and looked out over the grey waters. "I remember when I saw your father raise the sea boundary for the first time. I had never seen such a thing. That a man could raise his hands and the sea would respond."

Damien nodded. The first time he had raised a river, a feeling of euphoria had filled him. He could still remember how his hands felt weighed down, even though nothing sat in his palms. And how the river responded to his movement, rising up like a wall of water, reaching as high as the trees. Then, with a twist of his wrist, he locked the wall in place, effectively blocking anyone from the other side of the river from crossing. Of course, he only kept it up for a couple of weeks. It was all he could do.

He looked down at his hands. Since then, he had trained hard with his father, then alone, to make sure he was ready for this day: the day he would be called upon to protect his people with his mastery over water, the gift that had been given to his family over a millennia ago.

"I believe you can do it."

Damien glanced over at Taegis. The wind pulled at the older man's hair, tugging strands from the leather strip that held his hair back. Damien had known Taegis all his life; his earliest memories were of his father and Taegis laughing in the main hall over dinner. When his father died, Taegis became Damien's counselor, guardian, and friend, guiding him along the path of grand lord, teaching him the things his father would have when he was older.

To everyone else, Damien was Lord Maris, grand lord of the Northern Shores. To Taegis, he had a feeling he was the son the older man never had. And that suited him.

Taegis stepped back from the railing. "I don't think you've eaten all day. Come, let's find something for the both of us. This ship won't sail any faster with you standing here."

Damien straightened. "You're right." He would need all of his strength once they reached the place where he would raise the sea boundary. He cast one more look over the bow.

Water, as far as the eye could see.

Then he turned and followed Taegis.

Another wave hit the ship, spraying salt water up along the deck. Damien held on to the railing and let his body follow the movement of the ship. Thick dark clouds covered the sky blending in with the raging sea below.

The sea salt stung his face, and the wind pulled at his leather cloak. A rope was tied around his waist, a precaution should a wave prove too strong and try to sweep him overboard. Damien wiped his eyes and kept his gaze ahead, his gloved fingers curled around the wooden railing. The storm broke an hour ago, slowing them down just before the boundary. Hopefully that meant the empire's fleet had been slowed as well.

Another wave crested, sending the ship up for a moment, then plummeting down. Damien held on tight, feeling his insides move up into his throat, then rush down toward his middle. Quinn would have never been able to handle this storm. The slightest movement on the sea always made his little brother seasick.

An ache filled his chest, and Damien swallowed the lump inside his throat. Less than two years later and still the memories of his brother and parents affected him.

I need to focus. He pushed aside the feelings and breathed through his nose while he readjusted his feet. Right now, his people needed him.

The *Ros Marinus* pushed on through the storm. Once again Damien was thankful that Captain Stout was an excellent seaman and knew these waters well. Even so, if the welfare of the entire Northern Shores wasn't at stake, they would have turned back hours ago and sailed for cover until the weather passed.

A burst of wind hit the ship, sending Damien's cloak and hood flying back. Rain poured down, soaking his woolen clothes within minutes. He grit his teeth against the cold and tugged his cloak back around him. Even without the shore to tell him where they were, he knew they were close. He could feel it.

Moments later, one of the sailors crossed the deck to where he stood. "Captain Stout is preparing to drop the drogue and slow us down a bit," the sailor shouted. "With the weather the way it is, it's not possible to stop."

"That's fine," Damien shouted back. "I can raise the boundary from here."

"Yes, my lord. I shall inform the captain." The sailor made his way back.

Damien took a deep breath and planted his feet. Far off, a dark image appeared, darker than the storm clouds, riding along the waves. He narrowed his eyes. There was more than one.

The Dominia Empire's fleet.

His stomach hardened into a lead ball while his heart climbed into his throat, racing so fast it felt like it would burst out of him. Waves of adrenaline washed over him, leaving his body shivering and sweaty.

He only had minutes before the ships crossed the boundary.

Damien focused on the water between his ship and theirs. He pictured a line running between them. That was where he would raise the boundary.

"Light, Maker of Worlds," he whispered as he bent his knees and hunched down while raising his hands, palms up. "I bring before you my gift. Let me raise the water here and help me protect my people."

At once it felt like a heavy weight had settled across his hands, extending upward toward his arms, shoulders, and back, a weight so heavy that he could barely hold it. Every tendon bulged as sweat streamed down his face, mingling with the salt water and rain. The sea boundary was at least twice as heavy as any river boundary he had ever raised.

Damien closed his eyes and remembered all the days he spent on a cliff overlooking the sea, raising and lowering the waters. Time he had spent in communion with the Light and strengthening his gift.

He braced his body and prepared to raise the waters. His muscles screamed under the continual load. He panted and opened his eyes. The fleet was closer, close enough that he could see the outline of the leading ship. At this rate, they would get caught in the torrent when he raised the boundary.

What do I do? He grit his teeth and stared at the approaching ships. *I don't want to kill them. But . . . I don't have a choice. I need to raise the boundary. To protect my own people.*

Damien took a deep breath, his stomach heavy inside. *Don't think, just act. One. Two. Three—*

"Light, help me!" he shouted, his legs and back exploding up as he raised his arms upward. Along with his movement, the ocean in front of him shot up as well in an explosive display of water and spray. Within moments, a wall of water over a hundred feet high towered across the sea and spread rapidly left to right, tearing through the water like a fin.

He held fast on the deck, his hands raised, feeling the water rush as it surrounded the shores of his country.

Waves began to hit the ship as the ocean rebounded off of the newly made wall. Damien took a step back, keeping his balance and continuing to hold his hands up. Rain came down, pelting the deck and his body.

Almost . . . done . . .

Something dark appeared within the water-wall.

Damien strained against the surging power of the sea and peered at the torrential water-wall ahead. "No," he whispered.

Another dark object followed, then another.

Nausea swept through his body as he watched the empire's fleet rise and fall with quick succession inside the water-wall. Then, one by one, the bows went up while the stern tilted downward, plunging the ships into the sea and beneath the choppy waters like a child's toy in a stream.

Damien held back the bile building inside his throat. His only goal had been to raise the barrier and prevent the empire's ships from entering his nation's waters. Instead, it looked like he was going to take out the entire fleet—

Debris came rushing up through the water-wall. Broken parts of the ships—beams, planks, and poles—reached the top and bounced along the waves before being flung out in all directions.

A pole came sailing through the air and landed a few feet from the *Ros Marinus*. It bobbed for a moment before slipping down beneath the stormy water.

Damien gasped and took a step back but kept his hands up. The boundary had not quite reached the western shore, so he could not lock the water in place yet.

More wreckage flew through the air, landing around his ship. A splintered plank landed a foot away from where he stood. More pieces rained down. One hit his arm, sending surging pain across his forearm.

Damien blinked back tears and rain, his hands shaking as he held his palms up. Just a little bit longer—

A beam fell from the sky. He barely had time to step forward before it crashed into the deck, fracturing the planks before the bow. A crack echoed behind him. Damien twisted his wrists and locked the water-wall into place.

There. He was done—

The planks gave way beneath him, plunging him into the dark waters below.

10

Damien hit the water feet first. Frigid water sucked him down into the darkness beneath the waves, stealing his warmth away, the cold hitting his very core. Fear gripped his throat, but he kept it at bay. He opened his eyes to murky shadows and thrust out with his arms while clamping his mouth shut. With a couple of strong kicks, he started for the surface, the severed rope trailing behind him.

Something plunged into the water nearby. Out of the corner of his eye, he spotted a sailor, head down, a trail of dark liquid seeping from his body.

Damien broke the surface and gasped in a draught of air before diving for the body. He reached the sailor and grabbed hold of his collar and pulled him to the surface.

A wooden plank bobbed nearby. Damien reached for it with his free hand and pulled it under his arm. He looked back at the man. He was a Dominion sailor. The man's face was ashen, his eyes wide open in fear. A hole the size of Damien's fist was carved out of his chest, as if the man had been impaled on something, then freed of it. Dark liquid gushed from the wound, coloring the water around him while blood trickled out of the side of his mouth, mixing with the water running down his face.

With a cry, Damien let go of the man's collar and turned away, paddling with the plank beneath his arms. His whole body shook as he searched for the *Ros Marinus*.

His ship bobbed thirty feet away. Already sailors were scurrying across the deck and pointing in his direction. A wave crashed over him, pushing him beneath the water.

Damien held on to the plank and with powerful thrusts with his other arm, swam upward. When he reached the surface, he found the wave had pulled him farther from his ship.

More ship debris crashed around him, and he spotted another body. Dizziness swept across his mind and black spots appeared in front of his eyes. He could barely feel anything as tremors seized him.

I'm going to die! I'm going to—

No!

Damien struggled back up onto his plank as another wave washed over him.

No, I will not give up! Light, help me!

A small voice in the back of his mind chuckled softly. *Why would the Light help you? Look at all the men you've just killed.*

There was a break in the rain, and Damien looked around. Bits and pieces of a dozen ships were strewn across the waters. And in between broken masts and torn sails were bodies.

Hundreds of them.

Damien clung to the plank, frozen. He did this. He destroyed those ships. He killed these men. Father never told him how much destruction the water-wall could cause.

Oh, Light.

The *Ros Marinus* maneuvered its way through the carnage toward Damien. A rope was thrown over the side of his ship, a weighted board attached. It landed a few feet from Damien. At first, he stared at the board, his mind and body unable to move.

"Grab it!"

He faintly heard the shout over the waves and storm.

Grab it. He needed to grab it.

Damien blinked as if rousing from a deep sleep and moved. He kicked out with frozen legs, forcing everything from his mind but the board ahead. Finally, he reached for the board and let go of the broken plank.

He held on to the rope and board as a wave swelled beneath him. Once it passed, he placed the board beneath his arms and wrapped his arms and hands around the rope.

A moment later, there was a hard tug and the board began to move. Damien could barely feel his fingers and legs. And his chest hurt. Whether from the cold water or the carnage, he wasn't sure.

The board reached the side of the ship and began to ascend. Damien held on as the water tried to pull him back under. His arms screamed from the tugging and the weight of his soaked body. He locked his arms and pushed back the feeling.

Moments later, hands reached out and helped him over the railing and onto the deck. He collapsed, out of breath and out of strength. The rain had let up, but the wind raced across his soaked clothes and skin, sending shivers across his body.

One of the sailors knelt down beside him. "My lord, we need to get you belowdecks."

Damien roused himself and pushed up from the slick deck. Two of the sailors moved to help him, each grabbing him under his arms. Once he was on his feet, they led him toward the doorway where Taegis stood waiting.

"I'll take him from here," Taegis said, reaching for Damien.

Damien gave his consent, and the sailors moved away. His whole body was numb, and he shivered violently.

Taegis led him below to the captain's cabin. "We need to get you out of those wet clothes and into something warm. And I already have the cook preparing a broth for you."

"Thank . . . you . . ." Damien said between chattering teeth.

Taegis opened the door to the captain's cabin and led Damien inside. It was a small room, with a single bed built into the bulkhead, a small table nailed to the floor, and two chairs. A lamp swung above the table, the only light inside the room. Two portholes lined the other wall, but only dark clouds and rain filled their glass. Damien started stripping off the wet clothes as Taegis pulled dry, clean ones from the leather bag that sat next to the bed.

He placed the clothes on the table. "I'm going to get that broth for you."

Damien nodded as he tugged off his woolen shirt.

Taegis shut the door behind him.

Damien quickly changed into the dry clothes and climbed into the bed, tucking the thick covers and furs around his body. He knew only too well how the frigid seawater could steal away a man's warmth, health, and even life.

After a while, he stopped shivering and turned around so he could see the table and door. Doubts began to rise. Would his father have raised the boundary and let those men die, as he had done? Or would his father have found a different way to save their people?

Damien took a deep, pained breath and closed his eyes. His mind replayed the last hour over and over again, searching for anything he had missed, any way he could have done things differently. But with each recap, he saw no other alternative. If he had let the fleet get any closer, he could not have raised the boundary around the entire coast, and the fleet might have found a place to land.

Damien rolled onto his back and looked up at the wooden ceiling, clenching his hands. He did what he had to do: save his people, no matter the cost.

So why did he feel this deep-seated guilt?

The door opened, and Taegis walked in with a tray in hand. "I have both tea and broth," he said as he crossed the room. Damien sat up and leaned back against the headboard. Taegis placed the tray on his lap.

As Taegis went for a chair, Damien wrapped his fingers around the ceramic mug and breathed in the earthy scent. A matching bowl sat on the tray with wisps of steam rising into the air.

Taegis pulled the chair over and sat down. "I saw what you did."

Damien paused, his fingers tightening around the mug. "You were watching?"

"Of course. You did exactly what you were supposed to. You raised the sea boundary—and quite powerfully, I might add. Your father never was able to raise the wall that high."

Damien lifted the mug to his lips. He blew across the dark amber liquid before taking a sip. The tea warmed his insides on the way down, but he still felt chilled to the bone. "Did you see everything?"

"I did."

"And?"

"There wasn't anything you could do."

Damien worked his jaw. "It's all I've been able to think about."

"It is good to look back and consider if things could have been different. Sometimes they could have, and we learn from that. However, it is not wise to be too introspective. You did what you needed to do, and now the deed is done. In some ways, this was your first foray into war—a war that will inevitably come if the empire invades our land. And when it comes, more people will die."

Damien looked down into his mug. "I don't like it."

Taegis snorted. "I'm glad you don't like it. You're by nature a guardian. Your gift is to protect people. But . . ." He sat back and shrugged. "We no longer live in a time of peace."

Damien glanced up. "Did my father ever hurt others with his power?"

Taegis frowned. "Once, at least that I know of. There was a company of bandits roaming the Magyr Mountains years back, pillaging and burning their way across the country. They arrived at the Hyr River at the same time as your father. He had no choice but to raise the boundary with them close by, and the river washed the men away."

Damien paused, then placed the mug down and lifted the bowl of broth. As he gulped the meaty liquid, he mentally disagreed. It wasn't the same. Bandits were known criminals. Those sailors, however . . .

He placed the bowl down and wiped his mouth. They may or may not have believed in the empire's agenda. They might have even been conscripts. Damien had no way of knowing. But he still took their lives anyway.

He didn't like it. He didn't like it at all.

But Taegis was right. War would soon be upon them, and they needed to be ready or more people would die. Perhaps he could minimize that. "When we arrive back to Nor Esen, I'm going to send out messenger falcons to the seven Great Houses and call for an assembly."

Taegis's eyebrows shot up. "An assembly of the Great Houses? One has not been called since the end of the razing by the empire."

"I know."

Taegis eyed him carefully. "You will be required to exert your power and influence as grand lord of House Maris. Are you prepared to do that?"

Damien looked down at his hands. He had just raised the sea

boundary to save his people. If he had to face the other Great Houses in order to save more people, he would. "Yes. It is too long since the Great Houses met. We must unite and use what gifts we still retain. Perhaps a show of power will dissuade the empire."

"And if not?"

"There is still the coalition."

"Yes, but the coalition is made up of lesser lords and ladies and civilians. If you go against the Dominia Empire, you'll need the might of the Great Houses."

Damien sighed. "I know. I hope that this threat from the empire will be the catalyst that brings the Great Houses together. The wall between our lands and my water-wall will only hold the empire back for so long. If we cannot find a way to stop the empire now, we will lose everything." He looked up at Taegis. "In the end, we may need to fight back. Every one of us. Great Houses and citizens alike."

11

Lady Ragna sat on her throne in the great hall and read the message from House Maris. Young Lord Damien was calling for an Assembly of the Great Houses. She placed the parchment down and gazed ahead.

The massive room was empty, save for the two guards near the front doorway. Long narrow windows lined either side of the hall, allowing pale light inside. Thick columns, hewn from the obsidian stone found within the Magyr Mountains, held up the high ceiling. The air was cold, much too cold for an early summer morning, but the coldness helped keep her mind sharp, and so she welcomed it.

Lady Ragna tapped her finger against the thick wooden armrest. Lord Damien's message was surprising. This was a bold move for a new grand lord—and a young one, at that. No one had called for an assembly since the end of the empire's razing over four hundred years ago, after her house had been wiped out.

A bitter taste filled her mouth. Only after her family had been destroyed did the Great Houses finally come together. But by then it was too late.

"They thought too little of our gift," she whispered. "What

could Dreamers do compared to controlling water, manipulating fire, or brandishing light as a weapon? Even House Rafel and House Vivek were highly regarded due to their gifts of healing and wisdom. And so we were given over to the empire and wiped out."

She straightened and took a long, deep breath. It didn't matter now. All that mattered was protecting her family's legacy. She stood, the message still in hand, and headed for the door. The guards came to attention and saluted as she approached. She ignored them and headed into the hall.

She needed to know what the future held for her family before she responded back to House Maris. Would this assembly benefit House Ravenwood, or would it hurt her family in some way?

Her gown and cloak flew behind her as she hurried down the corridors toward the sanctuary. The priest would know. Surely by now the Dark Lady had spoken to him.

Twenty minutes later, she stepped into the sanctuary. The sanctum was even chillier than the great hall. Lady Ragna suppressed a shiver. The sanctuary was similar in design to the great hall, only smaller and darker. The windows were set north to allow maximum exposure to the moon and night sky in the evenings. Carved pillars lined the long room, cast in grey stone. There would be a new moon in one week's time, the best time to hear from the Dark Lady, but she couldn't wait until then. She needed to know now in order to respond to Lord Damien.

A shadow passed to her left, just beyond one of the columns. She slowed and watched as the priest made his way to the dais. His grey robes were a shade darker than the surrounding stone, and he wore a knotted rope around his middle. His head was covered by his cowl, concealing his face and hair. With his back to her, he stepped onto the raised platform and held out a long stick with a flaming tip. Inside the retable were dozens of candles of different shapes and sizes. With the glowing stick, he started to light each one.

Lady Ragna made her way across the inner sanctuary toward the dais, her gown barely whispering with each step.

The priest paused, his veined hand hovering over a candle. "Lady Ragna," he rasped before turning around. His watery blue eyes came to rest on her. "What brings you to the sanctuary today?"

She approached the dais and knelt down. "I desire your counsel, wise one. Does the Dark Lady have any words for me?" She did not need to say why. The Dark Lady would know.

The priest placed the stick inside a small silver vase between the candles, ember side up, and turned. He clasped his hands in front of him and closed his eyes. His lips began to move as he chanted silently.

Lady Ragna waited. The air around them began to change, becoming almost stifling, like a thick, invisible fog. The priest went stiff. He opened his eyes, now unfocused. "Hope will come from the north. A hope for the Great Houses. That which is hidden will come to light and the broken will be healed. But this hope carries with it the end of House Ravenwood. If this hope is allowed to come to pass, House Ravenwood will be no more."

Lady Ragna froze. She stared at the floor where her hands were spread out in supplication. The priest's words echoed inside her mind. *The end of House Ravenwood.* This . . . this was not what she was expecting.

If allowed to come to pass . . .

She curled her fingers. No, she would not let it come to pass. Too much had been sacrificed to bring her house back to power.

Beware the north.

She looked up. North . . .

Did the words mean House Maris? Or House Vivek? Both were northern houses.

The priest's body relaxed as he came out of the trance. He blinked his eyes several times, then looked down at her. "Those are the words from the Dark Lady," he rasped. "Did you need anything else, Lady Ragna?"

"No." She stood and brushed her gown with cold fingers. "Thank you, wise one." She bowed her head, then turned.

A heavy weight sat across her mind and heart as she made her way past the columns and back toward Rook Castle. These were not the words she had been hoping for. Since her mother had first revealed to her the history of House Ravenwood, she had worked tirelessly and sacrificed much to bring it back to power. For too long she had seen the derision in the eyes of the other houses and heard their whispers about Ravenwood. What those naysayers didn't know was that her house had not perished after the empire's razing. One heir had survived. Rabanna.

Lady Ragna made her way back to her own rooms and shut the door behind her. When Rabanna had first arrived back to Rook Castle after the betrayal of the other houses and years of exile in the Dominia Empire, she had found the mountain nation in disarray, with a new lord leading House Ravenwood. It took years of secret contracts and negotiations for Rabanna to finally find herself as lady of Rook Castle.

Lady Ragna looked around her suite. The rooms were expansive and richly decorated, thanks to generations of Ravenwood women, each one building upon the fortunes of the previous heir. Above the massive stone fireplace was a painting of Rabanna herself. She stared down at the sitting room with cold, dark eyes.

Lady Ragna approached the fireplace and placed a hand on the mantel. She stared down at the empty grate where only cinders remained.

The end of House Ravenwood.

She closed her hand into a fist. How could that be? So many generations of Ravenwood women had sacrificed to bring House Ravenwood back. Each marriage a political move, each daughter groomed to take House Ravenwood to the next level. Every heart hardened so that missions could be carried out.

"No!" She slammed her hand into the stone. "Whatever the hope from the north, I won't let it be the end of House Raven-wood."

But it will bring light and healing, a small voice whispered inside her head.

Lady Ragna laughed coldly. "What do I care of light and heal-ing? Where was this light when our house fell the first time? Where were the other houses when the empire razed our nation and killed most of our people? I only serve House Ravenwood, and I will not see it fall."

She turned away and began to pace the sitting room. Only House Maris and House Vivek dwelt in the north. And both would be at the assembly. She paused and stared out the long windows in front of her. The head of each house would need to be taken out quietly, in a way that no one would suspect murder. Given what she knew of each house, House Vivek seemed the greater threat, especially since it was House Vivek that orchestrated the betrayal that led to the capture of House Ravenwood by the empire those hundreds of years ago.

"But I can't let House Maris survive, either," Lady Ragna said softly. She tapped a finger gently across her mouth.

Selene.

Selene could take out the head of House Maris.

Lady Ragna spun around, her mind working faster and faster toward a plan. House Maris were followers of the Light, which meant it might be harder to break into the young new lord's dreams. She scowled at the thought. On the other hand, he was inexperienced, and perhaps not as strong of a follower as his predecessors. And Selene was powerful.

Lady Ragna stopped and smiled. Yes, Selene was very powerful. She glanced at Rabanna's portrait. Perhaps as powerful as Rabanna herself. Maybe Selene had been born for such a time as this. To save House Ravenwood.

"I'll need to work with her more," Lady Ragna murmured. "She will need more practice, though, before she is ready to tackle the grand lord of House Maris."

Breaking into the dreams of a Light-follower could be difficult. They were not always as easily manipulated by nightmares as others were. But Selene could do it. Even now she remembered how easily her daughter had been able to manipulate Petur and Hagatha's dreams. It had taken Lady Ragna herself many tries under her own mother's watchful eye before she could do what Selene had done in a single dream.

Lady Ragna headed for the door, the weight from the priest's words already lifting from her shoulders. She had nothing to fear. It had been prudent to seek out the wise one's counsel. In fact, since Rook Castle was centrally located amongst the houses, she would offer it as the location for the assembly. She now knew where the danger lay for House Ravenwood, and with Selene's help, she would extinguish it.

S elene stared at the fireplace ahead, her swords hidden beneath her cloak. Behind the hearth was the secret tunnel that led down to the training caverns. Her eyes felt like they had sand in them, and she gripped her upper arm. Her hair was pulled back in a haphazard braid. It was the best she could do since Renata—

She jumped back and glanced around. Her nerves crackled like lightning, sending tendrils of pain across her body. She glanced again at the hidden door and turned away. There was no way she could go down there anymore. Down into the darkness. Down where everything reminded her of what she was, and what she was training to become.

Selene fled the faux sitting room and hurried along the hall. She needed to get out of here, somewhere open, somewhere where there was light. There was an old training area south of Rook Castle, rarely used by the guards. She would go there.

She let out her breath. The thought of exercising slowly began to still her restless mind. Training had a way of allowing her to narrow her focus on the practice dummy and shove aside all other thoughts. And that was what she needed now. Something to take her mind off of that night. She would use the extra set of breeches and tunic from her room and hide her apparel underneath her cloak. No need to go down into the caverns.

After changing, she followed the corridors toward the southern side of Rook Castle and descended to the first floor. Near the back, she found the small door that led outside. As she opened it, warm summer air rushed to meet her face. A cheery sun hung overhead, bright against the spring sky. Just beyond the door was a small training area, the size of her bedchambers. On one side stood an old empty shed. The other two sides were hemmed in by Rook Castle and the surrounding outer wall. The northern side narrowed into a path that led to the main bailey of the castle. In the corner stood a hickory tree with a thick trunk and broad green coverage. Three practice dummies were set up near the outer wall.

The wind swept away the strands of hair that hung around her face. Selene took a deep breath, already feeling the tightness across her shoulders and the restlessness of her mind easing. This place was perfect. A quiet, out-of-the-way area where she could be alone with her thoughts and emotions.

She headed toward the weatherworn dummies, their canvas bodies stained and bulging in some areas. The target paint had faded and bits of straw poked out where the seams had come undone. Selene drew out her swords and stood before the middle one, raised her right arm while positioning her left arm across her body, and started her routine.

The sun made its way across the sky as Selene assaulted the dummy. With each hit, her strength and energy returned, burning away the fatigue from lack of sleep. Sweat soaked into her dark tunic and pants, and her hair stuck to her face.

Faster. Harder.

But the exercises only kept the demons away for a while. Soon, the memories of that night crept back. Renata's nightmare. The sound of her screams. The feelings of rage and helplessness exploding from Selene. The dreamscape shattering beneath her power. And Renata—

Selene stopped, her arms lifted. She saw Renata lying on the sleeping mat, pale in the moonlight, a trickle of blood beneath her nostril.

"I didn't mean to," she whispered, her eyes unfocused. "I had no idea. . . ."

It felt like a ball of lead was expanding inside of her, heavy and solid, pushing all of the air from her lungs and causing her heart to struggle beating. Her arms fell to her sides, and her swords dropped to the ground. Selene followed, landing on her knees. She crossed her arms over her chest and curled over her legs.

She rocked back and forth and sobbed. Each muffled cry felt like it was torn from her very soul. Instead of killing her, Selene had left Renata with a crippled mind. And she wasn't sure which one was worse.

"I wish I didn't have this power." She gripped her fingers and held her hands next to her chest. "I can't keep going on like this. It's going to tear me apart! Why can't there be another way to take care of our people? I don't think we even are, not if we are hurting the very ones—"

Another sob stole away her words. Where was the line? When did there come a point where their power was hurting their people more than helping? Was there any other way?

You must lock away your heart. You must never feel.

Selene stopped rocking as her mother's words filled her mind. As much as she loathed it, her mother was right. The only way she could survive the power inside of her was to close off her heart. To become cold. To never feel.

She looked up, her hands still clasped near her heart. For the first time, she wanted that coldness. It had to be better than this heart-wrenching agony she felt right now. Instead of locking her heart in a wooden chest, she imagined putting it inside a dark room. Then she shut the door—a thick iron door. But that wasn't enough. Inside her mind, she slammed one iron door after another until instead of anguish, all she felt was a deep numbness.

Selene took a deep breath and squared her shoulders. She slowly staggered to her feet. Every time she despaired over the bleakness of her future, she slammed another door shut. Maybe there was a way to escape her destiny, a better way than the one they were following now. But until she could figure it out, she had to keep her heart locked far, far away.

It was the only way she could survive.

"Selene, would you care to join me in my study this evening?"

Selene glanced up from her untouched soup—a cold concoction made of mashed beets—her spoon still beside the ceramic bowl. Father hadn't asked her to his study in years, not since Mother had taken over her education and training. Before that, she had spent almost every wintry evening with him, sitting beside the fireplace, quietly poring over books while thick snowflakes fell outside the windows.

The memory and the longing it brought in its wake for those simpler, quieter times came so vividly it took her breath away. "Yes," she said as she picked up her spoon. "I would like that."

She brought the spoon down into the red borscht, a lighthearted feeling spreading within her chest. As Mother's consort, Father held a lower role within House Ravenwood. But he never saw himself as anything but a father to her, Opheliana, and Amara, although as Amara grew older, she rebuffed their father's affection. Amara possessed the same pride as their mother did in the family name, and since Father was an outsider, he was not truly part of the family. But to Selene, he would always be her papa.

"Excellent." Father wiped his mouth with the linen napkin and placed it down beside him. "I will have a tea tray delivered for us."

Selene scooped up the red soup and brought it to her mouth. Her appetite had returned, just a little. After Father left, the dining hall grew quiet. Mother was gone for the next fortnight on a trip east to visit House Friere, and Amara had gone with her. And Ophie was too young to join family meals.

Slowly, the melancholy of the last few days trickled back. Selene ate a couple more bites, then pushed the soup bowl aside and stood. The light grew dim as the sun set outside, and the candles had not yet been lit.

"Lady Selene."

Her body tightened as she slowly turned around. "Captain Stanton."

Captain Stanton stood in the doorway, dressed in his usual dark clothes and leather garb. His dark hair hung in strands around his face as he stared at her through lidded eyes. Like a shadow, always following her. "Do you require anything of me this evening?"

Selene lifted her chin in a defiant way and gathered her gown. "No, but thank you for your concern."

He bobbed his head in a casual manner and stepped back as Selene walked through the doorway. She felt his eyes follow her as she made her way down the corridor. If there was one benefit to becoming grand lady of Ravenwood someday, it would be finding a new captain of the guard. She didn't trust Captain Stanton to watch a dog, let alone be concerned about her welfare. She might not know much about men, but even she knew what was in the captain's mind without needing to visit his dreams. She clenched her hand and jaw while looking directly ahead.

As she made her way through the hallways toward the northern end of Rook Castle, the heat of the day slowly seeped out of the castle. The day had been uncomfortably warm, even with the windows open to let the mountain air through. She dabbed her face with her handkerchief, then tucked it back into her sleeve. At the end of the third corridor, she opened the thick wooden door that led to her father's study.

The walls were stone slabs with windows encased around the room. A desk stood across the way between two open windows. The sky outside was a deep plum color, a contrast to the merry orange light from the candles lit around the room.

Selene stepped inside. The wooden floor was worn, with an old rug with faded colors set before the desk. The subtle hint of pipe leaf and vanilla hung in the air, mixing with the musty odor of a thousand years of knowledge. She closed her eyes and breathed it in. Everything here reminded her of her father.

"Selene."

She opened her eyes and spotted him sitting over on the right side of the room in one of two wooden chairs set up between a set of long, narrow bookcases. She recognized the leather-bound book he held carefully between his fingers: an account of the history of House Vivek before the razing.

"Father." Around the rest of the room were matching bookcases, all of them containing the books Father brought with him when he moved away from the lands of House Vivek, a traditional parting gift for a citizen of the nation of wisdom. Though not a direct descendant of the Great House, he was still the most knowledgeable man Selene knew. And she loved him for it.

"It has been a long time since you came to my study." He smiled as he rose and placed the book back in the empty spot three shelves up on the left. "I've missed you."

"And I have missed you." She took a seat in the chair opposite him. There was no need to say why they had been parted. She was sure it had to do with her mother. Which made this evening's meeting curious.

His silver hair was brushed back and his beard trimmed, as always. His eyes crinkled now in the corners, and there were additional fine lines across his forehead and around his mouth. He studied her for a moment before taking a seat. She couldn't miss the look of concern on his face.

"Since I was young, I always knew what my duty would be. As a member of a lesser house, I would be married off to a greater house and produce heirs for that house. But I wanted more. I wanted to be your father. As much as I could, I have done that, even as hard as it was to watch your mother groom you to be the next Lady Ravenwood." He folded his hands in his lap. "The last few weeks, word has reached my ears that you have changed, Selene. And I think I know why. Is it true? Has your gift come?"

The only other person besides her mother and sister who knew of the dreamwalking power was Father. His marriage to Mother had conferred to him that knowledge. When the oaths of matrimony were taken, all was revealed to the couple.

"It has."

"And it's not what you were expecting."

Selene glanced away. "No, it's not."

He nodded slowly. "I am not privy to the workings of House Ravenwood. And I'm not sure if you can even share what you are going through, if your mother has bound you to house secrecy. But if there is anything I can do, please let me know. I love you, and I would do anything for you."

Selene swallowed the lump inside her throat. He was so different than Mother. "Yes, I know."

But what could he do? She couldn't even tell him what Mother was training her to do. Was that her destiny? To be a killer? She clenched her hands until her fingernails dug into her palms as her eyes began to burn with unshed tears. She felt trapped by the dark future looming in front of her. If only she knew why they had been given this gift in the first place. . . .

Wait. Maybe he could—

There was a knock at the door.

"Yes," her father said. "Come in."

The door opened with a creak, and one of the servants walked in with a wooden tray bearing a small cast-iron teapot and two matching cups.

"Right here, Mira." Father pointed toward the table between the chairs.

The maid bowed her head and crossed the room. She placed the tray on the table and quietly backed away.

"Thank you."

Mira bobbed her head and left the room, shutting the door behind her.

Another difference between Mother and Father: the way they treated the castle servants. Her chest tightened as she remembered her mother's cold words about Renata. Selene pressed her lips together as she watched her father pour the earthy liquid into the two cups. No, she would not be like Mother. Not if she could help it. But was she destined to become just that? Could she remain loving and kind while closing off her heart? Or was she already turning into the coldhearted woman the servants were beginning to comment upon?

"Here." Father held out a small iron cup to her.

Selene took the cup and held it between her fingers, letting the aroma fill her nostrils. "How much do you know about the Great Houses and their gifts?" she asked, the cup remaining in her hand.

Her father paused. "Well," he said slowly as he turned and sat down with his own cup in hand. "Not much. Most of the Vade Mecum Library was destroyed during the Dominia razing. And in that library were the oldest recordings of the Great Houses, including the dispersion of the gifts."

"Well, what do you know?"

He shook his head. "Not much. Why?" He glanced at her shrewdly. "Are you wondering about your own gift?"

Selene looked down into her cup. "Yes."

"I'm afraid the dreamwalking gift is the one most lost to history. People don't even know it still exists."

"Except for you." Selene glanced at her father.

He nodded. "Except for me. And even then, other than what passed through the marriage bond, your mother has never shared anything with me and has bound me to the house secret."

Selene slowly took another sip. "Why did you marry Mother?" she finally asked.

There was another pause, this one more drawn out. Whether because of more house secrets or because her father was forming his words, she wasn't sure. He looked out the window, his tea cupped between his fingers. "I cannot tell you everything, but I can tell you that most marriages are not bound in love. Usually they are an arrangement to the benefit of each Great House or the greater house finds something they desire in the lesser house."

"And you? Did House Vivek bind you to my mother? Or did she want you?"

"Neither."

His answer took her back. Did Father actually love Mother at one point? Is that why he married her?

"There is a group of people who have been searching for a way to unite the Great Houses. This group has existed for many years, quietly working to bring every nation together. And there is another group who only wants power, also working covertly toward that goal."

Selene placed her cup down on the table, her heart beating fast. She recalled Mother speaking of a secret group of people who wished to merge the Great Houses and do away with the gifts. Was this the group her father spoke of?

Was he . . . was he one of them?

She licked her lips. He couldn't be. Such people were executed. Only last year a man had been thrown from the wall of Rook Castle for such sedition. And House Friere burned three heretics at the stake this past winter.

"I married your mother for peace. And"—he looked back at her—"to see if the dreamwalking gift still existed."

Selene stared at him. He married her mother to see if the gift of House Ravenwod still existed? But why? He couldn't tell anyone. He was bound to secrecy by her mother. "Why are you telling me this?"

"Because you asked why I married your mother."

"And why did you care if the dreamwalking gift still existed?"

"Because I believe it is an important gift, one that has the potential to unite the Great Houses."

"So you hoped to change Mother?" Selene almost laughed at that thought. No one could change Mother. And Mother was definitely not interested in uniting the houses, not after what they did to the Ravenwood family during the empire's razing.

"No. So I could help you."

She frowned. What did he mean by that? He married Lady Ragna to see if the gift was still there, hidden behind secrets. And then what? Have children who possessed that gift?

Selene looked down at her fingers, her tea on the table nearby. Wait. So Father married Mother because the only way he could find out if the dreamwalking gift still existed was by the knowledge he would receive through the marriage binding. Then she was born. And his hope was what? To use her gift? To somehow unite the nations through her? Was he truly part of that group that wanted to merge the Great Houses and do away with their gifts?

"You asked if I knew anything about the dreamwalking gift." She heard the gentle *thump* as he placed his own cup down. "I don't know much, but I do know a few things. House Ravenwood was once called the House of Dreamers. While the other Great Houses were given gifts to guard their people, instruct them, or fight to protect them, the Dreamers were different. They were given the gift of inspiration, the ability to enter the very hearts and minds of their people and encourage them. It is written that they could reach beyond the mountain nation and inspire all the nations."

Her heart beat faster. "How did they do that?"

Her father shook his head. "I don't know. That is all I know about the dreamwalking gift. Sadly, it was seen as inferior to the other gifts—ones like healing, courage, and the ability to use the light as a weapon. And so House Ravenwood was sold out to the empire as a way to appease the commander at the time and save the other nations."

"But we weren't wiped out."

"No, you were not. But I suspect the dreamwalking gift is used in a different way now, correct?"

Selene remained silent. Should she answer him? Could she trust him? After all, he had nearly admitted he was part of a renegade group of people who—if her mother knew—would be rounded up and tossed from the walls of Rook Castle. Father was living a very dangerous life, one that he'd planned out for a long time, it sounded like. Long enough that he found a way to enter the graces of the Lady of Ravenwood and marry her—just to find out about this gift.

But perhaps he could help her. This picture he painted of the

Dreamers, of what her family had once been, was ten times better than what they were now. Instead of taking lives, she could inspire them. How to do that eluded her, but she was willing to learn.

Selene opened her mouth to answer his question and found her voice had vanished. She closed it. It appeared it didn't matter if she trusted Father. Mother had their training bound within a house secret. "I-I can't say."

Father nodded. "I understand."

Secrets. So many secrets. Selene glanced out the window. It was dark now, and a cool mountain breeze blew through the opening. Sometimes it felt like all those secrets were going to choke her to death, if the darkness did not kill her first.

Did every Great House have this many secrets?

"Still, if there is anything I can do to help you, I will do it. I believe you have the ability to do what no one else can."

Selene glanced sharply back. "Why didn't you share any of this with me before?"

"As you can see, my position is a precarious one. I am a consort. That title would not save me if . . ." He shrugged and let her fill in the blanks.

No, he never came out and said it, but she knew now he was part of that renegade group. The coalition.

"I chose not to share with you until I knew you were ready, and the time was right. I had to be sure. . . ."

"Sure? Sure of what?"

"That you had the potential and willingness to change. House Ravenwood has a history of hatred—and rightly so. Your ancestors were given over to the empire and wiped off the face of the map—or so we thought. Your mother is a cold and bitter woman. Your sister Amara is heading in the same direction. The question is, what will you do, Selene? Will you be just like them—or will you be different?"

Selene clenched her hands. "But how? All you told me was my gift was once used to inspire others. How do I do that? And Mother—" Her voice vanished. Selene smashed her lips together in frustration. Secrets once again.

Father pulled on the end of his beard. "What if I could find a way to get you away from here?"

Selene narrowed her eyes. "From here? You mean Rook Castle?"

"Away from your mother's influence. A place where you would be allowed to hone your own gift and figure out who you are."

She shook her head. "I am the heir to Ravenwood. There is no leaving for me." As she said those words, they sunk deep inside of her. Her father's words, like rays of hope, disappeared as quickly as they'd come. There was no escape for her. Even if she ran, Mother would hunt her down and find her. Most likely she would be locked away and Amara would lead the family, leaving Ophie vulnerable to the family gift and all it entailed.

Selene stood. "Thank you for always caring for me. But we both know what my future holds."

Father stood as well. "Don't give up just yet, Selene."

She shook her head sadly and turned for the door. With each step, she closed off her heart so that by the time she reached for the latch, she was numb again.

"I will find a way to help you," he called after her as she left his study.

Just hopeful words. That's all they were. But she wasn't a little girl anymore. She could no longer go crying to her father and have him kiss away the pain.

The Dark Lady had set her course the moment the mark had been burned into her back. The Dreamers, whatever they had been, no longer existed. In their place now were the dreamkillers.

13

Selene!"

Selene turned around and found her father in the hallway with a stack of books in his hands the next day. She was thankful that she had washed and changed after her workout in the small outdoor training area in the back of the castle. Father, like the rest of the occupants of Rook Castle, did not know about the covert life the women of Ravenwood led. Apart from the secret being bound to House Ravenwood by her mother, it wasn't something she wanted him to know about. How would she explain she wasn't training to be a lady but an assassin? She couldn't bear to see the hurt in his eyes if he really knew what she was training to use her gift for.

He approached her with a soft smile on his face. "It's not much, but I was able to find a little bit about the Great Houses and their gifts. Most of the houses fiercely guard their secrets, but there is a little bit of information. And with the upcoming assembly, I thought you might want to know more about the houses that will be visiting."

Selene stared at the books, previous thoughts gone, replaced with the sudden desire to know more. She barely knew anything about the other houses. Most of the seven Great Houses kept to themselves, governing their own people, and only venturing beyond their borders in order to trade or forge alliances. She had only visited House Friere since her house and theirs often traded, especially back when the mines were active.

She reached for the books. "Thank you, Father."

He handed them over. There were four in all, each one bound in leather and as thick as three fingers.

"It's not much. Most of the books talk about the history and culture of each Great House and the nations they govern. And even then, the history is only after the empire's razing. But I thought you might find something. As the future grand lady of House Ravenwood, it is something you should know about."

Selene nodded. So far, Mother had covered very little about the other houses, perhaps because she wanted to focus on their training first. Selene's only knowledge came from excursions to the library, but nothing had turned up there. "I'll start reading this afternoon."

He gave her a firm nod. "Take as much time as you want. I don't need them back any time soon." Father turned and headed back to the west wing toward his own rooms.

Selene stared down at the books, eagerness filling her chest. Mother and Amara would not be home from their visit to House Friere for another day, which gave her at least this afternoon, evening, and the next morning to read.

With that thought, she hurried back to her own room.

Sunlight poured through the open window, illuminating everything inside Selene's bedchambers. She sat on a bench beside the window, her legs tucked up beneath her, her hair knotted at the back of her neck, a book opened on the cushion beside her. Father was right—there wasn't much information about the gifts the Great Houses possessed. So far, all she had discovered was House

Maris could control water somehow, House Luceras wielded light and was home to the famous paladins of light, House Rafel could heal with the use of special herbs, and House Vivek was famous for their wisdom. Nothing on House Friere, House Merek of the Southern Isles, or her own house.

Selene sighed and looked out the window. Summer would be over soon, and the time of harvest would be upon them, along with the Assembly of the Great Houses. Huge pine trees covered the mountains of Magyr, painting the mountain range in deep green. She watched an eagle glide high above the peaks, a speck against the bright blue sky. She remembered being a raven and how the wind felt beneath her, buffeting her, her wings spread out as she soared above the dreamscape. She marveled in the way freedom felt and the overwhelming sense of joy. If only she could always be a raven, flying high above the cares of this world.

But that was only in dreams—dreams where her job was to search out secrets or resurface old fears.

"That can't be why we were given the gift of dreamwalking." She closed the book and picked up another. Father said House Ravenwood was the House of Dreamers, and through dreams, her ancestors had inspired people. But how? And why? She opened the cover. Compared to the other houses, her own gift seemed small and insignificant. Other houses had heroes, men and women who fought with amazing power, protected their people, and healed those on the brink of death.

And House Ravenwood?

"Nothing," she whispered. Nothing about the Dreamers. No wonder Rabanna had chosen to take their gift in a different direction. Now they had power and wealth because of their dreamkilling. And if the other Great Houses turned against them like they did before the razing, she knew her mother would fight back. Her bitterness ran deep.

Selene spent the rest of the afternoon and evening looking over the last two books, only taking a break for dinner. By the time she finished the last book, night had fallen across the castle and the servants had lit the candles. A cool breeze swept through the castle, forcing out the hot summer heat and leaving behind a cool reprieve.

She placed the last book on top of the others and pinched her lips together. Again nothing. Her back and shoulders were stiff from bending over the tomes, and her head ached just behind her right eye. She rubbed the offending area and sat back, staring across the room.

The fireplace was cold and dark. Her bed, an ancient piece of furniture bought from merchants from the south and hewn from a single tree, sat near the fireplace, devoid of the usual furs and covered only by a single blanket. Next to the bed on a small table sat a string of black beads.

She gazed at the beads. She hadn't prayed to the Dark Lady in months, not since her gift had arrived. In fact, she hadn't even been back to the sanctuary. Before her gifting, she had been a doubtful—though dutiful—follower. Now . . .

Now something scared her about the Dark Lady. As if sensing her thoughts, a wind rushed through the room, and the light from the candlestick wavered before coming back to full blaze. A shiver ran down Selene's spine as she gazed around the room. It was almost as if she were being . . . watched.

She got to her feet and hurried across the room and picked up the beads. The small black orbs were cold between her fingers. Prayers from her childhood rose from the back of her mind but stopped at her lips. It was as if her mouth had been sealed. They would not form the rote words her mother had made her memorize years ago.

Was it possible there was no Dark Lady?

No, she knew the Dark Lady existed. Something deep inside her knew this. And yet . . .

And yet what about the other stories? The ones about an older god? And the old ways?

Who exactly gave the Great Houses their gifts? That was what Selene wanted to know. Had the Dark Lady? Another deity? The god of the old ways? The Light, which some of the houses served?

I want to know, but no one seems to have answers.

She held the beads up for a bit longer, then placed them back down on the table. Even fear could not make her follow that which she doubted. She no longer knew who or what she believed in.

She stared out at the night sky beyond her window, as a hollowness expanded inside her chest. All she knew was her future. She was a lady of Ravenwood. She would walk through the dreams of others, stealing or killing when she needed to. There was no other path for her, except for this long, dark, lonely one.

14

D amien stood on top of a narrow precipice that extended over the sea. Down below, waves crashed against the jagged coastline, sending up sprays of white foamy water with resounding crashes. Behind him stood the port city of Nor Esen and his home, Northwind Castle.

Deep blue water extended as far as the eye could see, spreading out beneath a lighter blue sky. Gulls glided through the air, buffered by the winds. The air was brisk this morning and scented with salt. Damien breathed it in deeply before lifting his hands and closing his eyes. He could feel the water-wall he had raised steadily siphoning energy from his power. It wasn't enough to drain him completely, but it left him weaker than usual.

He listened to the water and felt it sink into his soul. Then he started his daily ritual. First with one hand, then with the other, he lifted the water, sending the incoming waves higher and higher until the water crashed just below the ledge he stood on.

As he moved his arms in the familiar rotation, his mind lifted heavenward. *Light, Maker of Worlds, here is my gift. Let me use the waters to protect my people.* He started his morning prayers the same way every day as he practiced raising the water.

Then he planted his feet and moved his hands in front of him, this time pushing the waves away. As he started his next routine, he went through each servant, starting with Taegis, and let his heart pour over their lives, lifting up their fears, their happiness, and their longings to the Light.

Time went by, and he changed his position again, placing one foot back and one forward. He drew one hand in, turned his palm, and pushed out, rocking the waves below. A sandpiper flew by, disappearing along the beach to the east.

He savored the feeling of the water's motion and the strength in his body. He continued to commune with the Light, practicing his gift and petitioning for his people in the same way his father had taught him years ago.

Our gift came from the Light. And so we give thanks for our gift, always remembering that we were given this power not to lord over our people, but to serve and protect them.

He slowly let his arms drop as he remembered his father's admonition. Not too long ago, Damien had done just that: raised the waters in order to protect his people. He'd known he might have to do it someday, but to actually have done it, and to watch men die by his hands . . .

He clenched his teeth. Those were the hard choices of a leader. But it didn't mean he had to like what he did. He never wanted to come to a place where he no longer mourned the loss of life, whether for his own people or others.

Sweat soaked into his tunic and trickled down his cheeks as he finished his ritual. Then he took a deep breath and let it out slowly. Across the waters to his right, a low gong sounded. Moments later, the monks from Baris Abbey began their noonday chant. Their voices echoed across the sea, barely audible above the waves and wind.

Damien listened to their song, his body slowly relaxing as he admired how their chant and the natural sounds combined to create a unique harmony of man and nature. This was peace. The bridge between man and heaven.

He let out another deep breath, turned, and headed back toward Northwind Castle. There was much to do today, and he would need all the time he could get before his trip to Rook Castle and the Assembly of the Great Houses.

"Are you sure you want to travel this light?" Taegis asked, his arms folded across his chest. "Just a monk, two guards, and myself to accompany you?"

"Yes." Damien sat behind his desk inside his study, a quill in his hand as he finished one last missive to House Vivek. "I'm not heading to the summit to show off. I'm heading there to unite the Great Houses against the rising encroachment of the Dominia Empire."

"You know your opinion will not be popular. The Great Houses have functioned independently for hundreds of years. They won't want to start working together now. And you also know there has been a rise in deaths amongst the lesser houses across the nations. It's only a matter of time before whoever is behind these murders will go after one of the grand lords. I would feel more comfortable if we had more guards with us."

Damien placed his quill back into the jar. "That is the second reason I am going to the assembly—to talk to Caiaphas about these recent murders. I think they might be connected."

"Do you think the empire is behind them?"

Damien shrugged. "If they are, they are working with someone, or *someones*, on the inside."

"Who has that kind of skill and connections to move between the different nations? Do you think it's one of the Great Houses?"

Damien shrugged again. Taegis asked good questions. Whoever was behind these attacks, they were good, and they were able to move across borders and into the very strongholds of each house, which could definitely indicate someone inside one of the Great Houses. But who? And why? What did they have to gain in allying themselves with the empire?

"Caiaphas has been investigating a secret group for years, a group whose aim is in achieving power. I'm hoping that the letter he sent and his request to meet means he might have some information for us. The assembly gives me the perfect cover for visiting him."

"I still think we should bring a few more people."

Damien shook his head. "I want to travel fast and light. More guards and servants would mean more people I would need to look after."

Taegis huffed. "And who will be looking after you?"

Damien flashed him a smile. "You."

"And why a monk?"

"Abbot Dominick is considering Cohen as his successor, but the young man needs to see more of the world first. This trip will be a good chance for him to see the other nations and people beyond our border."

"Cohen? You mean that tall, gangly monk? The one with hair that looks like a thatched roof?"

"Yes."

Taegis laughed and dropped his arms. "Cohen looks nothing like a monk, and certainly not like the future abbot."

Damien's lips twitched. "True, but the young man has a kind heart and cheerful spirit. He might be just what the abbey needs. Father Dominick certainly thinks so."

"Well, no one can say that Father Dominick is a stick in the mud. I think he sometimes irritates some of his more faithful followers."

Damien stood and straightened the letter before carefully folding it. "That's probably why I like him. He's willing to give anyone a chance. Much like the Light of the old ways."

"Indeed."

Taegis grew quiet as Damien dabbed a small bit of wax on the crease and pressed his ring into it.

"So I can't convince you to bring more men?"

Damien picked up the letter. "I'm afraid not. We'll travel faster with just the five of us."

Taegis let out a sigh. "All right, then. I'll make the preparations for the trip."

"I would like to leave before the first day of Harvest."

"We'll be ready."

Damien stopped in front of Taegis before leaving the study. "Thank you, my friend."

Taegis bowed.

Damien headed for the aviary at the top of one of the towers. Taegis might not agree with all of his decisions, but when all was said and done, Taegis followed through. It couldn't be easy taking orders from a man half his age.

Damien ran a hand through his hair as he walked up the circular flight of stairs. Sometimes he felt like he was in over his head. He hadn't had nearly enough time to learn what it meant to be a grand lord before his father passed away. Taegis counseled him when he could, but it wasn't the same. Only Father had fully born the mantle of leading House Maris and its people.

His chest grew tight. He missed Father, Mother, and Quinn. Just when he thought he had moved on, something small would trigger a memory and his heart would grow heavy.

Damien reached the top of the tower where a half-dozen falcons waited inside a circular room with wide, open windows, each bird trained to deliver messages to each of the Great Houses. Fresh hay lay across the ground, and an older man stood near one of the windows, shoveling the area beneath the massive perches.

"Rufus, I have a letter for you."

The old man straightened and turned with the shovel in his hands. His silver hair was pulled back in a short tail behind his head, and his tunic and pants were stained from work and sweat. He wore a long leather glove across his right hand and arm. "My lord," he said and bowed his head while resting his hands on the top of the shovel handle. "I did not hear you come in."

"I needed to stretch my legs, so I thought I would deliver the letter to you personally."

Rufus looked up and smiled. "Where might your letter be heading today?"

"House Vivek." Damien held out the folded parchment.

Rufus placed his shovel aside and reached for the letter. "Sonya's ready to fly."

Damien frowned. "Sonya? I thought the falcon that delivered to House Vivek was Victor."

"It has been a while since my lord has visited the aviary. I'm afraid Victor passed away last spring, but Sonya was ready to fill in by then."

Damien looked around the aviary. Rufus was right, it had been a while since he'd come up to the tower. Fond memories of him as a little boy hurrying up the circular stairs so he could watch Rufus train the falcons spread across his mind. Sometimes Quinn came with him, hollering for Damien to slow down so he could catch up.

Damien smiled sadly as his throat tightened at the memory. Light, he missed Quinn. His little brother had been three years his junior and always tagged behind Damien wherever he went. Sometimes he found his little brother irritating, but most of the time he didn't mind the company.

What he wouldn't give to have Quinn with him now, even with his incessant questions and energetic ways.

"Everything all right, my lord?" Rufus asked.

Damien blinked and brought his mind back to the present. "Yes. Just thinking."

Rufus watched him for a moment, then nodded to himself and turned. He reached for the falcon resting on the perch to his left. The others preened themselves and one took off through another window, probably out to search for its meal.

Sonya was much larger than Victor had been and a beautiful specimen with her white chest and dark head and wings. She waited patiently as Rufus folded the letter twice over, then placed it inside the little box strapped to her chest. He stepped back, held out his right hand covered by the leather glove, and let out a small clicking sound with his tongue.

Sonya hopped from her perch to his arm. He walked toward the nearest window and held out his arm. He gave a couple more clicks, and Sonya took flight.

Damien came to stand beside Rufus and watched Sonya soar upward before taking off in a easterly direction, high above the cedar trees that lined the coast. "She's beautiful," he murmured.

"One of my best," Rufus replied.

Damien watched as she disappeared in the distance. Sometimes he wondered what it would be like to be a bird, with no responsibilities other than to hunt and fly. In his mind, birds represented freedom.

However, that was not the life he had been given. Instead, he had been born heir to House Maris, and the duty to take care of his people lay squarely on his shoulders, which meant stepping up and engaging the other houses at the upcoming assembly about the encroachment of the empire. He wasn't sure how much they would listen to someone as young as he was, but he had to try. He didn't want to live to see another razing like the one hundreds of years ago, or watch another house fall like House Ravenwood.

Not if he could help it.

15

The next day, Selene gathered up the books Father had lent her and headed out into the hallway. Servants rushed by, preparing the castle for the influx of guests as the Assembly of the Great Houses drew closer. Rugs were beaten, bed linens were changed in rooms that hadn't been used in years, and the windows were washed. The servants appeared enthusiastic about the upcoming gathering, despite the extra work.

"I've always wanted to see the lords and ladies of House Luceras," one of the servant girls said as she dusted an ornate picture frame. "I've heard they have hair the color of gold!"

"And their warriors are the famous paladins of light. Even the women are trained to fight!" the other servant said.

"I'm more excited to see House Rafel," said another servant girl quietly. "Lady Ayaka is said to be the most beautiful lady ever."

"I heard Lady Adalyn Luceras is the most beautiful lady."

"I think our own Lady Selene is the most beautiful," one of the servant boys chimed in as he hefted up a rug.

"Perhaps," the first girl said. "But she's not the same. Not anymore. She reminds me of Lady Ragna now."

"She's even colder than her ladyship," the second girl said.

"Aye," agreed the servant boy.

Selene hurried through the corridor before the servants realized she was there, her throat tight. Had she really changed that much over the summer, with each dreamwalk? Was she as cold as they said she was?

Like her mother?

"What are you doing with all of those books?" Amara's voice broke through her thoughts.

Selene slowed and glanced to her left. Amara stood in the juncture between the two main hallways. She still wore her riding habit, and her cloak was muddy along the fringe. She pulled her hood back and let her auburn hair loose. Every day Amara looked more and more like their father.

Selene shifted the books between her arms. "Amara. I thought you and Mother were supposed to arrive back this evening."

"We made good time." Amara flashed her a nasty smile. She probably thought she could make Selene jealous with a reminder that she had been chosen to accompany Mother and Selene had not.

Selene sighed internally. Her sister had no idea what awaited her when her own gift came. A part of her grieved for her sister. If only Amara knew that she cared. "How was your trip?" she asked, wanting to make light conversation.

Amara tossed her hair behind her shoulder. "I spent a good deal of time with Lord Raoul. He is not the same annoying little boy who used to come visit when we were young. Part of the reason we visited the House of Fire was to discuss the possibility of a stronger alliance."

"Stronger alliance?" Selene's eyes widened. "You mean a marriage alliance?"

Amara smiled. "Yes. And since I am not the eldest"—Selene noted the lack of bitterness for once—"I am a candidate."

"A candidate? To marry Lord Raoul?"

"Yes."

"Is that something you want?" Selene couldn't picture Raoul as anything but the stuck-up son of Grand Lord Ivulf who had a cruel side, especially toward animals.

Amara folded her arms. "I don't plan on being married to some lesser house. I have higher goals. Marrying into House Friere would enable me to be a grand lady—an opportunity I lack here."

Selene placed the books against her hip. "Did Mother say you were a candidate?"

"Not exactly," Amara fudged and looked away. "But why else would she have brought me?"

Selene frowned. Did Amara really not know their mother? Or did she only see what she wanted to see? There were many reasons Mother would have brought Amara. But to marry Lord Raoul?

Even though she knew she would be forced to marry someday, Selene hoped her consort would be a man she could eventually learn to love. Or at least tolerate, unlike the relationship Mother and Father shared. She had a feeling Raoul Friere had not changed from the malicious boy she had known, and she would not wish him as a partner on anyone, not even her sister, despite how much they disagreed.

Perhaps Mother wanted to talk to Lord Ivulf before the assembly. Their houses were close. By why bring Amara? Unless . . .

She remembered their fight over Renata. Maybe Mother was changing her mind about Selene. Mother could not control her, Selene had made that quite clear. On the other hand, Amara would do anything to be Mother's right-hand daughter. Was Mother secretly grooming Amara to carry on the family heritage, even though Amara's gift had not yet come?

Selene narrowed her eyes. She wasn't sure what she thought of that.

"What are the books for?" Amara repeated, interrupting her thoughts.

Selene glanced down as if noticing them. "I was reading up on the Great Houses before the assembly."

Amara raised an eyebrow. "Find out anything interesting?"

Selene shook her head. "No, not really."

Her sister smirked. "Well, I'm off to change." She turned before Selene could say another word and headed off toward her bedchambers.

Selene tightened her grip on the books and continued toward her father's study. She found the door slightly ajar, so she pushed it open. Sunlight poured in from the nearby windows. The air was hot and muggy and smelled faintly of Father's pipe. She crossed the room toward his desk, then she heard faint voices coming from the room next door.

Frowning, she placed the books on her father's desk. Who could Father be talking to? As she turned to leave, she heard her name. Selene stopped. She glanced toward the wall from which the voices were emanating. Her name was mentioned again. By Mother.

She bit the bottom of her lip. *I should leave. Nothing good comes from overhearing private conversations.* But with the way her body pressed against the bare wall near the bookshelves, she had already decided to eavesdrop.

It *was* Mother and Father. That alone piqued her curiosity. They hardly ever spoke to each other . . . and in Father's bedchambers, no less. Mother never visited Father as far as she knew. So why now?

"Are you sure this is the right time?" her father said, his voice muffled through the wood paneling.

"Every house will be here for the assembly. It's the perfect time. Selene is old enough to be married. And an alliance with

House Friere would make our ties stronger with the House of Fire."

"House Friere is bringing members of their lesser houses?"

"No. The negotiations would be between myself and Grand Lord Ivulf."

"So neither Selene nor her future consort would have a say?"

Selene could almost hear the bitterness in her father's voice, even though by his own admission, he had chosen to marry Mother. Did he regret his choice?

"Those decisions are always made by the heads of the houses. You know that," her mother replied.

Selene winced at her mother's callous words.

"Why House Friere?" her father asked moments later. "We already have a strong relationship with them. What about, say, House Maris?"

"House Maris?" her mother said, her voice rising. "We have no reason to align ourselves with them. And there is no eligible male."

"There is Lord Maris himself."

There was a long pause. Selene could almost imagine her mother's face, the way it grew dark and severe when she was angry, marring her beautiful features. "We do not marry other heads of houses."

"Why? Some of the other houses do, and it has benefited them both."

"You know why." Now it was Mother's turn to sound bitter. "Since the razing, my forebearers and I have kept our gift a secret. I will not allow our ability to be tainted by the gifts of others, or worse, be completely wiped out by another bloodline. Selene is the heir to the Ravenwood gift and will have complete control of our house someday. Secrecy has served our family for hundreds of years, and it will continue to keep our family safe. She will have a consort from a lesser house and preserve the dreamwalking gift. And no one will ever know it still exists."

"Except for the consort," her father replied.

"That is something I cannot control, but I can control who that consort is. Besides, what has House Maris ever done for us? Nothing."

Her father sighed faintly. "And when will this union happen?"

"In the next year. We are narrowing down the choices."

Selene felt like the air had been punched from her lungs. Her future—all the years left to her—was being decided on the other side of this wall. And she had no say in it. She would be bound to some man she didn't know, and most likely end up like her parents, distant and aloof from her partner in life.

"So why are you telling me all this?" her father asked.

"I came here because she is your daughter, too, and I thought you might want to know. But perhaps I was mistaken." There was a rustle as her mother stood up.

"Thank you," she heard her father say, his words soft through the wooden paneling.

Mother never replied and moments later, there was the soft thud of a door shutting.

Selene knew she should go, but she couldn't make her body move. Her mind was feverishly working through the words she had just heard while her heart swelled with love for her father. Always gracious, even under Mother's harsh and unkind attitude.

She swallowed and dropped her head. She did not want to marry a man associated with House Friere. Truth be told, she didn't want to marry at all and burden a future daughter with this terrible gift of dreamkilling and secrecy. But Mother would not allow that. House Ravenwood must endure, which meant producing the next generation of Ravenwoods.

And if she didn't, Amara or Opheliana would, and Selene would be discarded, the spinster daughter of Ravenwood, despite her powerful abilities.

Selene looked up. There were no choices for her. Either she became the woman her mother wanted her to be, inheriting the task of assassination and producing the next heir, or fade away.

Either way, her future was dark and bleak.

16

Selene stood by her father on the ramparts on a late afternoon during the first week of Harvest, awaiting the arrival of the Great Houses. A cool mountain breeze sailed along the castle top, sending the Ravenwood banners flying and snapping in the wind. She gathered her cloak around her body, being sure to keep her hood firmly over her head. Mother would not like the idea of her standing here watching the arrival of the Great Houses like some commoner. The official greeting would be taking place tomorrow in the great hall, with much pageantry and dignity, where each house would display their strength, power, and riches.

However, if she was going to really become the next grand lady of Ravenwood, she wanted to know more about the Great Houses, and that started with their arrival. How did they travel? What did they bring? What kind of atmosphere did they exude? When Father invited her to watch secretly from the battlements, Selene said yes.

The smell of smoke from the smithy combined with the pine scent of the trees that grew along the Magyr mountaintops created a pleasing autumn smell. She closed her eyes and felt the sun on her face, and she sucked in another lungful of air. Over the last few weeks, ever since she overheard the conversation through the wall, she had felt like a thick blanket had been pulled over her mind and body. She moved with a cold stiffness and barely talked to anyone. At night, she practiced her gift, keeping her heart locked behind iron doors so she felt nothing for the servants whose dreams she visited. Little by little, she could feel her heart dying, but it was the only way to stay sane both within the dreamscape and during the day when she interacted with the same servants.

In turn, the servants grew colder toward her, as well, but Selene held their whispers and actions at arm's length. If she let them inside, it would crack the doors she had hidden her heart behind, and she couldn't afford that. Indeed, she was truly becoming the Lady of Ice, as they had come to call her.

Father stood as a silent companion as they waited for the first house to arrive. Selene was grateful for his silence. That, and the beauty of the green mountains dotted here and there with orange and yellow, lifted the bleak burden she carried, even if for a moment.

A single horn blew high up along one of the towers. Selene looked toward the wide bridge that connected Rook Castle to King's Highway. It was the only known way to access the castle, as it was surrounded by steep valleys and ravines.

The entourage—too far away to make out who—left King's Highway and started across the stone bridge. The bridge was twenty feet wide and lined with a stone railing to keep those crossing from falling into the chasm below.

"Looks like House Rafel is first to arrive," her father said, pointing to the banner carried by one of the horsemen. Selene raised a hand to shield her eyes while keeping her hood in place and caught sight of the green banner with a white tree in the middle. "A long time ago, House Rafel was known as the House of Healing. The Rafel family was gifted with the knowledge of herbs and remedies. It was even said the grand lord or lady of the house could heal someone by simply laying his or her hands on the wounded."

"Is that true?" Selene asked.

Her father shrugged. "There were many miraculous things a long time ago, now forgotten. But I have a feeling there is some truth in the stories."

Selene watched House Rafel cross the bridge, particularly the older man dressed in fine dark green robes and the younger woman who rode beside him. His long, silvery hair reached below his chest and flew loosely around him. His daughter's hair was as dark as his was light, and even longer, bound on the right by what looked like a large pink flower.

Father spoke again. "The head of House Rafel is Grand Lord Haruk. The young woman beside him is his only daughter, Ayaka. Ah, it appears House Vivek is not too far behind."

Selene switched from the couple riding amongst the sea of green and spotted another group just rounding the bend farther down the mountain path. A dark blue banner led the way, white stars barely visible across the standard. The horn sounded again to announce the arrival of the new house.

"That was your house."

"Yes," her father replied. "The Great House of Wisdom. But it now pales in comparison to what it used to be."

House Rafel had finished crossing the bridge and was entering the gate below the ramparts when House Vivek started across. Both houses traveled with a large entourage of servants and guards, at least fifty people or more in each party.

Unlike House Rafel's long flowing robes and deep green colors, the members of House Vivek wore richly colored clothes trimmed in gold. Gold bands were wrapped around the muscular arms of the guards who carried the ornate litter that bobbed between the throng with swords and lances, the gold contrasting with the dark color of their toned skin.

"Grand Lord Rune and Grand Lady Runa must be in the litter. They are the only house with two ruling heads. When their father died, the brother and sister chose to rule House Vivek together."

Selene pulled her cloak closer to her body as she stood by her father and watched the procession of both houses toward Rook Castle. This would be the first time the seven Great Houses had met in hundreds of years—that is, if House Merek came as well. There still had been no word from the wyvern riders who lived on the Southern Isles. In any case, Rook Castle would be filled for the next fortnight.

A half hour later, as House Vivek finished entering the gate below, another house arrived. Her father's face brightened at the banner, white with a blazing sun of orange and yellow in the middle. It didn't take much to guess whose standard that was: House Luceras, the famous House of Light.

The entourage for House Luceras was by far the largest, with knights dressed in steel-plated armor riding on white steeds, their armor and lances glinting in the sunlight, and pages and servants dressed in white tunics covered in orange tabards. Selene silently wondered if the armor was crafted so that it reflected the sun's dying rays as a token to the house.

In the middle of the group rode three persons, dressed even fairer than those around them. Selene recalled one of the servants speaking of hair of gold, and indeed the servant was right. All three had hair the color of gold.

The two men were dressed in partial plate, which shone in the sunlight. The lady was dressed in a long white gown that flowed across the flank of her white horse. She held herself in a genteel way, with her legs to the left. Her hair, even more glorious than that of the two men, flowed down to her lower back.

A small fire sparked inside of Selene's chest as she gazed at the young woman. The servant girl was right. Lady Adalyn was the most beautiful woman she had ever seen. Her light skin and hair made Selene conscious of her own long black strands. And the graceful look on her face made Selene wonder if Lady Adalyn had ever experienced hardship in her young life. As the House of Light and the most devout followers of the old ways, she was sure House Luceras was blessed.

Father tugged at his beard. "I wondered if Grand Lord Warin would make it to the assembly. Last I heard, the pain in his limbs had left him bedridden. It looks like he sent his eldest son, Lord Leo, in his place."

"And the other two people?" Although Selene had guessed the woman's name.

Father intensified his gaze. "I'm not sure. The other young lord is either Tyrn or Elric. I would wager Elric. Tyrn probably stayed back to attend his father. And the lovely young lady is Lady Adalyn. She's a year younger than you, but already sought after by the other houses."

Selene swallowed the lump in her throat. What would it be like to be sought after? Maybe Lady Adalyn even had a choice in her suitors. A future of possibilities.

She glanced away and lifted her chin, her hand curling into a fist. *No use pining after another future. It won't change mine, it'll only make me feel worse. She has her path to walk, and I have mine.*

Still, she blinked back the tears that were forming.

As the last of House Luceras entered the gates below, her father turned toward the castle. "The other houses will arrive over the next few days—"

The horn sounded again. Her father glanced up and headed

back to their spot along the wall. Selene came to stand beside him. Far off, in the dying light, a smaller group could be seen. She counted again, then frowned. Only five people made up this group. It couldn't possibly be another house, could it? What kind of Great House traveled with so few people?

Selene squinted against the darkness, trying to make out the banner that one of the travelers held aloft to announce their approach. A light blue standard came into view with indigo waves enclosed in a white circle.

Her father placed his hands along the stone wall. "So House Maris was able to make it." He breathed out a sigh of relief. "Good."

Selene glanced at him from the corner of her eye. There seemed to be something unsaid in his sigh. "House Maris? The House of the Northern Shores? Were you not expecting them?"

"I was. But I wasn't sure when he would arrive. House Maris has experienced several tragedies over the last few years. Grand Lord Remfrey and Lady Serawyn died from a terrible sickness that swept across the shores two years ago. Shortly after, their youngest son, Quinn, also passed away, leaving Lord Damien as the youngest heir to be named a grand lord of a house in over four hundred years. His father and I were good friends, long before I met and married your mother. I was saddened when I learned that Lord Remfrey had passed away."

Selene turned her attention back toward the five riders as they approached the bridge and wondered again at so few people in the company. "How old is Lord Damien?" she asked. The standard of House Maris rippled in the wind, illuminated by the last light of the setting sun.

"Lord Damien is not much older than you. Four and twenty harvests."

"So young," Selene murmured. She couldn't imagine being the head of a Great House at such a young age.

"Yes. But he has shown tremendous responsibility toward his obligations and a good head for leadership. The people of the Northern Shores have not suffered. In fact, I think Lord Damien may become one of the greatest grand lords the seven nations have ever seen."

Selene glanced at her father in surprise. Such high praise for another house. Her father rarely said such words. Whoever this Lord Damien was, he had earned her father's approval, and that meant something. Maybe more than her own mother's opinion.

"What has House Maris done for us?" Her mother's words echoed in the back of her mind. What did Mother mean? Selene shook her head and glanced back as House Maris crossed the bridge. Her curiosity was now piqued.

"Why is he traveling with so few people?" she asked a moment later.

Her father shrugged. "I'm not sure. But House Maris has never been showy. Living on the rugged coast has made them hardy and with little patience for ostentatiousness."

Her eyes roved across the men, searching for Lord Damien. In the twilight and this high up, it was hard to make out individual people. Was he the man with the light hair? Or the lanky man on the left—

"He's the young man in the front riding on the black horse."

Selene focused on Lord Damien as he and his men approached the gates, but she could barely make out his features. His dark hair was short and he wore a long blue cloak. One of the men rode close beside him, his honey-colored hair pulled back, sword glinting at his side. No doubt Lord Damien's personal guard.

Just as they reached the castle, Lord Damien looked up. Selene froze. The ramparts should have hidden her, but somehow he had sensed her and her father and looked in their direction.

Their eyes met. Her stomach tightened at his hooded gaze, but she kept her face passive. Then his gaze switched to her father, which he returned with a nod.

Lord Damien dipped his head back down and entered the gates.

"He looks a lot like Lord Remfrey." Her father stepped away from the ramparts. The sun had now set and torches were being lit across the castle. "And he will lead House Maris well, just like his father did before him."

Selene nodded, her mind still in a whirl from that one glance. Who was this young man her father thought highly of and her mother detested? She straightened her cloak and tugged the fabric. She would be sure to be cautious around Lord Damien.

And yet at the same time, she wanted to know more about him.

17

Damien guided his mare through the tall gates into the courtyard of Rook Castle as the torches were lit for the evening. Up above, the sky went from a brilliant orange to deep purple. One lone star hung just above the walls, heralding the fall of night. He steered his mount toward a second set of gates and leaned over toward Taegis. "Caiaphas was watching us from the ramparts," he said quietly.

"I noticed. Who was the young woman with him?"

"I would imagine one of his daughters. She looked too young to be Lady Ragna. And I doubt Lady Ragna would be watching above the gates. I'm sure she has a lavish introduction waiting for us in the main hall when all of the houses arrive."

Taegis nodded.

Damien thought again of the young woman who stood with Caiaphas. Yes, she had to be one of his daughters. Which one? The older one and heir to Ravenwood—the name of whom eluded him at the moment? Or the younger one? He huffed quietly. No doubt he would be introduced to both. House Ravenwood was known for its schemes, although when it came to marriage, the ladies of Ravenwood always chose consorts from lesser houses. So, in that respect, he was safe from any possible matchmaking.

As he crossed the courtyard of Rook Castle, he looked around, admiring the ancient mountain fortress. It was more like a walled-in city than a single castle. Around the spacious outer courtyard, streets led toward other parts of the castle grounds. Homes, smiths, and shops were set up along the streets. It made sense. This high up in the mountains, away from other cities and villages, Rook Castle would need its own means to take care of its people.

The architecture gave the place a feeling of openness. Damien noticed the large windows, wide airways through the smooth, grey columns, open areas, and balconies high up. As if the fortress had been built to let the harsh mountain wind pass through rather than to keep it out.

Very different than the architecture of the other nations he had visited.

They approached another gate built into a smaller wall that surrounded Rook Castle itself. Inside was another courtyard with torches lit along the walls. Smoke from hundreds of fireplaces filled the air, slowly building a haze across the night sky.

The courtyard was a cacophony of sound and people. Horses neighed by the stables, servants scurried across the cobblestone, and knights dressed in steel plate from House Luceras stood by the staircase that led into Rook Castle.

Damien glanced at Taegis and Cohen. It seemed that the other houses had chosen this trip as an opportunity to show their affluence and wealth, while he had only brought a burgeoning young monk and three guards. Damien had no reason to impress the other houses. He knew who he was and the others knew as well. House Maris was master of the waters. Nothing else needed to be said.

He dismounted and held the reins in his hand as a man dressed in a dark grey uniform approached his party. "House Maris?" he said, his voice rising over the sounds in the courtyard.

"Yes," Damien answered, moving forward. Taegis and his other men dismounted and followed.

"The stable hands will come and retrieve your mounts. Then I will take you to your rooms. Your . . . er . . ." The servant glanced at Cohen, Taegis, and his two guards. "Your men will be shown to their own quarters."

Damien motioned toward his men. "If there is room, I would prefer my men stay with me."

The servant's eyebrows rose. "As you wish."

As they spoke, three young men dressed in work clothes crossed the courtyard on the right and approached them. One reached for the reins from Damien. "I will be taking care of your mounts during your time here."

Damien gave him the reins. "Thank you."

The young man bobbed his head and smiled. Damien got the distinct feeling the man had never been thanked before. He glanced up at Rook Castle. What was House Ravenwood like? In the past, Father spoke very little about the mountain house, and even though the two nations shared a border, there was little communication between them. He narrowed his eyes. Soon he would know.

The room the servant brought them to was rugged and yet lavish at the same time. Thick rugs and skins covered the cold stone floor. A massive fireplace sat on one end of the room, the mahogany four-poster bed on the other side, with deep blue damask curtains, dark furs, and a blue coverlet. On the walls were paintings of the mountainside encased in ornate frames. Two high-backed chairs stood in front of the fireplace, with a small table nearby topped with a bottle of wine and glasses.

Two additional doors led from the main room to smaller rooms for attending servants or spouses who did not share rooms. Taegis and the two guards took the one to the right and Cohen took the one on the left.

Double doors on the other side of the room led to a small balcony. Damien stepped out into the cool night air and placed his hands on the stone railing. He rolled his neck and sighed. Deep within, he felt the continual pull of the water-wall he had left up along the coast. It would continue to protect his people while he was gone, but it was beginning to wear on him.

One by one, stars appeared across the dark sky. He took in a deep breath, letting the cool, crisp air fill his lungs. These next few days would be his initiation into the role of grand lord. He knew the other houses had some misgivings about a lord as young as he was, and he was prepared for those who would try to manipulate him because of his age. They would soon find he was not easily swayed. He loved his people and would do anything for them. And more than that, he desired to see all the nations come together and be as one, like when the seven great nations had first formed over a thousand years ago.

Maybe this pending conflict with the Dominia Empire could do just that: cause the Great Houses to finally work together, not fall into schisms like what happened during the razing. But first, Damien needed to find who was causing the divisions in the first place and murdering those in the lesser houses. There could be no trust when fear ruled.

Damien headed back into the room and shut the doors behind him. One of the Rook Castle servants was placing his saddlebag and a woven chest in the empty corner near the bed.

"Thank you," he told the man.

The man bowed and left quietly. Taegis emerged from his room. "How long before you're summoned to the main hall for introductions?"

Damien shook his head as he looked through the sets of clothing inside the woven chest. "Not until tomorrow at the earliest. I'm sure Lady Ravenwood will wait until all the houses arrive before formal introductions are made." He pulled out a clean tunic, trousers, and a dark sleeveless jacket. "In the meantime, I plan on cleaning off the dust and dirt from our trip." He glanced over his shoulder. "What about you?"

"I'm going to finish my inspection of your room, then look over as much of the castle as I can. Sten and Karl will be here if you need anything."

Damien nodded. With unknown assassins on the loose, this would be a prime time to hit the Great Houses.

Cohen entered the room as well.

"And what are your plans, Cohen?" Damien asked as he stood and wrapped the clean clothes into a tight bundle.

"I'll stay in, at least for tonight. I had hoped to read more from the texts Father Dominick sent with me. Then tomorrow, I shall see if there are other priests or monks who accompanied the Great Houses. I look forward to exchanging opinions and ideas with others."

Damien gave him a thoughtful nod. "I'm sure a priest from the Temple of Splendor came with House Luceras. However . . ." His face grew dark. "I believe House Ravenwood follows the Dark Lady, so be careful."

"The Dark Lady?" Cohen paled, emphasizing the freckles across his long face. "I thought followers of the Dark Lady had died out years ago."

"No, there are still a handful of them here in the mountains. There might even be a few left in House Friere," Taegis said, entering the conversation.

"Interesting," Cohen murmured. Then he looked up, his face brightening. "Well, it should be an enlightening conversation with their leader."

The corners of Damien's lips twitched as he watched the gangly monk wander back to his room. Cohen was definitely different than most of the young men who entered Baris Abbey. He had a heart for the Light and for people and desired to share his passion with all, yet he possessed a gentleness some of the other monks lacked.

Damien nodded to himself. Yes, he could see why Father Dominick was grooming Cohen to replace him. Still, he had a lot to learn about the world. Once again, Damien was glad he had brought him along.

A small bell rang quietly through the halls the next day during the late afternoon. Damien looked up. He had barely retired to his room after spending the morning enjoying the architecture and mountain views around Rook Castle while Taegis talked to Captain Stanton of the Rook Castle guard.

The bell rang again, followed by a knock at the door. Karl, a younger guard from Nor Esen, exited his room and opened the door.

"A message for Lord Maris."

At the mention of his name, Damien stood and headed for the door. As he approached, he spotted one of the Ravenwood servants standing in the hallway.

Once he caught sight of Damien, the man gave a short bow. "Grand Lady Ravenwood would like to properly welcome you to Rook Castle this evening, followed by dinner."

The servant waited for his answer, his head still bowed.

"Tell Lady Ravenwood I will be there within the hour. Thank you."

The servant nodded and left.

An hour later, he returned. Taegis stepped out into the hallway, his hand on his sword and his eyes roving across the corridor.

Damien followed, along with Karl and Sten, the other guard from Nor Esen. It would be foolish to attack a nobleman in the hallway, but it never hurt to make a show of precaution.

The servant started down the hallway, Damien following, with Taegis and his two guards close behind. Their boots clapped quietly along the stone floor as they passed silver sconces with lit candles and doors that led into other suites.

At the end of the long hallway, the servant led them down a set of wide stairs and to the right. The ceiling arched above with wrought-iron chandeliers ablaze for the evening. Along the left side were long, narrow windows. Outside, a sliver of a moon made an appearance from behind hazy clouds.

Ahead, two guards stood on either side of tall double doors. One reached over and opened his. Damien nodded as he passed the man and entered the halls of Rook Castle.

Damien had been to a number of halls over his short life-span. The halls of House Luceras captured the essence of the House of Light with their wide windows, gold trimmings, and white marble floors. The halls of House Rafel were filled with thick wooden beams and columns, and lush green vegetation, reminding visiting dignitaries that House Rafel was connected to nature. He'd even visited House Merek, the famous wyvern riders of the Southern Isles. Their halls were tall, with rafters high above where young wyverns could swoop in and out.

As Damien looked around the hall of Rook Castle, only one word came to mind: cold. Smooth grey stone walls, narrow windows lined in lead panes, and dark ornate furniture surrounded the cavernous smoke-filled hall of Ravenwood. The air itself was not chilly, but it felt like it nonetheless.

Large groups of people were gathered beneath the high ceiling, most likely a collection of rich families and lesser houses with connections to House Ravenwood. He spotted House Luceras near the front, the golden hair of the members from the House of Light standing out from amongst the crowd. However, he could not see any other of the Great Houses. Apparently he was the second to arrive tonight.

At his entrance, a courier rang a bell. As the tones echoed around the hall, the room became quiet. "Announcing Grand Lord Damien Maris from the Northern Shores."

Damien started forward as the people parted for him. At the front of the hall, Lady Ragna stood upon a dais, in front of a lavish black throne with a raven carved into the stone on each side. She was dressed in a long dark gown and wore a sleek black cloak lined with black feathers. Her hair hung around her face and over one shoulder, reaching down to her waist. She exuded a dark beauty, marred by something hidden within her eyes.

Caiaphas stood at her side, one step behind, in the proper position of a consort. His silver hair was slicked back and his beard neatly trimmed. He barely gave Damien a glimpse before setting his eyes ahead.

On Lady Ragna's right stood two young women, one slightly taller than the other, with long black hair with almost a blue sheen to it that matched her deep blue gown. She held her head high and watched him approach with an indifferent, almost chilling gaze. The other young lady looked to be her sister, but with auburn hair gathered over one shoulder. Her dress was a deep crimson trimmed in fur. Her gaze was inquisitive as she watched him.

No doubt they were the daughters of House Ravenwood. His guess would be the one who had stood with Caiaphas on the battlements was the one in blue. Though both women were striking, once again he found himself thankful that House Ravenwood chose consorts from amongst lesser houses. They appeared beautiful, proud, and dangerous—not the kind of women for him.

As Damien approached the dais, Lady Ragna beckoned him

up the steps. Taegis stayed close behind, like a shadow along Damien's back.

"Grand Lord Damien, House Maris is welcome to Rook Castle," Lady Ravenwood said with her hand raised. "Thank you for answering the summons of the seven Great Houses during this time of crisis. Through our combined knowledge and resources, I hope we can find common ground. The assembly will commence in two days. In the meantime, you are welcome to the hospitality of House Ravenwood. If you need anything, please ask."

Damien bowed stiffly. Already House Ravenwood was positioning itself as the leader of the assembly, never once mentioning how it was he who had called the assembly in the first place. *Light, give me patience*, he prayed. "Thank you, Grand Lady Ragna."

"Please join us in the dining hall after all of the Great Houses have been announced."

"I will."

The raised voices behind him alerted Damien that one of the other houses had arrived. Quietly he headed toward the left and watched as House Rafel entered the halls.

Grand Lord Haruk walked between the crowd, assisted by his daughter, Lady Ayaka. Both were clothed in deep emerald green. Servants dressed in similar coloring followed behind, carrying the trains of their flowing robes.

Damien tuned out Lady Ragna's greeting to House Rafel and studied her daughters again. The taller daughter appeared to be older. He could almost see the weight of House Ravenwood resting on her proud shoulders and wondered if the burden was as heavy as his own. However, chances were it would be many years before she would need to take up the mantle of her family.

Her eyes glanced at him and he stared back. Neither moved as House Rafel took its place beside House Luceras over on the right side of the room. Suddenly he wondered if what he took for cold indifference was something else. She blinked and looked away.

Damien frowned as House Vivek was announced across the great hall. There had been a flash of hopelessness within the young woman's dark eyes. Every house had their secrets, except perhaps his own. So what secrets did she hold inside? He glanced at the other daughter as House Vivek approached the dais. She did not share her sister's coldness. Instead, there was a fire in her eyes, a hunger for something more.

Damien mentally shook his head and took a deep breath. In either case, both women were dangerous. But he couldn't help that a small part of him went out toward the lady in blue.

18

Selene followed her mother and father to the dining hall after the two-hour greeting of the Great Houses. Her neck and shoulders felt stiff, and fatigue hung across her mind like a thick fog from another late night of dreamwalking. All she wanted to do was head back to her rooms and lay her head down. Instead, she would be seated with strangers from the other houses and forced to endure a meal filled with unspoken probing hidden behind tedious talk. House politics at its best.

Unlike the room the Ravenwood family used for private dining, the formal dining hall was almost as big as the main hall, with high ceilings and rafters from which hung the Ravenwood crest on banners of deep purple. Beneath the fluttering banners were three long tables set up in a U shape so that the diners could view each other. The room could easily seat over one hundred people. Thick wooden chairs were pulled back, and settings of elegant silver were ready for the dinner guests.

Candles filled the area with soft light. A fire roared in the massive fireplace on the other side of the room, burning the autumn chill from the air.

The servants directed those entering to their seating arrangements. Selene was led to a chair along one side while Father and Mother were seated at the front table, with House Vivek on the right and House Friere on the left. The members of House Luceras were seated across from Selene, their golden hair glinting in the candlelight. Her heart dropped as Lady Adalyn graciously took a seat almost across from her. The last thing she wanted was to view the beautiful lady of light all evening.

As Selene sat down and the servant pushed in her chair, she caught the young lord of House Maris being directed to the chair beside her. Interesting. She reached for the dipping bowl and placed her fingers within the tepid water. Why had she been seated beside Lord Damien? Surely Mother would have used this opportunity to acquaint her with House Friere since she hoped for a pairing between the two houses. Instead, Amara had been seated beside Lord Raoul, near the eldest Luceras lord.

Selene wrinkled her nose and reached for the cleaning towel as she watched her sister and Raoul begin a lively conversation. Raoul certainly had grown into a handsome young man. Not surprising. The men of House Friere were famous for their thick dark hair and sultry looks. Raoul wore his long hair up in a knot at the top of his head, pinned there by a small ornate gold piece. His white tunic was open at the chest, exposing toned muscles, and a thick leather cord hung around his neck with what looked like a golden skull pendant at the end. A black leather jerkin studded with gold completed his ensemble.

He glanced over at Selene and grinned before downing the contents of the crystal goblet beside him. Amara tugged on his arm and he turned his attention back to her.

Selene looked away in disgust, only to find all three siblings from House Luceras staring curiously at her. Lady Adalyn's eyes were large and innocent-looking. Her brothers—one on either side of their sister—had the same hair color, like wheat on a summer's day.

The older one's gaze grew guarded, and he pulled his sister's attention to himself while the younger—Elric, was it?—watched her the same way a raven looked when it spotted something sparkly.

Selene breathed in through her nose and reached for the nearby goblet—

Her hand brushed warm fingers, and she pulled back with a gasp.

"Pardon me," Lord Damien said as he took his hand away from the goblet between them. "I did not realize you wished to drink first."

His soft tenor voice surprised her. She had expected something deeper, something more commanding from the young grand lord. Her cheeks burned as she prayed the candlelight hid the color across her cheeks.

His dark gaze moved across her face, settling again on her eyes. He had short dark hair brushed to the side, exposing a small, white scar that ran through his eyebrow. His face was clean shaven, and he had a strong jaw. But it was his eyes that captured her attention. They were the deepest blue she had ever seen.

Heart beating faster and her face growing a deeper shade of red, she pressed her lips into a fine line. "No, you may go first." *Dart'an! He was a grand lord, not some commoner! Get your head together, Selene!*

Lord Damien chuckled and gently pushed the goblet toward her. "It is all yours, my lady. I will ask for a new goblet when the servants come by."

Selene spotted her mother down at the end of the table glancing her way. She thanked him and took a gulp of the tart red liquid, feeling it burn down her throat. She hated these kinds of gatherings. They always brought out an inelegance in her.

Moments later, platters of various meats, large round loaves of dark bread, and tureens filled with soup and sauces were placed along the table. Selene placed the goblet down, thankful for the distraction. But her nerves would not let her settle as her stomach twisted. Even the rich smell of venison and pheasant mixed with fresh bread could not awaken her appetite.

More wine was poured into the crystal goblets set around the table. Conversation began as bread was broken and meat was sliced and placed on plates. She overheard Damien quietly asking for another goblet before the servant left. She knew she should offer the use of the one between them, which was common practice. But in this instance, she desired her own.

Lord Damien finished cleaning his fingers in the water bowl and placed his towel on his lap. Every time he moved, his tunic brushed Selene's arm, making her aware of his presence, compounding her discomfort as she remembered her etiquette error. It wasn't the first time she had sat with a nobleman. In the past, she had been seated with Lord Raoul and even his father, Lord Ivulf.

But this was different. There was something about Lord Damien. Even his scent was different. Just the barest hint of clove, cinnamon, and sandalwood. Difficult ingredients to obtain at Rook Castle, especially cinnamon, since fewer and fewer tradesmen traveled King's Highway through the mountain region. But she would never forget the smell.

"Would you like a slice of venison?" Lord Damien asked as he captured a piece with a two-pronged fork and knife.

Selene looked at the meat and her stomach rolled. However, he was kind to offer, so she should accept. "Yes," she said. "Thank you."

He placed a slice on her plate, then two on his. "I know my name was announced earlier this evening, but that doesn't make it a formal introduction." He placed his utensils down and turned toward her. "I am Lord Damien from House Maris."

Selene placed her own down as well. "Lady Selene, heiress to House Ravenwood."

Lord Damien nodded and picked up his fork and knife. "So you are the eldest Ravenwood?"

"I am," she said slowly. He wasn't sizing her up as a possible marriage match, was he? Surely he knew that House Ravenwood did not marry the heads of other Great Houses.

She cut the meat into tiny pieces and placed one in her mouth. She could feel Lady Adalyn and Lord Elric watching her again from across the gap between their tables.

"If I may be so bold, part of the reason I am here is to get to know the other houses. Would you mind telling me a little about yourself?"

Selene paused her fork halfway to her mouth. About herself? What could she say? All she could think about were the late nights spent walking in the dreams of others, learning how to twist those dreams into nightmares.

"I'm sorry," Damien said a moment later, turning back to his own food. "I shouldn't pry—"

"No, it's all right. I'm at a loss at what to say about myself. I'm afraid there's not a lot about me that you would find interesting." At least anything she could share with him. And it sounded like the type of thing a lady would say.

However, she was sure he would find her dreamwalking gift very interesting. But that was a secret she could never divulge—and never wanted to. She never wanted anyone to know about that secret part of her.

"Well," he said thoughtfully, "what's it like growing up in the mountains? I'm from the coast. We have mountains there, but nothing like the Magyr Mountains."

At the word *coast*, Selene's eyes lit up. Being a landlocked nation, and having only traveled to the lands controlled by House

Friere, she had never seen the coast. Her father said that there was water "as far as the eye can see."

She hurried to answer Damien's question so she could pose her own, sharing a little about the seasons and the wild creatures that lived in the mountains, including the timber wolves. "However, I don't think the mountains can compare to the coast. Please," she said, her meal forgotten as she placed her complete attention on Lord Damien, "tell me what the sea is like. I've heard there is so much water that the sea touches the sky."

"Yes, that's true," Damien said and put his fork down, a smile on his face. "If you take a ship out to sea, there is nothing around you but water and sky. And if you happen to be out when the sun is rising or setting, the water reflects the most beautiful colors."

Selene leaned closer. "And what about the animals? What kinds of creatures live in the sea?"

"Well, there are turtles the size of a shield and fish bigger than this table—"

"This table? And you saw them?"

"Yes."

"Amazing," she murmured as she sat back. "And what is your home like? Do you live next to the sea?"

Lord Damien chuckled softly. "Yes. In fact, the balcony from my bedchambers overlooks the sea."

Her eyes lit up again. "So you can see it every day?"

"Yes."

Selene turned back to her plate and picked up her fork. It was exactly how Father had described it, only even better coming from Lord Damien. She could hear the pride he had in his homeland in the way he spoke. She poked at the last bit of meat on her plate and tried to picture it, but all she could imagine was a mountain lake, only much bigger. She let out a sigh. What she wouldn't give to see the sea. To see anything. To visit the other lands, to see the

Northern Shores, or the rolling green hills of House Luceras, or the vast forests of House Rafel.

And I will, she thought as she stabbed at the meat. *Only for a very different reason. To carry out missions.*

"Perhaps some day you can visit Nor Esen, my home city," Damien said.

Selene smiled sadly without looking up and lifted the meat up from the plate. "That would be nice," she said before placing the piece into her mouth. But the only reason she would be going was if his name—or the name of a lesser house within his nation—was assigned to her. The thought made her throat tight, and she found it difficult to swallow.

The rest of the dinner went by quietly as Lord Damien turned his attention to the guest on his right. Amara glanced in Selene's direction once in a while, her gaze darting between her and Lord Damien. The Luceras siblings talked quietly amongst themselves or with Lady Ayaka of House Rafel, who sat next to Lord Elric.

Selene watched Lady Ayaka from beneath lidded eyes. The heiress of House Rafel appeared to be at least twenty winters, with pale skin and hair as dark as her own. Her father sat beside her, his skin weathered and creased, appearing almost as if he could be her grandfather. His beard was gathered midway down his chest in a slender silver chain, and his hair hung over his shoulders in thin white wisps.

As Selene's gaze wandered, she wondered if Mother had ever been assigned to walk in the dreams of the people gathered in this hall. If so, who?

Her gaze stopped on the elder Luceras lord, and she tried to imagine what it would be like to be assigned to him. He spoke quietly, seemed to mistrust everyone in the dining room, and was overly protective of his siblings.

That meant he was the cautious type, and it would be more difficult to infiltrate his room in order to enter his dreams.

Lady Adalyn, however, exuded innocence and beauty. The paragon of a lady. Selene narrowed her eyes. It could all be an act. But if not, Lady Adalyn would be an easy target, apart from the guards who no doubt defended her chambers from the outside.

But what if she were assigned to kill her target, not merely find out information? Could she do it?

She glanced again at the oldest Luceras brother. He was bigger than the other brother, broad in the shoulders, with toned muscles and strong hands, the kind of hands that could choke her with a single squeeze. But none of that mattered if he never woke up.

She watched him, almost mesmerized. What were his nightmares? What scared a young lord like him? What could she twist inside of him to the point that it made his heart stop?

And could she do it? Could she kill him? Or would she end up shattering his mind like she did to Renat—

Selene sat back, her eyes wide. Why was she thinking these thoughts? Assessing those around her, looking for their weak spots before even entering their dreams? Her heart thudded madly inside her chest as a cold sweat coated her back. Was she finally becoming a killer?

With a shaky hand, she reached for the recently filled goblet and held it up. In the candlelight, the crimson liquid sparkled inside the cup. Such a dark, deep red.

Like blood.

Selene let out a loud gasp and the goblet tipped, spilling the crimson liquid across the table. This time, everyone turned to look at her. With swiftness she grabbed hold of her emotions and slammed them behind her mental iron doors.

"Is everything all right, Lady Selene?" Lord Damien asked beside her.

Selene lifted her chin. "Yes, I'm fine. Just a little clumsy." She let out a simpering laugh and waved to one of the servants. Her mother stared at her from the end of the table with a glare so hot she could almost feel it scorching her skin.

Don't think. Don't feel. She chanted those words inside her head as she slammed the doors of her heart shut and mentally adjusted the cold mask across her face.

A servant mopped up the spilled wine. Shortly after, everyone went back to their conversations and she felt alone. So alone. Selene swallowed and glanced down at her empty plate, one thing pressing at her from within: the overwhelming desire to be done with this evening.

D amien stared at the unfamiliar ceiling inside his guest room later that evening, his hands resting behind his head. A cool breeze swept through the room, ruffling his shirt and his hair. He could hear Cohen in the next room preparing for bed. Taegis was still out in the hall. Karl and Sten were on break.

His mind began to replay the evening, from his appearance and introduction to the other Great Houses, to the dinner served, then to the people in the room that night.

Tonight was his first view of House Friere, and both Grand Lord Ivulf and his son Raoul were everything he had heard from his late father: loud, arrogant, and dark. The younger Ravenwood daughter seemed taken by Lord Raoul. Perhaps there was a match in the making there.

His mind moved onto the next family. It was good to see House Luceras again, although Lord Leo had been overly cold and suspicious of everyone. Of course, Leo had always been like that, even when they were kids.

Lady Adalyn was as beautiful as ever. A smile touched his lips. Long ago, there had been talk between their fathers about an alliance between their houses. He wasn't ready to settle down yet, but he wouldn't be surprised if the brothers approached him during this trip.

Lord Elric was now a young man and reminded him greatly of Quinn. Damien sighed and ran a hand through his hair.

Then his mind turned to Lady Selene Ravenwood.

His first assessment of her had been right. She was cold and quiet. Almost haughty even. But the longer he thought about it, the more it seemed like a mask than her real self. The moment he spoke of the coast, her dark eyes had lit up, burning away her cold visage, bringing life to her features. The way she asked questions, hanging on his every word, he could almost see her imagining the sea.

But when he spoke of a visit someday—and it wasn't that uncommon for the Great Houses to visit one another—the mask fell right back into place, followed by her polite, yet cold response.

With any other person, he would wonder at the change, then move on. But something about Lady Selene kept tugging at him, making him ask why. The only other time he could recall seeing such a face was . . .

He suddenly sat up. The look she gave him he had seen once before when he was a boy. A messenger arrived at Northwind Castle to announce that one of House Maris's ships had been lost at sea. He remembered going to the memorial along the beach to commemorate those lost during the storm and spotting a little girl his age. She didn't cry, just stood there by the rippling waves holding a ragged doll in one hand, a look of death on her face.

It was so different compared to the others grieving there along the beach that it burned an image inside his mind. It was as if she too had died and only a shell of herself remained.

The memory came back so vividly it felt like he had been punched in the midsection.

Damien glanced toward the balcony where the moon sat just

over the mountain peaks. He rubbed his face and sighed. What had happened to Lady Selene? He thought back but could not remember hearing of any tragic happenings at House Ravenwood in recent years. That didn't mean she hadn't experienced something devastating, but what could it be?

And why did he care?

He lay back down. *Why do I care?*

Because you want to save everyone.

For as long as he could remember, he was always trying to save things: birds with broken wings, his little brother's toy boat, even a bat that had once gotten caught in a chimney. When he couldn't save them, he would become crestfallen and ask his father why it hurt inside.

"Because you want to save everyone, my son. You have a big heart. And it hurts to see the pain in this world. But that's not a weakness. It is your hidden strength. Never forget that."

Was it possible that it was both his strength *and* his weakness? When others were able to move on and let go of what they couldn't change, Damien stubbornly held on. Sometimes the pain felt like a black pit sucking him in. He could put on a smile, and sometimes even shove his heartache aside, but it was always there, waiting for him in the dark watches of the night.

He still grieved over his parents' deaths. And Quinn's death. He couldn't let go, even almost two years later. And because of that, the pit grew bigger inside of him. Would it someday suck him in completely?

He rolled over onto his side. If only he could turn off the pain and not feel so much. He didn't want to stop caring for people, but he just couldn't let go when he couldn't take their pain away.

He thought again of Lady Selene and her mask of despondency. *Whatever it is, I can't save her from it.*

20

S elene entered her mother's bedchambers and bowed her head. "Mother."

Mother stood from a chair set near windows that overlooked the Magyr Mountains and turned, her dark gown flowing with her movement. Hagatha took a step back. The scent of rosewater permeated the room. Sunlight streamed through a window, spreading light across the ornate chairs set near the empty fireplace.

"That is all, Hagatha. You may go."

"Yes, my lady." Hagatha bowed as she took another step, then slowly made her way to the door, bypassing Selene on her way out. Her posture seemed even more bent and the wrinkles on her hands and face more pronounced. Selene kept her eyes on her mother and away from Hagatha, but that did not prevent the flash of memory of Hagatha's nightmare and the timber wolves descending upon the woman. Wolves set upon her by Selene's own command.

Selene breathed in through her nose and shoved the memory aside.

As Hagatha latched the door shut, her mother beckoned Selene toward the sitting area near the sunlit window.

"How was dinner last night?" her mother asked as she placed a hand on the back of one of the chairs.

Selene came to stand behind the other chair. She recognized the gown Mother wore. Regal, yet not ostentatious. The gown she wore for negotiations. So the first of the talks between the Great Houses would begin today. "It was no different than any other dinner."

"And what about Lord Maris? What did you think of him?"

Selene frowned. If she had not overheard her father and mother's discussion weeks ago, she would almost suspect her mother had ulterior purposes. But she knew that wasn't the case. So why was she asking? "He seems like a capable grand lord, despite his young age."

"Capable?"

"Yes. And seems to have a love for his land." She thought again of the way he spoke of the Northern Shores. She had a feeling that love extended past the land and to the people as well. The thought warmed her.

"Do you think he is a threat to our nation?"

Selene blinked. "Threat?" Her mind rushed through her limited knowledge of the Great Houses. House Ravenwood and House Maris had little interaction with each other since the razing hundreds of years ago. But the houses had never been hostile toward each other either. Just civilly cold. "I don't believe so. Why?"

Her mother ran her fingers along the back of the chair. "I received a message from the Dark Lady when I first received the summons for the assembly from House Maris."

A shadow fell across Selene's heart, stealing away the warmth from moments ago. A message from the Dark Lady? "What did she say?"

"That a threat comes from the north."

"The north? And you think it is House Maris?"

"Or House Vivek."

Selene looked down at the back of the chair. "Have we been assigned to take care of this threat?"

"In a way, yes."

What does that mean?

"It is time for you to begin your journey toward becoming head of House Ravenwood." Her mother came around the chair and sat down, then waited for Selene to do the same.

Selene sat down and waited.

"Part of becoming a grand lady is putting your house above all other houses. For generations, the ladies of Ravenwood have done everything to bring House Ravenwood back to power. We have married those we did not love, sold our gift to provide for our people, and even made alliances with our enemies."

Selene knew of the first two sacrifices, but what did Mother mean by alliances with enemies? Yes, the Great Houses did not always get along, but she would not consider them to be enemies.

"Five years ago, during a visit to House Friere, I met with emissaries from Commander Orion of the Dominia Empire."

Selene felt like she had been hit in the chest. "The Dominia Empire? I don't understand. Why would you meet with emissaries from the empire when you know what they did to us? To our house?"

"Times have changed. They have offered to help us in exchange for our assistance."

Selene frowned. "What do we need help with?"

"The empire will return to us what they stole all those years ago: land and power."

Selene's mind was a swirl of colors and thoughts. "I don't understand. We have land. We have the Magyr Mountains and Rook Castle. And what do we need power for? Our people, though few, are taken care of and work willingly and diligently for House Ravenwood. What more do we need?"

Her mother's eyes flashed. "Before the razing, House Raven-wood was one of the greatest amongst the seven houses. We were revered and our dominion lay beyond the mountains. The other houses took that away when Ravenwood was betrayed and handed over to the empire."

Selene stared at her mother. This had nothing to do with gaining back what House Ravenwood had lost. Yes, the other houses betrayed them years ago. But aligning with the empire? That went beyond simple hatred. This was about her mother's ambitions—ambitions that had been passed down and fed to each Ravenwood generation until it had bloated into the monster before her. If Father was correct, Ravenwood never had power, only influence because they were Dreamers and had the ability to inspire the other nations. Then the razing happened, and now House Ravenwood was power-hungry and willing to destroy everyone around them.

Selene flexed her fingers as her body tensed. She wanted no part of this. "How?" The word came out in one hot breath. "How exactly will they give us this land and power?"

Her mother pressed her fingers together. "No matter what we do, we cannot stop the empire. Commander Orion has built up the empire's forces, and they possess weapons we cannot defend against. This conflict has been in the making for many years. By aligning our house with the empire, I am ensuring our survival and victory. In return for our help, they will let us rule the land on this side of the wall."

"And how exactly are we helping them?" Wait. The covert assignments, the assassinations . . .

"I think you know." Her mother watched her with a keen eye. "We have slowly whittled away the other houses, sometimes choosing our own victims, sometimes hired by them to take out one of the other houses. In some ways, the Great Houses have brought about their own destruction. In fact, every house but House Maris has sought to eliminate someone from another house and unknowingly hired our skills. Oh, the delicious irony. In the end, they made our job easier."

"Even House Luceras?" Selene asked. She could not imagine the holy House of Light had secretly sought the death of someone.

Her mother smiled that not-so-nice smile. "Even House Luceras."

"But not House Maris," Selene confirmed.

Her mother's smile faded. "No. Never the water nation."

"And that's why you think House Maris is a threat?"

"That, and because of the Dark Lady's message."

Selene stared down at her lap. She felt like she had walked into the midst of a spider web and could not escape. Instead of fighting the empire, her mother had made an alliance with the very nation that had almost wiped out their family. An alliance of blood.

Selene brushed a shaky hand across her face. And now she was being dragged into it as the heir to House Ravenwood. "How could you do this?" She wanted to jump to her feet and scream at her mother, but she kept her body firmly planted in the chair.

Her mother lifted her chin and stared coldly at Selene. "I do not owe an allegiance to the other houses. I only have an allegiance to my own."

Selene's nostrils flared. "And what about our people? What happens to them when the empire marches across our lands?"

"They will be safe under my protection."

"And the other nations? What about the other peoples?"

"They are not our concern."

Her mother's harshness and callousness shocked her, even though she knew it should not. Her mother had lost her heart a long time ago, having buried it so deeply that it finally died inside of her. Selene gripped her fingers together. "So why allow the Assembly of the Great Houses—and here, no less? To spy on them?"

"No. To start eliminating them."

Selene's mouth fell open in a silent O. The room dimmed, then came back into focus. This . . . this was all wrong. Selene thought she was going to faint, but she fought against the darkness scrolling across her vision. She pressed her fingers deep into her palms until her eyesight came back. "If you are eliminating all of the Great Houses, then why does this threat from the north matter?"

"I wish to deal with it first, here, during the assembly."

A threat from the north. Two houses. House Maris and House Vivek. Two dreamkillers. Her mother . . . and her.

This would be her first assignment.

Selene tightened, then loosened her fingers. "So we will kill the grand lords and ladies of both House Vivek and House Maris."

"Yes." Her mother nodded, her devilish smile coming back.

Selene let the numbness slide over her, stealing away her mind, her heart, until she felt nothing. "And which house shall I take?"

"House Maris. I shall take House Vivek. I want you to begin walking in Lord Damien's dreams tonight. Find his fears. Find his secrets. Then, on the last night, we strike."

"And you don't think the other houses will suspect anything?"

Her mother stood and brushed out her long gown. "Oh, they will. But I will make sure all accusations are pointed toward the empire. After all, this assembly is here to discuss what to do with the empire's encroachments on our land. So there was bound to be an assassin from the empire present. No one will suspect it was one of the houses." Her mother turned, then paused and looked back. "I do not need to tell you that what I've shared is bound to our house secrets. You may never speak of this to anyone."

Selene bowed her head and nodded.

"Now I must go. The first of the talks begin this morning."

She headed toward the door. "But tonight," she called back, "*we begin.*"

Selene left her mother's bedchambers shortly after, her body still numb. Her mind went back to last evening, to Lord Damien who sat beside her, with the short dark hair and deep blue eyes. To the young man who spoke of the ocean with a soft smile.

"Don't think, don't feel." She chanted those words under her breath as she went to her room to retrieve her swords and black clothes and prepare herself for her first mission. But when she reached her room, the numbness could no longer contain the swirl of emotions inside of her. All she could see was Damien's face and hear his tenor voice, and know that soon she would be the one to end his life.

Selene shut the door behind her, covered her face with her hands, slid to the floor, and cried.

21

Selene spent the rest of the day in the small training area on the southern side of Rook Castle until it was too dark to see and her body was thoroughly tired. Then she bypassed most of the castle, avoiding the dining area, and slipped to her bedchambers. Long had her tears dried, but she felt heavy, like a block of ice was inside of her. She shut the door to her room and rubbed the skin above her heart. Maybe she didn't have a heart anymore. Maybe it was beginning to shrivel up and die like Mother's.

Every time she remembered their conversation from this morning, Selene shoved the memories away. She wasn't numb enough yet to face what her family had become: traitors to the other houses and traitors to the people around them. And allies of the Dominia Empire—

Selene clenched her hands and marched across her room to the small table that stood by the changing panels, topped with a ceramic pitcher and bowl. She stripped off her loose tunic and beige pants. After dumping the soiled clothing in the corner, she poured tepid mint-scented water from the pitcher into the bowl and began to wipe away the sweat and grime that had accumulated from her exercise. She finished with her hair, then placed on clean underclothes and black attire for this evening's mission.

It was fully dark now, barely light enough in her bedchambers to see what she was doing. In some ways, the darkness soothed her, allowing her to hide who she really was in the shadows and become the dreamkiller.

Selene secured the small curved blades to her side and glanced out the window. Tonight she would see what kind of security Damien had, then begin to explore his dream world. But just in case something went wrong, she was ready.

The moon was now rising swiftly over the Magyr Mountains, bathing the peaks in its pale light. She secured her scarf across her face and pulled her hood over her head. Everything in place. But inside, her stomach seemed to have broken out of its ice block and was now writhing like a nest of snakes.

She placed a hand on her midsection and closed her eyes.

Breathe in. Breathe out.

Emotions had no place on her mission. She imagined shoving down every feeling inside of her until she felt nothing but cold and her stomach grew hard again. The chill was her friend. It kept the thoughts and feelings that would interfere with her work at bay.

She was in control.

Satisfied, Selene headed toward the door. The hallway was silent, and only the subtle flare of candlelight lit her way. Even that was more than she needed. She knew these halls and could find her way blindfolded.

After two turns, she headed down a fourth hall to a small storage room once used by her grandmother's personal servant. Inside, she followed a stack of wooden crates to the back wall and pressed down on a small lever located near the corner. The wall slid to the side, leading into a narrow tunnel. Selene entered and moved the wall back into place behind her before continuing on to the tunnel that would lead her beneath Lord Damien's balcony.

The air was cold in here and smelled of dust. There was no candlelight now, just the darkness and her own memory of the path. Quietly she made her way along, her fingers brushing the sides of the cool rock wall. Ten minutes later, she met the first curve and rounded it. A minute later, another turn. The air grew colder and the scent of pine replaced the dust smell. Almost there.

A moment later, she stooped down and emerged through the tiny opening in the rocky face of the cliff, the moon her only light. Right above her was the balcony that led to the guest room Lord Damien had been given. Mother must have been planning this mission in advance if she had placed the grand lord here.

Glancing up, Selene spotted the footholds within the rock wall and scurried up the boulders to the balcony above without a second thought. Somewhere in the valley below, a timber wolf howled. Seconds later, it was answered by another wolf farther away.

Selene ignored the nightly noise as she grabbed the lip of the stone balcony and swung her body up gracefully. She was over the railing before she took a breath and paused next to the curved doorway. Lord Damien had not bothered to shut the door. Given the heat, she was not surprised. The cool mountain air was refreshing after a warm autumn day.

Silently she peered around the doorway. The bedchamber was one of their more lavish ones, with a four-poster bed against the far wall, massive stone fireplace to the left, a mountain bear rug across the stone floor, and opulently framed paintings of the Magyr Mountains along the walls.

Selene narrowed her eyes and gazed across the room. There were two other doors, each one leading into separate rooms, apart from the one that led into the hallway. Who slept in the rooms beyond? She recalled Lord Damien had come with a small party of four other men. Most likely those men were in the other rooms.

She then focused on the large four-poster bed where a single body lay. There was a small space on the other side of the bed by the wall—facing away from the doors—where she could crouch down and not be seen. That was where she would position herself.

Her soft-skinned boots made no sound as Selene stole across the room to the bedside. Lord Damien lay on his back as if he had passed out. A wry smile crept across her lips. Good. It appeared the talks had taken everything out of him. He hadn't even bothered to change out of his clothes or crawl beneath the covers.

She took a moment to gaze at his face. Her stomach did a small flip. Up this close, and without his own eyes staring back, she was able to fully take in his features. Lord Damien was indeed a handsome man. His dark hair, kept shorter than was common, was thick and full. His face held traces of his youth, but the stubble across his jaw indicated he was fully man. And not just a man, but one who kept his physique in top condition as indicated by the tight, lean muscles beneath his thin tunic.

Selene brought her thoughts to bear and pushed them away. She had a job to do.

She knelt down beside his bed. His sleeves were rolled up to the elbow, leaving his forearm exposed. That was where she would make contact.

Her heart started thumping inside her chest, and a cold sweat broke out along the back of her neck and back. It was one thing to enter a servant's dreams, but quite another to enter a stranger's. And not just any stranger, but the head of a Great House.

Focus, Selene. He's just a man. A man with fears just like any other. You're here to find out what his are and nothing more.

Still, her hand shook as she reached for his arm. Would his

dreamscape be like Petur's, filled with horrific secrets? Or dark and bloody like Hagatha's with the timber wolves?

Or like Renata's?

She squeezed her eyes shut at the last memory, guilt clawing at her. No matter what she found inside Lord Damien's mind, she would make sure to keep her emotions under control. Never again would she shatter another person's dreamscape.

After she took some deep breaths, her hand stopped shaking. Selene opened her eyes, reached up, and gently wrapped her fingers around his forearm. His skin was warm against her cool fingers. Before she could form another thought, she was drawn into his dreamscape—forcibly so, as if she had been pulled inside by his own will.

Selene gasped. That had never happened before. Bright light filled her vision as her body took its raven form. Her talons hit the ground and she stumbled back, holding a wing over her eyes.

It took a moment for her eyesight to adjust to the light, then she slowly brought her wing down. The air around her was warm, in a comforting way. She had never felt warmth like this, not even on the fullest day of the sun month. It was like submerging beneath the waters of one of the hot springs around Rook Castle. Even the air here was sweet and heady. And light-filled. Not dark like Renata's dreamscape. Not monochromatic like Petur's.

She felt a pull again from deep within, drawing her into Lord Damien's dreamscape. Almost as if it wanted her here. She gave her body a shake, then spread her wings. Such a strange sensation. And unlike any other dreamscape she had visited.

She lifted lightly from the ground. As she rose, the dreamscape spread out before her, its appearance like one of those oil paintings that hung in the east wing, the one with the beautiful beaches, long stretches of blue water, and white sand. Is this what Lord Damien dreamed of? Was this his essence—water and light?

How would she find what he feared if this was who he was? Did he even have any fears?

She snorted at her own thoughts. Of course he did. Everyone feared something. She might have to dive deep into his dreams, but she would find it.

She flew higher, letting the wind currents carry her along the dreamscape. On and on she flew, along the white sandy coast, the sweet air brushing past her face and feathers. So . . . beautiful. Was this what the Northern Shores looked like? If so, she wanted to visit it in the real world more than anything. A part of her wanted to land, change back into her human form, and simply walk in the light along the edge of the water.

She gave her head a shake and pumped with her wings. That wasn't what she was here for.

A minute later, a bright light appeared along the horizon, even brighter than the sun-like light around her. Selene flapped her wings and steered toward it.

The closer she drew, the more it looked like a bonfire along the beach, only the flames were white, not red and orange like the physical fires she was used to.

She angled her body and started down in a slow circular descent. The white fire entranced her, as if drawing her toward it with invisible tethers.

A second later, she pulled up hard and fast. The fire lay fifty feet beneath her. Selene breathed hard and stared. At this range, she could see each flame dancing upon the other, a revolving orb of white light.

It couldn't be. But it was. She could feel it now.

Damien's soul.

Selene swooped down onto the sand and hovered ten feet away and stared at the white fire. His soul was nothing like Petur's or Anna's. So alive, so full of light.

Mother said to never touch the soulsphere, but it was if her dream body was moving of its own accord. Selene slipped out of her raven form and her bare feet stepped upon the sand. She stood before the ball of light.

More than anything she wanted to touch it. The desire was like a fierce wolf inside of her, lunging at the chance to touch the gleaming sphere. She reached out her hand. It was like standing before a roaring fire on a cold winter's night. One touch, just one finger.

So different than her own cold, dark soul.

She pulled her hand back and spun around. What was she doing? One touch and he would've sensed her presence.

I've got to get out of here!

Selene transformed back into a raven and sped toward the breach in the dreamscape, her heart pounding and breathing ragged.

A second later, she found herself back in the bedchamber, her knees numb from kneeling on the stone floor.

Damien gave a low groan, and one of the doors on the other side of the room opened.

Selene froze, her head below the mattress.

Footsteps, barely a whisper across the stone floor, approached the bed.

Sweat spread across her body, soaking into her clothing. She could feel the weight of her blades, ready to be drawn at any notice. Her mind switched to a layout of the bedchamber, calculating a path to the balcony and how long it would take to sprint across the room and disappear over the railing.

The footsteps stopped near the bed.

Damien groaned again and moved across the mattress.

Whoever stood nearby let out a sigh, and the sound of footsteps grew distant.

Selene waited, every part of her being focused on the other person in the room. A door opened and shut moments later.

Selene listened. The only sound now was Damien's gentle breathing and the distant howl of a timber wolf outside.

Quietly, she lifted her head and scanned for the two doors on the other side of the room. Both were closed.

She slowly stood on shaky legs, ready to run at the slightest provocation, her heart still thrashing inside her chest. Only adrenaline was keeping her mind and body from freezing. She glanced again at Damien and shook her head. She was not in a state where she could reenter his dreamscape. She needed to get back to her room and collect her thoughts and emotions. She would just have to try another night.

She turned and silently stole across the room to the balcony. With one swift movement, she launched herself over the railing and landed on the small rocky lip, her knees bent, her hands spread out across the cold surface. She stared down at her hands, her mind freeing itself from the fear from moments ago and drawing back to the scene she had stumbled upon in Damien's dreamscape: his luminous soul.

Who exactly was this man? Why did his soul look like that? And why did she want to touch it so badly?

22

Damien pulled on a clean light tunic while fighting back a yawn. Yesterday's talks were long and tedious, with each house positioning themselves with words. The Dominia Empire barely came up. He tightened his belt around the tunic, then shrugged on his sleeveless leather jacket. Today he would need to keep the conversations on topic. There were only a couple of days remaining to figure out a plan before some of the houses left. Time was already ticking.

"Lord Damien, good morning."

Damien glanced back and spotted Taegis with the guards Sten and Karl exiting the room they shared. The three men bowed to him. Taegis dismissed Sten and Karl, then approached Damien while the two guards headed for the door.

"We will be taking shifts outside the meeting hall today, so if you need one of us, we will be there."

Damien nodded as he secured his sword at his side.

"You appear tired. Is everything all right?"

Damien glanced up. Did it show on his face? "Yes. I had the strangest dream last night. I was walking along the shoreline near Nor Esen when a raven appeared. It continued to follow me. I'm not sure what it means—if it is an omen or my mind simply adjusting to Rook Castle. I've seen more ravens here than I have anywhere else."

Taegis looked at him thoughtfully. "I would wager the latter, but I also would not discount it being an omen. If so, watch out. It could be warning you."

"Of what?"

Taegis shrugged. "Perhaps the talks, perhaps of one of the houses. I know little about dreams, but my grandmother used to be leery of all black birds, especially ones in dreams. Then again, she hated ravens, so who knows."

Damien thought again about the dream from last night. The raven had not appeared portentous. "I will keep that in mind."

The two men left the guest chambers and headed for the meeting hall. As Damien glanced around at the architecture, furniture, and artwork in Rook Castle, the more he was convinced the raven was merely an intrusion of his surroundings on his mind rather than something more.

At the double doors, Taegis stepped to the side and folded his hands in front of him. He was not alone. There were guards from the other houses, all here to secure the safety of their lords and ladies.

A servant opened the door and allowed Damien inside. The room was circular and two stories tall, with arched columns along the first and second story. An enormous round table stood in the middle of the room, surrounded by high-backed chairs. A silver chandelier hung above the table and twinkled with the light of dozens of candles. Past the columns were narrow windows filled with pale light.

Most of the houses were already gathered. Lord Haruk Rafel was already seated, his silver hair flowing around his dark green robes. Lord Leo Luceras leaned against one of the columns to the left with his arms folded across his chest, his golden hair standing out beneath the candlelight. Lady Ragna stood behind her chair, talking amiably with Lord Ivulf Friere. With a cloak trimmed in grey timber wolf fur and his dark hair captured beneath a thin steel circlet, Lord Ivulf presented an imposing figure. Lord Rune and his sister Lady Runa sat on the right side of the table, talking quietly between themselves.

Lady Ragna glanced up and spotted Damien. "Grand Lord Damien, thank you for joining us this morning."

Damien bowed stiffly. Once again, Lady Ragna was taking control, and it left a bitter taste in his mouth.

At her announcement, the other grand lords and ladies took a seat around the table. Damien sat with his back to the door. The air held myriad smells, from perfume and scented water to the more earthy smell of mint and hibiscus. He sniffed again and glanced to his left. Lord Haruk looked like he was about to go to sleep with his eyelids half raised and his breathing an even tempo.

Before Lady Ragna could say any more, Damien spoke up. "House Vivek, please share what has been going on along your borders and the wall." He sat back and folded his hands across the table. No more getting off point. It was time to direct the talks toward the growing threat of the empire.

Lord Rune stood, his regal deep purple robes cascading down his wide-set shoulders and long body, accenting his dark skin. He bowed politely to Damien, then the rest of the assembly, then in a deep voice began to talk about the skirmishes along the wall.

The morning went by, each hour bringing more and more heated discussions. By afternoon, it became apparent to Damien that there was a split between the houses. His house, House Vivek, and House Luceras wanted to start taking action against the encroaching empire. But House Ravenwood, House Friere, and

House Rafel did not see any imminent threat. House Ravenwood went so far as to ask if the threat was even real.

Damien could feel a pulsing headache forming behind his right eye and not for the first time wondered why seven houses had been given gifts to rule the peoples when perhaps only one house would have sufficed. He glanced again at Lady Ragna. Her house did not even have their gift anymore.

"Harmony is a beautiful thing, my son." His father's words echoed in his head. *"Yes, it would be easier if there was only one house. But the Light bestowed seven gifts that—when used together—nothing can stand against."*

Damien rubbed his throbbing eye and sighed. His father had believed so strongly in the unity of the houses that he had formed a secret group to work toward that end. But would his father's hope come to pass? Looking around, Damien wasn't so sure. And what about the missing gift? The original members of House Ravenwood had died in the razing, leaving it a Great House in title and land only.

Could six gifts accomplish what seven gifts were originally supposed to do? And House Merek had not even bothered to show up for the assembly, bringing those gifts down to five, assuming the houses present could even cooperate with one other.

I wish I knew what you had planned, Father, Damien thought silently.

By late afternoon, it was clearly time for the discussions to end for the day. Damien motioned for an adjournment, and Lady Ragna invited the houses to dinner.

He stood and stretched his arms up, releasing cramped muscles along his back and shoulders. What he needed was a bit of exercise to loosen up muscles not accustomed to being lethargic. Perhaps there would be time for that tomorrow, before the talks resumed.

Damien followed the other lords and ladies out. Moments after he exited the doorway, Sten joined him. As they headed back to their own rooms, a muffled horn rang out across Rook Castle.

He glanced toward the open archways that overlooked the main part of the castle. Far off in the distance, past the ramparts and above the Magyr peaks, three dark shapes glided along white clouds.

Damien stepped closer to the nearest archway and watched the shapes approach. They looked like large birds, only the wings were wrong. More like a bat, but scaly—

His eyes widened and a ball of warmth expanded across his chest. He grinned and clutched the edge of the archway and leaned out. There was no mistaking those creatures. The famous wyverns of the Southern Isles. And upon them rode the lords of House Merek.

He wanted to whoop and thrust a fist into the air, but it would appear too youthful, so he contented himself with smiling and watching the approaching entourage. So Grand Lord Malrin had decided to come after all. Although, given the few wyverns approaching, he had chosen to come with a small company.

The horn sounded again as the wyverns changed course and began to approach Rook Castle. Damien stepped back. Most likely House Merek would land in the inner courtyard.

He took off at a brisk walk toward the courtyard, Sten behind him. By now servants and guests alike had begun to gather in the hallways, asking questions and pointing toward windows.

"What are those?"

"Are they safe?"

"They aren't really going to land those creatures here, are they?"

Outside, Damien went down a few more steps, then looked up. Against the cloud-riddled sky, three wyverns began their descent as the third horn sounded. There was no banner flapping from one of the saddles, nothing to indicate what house the riders represented. Then again, no introduction was needed. Only one group of people rode the wild wyverns of the south, and that was House Merek.

A dull roar filled the air as huge wings lowered the beasts to the ground. The first wyvern was a giant, with burnished copper scales and riding gear made of leather and iron. By now, a crowd had gathered around the courtyard, including the siblings from House Luceras and Lady Ayaka Rafel.

The copper-colored wyvern touched down, its wings sending up a cloud of dust before settling. A lithe figure jumped down from its back and started toward the main stairs where Damien stood.

Damien narrowed his eyes. That wasn't Lord Malrin Merek. It was his daughter, Lady Bryren. Her hair matched the copper tones of the wyvern behind her and hung around her face and shoulders in a dozen loose pieces and small braids. She wore black kohl around her eyes, accentuating her light brown irises. Her clothing consisted of leather pants and jerkin, a light tunic beneath, and soft-skinned boots.

She spotted Damien and a smile spread over her full lips. "Lord Damien Maris," she said as she approached the stairs. "Last time I saw you, we were trying to catch wyvern hatchlings outside my father's hall."

Damien bowed. "Lady Bryren. What a surprise." He looked up. "Where is your father?"

A shadow passed over her face as the other two wyverns landed and their riders disembarked. "He passed in the night a couple of weeks before we received your summons for the assembly."

"I'm sorry to hear that." Lord Malrin dead? How? The man was as fit as they came the last time Damien had corresponded with the grand lord of House Merek. Granted that was months ago. "How did he pass, may I ask?"

"The healer believed his heart gave out."

Damien frowned. A young woman from one of the lesser houses under the protection of House Luceras had met the same demise a few months ago, and a man from House Vivek earlier than that. Could they be connected? Did Caiaphas know about Lord Malrin's demise?

One of the riders approached while the other secured the bridles, saddles, and saddlebags from the wyverns. He was taller than Damien, with spiky coal-black hair and a small braid that hung over his right shoulder. He had the same dark lines around his eyes as Lady Bryren and was dressed in similar fashion.

Lady Bryren placed her hand out, palm upward, and the man took it. "Lord Damien, let me present to you my consort, Reidin, of the lesser House of Ral."

"Consort?" Damien's eyebrows rose. "When did you marry?"

Her face tightened. "Shortly before my father passed away. I'm glad he was able to be at our binding."

Reidin did not say a word. He simply watched Damien with hazel eyes.

"Welcome, House Merek."

Damien stiffened as Lady Ragna came to stand beside him on the staircase. The scent of her rosewater and the musk from the nearby wyverns created an unpleasant aroma. He choked down a cough.

Lady Bryren and her consort bowed their heads. "Lady Ragna. Thank you for extending the hospitality of Rook Castle for the assembly. Please pardon our tardiness. We ran into some bad weather south of here."

Lady Ragna sniffed unpleasantly. "Do your mounts need any special treatment?"

Lady Bryren lifted her head. "No. Our wyverns do not require shelter or food. They will be quite content to hunt and rest in the Magyr Mountains, if that is all right with you."

Lady Ragna looked over at the three beasts. "As long as they do not harass my people."

Lady Bryren grinned. "They do not like most people, so there is no fear of that." She looked back and gave out a shrill whistle. At once, the three wyverns—bereft of their saddles and bridles—lifted into the air and took off over the ramparts in a great wind.

As Damien watched the majestic creatures fly off, he noticed a single figure standing on the topmost ramparts. Lady Selene stood atop one of the towers, a silhouette against the darkening sky, dressed in black, her long hair unbound and flying behind her like the wings of a raven as she watched the wyverns fly toward the setting sun.

Something shifted inside of him at the sight of her. She appeared alone at that moment, a single pillar high above everyone else. Powerful, beautiful, and vulnerable at the same time.

Seconds later, she dropped her head and turned, disappearing from sight. Damien blinked at the strange emotion and brought his attention back to Lady Ragna and Lady Bryren.

"You are invited to join us for dinner this evening, where I will announce the arrival of your house," Lady Ragna said to Lady Bryren.

"I will be honored. But first, my companions and I would like to clean up."

"I will send my servants out to show you to your rooms and to take care of your needs."

Lady Bryren bowed again. "Thank you, Grand Lady Ragna."

Lady Ragna turned and disappeared into Rook Castle.

Lady Bryren looked up with a smirk on her face. "Apparently House Ravenwood still dislikes our house and our ways." She shrugged and headed for the third rider, who stood beside their saddlebags. "No love lost on our part either. Terric! Look who I found! Lord Damien! Do you remember him?"

The third rider looked up. His deep red hair ran toward the back of his head in thick spikes. He also wore kohl around his eyes, accentuating his green eyes and matching his black leather attire.

Damien swore if Lady Bryren could, she would have been skipping across the courtyard. At least she had acquired a modicum of decorum, but he had a feeling she would always be young at heart, no matter her age. She was just as spirited and vibrant as he remembered when they were young.

Terric glanced at Damien, then back at Lady Bryren. "Lord Damien. You mean from House Maris?"

"Yes! Except that's grand lord now, right?" She looked over at Damien.

Damien winced inside but managed a faint smile. "Yes." He recognized Terric now. It was the hair. He was one of many cousins to House Merek and was always a shadow to Lady Bryren when they were young. Damien noticed the siblings of House Luceras were now approaching.

"Lady Bryren." Lord Leo bowed. The stiff coldness from this morning was gone, replaced with genuine affection. Lady Adalyn and Lord Elric bowed as well. "It is good to see you."

Lady Bryren's face brightened even more. "Lord Leo, and Lord Elric, and—oh my, Lady Adalyn, you have become such a lovely lady!"

Lady Adalyn blushed. Damien glanced over. Yes, Adalyn was quite lovely today, with her long golden hair gathered to one side and swept into a thick braid. Her white gown looked almost ethereal in the dying light. Elric smirked, bringing out his dimples.

It felt like a family reunion, with Lady Bryren gushing over the Luceras family, her consort and cousin looking on. For as long as he could remember, their three houses had always been close, visiting each other every couple of years.

Damien stood back and watched. This was what unity should

feel like: warmth, friendliness, and genuine love. He looked back at Rook Castle. Lady Ayaka was already gone, along with most of the servants and other houses. If only all seven houses could get along like these three did.

He let out a long sigh. However, if the talks were any indication, the seven Great Houses were far from it.

D inner that evening was a loud, boisterous affair with Lady Bryren's arrival. Damien watched her from the other side of the dining hall as she chatted away with whomever would listen, while her consort and cousin sat quietly.

"It is good to see her again, isn't it?" Lady Adalyn's silvery voice flowed from his right.

Damien reached for the nearby goblet. "Yes, it is. I'm glad House Merek was able to come." However, he was still disturbed by the news Lady Bryren brought about her father. He took a sip, his mind going over her words.

"How are the talks going?"

Damien blinked and placed the goblet down. He glanced over at Adalyn. In the candlelight, her hair fairly glowed, and the golden gown she wore made her appear as if she were made of light. Her eyes, usually a light blue, appeared darker and deeper as she looked back.

A shy girl, Adalyn rarely spoke, even when they were young. She was more content to observe and listen while her older brothers carried on the conversation. The fact that she was asking him questions meant she was trying to engage him in conversation. Interesting.

"As well as I expected. I'm afraid I cannot share more."

"Oh." Her face blushed. "That's all right." She picked up her cleaning cloth and carefully cleaned her fingertips.

"And how is everything back home?" Damien asked. She was trying, he could tell, so he would help her along.

"Very well. We have more pilgrims arriving every day to learn at the Temple of Splendor." Lady Adalyn bubbled along, sharing with him the latest news and goings-on in the hill country. A servant came by and placed a plate in front of each of them: quail with a light sauce.

Lady Adalyn began to daintily remove the meat from the bird. "There was talk of cutting down the old oak tree in the city square. I persuaded Father not to do it. There are too many memories there. Especially of Elric and—" She paused, her fork in midair.

Damien knew what she was going to say. Elric and Quinn. The two were thick as thieves when House Maris would visit House Luceras.

"I'm sorry, Lord Damien," she said quietly.

Damien swallowed the lump in his throat. He placed his silverware down and lightly patted her hand. "It's all right. Those are good memories. I'm glad you can remember Quinn that way."

She nodded, but her hand shook beneath his. "We miss Quinn. Every time I pass the old oak tree, I see him and Elric climbing along the branches, trying to see who can go the highest." Her hand tightened around the silverware, almost as if she were consoling herself. "Thank you," she whispered, then went back to cutting up the bird.

Damien took up his own silverware. He always secretly wondered if Lady Adalyn had possessed feelings for his brother, Quinn. Now he would never know. It was one reason to put off any offers of marriage her brothers might bring to him. He wasn't sure if he could marry Lady Adalyn if her heart had belonged to his brother.

Then again, he might not have a choice. As only heir to House Maris, his choice in spouse would be very important. And a stronger alliance with House Luceras would be beneficial to his people.

Damien slowly chewed on a piece of quail and looked over the other dinner guests. Lady Bryren continued to talk exuberantly with those around her. Lord Rune of House Vivek seemed to be entertained by her words. Damien's lips curled to the side. Rarely did he see Lord Rune so diverted. His sister sat beside him, picking at her bird.

The other dinner guests seemed occupied as they spoke to each other in amiable chatter. Except for one. His eyes were drawn to the end of the table across from him where Lady Selene sat next to Lord Raoul from House Friere. She wore an elegant but simple blue gown, a stark contrast to the more ostentatious wardrobes of the other women present.

He could tell Lord Raoul was trying to get her attention, but to no avail. She appeared cold and aloof, with her chin set and her movements precise and orderly.

Lord Raoul leaned closer to her, his dark eyes glittering as he spoke more fervently. The gold jewelry along his fingers and the skull pendant around his neck glistened in the candlelight.

There was a hint of anger, just a flash of emotion, before the cold veil descended back upon Lady Selene's face as she answered him. Whatever reply she gave him made him back up and begin to ravage his quail with a sullen look on his face.

Once Lord Raoul's attention was elsewhere, Lady Selene seemed to sag forward infinitesimally, as if she had been holding herself together, and her eyes glistened. Damien reached for the goblet nearby and studied her over the crystal rim. He felt that same strange tugging sensation from earlier when he'd spotted her at the top of the tower when House Merek arrived. She appeared now as she had then: alone and vulnerable.

As if sensing his perusal, she looked up and over at him. They stared at each other, the other dinner guests forgotten. A flicker of life came back into her dark eyes before she glanced away.

Damien tipped the goblet and took a sip of the wine. People were usually easy for him to figure out. Lord Raoul was a spoiled heir, Lady Adalyn was shy and acquiescent, Lord Haruk from House Rafel was tired and ready to place the mantle of ruling onto his daughter, Ayaka, but was probably waiting to find a consort for her first, and Lady Ragna was driven and ambitious, despite her lack of real power.

But Lady Selene? He placed the goblet down. One moment she was cold and aloof, the next moment vulnerable. She was an enigma to him.

And he found himself wanting to know more.

Selene stared down at her barely touched quail. One moment, Lord Raoul was pressuring her to spend the evening with him and she was lashing out at him. The next moment, she found Lord Damien staring at her. . . .

That one glance was all it took for her to remember his dream-scape and the way his soulsphere radiated light across the expanse of his mind and body. She wanted to look at him again and search his face for any trace of that light in this reality. Where did the light come from? Why was his soul so different than others she had encountered?

And why was she drawn to it like a moth to a flame?

"Dart'an!" she whispered. She was supposed to go back into his dreams tonight, but already she was distracted by thoughts of his soul. Not good.

"Did you say something?" Lord Raoul said in a husky voice.

"No," Selene said through tight lips. She did not need Raoul pressuring her again. She had a job to do, and even if she didn't, she would not waste her precious time on him. There was no future between them. Her house did not marry the heirs of other houses. And he most likely knew that. She glanced at her mother at the head of the table. Why in the name of the Dark Lady had her mother placed her beside him? She knew her mother was considering an alliance with House Friere, but it would be with one of the lesser houses and not with Raoul himself.

Mother never glanced her way. Instead, she seemed to be in a deep discussion with Raoul's father, Lord Ivulf. Selene fought back a grimace. She'd never liked Raoul nor his father. Both men gave her a feeling of dread. She spotted her father on the other side of Mother and an ache filled her throat. He was the silent, forgotten partner.

Selene went back to her cold quail, but her appetite was gone. Was that how her own marriage would be? Two strangers forced to live life together?

She shoved the plate aside. *I hope not.*

After dinner, Selene made her way out of the dining room, escaping through the throng of sociable chatter and laughter. She couldn't help but notice how everyone seemed to get along, especially the younger lords and ladies. The newest arrival, Lady Bryren, had a way about her, lowering barriers and bringing smiles to people's faces. A small part of her was jealous of the young woman's ability, and another part of her wanted to stay and linger with the others. To just be normal and have normal conversations, and laugh. Even her sister Amara had joined in, her voice almost as loud as Lady Bryren's.

Selene wanted to glance back to see if Lord Damien was staying as well. Was he laughing with the others? Did he enjoy their company?

No. She didn't want to know. It would make her feel even more like an outsider.

Selene took a deep breath and pressed on ahead toward the doors that led out into the corridor. With each step, as she made her way to her bedchambers to prepare for that evening, she felt the mantle of House Ravenwood settle once again across her shoulders.

When she was dressed and ready, she paced her room. The other houses had taken to staying up late, and she had a feeling tonight would be no exception, which meant she would have to wait longer to sneak along the halls to Lord Damien's room.

Back and forth, back and forth, her boots barely whispering across the stone floor. A cool breeze entered her room from the nearby windows, and the sound of voices echoed across the castle. She finally sat down at the end of her bed and held her face in her hands.

Every time she thought of the burning ball of light inside Lord Damien, her heart quickened. It was all she could think about. Even tonight when she looked at him, she didn't see him, but the light inside of him.

What ignited his soul? What made it burn so brightly?

She curled her fingers against her cheeks. Never had she longed for something so much that her body ached for just one touch of that light.

Selene ran a hand across her face and dropped her arms. How was she going to accomplish her mission if all she could think about was his luminous soul?

"I just won't go there," she whispered into the night air. If the coast was there again, she would not follow it. Instead, she would find his stream of memories and follow them instead. Mother was expecting a report in the next day or two, and she did not want to show up empty-handed. She needed something—a fear or a regret—to present to her mother. Something she could twist enough to damage his mind—

Bile flooded her throat as she curled forward. The bit of quail and bread she had eaten came rushing up, threatening to exit her mouth. *Don't feel, Selene!* She clenched her hands into two tight fists. *Don't think, don't feel, only act.*

Breathe.

She breathed in.

Breathe out.

She breathed out.

Slowly her body loosened, and her dinner settled back down. She looked over at the windows. A crescent moon rose above the mountain peaks. She watched it, waiting and listening for the night to settle across the castle. When it was about to reach the topmost summit, she stood. Time to go. She double-checked her swords, then readjusted the black cloth across her face and tugged her hood up over her head.

The moment the moon crested over the final peak, Selene moved toward the hallway. Soundlessly she made her way through the castle, into the secret room on the second floor and through the tunnels beneath Rook Castle until she reached the opening below Damien's balcony.

Just like before, she gracefully made her way onto the balcony and peeked inside. The doors to the other rooms were closed, and Damien lay on his bed. She closed her eyes and listened. No sound. But just to be sure . . .

She double-checked the room, then stole across the floor to the opening between the bed and the wall and crouched down. She listened again. She could hear the even, deep breaths of sleep. She waited a moment more, then stood.

He had removed his sleeveless leather jacket, but he wore the same tunic and trousers from dinner. He even still had his boots on. And this time his sleeves were down, leaving only his neck exposed.

Selene watched him sleep, the gentle rise and fall of his chest and the way his face relaxed. He was even more fascinating tonight. She frowned. Was that because of what she had seen inside of him? Or was she becoming more aware of his features?

She let out a small sigh, the sorrowful ache from earlier tonight returning. Could she do it? Could she really turn his fears against him? An invisible hand tightened around her throat, pressing against her airway.

She shook her head to clear away those thoughts and focused on the mission at hand. She reached for his right arm and carefully pulled his sleeve up until his wrist was exposed, then settled down beside his bed. She would be sure to maintain a conscious presence of both his dreams and the room, given how someone had walked in last time. She would not be caught.

She took a deep breath and wrapped her fingers around his skin—

At once she was pulled into Damien's dreamscape as if he had grabbed her hand and yanked her inside.

24

Selene's body shrunk as her arms elongated and transformed into black wings. She gave her body a shake, this form both familiar and unfamiliar at the same time.

Lord Damien's dreamscape had changed. There was no white sand, no gentle sea waves. Instead, she found herself in an unfamiliar room, dark save for a fire that burned in the stone fireplace nearby.

Whatever had happened to him since her last visit, it had changed his dreamscape into something darker. Perhaps this was fortuitous. The dreamscape already held that ominous sense that came with nightmares.

Selene focused on the world outside the dreamscape, seeing and hearing Damien's room as if looking through a curtain of water. There was no movement, no doors opened. Satisfied, she sunk once again into the dream.

The room looked like a bedchamber, with a large four-poster bed against the far wall, a bearskin rug on the floor, and a sitting area to the right, beneath three long windows carved out of the light, smooth stone wall.

Selene lifted off the floor and flew to the nearest bedpost and looked down. A couple lay in the bed, and her heart gave a sharp warble. She had no desire to intrude on an intimate moment.

On second glance, she realized the male inhabitant was not Damien, but a much older man who looked like Damien, only with a full black beard and aged features. His face was pale and glistened with sweat.

Next to the man lay a woman with long chestnut hair spread out across a pristine white pillow. Thin streaks of grey peppered her hair and dark circles formed below her closed eyes.

There was a low groan nearby.

Selene turned and found a younger Damien sitting in a dark corner near the bed, his head held in his hands. He appeared broken. He glanced up and wiped his eyes with the back of his hand.

Selene paused, feeling the atmosphere around her. There was a gnawing fear here, fed by the unknown and grief. She glanced again at Damien's ghostly figure. For one moment, he appeared dark, almost black, like a hole had opened up, a bottomless pit where he sat, then his image appeared again and the hole was gone.

She narrowed her eyes. Had she seen something, or was it just a trick of the dreamscape? Before she could think on it more, the room began to spin until it was a whirl of shadows and muted colors. Selene flew up from the bedpost and waited for Damien's mind to settle. But she tagged the memory within her own mind. Whatever that had been, it could prove useful when she went to reconstruct his dreams later on, if she could figure out what she had seen.

The shadows and faint light settled down into a new image. Grey water spread out as far as the eye could see, beneath an equally grey sky. Below her, a large ship moved along the undulations of the sea. She swooped down and landed on the rigging. About thirty people gathered on the deck around three narrow wooden boxes.

A young Damien stood beside a man dressed in burgundy robes, with thin white hair and clean-shaven face. Behind the crowd stood the older Damien. It looked like he was revisiting another memory through his dreams.

The old man in burgundy robes spoke a prayer over the wooden boxes. Then the crowd parted as the railing was opened and the boxes were lifted and carried one by one to the edge of the ship, then gently dropped into the sea.

As the third one was cast into the sea, the cold, gnawing fear sensation spread across the dreamscape. Again? She looked around, but Damien did not change form. However, the fear seemed to be spreading, like cold fingers, entering her small feathered body and causing her to shudder.

The boxes bobbed along the water's surface before sinking below the lapping waters. Selene turned away. Perhaps the chill was coming from the death scene below. It didn't take much to realize that what she was watching was a burial of sorts, and she had a feeling that two of the boxes held the couple she had seen from the previous dreamscape.

Mother would be pleased by this. Selene still hadn't located a tangible fear-memory or figured out what the gnawing coldness was, but these dreams had certainly revealed Damien's sorrows, and she could work with that.

Selene cringed at the thought. The memory of Damien looking up and wiping his eyes filled her mind. She had never seen a man cry before, and she doubted the heir of House Maris cried in public. Even now, his younger self was standing stoically on the ship's deck.

What would Selene be made to do? Make him endure the death of these people over and over again? Trap him in an unending loop in his mind? It wouldn't kill him, but it certainly would make him go crazy.

But I don't want to do that.

Her throat tight, she spread her wings and lifted off the rigging. For one moment, Damien looked up. Selene ignored his glance and flew away. She flew until the ship was only a speck across the grey waters and still she flew.

There had to be something else she could use, something other than this desolate scene. She glided high above, watching the ever-changing landscape of Damien's dreams, being careful not to go near the shoreline where his soulsphere was.

Then she felt it: that cold, tingly feeling of fear. It wasn't as strong as the gnawing coldness from the death scenes, but she couldn't mistake the tinge of terror that lined the memory.

She dove back down toward the water's surface and sailed along the wind. The wind began to blow harder and waves rose along the top of the sea. The clouds above grew dark and ominous. She pumped her wings and flew on. Higher and higher the waves grew the farther she went, and the wind buffeted her body, pushing her off course.

What is going on? Another gust of wind caught her and tossed her into the air. Then the rain came, hard and strong. She could barely stay above the water. Each time she dipped down, a wave would reach up and almost grab her by the talons. She began to shiver as the torrential downpour soaked through her feathers and skin.

A part of her wanted to change the dreamscape, but she couldn't, not if she wanted to see what exactly Damien feared. She had to experience his fear in its entirety if she hoped to replicate it. She sucked in another breath and pressed on.

Just when her wings felt as if they would give way beneath the storm, she spotted a dark shape in the distance, beyond the tumbling waves.

A ship.

The sense of dread was coming from there.

Selene pumped her wings with all her might and steered for the ship. Twice the wind blew her to the left, but she fought against it and made her way forward. Once she reached the ship, she dove for the nearby doorway and landed on the wooden planks.

The ship lurched to the side.

"Dart'an!" Selene said as she changed into her human form. She grabbed the side of the door and held on for dear life. Never had she experienced a storm like this before.

Ahead, she could see a figure standing at the helm of the ship. Her senses expanded. It was the owner of this dream. Damien.

He stood at the prow, his arms and hands extended up as if he were holding the storm.

Selene looked past him, then gasped. She leaned forward. Was she really seeing what she was seeing? Was that a wall of . . . water?

Things started falling out of the sky, crashing onto the deck around them. Large wooden planks and barrels. Torn canvas sails. And . . .

Selene wiped her face and looked back. A body lay sprawled across the deck. She looked up at the sky, then back at the body. Where did that come from?

A beam fell from the sky and hit the deck near Damien. The prow gave way, sending him out of view.

"No!" Selene changed into her raven form and tore across the deck and over the ledge. She looked back and forth frantically across the dark waters while fighting the wind and rain. Where was he? Where did he go? All around her broken parts of ships and bodies lay scattered across the waves. Her breath burst in and out of her chest. Where did these people come from? One rolled onto his back, and Selene bit down a scream as she veered away from the sightless eyes and ashen face floating across the water.

Did Damien do this? Dark Lady, what kind of gift did he possess?

Damien surfaced thirty feet away and started swimming toward one of the floating bodies. He grabbed the sailor and a plank nearby. Dark liquid gushed out of a hole within the dead man's chest.

A moment later, Damien cried out and let the man go, then turned and used the plank to swim back toward the ship.

Selene watched the dead man bob for a moment, then sink. More bodies began to sink around her.

She could feel blind panic bubbling up inside both dream Damien and sleeping Damien. A wave crashed over him, pushing him beneath the water. He held onto the plank and rose back up. But the water had taken him farther from his ship. As he looked around, Selene sensed his guilt and remorse. She was right. He did do this. Moments later, a darker, more menacing feeling arose inside of him, spreading to her.

His desire to give up and let go.

"No, don't!" she screamed, but it only came out as a loud caw.

A second later, the feeling was gone. But this time she knew it wasn't a trick of the dreamscape. Despite the light inside of Damien, there was something dark lurking underneath. What it was, she wasn't sure. But she was wary of it.

Damien's ship approached and a line was thrown out to him.

Selene soared upward, not waiting to see if Damien was rescued. She already knew he survived this event. What she needed was to get out of here. There was too much going on, too many feelings, too much fear and darkness.

She flew until she was beyond the storm and wreckage below, then she turned and headed in the direction of the white sandy shore. All she wanted was to see Damien's luminescent soul, to be reminded that there was light inside of him, and to sit beside it and be warmed by its presence.

She shivered as the cold wind swept across her feathers. Usually flight brought a feeling of power and joy. But not this time. Instead, she felt frozen and hollow inside.

Did Damien feel the same way about his gift? Whatever he did back there killed a lot of men. Did he also feel cold and empty every time he called upon his gift?

Fatigue crept across her body. She scoured the horizon in hopes of seeing a glimmer of those white sands. But nothing appeared.

Finally, Selene soared upward until she burst past the dreamscape.

With a gasp, she sat back and dropped her arms. Her knees tingled from kneeling on the floor for so long. Damien never stirred. And the doors beyond the bed remained shut.

Slowly, painfully, she rose to her feet. Mother would most likely expect a report first thing in the morning, which meant forgoing her usual morning routine out on the training grounds. And more than anything she wished she could practice her swords and clear her mind of this most recent encounter.

Selene swallowed and looked down at Damien's slumbering face. She would have never guessed he held such sorrow inside of him. The death of what appeared to be his family, the death of all those men, then almost dying himself . . .

Before she could stop herself, she bent down near his ear. "I'm sorry," she whispered. "I'm so sorry. I wish there was some other way." But there was no other way. Soon she would return and when she did, she would use these awful memories against him to take his life.

First, one hot tear, then another coursed down her cheek. Her chest ached with a deep heaviness. She pressed her hand against her chest to make the hurt go away, but it just pulsed beneath her fist. No matter what she did, or how many times she tried to hide her heart away, it seemed to always be there, breaking.

She slowly rose to her feet and wiped her eyes.

Maybe that meant she was still human. That was a good thing, right?

She glanced one more time around the room. Everything was quiet. Damien was still fast asleep, although restless now, and his companions were still in their rooms.

With a heavy sigh, Selene silently left his bedchamber.

W hat have you found out so far?" Lady Ragna stood beside the fireplace in her room, still dressed in her dark tunic and leggings. Her hood was pulled back and her face scarf hung over one shoulder. Apparently Mother had been out dreamwalking last night as well. Most likely visiting the dreams of either Lord Rune or Lady Runa Vivek.

The first rays of daylight trickled through the nearby windows. Morning would soon be here, and Selene hadn't slept since yesterday. Fatigue lay heavily across her mind, but a nervous energy filled her being and her body refused to rest. She stood rigidly in the middle of the room and gave her report.

"Lord Damien still holds on to grief for his family." The heaviness and the strange darkness she had observed an hour ago still hung upon her heart, but she kept those buried and away from her mother's perusal.

Her mother nodded. "That is to be expected. House Maris was always quite close."

Selene pondered her mother's words. What would it be like to have a close family? To actually love one's parents and grieve over their deaths? A small part of her wondered if she would actually be sad at the departing of her mother.

"However, I'm not sure if grief is strong enough to turn a person like Lord Damien," her mother continued.

"Why?" Selene blurted out before she could stop herself.

Her mother paused, carefully taking in Selene. "House Maris is powerful in their own right. And their minds are quite strong." She smiled faintly. "I'm impressed that you were actually able to dive into Lord Damien's grief. Did you see anything?"

"Yes, I saw the day of his parents' death. And their burial." Selene didn't mention the fact that the moment she touched Damien, it felt like he pulled her in. If his mind was that strong, then why would he do that?

Her mother's eyes widened. "You did? Very impressive."

Selene narrowed her own eyes. Mother seemed to know a lot more about House Maris than she was letting on.

"Still, that kind of knowledge might shatter his mind, but not his body. And we can't afford to have another Renata incident. If Lord Damien remains alive, his people will still rally around him, broken mind or not. He could still be the threat from the north that the Dark Lady warned me about."

Selene felt like her mother had just punched her in the gut at the mention of her servant Renata. She fought the urge to suck in a breath or turn away. Instead, she curled her hands tightly at her side.

"Is that all you found?"

Selene was done with this conversation. She wanted to leave this instant and hit something really hard. But Mother pinned her to the spot, her dark gaze fixed on her. Selene had no choice but to continue to divulge Damien's secrets, ones she did not want to share. She lifted her chin. "No. I also discovered his fear." At least one of them. She had yet to figure out what else she had witnessed.

"You did?" The faint smile widened upon her mother's lips and a spark entered her eyes.

Once again, Selene felt like her mother was leaving something out. She seemed too eager about Selene's progress with Lord Damien—

Wait.

Was it possible her mother tried to dreamwalk within the mind of a member of House Maris . . . and failed?

Selene blinked with this newfound thought, a rush of questions entering her mind. Who? When? Was it Damien? Or someone else? Possibly his father? Her mother mentioned failing at a mission once. Just one. Had it been with House Maris?

"Selene?" her mother probed.

"Yes?" Selene said, trying to bring her mind back to their conversation.

"What is it young Lord Damien fears?"

Selene froze. Everything inside of her told her not to tell her mother. If Damien's greatest nightmare was the carnage he left after using his power, then she had no desire to share that with her mother because . . .

It was the same fear Selene had.

"Selene?" Her mother's voice took on a rougher, darker tone.

"I found a memory of Lord Damien in a storm. He fell from a ship and the waves almost took him away."

Her mother waited for her to continue, but that was all she was going to share.

"So," her mother said a moment later, "is Lord Damien afraid of storms? Or of drowning?"

"I . . . believe he is afraid of both."

"Is the fear strong enough?" There was doubt in her mother's voice.

"Yes. I felt his fear. He sunk under the water twice and thought he was going to die."

"Interesting, considering his gift involves water," her mother mused. "Yes, I think that would work. Do you think you can pull it off?"

Selene swallowed the lump in her throat. Now it came to this. She knew Damien's true weakness, something he feared strongly. And she knew her power. It would be a simple task to repeat that stormy day, and then let him drown. And if that didn't work, she could add in the men he killed. Remind him what happened when he used his gift. Drive it like a spike into his mind until it cracked and his heart gave out.

Her hands began to shake. Oh yes, she could do it.

Or could she?

Could she kill the only light she had ever seen inside a person? Could she kill Damien?

"Yes, I can do it," she answered, pushing the words through tight lips. What choice did she have? There was no way out, no other solution. If she didn't kill him, her mother would, and Selene would be locked up—or worse. And her sisters would be left to fulfill the Ravenwood legacy.

"Good. I plan on striking against House Vivek near the end of the assembly. You'll do the same. We'll talk one more time before that night comes. Now, I must go." She let out a tired sigh. "The talks are later this morning, and I need some rest before they begin."

Her mother turned without bidding her good-bye and disappeared into her private chambers.

The moment the door shut, Selene spun around and left her mother's rooms. She needed rest as well, but she knew it would not come, not with her mind full and body on edge. Instead, she headed for her room to pick up her twin blades, then she would head out to the private workout area and exercise until her body could no longer move.

Selene no longer saw the straw-stuffed dummy in front of her, nor felt the blades in her hands. Instead, her body moved without her while her mind feverishly went over Damien's dreamscape and how soon she would be taking his life.

Every time she pictured how she would do it, the lump inside her chest expanded, reaching all the way to her throat. She hit the dummy harder.

Why, why, why? What good will his death bring? Yes, Mother says he's a threat, but is he really?

Selene dropped her arms and panted as she stared at the dummy. It was Lord Damien who had called the Great Houses together, who led the talks, and, if she guessed correctly from his memories about the dead men she had seen, had even stopped an invading Dominion fleet.

And he was the youngest of the house lords.

Selene frowned. Was that why he was a threat? Because he was actually taking action when the other houses had been content for years to sit back and only take care of their own? Even with the threat of another empire razing under Commander Orion's authority?

She started her exercises again.

I don't get it. Lord Damien is doing more good than anyone else. Is it because he's different?

So far she had only dreamwalked within the minds of the servants in Rook Castle and Lord Damien, so her experience was limited. But she had a feeling that even if she walked in the dreams of multiple people from different nations, she would still find he was different.

What made him that way? Why was his soul like white fire while others had souls that were dark and bound in chains? Even that hint of darkness could not extinguish the blazing light inside of Damien.

Selene paused and looked down. She couldn't see her own soul, but she could feel it. If it had a form, most likely it would look like a revolving orb of dark storm clouds. At least that's how it felt. And she could guess why Renata's soul was the way it was: she was still chained to her past, tainted by actions forced upon her.

Could a person's soul change? Could Renata be freed of her shackles? Could Selene's own soul be filled with light?

Or were only some people given luminous souls?

Selene swallowed. She hadn't visited Renata since that day. She couldn't stand to see the young woman's blank eyes or face the knowledge that she had done that to her. She was just as bad as those men from Renata's dreams.

No, I don't deserve such light. Selene lifted one blade and brought the other horizontal across her body. *My destiny most likely will paint my soul blacker than hell. But Renata does deserve it. And sweet little Ophie. And even Petur. They deserve freedom. They are kind and generous people.*

She pressed her lips together and continued her exercises. Sweat ran down the contours of her face and neck, soaking into her back. Her braid swung back and forth as she hit the dummy harder and harder. The sun rose higher in the sky as morning spread across the castle.

But no matter how hard she used physical activity to purge her questions from her mind, it didn't stop her deep longing for Damien's soul. To see it and sit beside it. Be warmed by it. To understand how it came to be like that and know where the light came from—

Selene sensed someone behind her. With a sharp twist, she brought her body and blades around . . .

And found the one man her mind had been on all morning standing in front of her.

26

"How did you sleep?"

Damien rubbed the back of his neck as he and Taegis followed the long corridor toward the southern side of Rook Castle. A cool mountain breeze blew through the open archways, bringing with it the scent of pine and smoke. "Not well." He dropped his hand and twisted the family ring around his finger, his chest tight and heavy from the dreams.

"Oh?" Taegis glanced at him from the corner of his eye.

"The nightmares came back."

Taegis was quiet for a moment. "Which ones?" he finally asked.

"I saw my parents again, the last few days before the plague took them. And the day—" His voice hitched, and he twisted the ring faster. It had been almost two years. Why couldn't he get over the deaths of his parents and brother?

"The day Lord and Lady Maris and your brother, Quinn, were taken out to sea."

"Yes," Damien said through tight lips.

"I wondered if seeing those whom your family interacted with over the years would bring back memories."

"I don't know. These dreams seemed different than the ones I used to have. And there was a raven again, following me."

"A raven?" Taegis scratched the side of his face as the two men made their way to the inner bailey. "You mean the same one you told me about a few days ago?"

"Yes."

"That is odd. Perhaps there is more to this raven than just an intrusion of our surroundings. I overheard some of the Raven-wood guards talking about a legend involving a raven yesterday morning."

Damien glanced over at Taegis. "What did they say?"

"Every few years, a raven haunts the dreams of those who live here. It seems the raven has been seen again over the last few months."

"A raven who visits dreams," Damien murmured, his mind flashing back to the nightmares from last night. That was exactly what it did. It had followed him, watching him with beady black eyes. But why? And where did it come from? Did it bring bad tidings? He shuddered at the intrusion. Maybe he would see about procuring a sleeping draught for tonight.

Sunlight streamed through the breezeway as they made their way downstairs and outside. Young maple trees were already changing out in the courtyard, adding color to the dull grey castle walls. Damien breathed in deeply and let his breath out with a sigh, letting the morbid thoughts from earlier fly away. It might not be the ocean, but the mountains in the autumn were the second best thing.

As they neared the area where Captain Stanton had indicated they could train, the sounds of wooden thumps and metal clashing echoed through the narrow area.

"Sounds like someone already beat us to the training grounds," Taegis said.

Damien frowned. "I thought this area was supposed to be for private practice, not for soldiers."

"Then we should see who it is."

They walked between Rook Castle and the outer wall toward the sound. Beyond the corner of the castle was an old hickory tree in full array of yellow and orange leaves. Beyond the tree was a small weatherworn shed. Three dummies were set up next to the wall. A lithe form dressed in black attacked the first dummy with a flurry of hits.

Damien did a double take as the figure straightened up and prepared for another round. Wait . . . was that a woman?

She held two swords in her hands, one slightly shorter than the other, both curved. With one swift movement, she swung her arms across her body, the shorter sword ahead of the other one. When she reached half an arc, she brought the longer sword back. The swords hit the dummy in lethal succession.

Taking a deep breath, she brought her swords back into position, refocused, then held the longer sword above her head, and the shorter one across her body. In a flash, she brought the long sword down at a steep angle while swinging the shorter one slightly upward and across her body.

Each time she performed a move, she repositioned herself to start another set of sword movements.

Damien watched her, mesmerized. The way she moved was like a dance. Each movement, each part flowing with graceful ease. Even her loose black clothing and long braid moved in synchronization with her blades.

Taegis whistled quietly. "I've never seen a fighting style like that."

"Neither have I."

As if sensing their presence, the woman spun around, her blades out and ready. She panted as sweat trickled down the side of her face.

Damien felt like he had been punched in the gut. He wasn't sure who he had expected the woman to be, but he definitely didn't expect Lady Selene Ravenwood.

The moment she laid eyes on him, her whole body stiffened. Her face, already flushed from her workout, turned even rosier.

"I'm sorry we disturbed you, my lady," Damien said, taking a step toward her.

She moved her blades between herself and him in a protective manner.

Damien stopped, puzzled. Did she fear him? "We were told we could practice here by Captain Stanton."

Lady Selene took a few deep breaths and slowly lowered her swords. "I see. Most people do not know about this training area. Forgive me, your presence startled me."

Damien got the feeling there was more to what she was saying. "If you like, we can come back later."

She shook her head. "No. I was just finishing my routine."

His eyes slid back to the swords. The morning light glinted off the sharp blades. "I've never seen a fighting style like the one you were using just now. Where did you learn it?"

Lady Selene tucked the shorter sword into the scabbard located near the middle of her waist, then the longer sword on her left side. "It is my family's. And one we do not share."

Her tone made it clear that she would not be answering any more questions. A part of him wished he had not interrupted her routine. It had been a beautiful sight to behold.

"Please excuse me, Lord Damien." She gave him a small bow, then headed right and exited the training area.

Damien watched her leave, unable to take his eyes off her. She possessed a dark beauty so unlike any other lady of his acquaintance, especially Lady Adalyn Luceras. Like an exquisite deep red rose surrounded by thorns.

"Do you need a moment, or would you like to start?"

Taegis's voice interrupted his musings. Damien turned back. "Lady Selene is an interesting woman, one whom I cannot peg. She appears cold, but I sense there is much more to her beneath the surface."

"I think you should be wary of anything that involves the Ravenwood family. That goes for both Lady Selene and her father."

Damien caught the reference to Caiaphas. "I will. However, I find myself wishing to know more about Lady Selene."

"And what of Lady Adalyn?"

Damien frowned. "What of Lady Adalyn?"

Taegis drew out his sword and studied the edge. "I'm sure you're aware that House Luceras will most likely approach you about an alliance during our stay."

Damien snorted. "You could say that of almost any house here. What makes you speak of House Luceras specifically?"

"Out of all of the houses, it would be the best union for House Maris."

Damien nodded and drew out his own sword. "Yes, you are right. But House Maris has always married for love, and I do not feel that way toward Lady Adalyn."

"But perhaps your affection could grow."

"It could. But I think she loved my brother, and that would be hard to overcome."

Taegis stepped into the inner circle. "Well, it's something to think about."

Damien raised his sword and approached Taegis. "We'll see."

An hour later, Damien headed back to his rooms to wash up and change before the house talks began. Already his mind felt clearer and his body refreshed from the exercise. Too bad he couldn't start every morning this way. Once inside his room, he stripped off his sweaty tunic and headed over to the table in the corner where a washbasin and pitcher were set for his convenience, along with soap and a fresh linen cloth. He poured the water into the basin and began to wipe down his body.

When he reached his left side, he stopped and glanced at the marks just above his hip. Three small white waves lay across his skin, the symbol of his house. His mind went back to his conversation with Taegis earlier that morning. He was the only member left of House Maris, the only one with these marks and gifts given to his ancestors, which meant it was important for him to marry—and marry soon—in order to carry on House Maris.

He let out a long breath and finished his washing. Taegis was right, Lady Adalyn was a good choice. Their union would strengthen the ties between their families. And as the fourth child of House Luceras, it wasn't necessary for her to carry on her family line. But their bloodlines would still compete, and there was no certainty that their children would inherit his gift.

A better choice still would be a woman from a lesser house. Then he would be assured of passing on his gift.

"But I'm not interested in either," he said quietly as he wrung out the cloth and hung it on a peg. He closed his eyes and lowered his head. *Light, Maker of Worlds, please guide me.* He had witnessed the love between his parents and hoped for the same. But he also knew that kind of love was rare between grand lords and ladies and their consorts.

If he couldn't marry for love, then he at least wanted to marry for a greater good. And the greater good at this moment was uniting the Great Houses and figuring out who was working behind the scenes and assassinating those of lesser houses.

As Damien finished changing into clean clothes, there was a knock at his door. As he turned, Sten, one of his guards, emerged from the room to the right and headed for the door. There was a small exchange between Sten and the servant outside, then he closed the door, a small piece of paper in his hand.

"A message for you," Sten said as he crossed the room. The guard was a short, stocky man, the same age as Taegis, with thick grey hair and callused hands. He was fiercely loyal to House Maris, and one of the few guards Damien had known since he was a young boy.

Damien took the note from Sten and opened the folded parchment.

If you are still willing, I would like to meet with you. I have information and a request relating to our coalition. My servant will meet you at your room tonight after dinner and will escort you to my private rooms. He can be trusted and will ensure that you are not seen.

Caiaphas

Damien's stomach tightened as he refolded the note and tucked it inside his jacket. Ever since he'd sent the note weeks ago, he'd wondered when Caiaphas would approach him about a meeting. Looked like he'd found an opportunity. Damien was still willing to meet with his father's friend and fellow cohort, but Taegis would not be happy.

Still, Damien would not miss out on an opportunity to find out what Caiaphas knew, not with the importance of these talks and the encroachment of the empire. Someone—or someones— were working against the unity of the Great Houses, and if he was to help lead the houses toward collaboration, he needed to know who or what he was fighting against.

He would finish the work his father had started.

27

Lady Bryren stood and leaned across the meeting table. Her copper hair hung wildly around her shoulders, small braids and beads woven within the strands. Her leather and fur attire stood out amongst the silk and dyed-wool tunics and dresses. Her light brown eyes were accentuated by the dark kohl painted around her eyelids, giving her a fierce appearance. Not that she needed the barbaric attire to make her appear menacing—her very being exuded the raw power and courage her house was known for.

"Is House Friere blind? Is that why you cannot see the threat on your doorstep? Or are you cowards, hiding your heads behind your fingers and hoping Commander Orion will be content to stay within his borders?"

Lord Ivulf's lip curled, making him appear more wolfish than usual. His amber eyes seemed to almost smolder as he stared at Lady Bryren. "And what does House Merek know of the wall? It is my house that has kept the wall intact between our lands and the Dominia Empire for these hundreds of years. We live on the very edge of the empire. You and your house live on islands, far from the supposed conflict. Your understanding is based on the words of House Vivek and House Maris, not on facts."

Damien bristled at Lord Ivulf's accusation, and his hand curled along the tabletop. Sunlight streamed through the narrow windows that encompassed the round meeting room, yet the light did not reach the center table. Only the chandelier overhead lit the area, doing so in such a way that it left shadows between the different houses in an almost foreboding manner.

Lord Rune Vivek narrowed his eyes at Lord Ivulf. "You seem to forget that it is my people as well who live in the shadow of the wall and of the empire. We also have the 'facts.' And the fact is, Commander Orion is testing our defenses, searching for a weak spot where he can cross over to our lands."

"There is no weakness to be found along the wall."

Lady Bryren sat back down and sneered. "No, the only weakness is House Friere."

Damien grit his teeth. As much as he admired Lady Bryren's fearlessness, sometimes it bordered on recklessness. Her hot words were doing nothing to bring the houses together.

Nearby, Lord Leo Luceras pinched his nose, annoyed. Lord Haruk Rafel looked on the scene grimly from beneath his deep green cowl. Lady Ragna stared icily at Lady Bryren from Lord Ivulf's side.

Lord Ivulf slowly stood, his fur cloak towering around him. "Weakness, you say? We are weak because we choose not to pick a fight with the Dominia Empire? We are weak because we are not warmongering like some of the houses here? We are weak because we see the foolishness in starting a war with the empire? A war that would wipe out our people first before the empire ever reached your shores?"

Lady Bryren lifted her nose. "You are weak because you will not fight the danger that is clearly encroaching on your land. You claim to protect your people? Then do it!"

Lord Ivulf's hands curled. Like metal heating in a blacksmith's fire, his fists began to turn red and burn. A slip of smoke wafted up from his clenched fists.

Lady Bryren's eyes darted from Lord Ivulf's hands to his face. "Do you think I'm afraid of your power?"

"Your gift of courage has always been a double-edged sword for House Merek. You are brave, Lady Bryren, but you are also foolhardy to mess with the House of Fire." His fists now burned with a white heat, edged in red. However, there wasn't a burn mark on the table beneath his hands.

"Lord Ivulf." Lady Ragna placed a hand on his forearm, her dark eyes firmly planted on Lady Bryren. "This is not the place for accusations. This is a place to find out the truth, and then to act on it."

Damien sat back, one leg over the other, his fingers steepled in front of him. He exuded a persona of calmness, but inside he was shaking. Why were House Ravenwood and House Friere so adamantly denying the advancement of the Dominia Empire or what Commander Orion had already done to the eastern continent?

"What truth are you talking about, Lady Ragna?" Damien asked. "The one that is visible, that has been observed by countless people? Or the one you want to believe?"

Her eyes grew even darker, almost black. "What one can see can be manipulated, Lord Damien. Because of that, observation alone is not a basis for truth."

Lord Rune slammed his hands onto the table, startling his sister Runa beside him. "We are getting nowhere! We are running around in a verbal circle like a wild dog chasing its tail. And while we fight amongst each other, the empire will come and destroy our land and people."

"Lord Rune is right." Damien looked around the table. "Whether the empire is coming or not, one thing is certain: we are not united.

We are fractured and cracked along the seams, which makes us vulnerable. And when we are vulnerable, our people and lands are vulnerable. We must repair that first before any other action can be taken."

"And how exactly do we do that?" Lady Ragna asked. "Do some of us simply forget offenses committed against our houses? Do we trust again and hope we will not be wiped out?"

"Eventually we need to get to that point, yes," Damien said.

"Easy for you to say, House Maris. Your house was never destroyed. Same with all of you." Lady Ragna glanced at each head of house. Lord Leo returned her stare with a stoic one of his own while Lord Rune and Lord Haruk glanced away in shame. "No one came to the aid of my ancestors. It is hard to trust when such is our history."

"And yet, like you said, it is in the past. If we cannot move on from the past, then in the past we will always remain. Trust takes faith. Will you take that step, Lady Ragna?"

"I must have a reason to. And I have not found that reason yet."

Damien rubbed the side of his forehead. Such stubbornness!

"I am with Lady Ragna." Lord Ivulf glared over the room. "Show us why we should trust all of you."

Lady Bryren's nostrils flared. "The same could be said of you as well. Why should I trust you?"

Lord Ivulf smirked. "Like Lord Damien said, you would have to take a step of faith."

"I would rather kiss the back end of a wyvern."

Lord Ivulf stood to his feet and stared daggers at Lady Bryren. "You call yourself a grand lady of a Great House, but you appear and talk like a barbarian."

Lady Bryren shot to her feet. "At least I am honest about who I am and where I come from, instead of dressing brazenly and putting on an air of superior importance."

Lord Ivulf's hands blazed again as he shouted out a retort.

Lord Leo crossed his arms, his jaw tight. Lord Haruk bowed his head and sighed. Lord Rune looked like he was going to burst a vein along his forehead.

Damien scrubbed a hand over his face. *Dear Light in heaven!* Were they lords and ladies of the Great Houses or squabbling children? He would need to talk to Lady Bryren later about how easily she rose to Lord Ivulf's taunting. It was up to them, the younger leaders of the Great Houses, to show the elder leaders that they were capable of leading and maintaining a level head.

But as he watched the shouting match start anew between Lady Bryren and Lord Ivulf, with comments thrown in by Lord Rune, he wasn't sure that could happen. And if that couldn't happen, then uniting the seven houses was beyond the realm of possibilities.

Were they destined to lose in the end—either to the empire or to their own contentious ways?

28

Damien barely ate a bite at dinner that night, and almost contemplated excusing himself from the meal early, but he didn't need any extra attention on himself. The talks had grown even more divided, and the yelling match today between House Friere and House Merek only emphasized how much.

He rubbed his temple and sighed. Not surprising. Both houses were known for their hot tempers. Even now, Lady Bryren refused to look at the head of the table where Lord Ivulf sat next to Lady Ragna—

Damien sat up and watched the head table covertly. Every night, Lord Ivulf was seated at Lady Ragna's left. All the other houses were moved around the dining hall, but not House Friere. He narrowed his eyes. Why?

His gaze moved to Caiaphas. The man sat as regal as usual at Lady Ragna's side, but anyone could see her attention was fully on Lord Ivulf. She never spoke a word to Caiaphas. Instead, he ate quietly beside her.

The consummate consort.

Damien glanced away and swallowed the bitter taste in his

mouth—and caught Lady Selene watching him from the end of the table. She looked so different tonight than she had that morning. Her dark hair was pulled up in a noble manner, held in place with a silver circlet. A thin silver chain hung around her neck with a single diamond pendant. Once again he was struck by how simply Lady Selene dressed compared to the other women present, even Lady Bryren, yet she still came across as the most ladylike of them all.

He also remembered how she looked this morning with her hair bound in one long braid, her face shining from her exercise, her body moving in harmony with her swords. She was an entirely different creature compared to the one who sat at the table tonight.

Lady Selene looked away and lifted a crystal goblet to her lips.

Damien picked up his two-pronged fork and knife and prodded the fish on his plate.

Where did she learn to fight like that? And why? House Luceras and House Merek taught their women to fight, but he had never heard of House Ravenwood fighting. And her style was so foreign . . . and so beautiful.

"So how are things along the Northern Shores?" Lord Elric asked as he took a bite of bread. The younger Luceras lord was so casual compared to his older brothers, Leo and Tyrn. Just like Quinn had been.

Damien took a bite of the fish and chewed, allowing a small bit of time to compose his emotions. Then he answered, carrying on a light conversation with Elric, but moments later his thoughts were drawn back to Lady Selene and the mystery she held.

After dinner, he retired to his rooms and waited for Caiaphas's servant to come for him. He did not have to wait long.

Taegis answered the door, then glanced back at Damien with

a puzzled look on his face as Damien approached the door. "The servant says he's here to escort you to Caiaphas's study," Taegis said quietly.

"Yes, I received a message from him this morning."

The frown on Taegis's face deepened. "Do you think this is wise?"

"I want to hear what he has to say."

Damien could see disagreement all over Taegis's face. But Damien owed it to Caiaphas—and to his father—to hear the Ravenwood consort out. It was his father and Caiaphas who had first cast the vision of the houses working together and put in place a coalition for that purpose.

Taegis sighed. "Then let me come with you."

"I don't want any attention. Stay here. I will be there and back before the evening expires."

Before Taegis could protest, Damien headed out into the hall and followed the servant. It was moments like these where it was difficult to be a grand lord and make decisions that his elders did not approve of. Especially Taegis.

The servant led Damien through the darkly lit corridors to the west wing where the Ravenwood family resided. They ascended a staircase to the second floor, then the servant stopped and opened the nearest door.

"Thank you," Damien said as he stepped inside.

The servant nodded and shut the door behind him.

Bookcases filled the room, taking up almost every inch of stone wall available. Between the bookcases were lead-paned windows overlooking the night sky and Magyr Mountains. A desk stood in one corner, and two comfortable chairs were in the other. Candles were lit, filling the room with a soft glow. The air smelled of pipe weed, vanilla, and wood—comfort smells. Caiaphas gently placed a book down on the table between the chairs and stood. The dim light accentuated the dark circles beneath his eyes, and he looked older than his fifty winters.

He gave Damien a tired smile that reached his eyes. "Lord Damien, thank you for coming."

Damien bowed his head. "Thank you for inviting me. I admit, your message from a couple of weeks ago piqued my curiosity."

Caiaphas was quiet for a moment as he studied Damien's face. "You really do look like your father did at your age," he murmured. "How I miss Lord Remfrey. He was a good man and a good friend."

Damien swallowed. "I miss him as well."

"I'm sure you do." Caiaphas came around the chair to stand next to Damien in the middle of the room. "The role of a grand lord is not an easy one, and I can imagine to have that responsibility thrust upon you at such a young age is hard. But from what I've seen and heard, you're doing an extraordinary job."

"Thank you. I only hope to do as well as my father did before me."

"And you will. Now, to get on to business. Please take a seat." Caiaphas motioned toward the chairs near the windows. Damien took the one on the right, and Caiaphas sat down on the left.

Caiaphas leaned forward and folded his hands across his knee. "First, how are the talks going?"

Damien shook his head. "No matter what information House Vivek or I share about what the empire is doing, some of the other houses do not see the Dominia Empire as a threat."

Caiaphas pursed his lips together. "Not surprising. Strife between the houses has been there since the creation of the seven houses." He stared at Damien. "Some houses would rather allow the empire to invade our lands than work with each other."

Damien narrowed his eyes. There was a cryptic tone to Caiaphas's voice and manner. Was the older man trying to tell him something? Something bound by a house secret? "I had hoped it would be different. Especially with the Dominia Empire testing our boundaries, both on water and on land."

"Tell me how each house is reacting." Caiaphas sat back and waited.

Damien rubbed his temple and sighed. Taegis would caution him about what he shared, but his father had trusted Caiaphas. Despite his submissive demeanor when Caiaphas was around Lady Ragna, there was a keen intellect in those steel grey eyes of his. Damien wondered if Lady Ragna knew what manner of man she had married—and who was playing who.

"House Vivek and my own house see the Dominia Empire as a threat. Not only have they tested our boundaries, but from what I've heard, the new commander, Orion, seems as bent on domination as his predecessor, Commander Tolrun."

"I've heard the same thing. The people of Dominia support Commander Orion. He has brought wealth and prestige back to their empire. And he has done away with the old ways of monarchy and has set a new precedent: those who fight receive the spoils. So it's not surprising that the Dominia Empire has its sights set on us. If the people conquer us, it's more wealth for them."

"But hardly anyone is listening at the table. House Merek is siding with us, but House Luceras and House Rafel seem swayed by House Friere's arguments."

Caiaphas quirked an eyebrow. "Interesting."

"They believe the wall between our lands and the Dominia Empire is doing exactly what it's supposed to: keep the empire out. And that is enough."

Caiaphas narrowed his eyes. "What about the skirmishes some of the lesser houses of Friere are claiming? And House Vivek's observations along their borders? And the small fleet that sailed for the Northern Shores?"

Damien's chest tightened as he remembered his most recent

dreams and the ships he had destroyed. "Lord Ivulf denies any claims from the lesser houses within his land. And he went so far as to accuse House Vivek of provoking the empire along their own border."

Caiaphas pulled on his beard. "I expected some pushback from some of the other houses. But outright denial? That's bold."

"House Ravenwood agrees with House Friere," Damien said carefully.

Caiaphas's face darkened. "I'm not surprised."

Damien could hear his unspoken comments in his tone. "Is that why you wanted to meet? Does it have something to do with House Ravenwood?"

"Yes. Partly. As you know, I cannot speak of house secrets. But I believe I can share some things that might help our coalition and give you answers to the questions you have. But you must listen carefully. Your father dreamed that one day all of the Great Houses would unite and work together as one nation. There are a handful of us who desired that as well, and we have been working together for many years toward that goal. My marriage into Ravenwood was part of that plan."

"Your marriage? Can you explain?"

Caiaphas shook his head. "All I can say is that my union has brought forth fruit."

Damien wrinkled his brow. What did that mean?

Caiaphas went on. "You will need every house on your side if you hope to stop the empire. That includes Ravenwood *and* Friere."

Damien curled his fingers around the arms of the chair. "I'm not sure how that's going to happen. House Friere is adamantly denying any threat from the empire. And House Ravenwood agrees, which makes me ask why House Ravenwood is denying the encroachment of the empire. I would think Ravenwood would do anything to prevent the obliteration of another house, unless . . ."

He frowned. Unless there was so much hatred within Ravenwood toward the other houses that the empire paled in comparison. Caiaphas's words came back to him. *Some houses would rather allow the empire to invade our lands than work with each other.*

Was that what the older man was hinting at?

No other house came to the aid of Ravenwood hundreds of years before when the empire obliterated House Ravenwood. Even his own house held back until the damage was done, much to the chagrin of future lords of Maris. If only they had stepped in and led the charge toward saving House Ravenwood instead of hiding behind their borders and power. If there was one regret his ancestors held, it was that they allowed one of the Great Houses to fall.

"Ravenwood hates all the other houses, doesn't it?" Damien said quietly.

"Yes."

The fact that Caiaphas could answer meant that Ravenwood's hatred was no secret.

"Does that mean that if the Dominia Empire continues their hostilities toward the border nations, Ravenwood will not step in and help?"

Caiaphas's face hardened. "I believe so."

Damien stared at him, a tangle of emotions. If that was the case, then there could be no unity. House Ravenwood would never work with the other houses. But did it matter? Ravenwood no longer possessed their gift. "So why did you bring me here? To tell me that Ravenwood will never ally itself with the other houses?"

"Yes, and no."

"No?"

"Lady Ragna will never work with the other houses. In fact, I suspect——" His lips moved, but no words came out. "Dart'an," Caiaphas muttered. "Apparently that information is bound. Give me a moment." He pursed his lips in thought. "Follow the murders," he finally said.

"Follow the murders?"

"Yes. That is all I can say on the matter. Look into them closely."

Damien leaned back into his chair and rubbed his chin. He was already doing that, but he would look into them again, especially Lord Malrin Merek's recent death.

"And don't discount House Ravenwood."

"But you just said Lady Ragna will never work with the other houses. Besides, you know that House Ravenwood no longer possesses their gift. I'm not sure how much help they can be."

Caiaphas shook his head. "Don't give up on House Ravenwood yet. The Great Houses need Ravenwood, whether they know it or not."

"I'm not sure how that will happen, given what I've observed during the talks and what you've shared about Lady Ragna——"

"Lady Ragna is not the only one who represents House Ravenwood. I believe my daughter, Lady Selene, could help us with our cause."

Damien flashed back to watching Lady Selene move with such grace and lethality in the bailey. Then again to this evening with her cold reserve. "How?"

"She is . . . capable . . . of more than you know." Caiaphas seemed to be choosing his words carefully, testing them to see if they were bound.

Damien already knew that, having stumbled upon her this morning.

"But we would need to approach her soon. Each day she is turning more and more toward her mother. Eventually, I fear she will be too far gone."

"You mean recruit her into the coalition? What can she do for us that you cannot?"

Caiaphas looked straight at him. "There is more to her than I can reveal. But I can tell you that she would bring more to the coalition than I can. In fact, I believe she could possibly unite the Great Houses more than anyone else."

Damien looked at him, puzzled. Although she was intriguing, from what he had seen of Lady Selene, she ultimately had a coldness about her, not the kind of personality that would bring the Great Houses together. "I don't understand how."

"And I can't tell you. I am bound—body and soul—to House Ravenwood. But you must believe me when I say that the coalition needs my daughter. The Great Houses need my daughter. *You* need my daughter."

Damien narrowed his eyes, studying the man before him. There was an earnestness to Caiaphas. Was it real? Or was Taegis right in his warnings about House Ravenwood? "Why Lady Selene? Why not Lady Amara?" he asked.

Caiaphas sighed and shook his head. "Amara is deep within her mother's influence. She would never go against Lady Ragna. She is also ambitious and reckless. But Selene has been asking questions. She has a searching heart. I believe she could be persuaded to join us."

"You trust her?"

"I do."

"But you still haven't answered why Lady Selene could do more for us than you are doing already."

"I can't share house secrets, not even on pain of death."

"And neither can Lady Selene. She is bound just as much as you are."

"But there is a way around that. . . ."

"A way around . . . ?" Wait. Damien's eyes went wide. Caiaphas surely didn't mean . . . "You're not suggesting a marriage between our houses, are you?"

"It would be a way around the binding. House secrets are revealed when the vows are spoken. You would know what I cannot tell you. And you need to know. The knowledge she carries would not only help you, it would answer many of your questions."

"But you don't have the authority to approve such a matter. And I—" Damien ran a hand through his hair and glanced away toward the window. He could barely make out the Magyr Mountains beneath the starry sky. Caiaphas couldn't be serious. Marriage? Between House Maris and House Ravenwood?

"And it must be a willing union, or else the house secrets would remain in place. By both of you. Then you will know all of House Ravenwood's secrets. As the leader of the coalition, it has to be you she bonds with."

"You're asking too much."

"Am I? Many of us have married for reasons other than love for the sake of our people and for the sake of the coalition. Would you do any less?"

Tonight proved just how true Caiaphas's words were. There was no love between him and Lady Ragna, Damien had seen that. And given what Caiaphas had shared earlier, the man married into Ravenwood to help the coalition.

Caiaphas was right. Could Damien do any less than that?

And yet something inside stopped him. He did not want a loveless union like Caiaphas. Unlike the other Great Houses, House Maris did not divorce. His would be a marriage unto death. Yes, knowing the Ravenwood secrets could help the coalition, perhaps. But if and when the nations united, everyone else would go back to their lives but him. He would be forever bound to Lady Selene.

Could he marry a woman he did not love?

"I can tell by your silence right now that marrying my daughter is not an option. So I will ask this of you: keep Selene safe. She must be protected at all costs."

Damien looked up and studied the older man. There was something going on, something Caiaphas couldn't tell him. Something to do with whatever secrets House Ravenwood held. But the cost to know those secrets was too great. However, he could promise Caiaphas to keep his daughter safe. Perhaps that was what was driving the older man. "Yes, I can do that. You have my word."

Caiaphas gave him a firm nod in return. "Thank you. You have no idea how important that is. Perhaps in time you will come to see what I see: though Selene may appear cold on the outside, inside of her beats a strong and passionate heart. You could do worse for an arranged wife."

Damien stood. "Perhaps so, but I stand by my decision. I hope that she might join us in uniting the houses. But at this time, I will not marry her."

Caiaphas also stood. "Then that will have to do for now. I wish you the best with the rest of the negotiations. And I will see you tomorrow at the gala."

Damien frowned. "Gala?"

"Yes. Did you forget?"

Damien ran a hand along the back of his neck. "I did. My mind has been on the talks and nothing else."

"I will see you then. Use the gala as an opportunity to look into the deaths surrounding the Great Houses. And Lord Damien, thank you." His grey eyes glistened in the candlelight.

Damien bowed. "I wish I could have been more helpful," he said. And he meant it. But like Caiaphas said, the marriage union would have to be willing, and at this point, he was not.

"You and your family have done more for the people of these lands than most will ever know or realize," Caiaphas said. "I'm glad I can be a part of it. If I find out anything more, I will send word in my usual way. Good night, Lord Damien."

"Good night, Caiaphas." Damien turned and left the study. As he followed the servant back through the corridors to his rooms, his mind mulled over the last half hour. If Caiaphas's hints were to be understood, then House Ravenwood, and perhaps House Friere, would never unite with the other houses, even if the Dominia Empire invaded their lands and wiped everyone out.

He shook his head. He did not understand such hatred, the kind that would rather see the world burn than help others. But Caiaphas was adamant that there was a way around that.

Lady Selene.

House Ravenwood held many secrets within their house, secrets that held answers to the questions he had, secrets that could potentially help the coalition. They could be his if . . .

He shook his head. No. Even if he were willing, it was not right to use Lady Selene in such a way. She would be bound as much as him. And he doubted Lady Ragna would concede to such a union anyway.

Which left him the promise he'd made to Caiaphas. Damien would keep Lady Selene safe. He wasn't sure what that would entail or what danger she could possibly be in, but if there was something he could do, he would do it.

29

Damien pulled the long blue tunic over his linen shirt and secured it around his waist with a black leather belt. The tunic was trimmed in silver thread, making the edges of his sleeves and waist look like sea waves were woven within the cloth. He completed his ensemble with a pair of dark breeches and leather boots. It was simple attire easily packed within his saddlebags but formal enough for the gala that evening.

He glanced in the long mirror near the changing screens. The few bright rays from the setting sun glanced off the smooth surface, illuminating his room with yellow light. He straightened his tunic and belt, then ran a hand through his dark hair. It was longer now and would need a trimming when he arrived back at Northwind Castle.

His heart twisted again at the thought of home. Tomorrow the final terms of the treaty would be discussed, then signed the following day. Then he would be heading home. Even though he had only been gone for over a fortnight from the Northern Shores, it felt much longer. And he was tired. He had been met with nothing but resistance and cold civility from most of the houses concerning any kind of unity. Most were content to stay within their borders and bury their heads where the Dominia Empire was concerned.

In some ways, it felt like it had been a waste of an assembly, and secretly he wondered if the other houses viewed him as a young and foolish grand lord.

He took a deep breath and closed his eyes. It didn't matter. He would never have been able to live with himself if he hadn't at least talked to the other houses about the impending war, even if they didn't see it as such. He would enter into the treaty terms tomorrow with hopeful determination and stand alongside those who chose to be a part of it. Still, he couldn't quite suppress a small hope that all seven houses would agree to help one another.

He took another deep breath and opened his eyes, shoving aside his political thoughts. Tonight was a time to simply enjoy the company of the other houses. Something he planned on doing.

The sun had dipped behind the mountains by the time Cohen stepped out from his own room, dressed in his long burgundy clergy robes, his thick wheat-colored hair brushed back. A broad smile filled his young face. "I am looking forward to this evening," he announced as he crossed the room.

Damien smiled back, his morose and depressing thoughts disappearing by the second. "I'm glad Lady Ragna chose to invite more than the Grand Houses. Do you plan on dancing?"

"Well, no." Cohen blushed and glanced away. "I don't think it would do for a monk to partake in dancing."

"No, probably not."

Taegis exited his own room at that moment, followed by the second guard, Karl. Karl was the same age as Damien, with unruly black hair and a gruff personality. His dark eyes appeared guarded as he glanced around. Both men were dressed in House Maris colors, swords at their side.

"Sten will be joining us this evening, and all three of us will be on guard duty," Taegis said.

Damien nodded and headed for the door. "Then let's go."

Cohen joined him in the corridor, Taegis and Karl close behind. The men made their way through the cool stone corridors of Rook Castle. Candles were already lit for the evening, and the gentle hum of voices echoed throughout the hallways. Having been here for over a week, the castle had become somewhat familiar to Damien. The hall to the left led to the inner courtyard. The hall to the right led to the meeting and dining halls. And the hall in front of him continued toward the west wing.

At the junction of the four main corridors, Damien turned right and headed for the dining hall. He spotted Lord Haruk Rafel and his daughter ahead of him, along with a handful of guards and members of a lesser house who had accompanied the grand lord. All were dressed in various shades of green in representation of their house.

Past House Rafel, the double doors that led into the dining hall were open and welcoming. Music drifted from the hall, combining with the sound of conversation. Damien and Cohen entered the hall while Taegis, Sten, and Karl took up positions on either side of the doors along with the other guards.

The chandeliers were lit along the high-arched ceiling and dark candlestands were set around the perimeter of the room, casting the cavernous hall in soft candlelight. Chairs were set up along the walls, but the middle of the hall had been emptied of tables in order to accommodate the guests arriving for the gala.

The hall was already full of people chatting quietly, slender crystal goblets in hand. Dazzling gowns, doublets, and tunics of every color filled the room, almost to a dizzying degree. The narrow windows set around the room were open to let in the cold mountain air, but the room still felt warm to Damien, and the scents of rosewater, sandalwood, lavender, cinnamon, and pine filled the air.

Damien made his way to the closest window. He was not used to so many people and needed a cool breeze to clear his muddled mind. Cohen joined him, his eyes wide as he took in the room.

"Amazing," Cohen said softly. "So many people, so different from each other, and yet we are all connected, a part of one people."

"Yes." Damien breathed in the mountain air, letting it relax his mind and body. The last time the seven Great Houses were together was hundreds of years ago. To see every nation here, now, under one roof, was exactly what Cohen had said: amazing. Damien smiled wistfully, wishing again that his father could see this. It had been his passion in life to see the nations together as one.

But in reality, they were still fractured, and tomorrow's treaty would reveal just how much.

No. Damien gave his head a shake. He was not going to think about that tonight.

"Lord Damien." He turned to see Lady Bryren Merek approaching him with her consort at her side. Unlike the other ladies in the room, her gown consisted of soft leather pieces layered over dyed red and flaxen-colored linen.

Reidin stood beside her, as quiet as ever. His leather and dyed linen attire matched Lady Bryen's. His black hair stood in spikes around his head, matching the kohl around his eyes.

Damien would think their relationship was similar to Lady Ragna and Caiaphas's, what with Lady Bryren's outgoing, fiery personality and Reidin's more quiet reserve, except that he often caught the glances they sent each other when they were together, and he had spotted them one evening hand in hand atop one of the towers.

It appeared the stoic man was a good fit for the wyvern lady.

Damien bowed his head. "Lady Bryren, Reidin."

Reidin's eyebrow quirked, apparently surprised that Damien had remembered his name.

Lady Bryren flashed Damien a bright smile. "You look striking this evening. That tunic really brings out the color in your eyes."

For one second Damien was taken aback by her blunt comment, then laughed. "Thank you," he said.

"I expect almost every house in this room will be seeking you out tonight to inquire about a possible alliance with House Maris."

Damien cleared his throat, thankful for the cool breeze flowing through the window behind him. "Yes, I suppose so."

"Are you ready for the onslaught of invitations?" Lady Bryren's eyes twinkled in merriment. Damien caught Reidin looking away, trying to hide the smile dancing across his lips.

Cohen gave Damien a wide-eyed look. No doubt the monk did not realize one of the more subtle reasons for galas like these was to negotiate marriages between the houses. Even his own father and mother's engagement was formed during a smaller gala held at Northwind Castle.

Damien's own humor returned. "Armed and ready, Lady Bryren," he said and smiled back. But his insides still squirmed. No doubt she was right. He casually glanced around the room.

Lady Bryren turned and grabbed two goblets from a tray held by a nearby servant and held one out to him. The red wine sparkled inside.

Damien accepted it gingerly. "May I speak to you for a moment, Lady Bryren?"

The smile on her lips dipped. "Certainly. From the look on your face, I assume it is something serious."

"Yes, it is." He moved to an empty corner and Lady Bryren followed after whispering instructions to her consort. "Does anything stand out to you about your father's death?"

Lady Bryren's eyes narrowed and her lips tightened. With any other person, Damien would have crossed a line with his blunt question, but Lady Bryren preferred frankness.

"Why are you asking?"

"I was shocked to hear of his passing. And the more I thought about it, the more it seemed . . . convenient."

"Are you implying something?"

"My house has been following the deaths of various lesser lords and ladies over the last five years. At first, none of them seemed to be related. But lately I've been wondering if there is something going on. They all passed away in the same way: during the night their hearts gave out."

Her face darkened further. "I have not heard of these deaths."

"Most have not since we each keep our own counsel within our borders."

"So how do you know about them?"

"As someone who wishes to see all seven houses unite, I have kept track of news within each nation. And there are others who have been helping me."

Lady Bryren glanced over the room. "So you're implying that my father may have been murdered."

"I don't know. But the timing seems convenient."

Her nostrils flared. "I did wonder at the death of my father. He was in perfect health. But the healer assured me that even the hardiest men can die unexpectedly. And my father was never the same after my mother died, but certainly not changed enough to pass away so suddenly." She looked at him. "What are you going to do with this information?"

"I'm going to continue to search for who is behind these deaths. I think they are trying to weaken the Great Houses, one by one. But this would be the first time a grand lord was targeted."

"Weaken? For what purpose?"

"I don't know. But it would be convenient for the Dominia Empire if our houses were splintered and fragile."

"Like a wounded animal unable to escape a trap," Lady Bryren murmured.

"Exactly."

"And you didn't bring this up during the talks because you think one of the Great Houses is behind it?"

"I'm not sure who else could move across the borders of our countries so easily or know who to hit so precisely."

Lady Bryren nodded grimly. Then her face changed and she raised her cup and said in a loud voice, "May you find happiness, Lord Damien."

It took Damien a moment to realize Lady Bryren had noticed someone watching and was covering for them.

Damien raised his own goblet and forced a smile. "And you as well, Lady Bryren."

She pointed at Reidin and her smile grew wider. "I already have." Then she placed her goblet near her lips as if to take a sip. "I'll think about what you have shared and write later," she whispered.

Damien took a small sip and then held the cup between his hands, watching as Lady Bryren grabbed Reidin's hand with her free one and led her consort away toward a table where a lesser house from Rafel stood in their long green robes.

Cohen approached him, the monk's gaze following Lady Bryren. "House Merek is not what I thought it would be. Lady Bryren does not appear as fierce as I had imagined."

"Oh, trust me, House Merek can be as fierce as the wyverns they ride if you get on their bad side." Damien took another sip from the goblet as he remembered the shouting match between Lady Bryren and Lord Ivulf. Pity the person who murdered her father, if that was truly what had happened. Lady Bryren would not stop until she captured the killer and dropped them from the back of her wyvern to the sea below.

The music across the room changed as he took another sip from the goblet Lady Bryren had offered him. He scanned the room, searching for the other houses. Lady Ragna stood on a low platform at the head of the room, dressed in a long black gown that reminded everyone that even though she was older now, she was still one of the most beautiful women of the seven Great Houses. He spotted Caiaphas beside her, dressed in silver and black, and their second daughter, Lady Amara, at her side.

Lady Amara's dress was similar to her mother's, but a deep garnet color trimmed in gold with a much more daring cut along the front. Her hair hung over one shoulder in a cascade of auburn strands. Along his periphery, Damien could see the second Ravenwood daughter was attracting the attention of many of the male guests. Not surprising. He secretly wondered if House Ravenwood was propping Lady Amara up as a possible alliance. His nose wrinkled at the thought.

Then he wondered where Lady Selene was. He scanned the platform again but did not spot the oldest daughter and heir to the Ravenwood house. His thoughts drifted back to his conversation with Caiaphas the previous night. Caiaphas had been deadly serious about his daughter and marriage.

Damien narrowed his eyes and studied Lady Ragna again. There was a darkness to her and to a more subtle degree her daughter as well. *"Amara is deep within her mother's influence,"* Caiaphas had said. Damien could see that now as he watched the mother and daughter look over the room together from the platform.

But Lady Selene was different. Cold, but not necessarily dark. Not like her mother or sister.

"Lord Damien. I hoped I would have a chance to speak to you tonight."

Damien turned to find Lord Leo behind him. The oldest Luceras sibling and heir was a few inches taller than he was. His blond hair was brushed back, revealing his strong, clean facial features and light blue eyes. He wore a matching light blue tunic with a small cape clasped around his neck.

Damien gave him a small bow. "Lord Leo. What can I do for you?"

"I wish to speak about my sister."

Damien's stomach clenched as he straightened from his bow, and his hand tightened around the goblet. Lady Bryren was right. He'd barely been here for five minutes and already the other houses were seeking him out.

"It is my father's wish that I talk to you while I am here about a possible alliance between our families; that is, if you do not already have a union in mind." He watched Damien with keen eyes.

"No, I have not made an agreement with anyone yet." Still, he couldn't help but remember Caiaphas's urgent request. As of now, he would protect her, but nothing more.

"I see," Lord Leo said quietly. "Are you open to the possibility of aligning your house with ours?"

Damien stared down into the deep red liquid inside his goblet. Normally, it would have been his own father and mother inquiring after the other houses, then presenting him with the possibilities, but still allowing him a choice, one that left room for love.

Instead, here he was, grand lord of House Maris with the weight of this decision resting solely on his shoulders—a decision that did not just impact him, but his people as well.

He let out a long breath and looked up. "I'm willing to consider the possibility," he said.

"Thank you, Lord Damien. Please spend some time with my sister this evening. I think you will find that she is a beautiful, kind soul."

He already knew that but didn't say anything.

Lord Leo bowed and departed, making his way toward the other side of the room where Lord Haruk and Lady Ayaka Rafel stood. Both father and daughter were dressed in emerald green gowns trimmed in gold. Lady Ayaka's long black hair hung down her back, held in place by a large white flower. Damien narrowed his eyes as the Luceras lord spoke with Lady Ayaka. Perhaps Leo was negotiating his own alliance.

"Fascinating," Cohen said beside him.

"What is fascinating?" Damien asked.

"Life in the abbey is nothing like the life the Great Houses lead."

"I would think it is simpler."

"It is. I do not envy you, Lord Damien." Cohen paused. "Ah, there is the priest from House Luceras. I think I shall join him."

Cohen headed for a short, stout man dressed in white robes standing near the musicians. He looked out of place, his bald head glistening with sweat.

Damien shook his own head and smiled. Poor man. Hopefully Cohen could put him at ease.

A moment later, he spotted Lady Adalyn with her other brother. Lord Elric was shorter and slimmer than Leo but still had the same light-colored hair and eyes. And he was never without a grin on his face. He stood beside Lady Adalyn, that charismatic smirk on his face as the two spoke with members from a lesser house who had traveled with them.

Damien watched Lady Adalyn. She wore a long white gown with a golden-trimmed bodice. Her golden hair was held back with a jewel-studded comb, accented by the candlelight around her. She had a delicate grace to her form and manners. Her smile was tender and gentle, her eyes kind. Almost everything about her exuded the very virtues of House Luceras: purity, integrity, and light.

And yet . . .

He let out a long breath. He wasn't attracted to her. Yes, she was beautiful, but she did not pull at his very soul. The fact that he felt so disconnected from her concerned him about a possible alliance. Still, he'd promised her brother he would consider the possibility.

Damien finished the rest of his wine and placed the goblet down on a nearby table, then made his way across the room. The music changed again, a more upbeat tempo, and couples began to gather in the middle of the floor for the first high dance.

Lord Elric held out his hand to the lady next to him—a blushing, freckled young woman—and led her to the floor to join with the other couples. Damien took his place beside Lady Adalyn.

"Good evening, Lady Adalyn," Damien said with a bow.

"Grand Lord Maris," she answered softly and bowed back.

He noted her use of his formal title and wondered why she was using it. "Have you enjoyed your time here?" he asked, starting with small talk.

Her eyes dimmed. "Rook Castle and the Magyr Mountains are beautiful, but I miss the rolling hills and white coastline around Lux Casta. I also miss my father. His health is stable, but not good. I do not wish to be away from him much longer."

"I understand." He was thankful she answered honestly instead of couching her words in order to hide her homesickness. But it also made him wonder how well she would do moving away from home, something that needed consideration in a potential alliance.

The long line of couples in the middle of the room began a lively dance, filled with steps and bows.

Damien watched them for a moment, then glanced at Lady Adalyn. "Do you like to dance?"

A soft blush touched her cheeks. "Yes, I do. Elric taught me when we were younger."

"Then let me do the honor of asking for your hand for the next dance."

She smiled and looked up at him from beneath long lashes. "I accept, thank you."

Yes, she was definitely beautiful, but he still did not feel that tug. And he was having a hard time coming up with things to talk about. He fought the urge to run a hand along the back of his neck. Instead, he steered their conversation toward her daily pursuits. Her answers were the typical ones of a lady of her stature: classical reading, painting, embroidering, and the running of a household . . . and paladin training.

Damien's eyes lit up at that last one. "Tell me more about your training."

"I'm not as experienced as my brothers, but my father felt it was important that I know the basics of our gift and the training that comes with it. My use of the light is more for defense. I can summon a shield, but I'm afraid that's all. My brothers' abilities are more impressive. Elric wields a polearm he can summon from the light. Tyrn creates a shield that can expand over multiple people. And Leo inherited Father's broadsword and can manipulate light spheres."

"Fascinating," Damien said, his eyes wide. "I know little of House Luceras's light abilities."

Lady Adalyn blushed and glanced down.

The first song ended and the couples in the middle of the room either walked toward the perimeter or lined up for the next dance.

Damien held his hand out to Lady Adalyn. "Shall we?"

She looked up, her eyes sparkling. "Yes."

She was like an angel, and he knew he should be captivated by her beauty and innocence, like half of the men present. But he felt only a camaraderie that came from knowing her family all of his life, and nothing more.

As the music started and they began to move around the room in a lively step, he wondered if a marriage could be built on that kind of foundation. He watched her from the corner of his eye as she joined the women in a five-step movement that included a small kick and hop. The gentle smile she wore graced her face and her golden hair shone in the candlelight.

Any man who wedded the beautiful lady of light would be fortunate. So why was he hesitating? He mentally sighed as he danced with the men as Lady Adalyn watched. He wasn't sure. Perhaps it was because there were more pressing matters like the Dominia Empire and the coalition. Still, that did not stop the fact that eventually he would need to marry and carry on his line. He just wasn't ready to think about that at the moment.

He reached for Lady Adalyn's hand as they joined up again in the middle of the room and gave her a small smile. She at least deserved that much. Their fingers touched, then his eye caught a figure standing along the edge of the crowd.

Lady Selene Ravenwood.

The moment he spotted her, something shifted inside of him. He continued to dance with Lady Adalyn, his body moving in the remembered steps, his voice quietly speaking to her. But his mind was fully on Lady Selene.

She stood in the farthest corner where the candlelight barely reached. Her gown was as dark as the shadows she stood within, save for her bodice, which was trimmed in what looked like a thousand tiny diamonds, like stars against a night sky. Her hair hung in dark sheets around her face and across her shoulders, reaching almost to her waist. A single silver circlet held her black hair back and a small diamond twinkled at her throat.

Damien lightly held Lady Adalyn's hand as they followed the

other couples in finishing the dance. From the corner of his eye, he spotted Lord Raoul Friere approach Lady Selene. Her body stiffened as she answered his question. Then they disappeared behind the crowd approaching the dance floor.

Damien led Lady Adalyn to a window, grabbed a goblet from a nearby tray, and held it out to her.

"Thank you," she said. She sipped the dark wine as a cool breeze pulled at her hair. Damien glanced back, hoping to spot Lady Selene again, but she was still hidden behind the crowd.

Lady Adalyn asked him a question. He turned back and answered, only half of his mind on their conversation. The music started again. Moments later, he spotted Lady Selene with Lord Raoul joining the new set of couples in the middle of the room. If looks could freeze, Lady Selene would have encased Lord Raoul in ice. The young lord did not seem to notice. Instead, he held her hand in a firm grip with a haughty smile on his face. His long black hair was pulled back in a knot at the top of his head, held in place by a golden band. His deep red tunic stood out against Lady Selene's dark gown like fire against the night sky.

Lady Adalyn continued to speak, and Damien continued the conversation, his attention split between Lady Adalyn and the dancing couple. The longer he watched, the more he realized the frozen appearance on Lady Selene's face was a mask. In fact, it had always been a mask. Her movements were stiff, almost forced. So unlike the way she moved with her dual blades. And on closer inspection, it appeared that what he had taken for coldness was actually unease.

She did not want to be with Lord Raoul.

One of the young men who had accompanied House Luceras to Rook Castle approached Damien and Lady Adalyn. He bowed to Lady Adalyn and held out his hand. "May I have the next dance, my lady?"

She glanced at Damien, almost as if to ask permission.

"Thank you for the wonderful dance, Lady Adalyn," Damien said. "Enjoy the rest of your evening."

She bowed her head, a slightly disappointed look on her face. "Thank you, Grand Lord Maris." Then she took the young man's hand, and he led her to the crowd waiting for the next dance.

Damien frowned, wondering at her look, before turning his attention again to Lord Raoul and Lady Selene. At the end of the song, Lord Raoul led Lady Selene from the floor.

He could barely see the couple now as they stood across the room in a shadowed corner. Damien headed toward them, following the perimeter and avoiding the couples lining up to dance. As he drew closer, he could tell Lady Selene and Lord Raoul were deep in discussion.

He paused. Perhaps he should not intrude—

Lady Selene's chin shot up, and her eyebrows converged into a V. She raised her hand as if to slap Lord Raoul, then seemed to think better of it. Damien could not hear her words, but he could tell they were scathing.

Lord Raoul laughed and turned away, but he did not see Damien. Instead, he sauntered away with a satisfied look on his face.

Damien ignored the crowd around him and the buzz of conversation and laughter. He watched Lord Raoul walk away, then turned toward Lady Selene. Her back was to the people, her face toward the wall. She raised a hand as if she were wiping something from her face. Then her shoulders straightened and he could almost imagine her cold mask falling into place.

She turned around and lifted her chin. Yes, the mask was back. He realized he had never seen her smile before, and he doubted she would smile tonight.

Damien straightened. He didn't know what he was going to do or say. But he would do something to lighten her spirits.

Even if it was just a little.

L ord Raoul stood before Lady Selene, blocking her view of the dancing couples and people around the room. "Why do you fight me, Selene?" he asked.

Selene narrowed her eyes at his casual use of her name. "*Lady* Selene," she corrected him. "And as I've said before, I have no interest in marrying you. I only danced with you because it was the proper thing to do."

Lord Raoul snickered, his smoldering amber gaze set on her face. "You do not know yet, do you? Then let me inform you. For generations, House Friere and House Ravenwood have been lovers. Our houses are intertwined."

Selene curled her lips. Raoul's delusions were even more pretentious than she had thought. Lovers? Bah! "Then marry my sister Amara. There is already talk that our families are looking to align with each other."

He snorted in a derisive way. "Amara? She is hardly gifted. You, on the other hand . . ." He lifted his hand and ran his fingers along her arm and leaned in. "I know the mark you bear on your back," he whispered. "It is you I want. The most powerful Ravenwood lady."

Selene sucked in a breath as she took a step back and raised her hand. "Don't you ever touch me," she said through clenched teeth while her heart raced. How did he know about her mark? Forget that, how did he know about her gift? No one knew about the Ravenwood gift unless . . .

Unless Mother had told them.

Did that mean Lord Raoul's words were true? Were Mother and Lord Ivulf close enough that she had shared their family's most sacred secret? Were they . . . lovers?

Mother said Lord Ivulf only suspected their gift. Did she lie?

Lord Raoul laughed. "Now you're beginning to understand. We will be together, mark my words. Every Ravenwood lady before you has joined together with the lords of Friere. Eventually, someday, you will come to me, no matter who you marry. You'll see. You cannot fight destiny."

Before Selene could say another word, he turned and walked away. She spun around and faced the wall, her hands clenched. He was wrong! He only said those things to hoodwink her into believing some perverted lie.

But that didn't explain how he knew about her mark and gift. And her mother sat with Lord Ivulf at every meal, smiling and sending meaningful glances. Like two admirers. No, more than that. Like two lovers.

You cannot fight destiny.

Her heart clenched and her stomach coiled. *Never!*

Every Ravenwood lady has joined the lords of Friere.

Every single one of them.

It was true. She knew it deep within. Mother with Lord Ivulf. Her grandmother with Ivulf's father. Every generation. And together, they exploited the gift of dreaming.

She bit back a sob, but still a tear escaped. Raoul had voiced her deepest, darkest fear: that she could not escape her destiny.

No matter what, she would eventually become a murderer. Did that also mean she would follow in her family's footsteps and join with House Friere?

She wiped the erroneous tear away and breathed in deeply, letting the air fill her lungs, clearing away all emotion, willing herself to become cold. She embraced the numbness as it rushed over her, taking away the confusion and pain of moments earlier. She turned, her mask fully in place, a mask chiseled in ice.

No. She would find a way to escape her destiny. Someway, somehow. She just needed more time.

"Lady Selene."

Selene started and glanced to her left to find Lord Damien bowing in her direction.

A longing filled her being as she stared at his face, a face she knew well from walking in his dreams. She could almost see the light inside of him, a light she so desperately wanted to embrace.

But all those nights had been spent preparing for her mission. A mission to extinguish that light.

He looked up and the candlelight caught his deep blue eyes. Selene wanted to turn away and run. Instead, she clutched her arms in front of her, shielding herself from his intense gaze.

"Is everything all right, Lady Selene?"

"Yes." The word came out so fast she didn't have time to think about it. She blushed at his skeptical look. "I'm afraid I don't do well at parties like this."

"I understand. Growing up along the coast and away from most of the houses, my own experience with galas is limited."

He was smiling softly at her. Lord Damien was so different from Lord Raoul. Was that because of the light inside of him? Her throat grew tight and her stomach heaved as she once again remembered her deadly mission.

Don't feel. Don't feel.

But her mantra did not seem to help this time. All she could do was feel. The anguish, the remorse, the entrapment . . . and something more.

"May I have the next dance?" He held out his hand.

Selene stared at it. His hand was strong and masculine, with a thick silver ring on one finger.

Common sense told her she should stay away from him. Familiarity would only make her job tomorrow harder. But her body seemed to have a mind of its own. Before she could think, she was already extending her hand toward his.

He took it with a smile.

Something fluttered inside of her at his touch. His hand was warm and smooth, so unlike Lord Raoul, whose touch had been hot and sticky.

"You look lovely this evening," Lord Damien said as he brought her to his side.

Her eyes widened at his words. "Thank you." Once again, she was struck by how different Lord Damien was compared to Lord Raoul. His words had made her feel exposed; Damien's made her feel beautiful. Like a lady.

Even if she was anything but.

I shouldn't be doing this. I shouldn't be here. She swallowed as bitterness rose up inside her chest. *And yet I want to.* She clung to that last thought as it fed strength into her resolve. *I want to dance with Lord Damien.*

Selene straightened, throwing off the darkness from earlier that evening. Lord Damien skillfully led her toward the crowd at the edge of the dancing couples. The longer they stood there, hand in hand, the easier it was for her to imagine this was her life. No dark destiny loomed before her. Instead, she was simply a lady of a Great House dancing with the lord from another house.

"How has your time been here at Rook Castle?" she asked as they waited for their turn.

"It's been interesting," he said in his soft tenor voice.

"How so?" She glanced at him, curious about his appraisal of her home and the assembly.

"This is my first time meeting some of the Great Houses. Growing up, my family would visit House Luceras, and I've had the pleasure of visiting the grand halls of both House Rafel and House Merek. But I've never met House Vivek, even though we are neighbors, or House Friere. Nor your own house." He looked at her. "Perhaps I find yours the most intriguing."

She raised an eyebrow. "Even though we are the lowliest of the houses, bereft of gift and ruler of the smallest nation?" Her chest tightened at her outright lie. No doubt her words had just added another black link to the chain surrounding her soul.

"My father taught me the Great Houses were each given a gift to help serve their people. But even without a gift, a leader can still serve his or her people through sacrifice and love. In some ways, your house has the greatest ability to show that truth."

Her mouth fell open as her mind grappled with his words. "I-I've wondered that myself." But how, exactly? All her mother had taught her was how to manipulate others with her gift. Instead of loving and sacrificing, she hurt others with her dreamwalking.

How do I do that? How do I change?

The song ended, and the couples exchanged places on the dance floor. With gentle guidance, Lord Damien led her to the line of couples waiting for the next melody. She caught sight of her father near a group of older men. His surprised gaze moved between herself and Lord Damien, then he smiled approvingly at her.

The music began, a slow, soft piece indicating the dance would be a low one. Selene held her dress up by her right hand as Lord

Damien lifted her other hand up with his own. They bowed to each other, then bowed to the crowd, then started forward in smooth, small steps.

Every time Lord Damien faced her, he greeted her with his soft smile and deep blue gaze, twisting the feelings inside of her. She never let it show, keeping the icy veneer across her face. But deep down, with every step, half of her knew she was being drawn to the lord of House Maris. And the other half screamed that this was a mistake. She should have stayed far away from him and kept her heart locked away.

Because no matter what, tomorrow would come and she had a mission to do.

A leader can serve her people by sacrifice and love.

Lord Damien's words played in the back of her mind like a haunting melody. But wasn't that what she was doing? The Dark Lady—Selene winced at the thought of her family's patroness—delivered a message to her mother that there was a threat from the north, a threat to their family and people. At least, that was how Selene remembered it. By eliminating Lord Maris, she would be eliminating that threat. That was sacrifice and love, right?

Selene wrinkled her brow. Wait, was the threat to their people, or only their house—

"Are you enjoying the dance?"

What? Selene sucked in her breath and found Lord Damien staring at her, his face inches from hers. She pulled away and blushed, their hands still together and their shoulders still touching. She had been so consumed with her thoughts that she hadn't noticed how close he had drawn during the dance.

Dart'an! Where was her composure? "Yes, I am," she said a second later, grateful that her voice sounded cool and calm.

"You were frowning a moment ago."

"I was thinking."

"About?" he asked as he held their hands up and stepped back, then forward in cadence with the music.

"About what you said earlier. About the reason gifts were given to the Great Houses."

"I see." His grip tightened around her hand. "I'm sorry if I hurt you with my words. I meant them as an encouragement to you, not a reminder of what your house has lost."

Warmth filled her entire being. "I was challenged by them. I wonder how what you said fits into who I am and the leader I will become."

"And what have you discovered?"

The euphoria from moments ago melted away like a warm breath in the winter. "I'm not sure. I need more time to think." She could feel herself withdrawing into her cold, dark self. Because if her conclusion was right, then killing the man beside her would be a true act of a leader. A sacrifice of love for her house and people.

Or was that just for her house?

If so, was House Ravenwood worth saving?

Had centuries of hate become a poison across the nations?

The music tapered off, ending the dance. Damien led her through the crowd and away from the floor. As they passed through the throng of heavily scented gowns and doublets, Selene caught sight of Amara only a few yards away standing with Lord Elric Luceras.

Her sister looked tragically beautiful in the deep-cut scarlet gown. Instead of enhancing Amara's natural beauty, it made her appear predatory. Selene wondered who had chosen the gown: their mother or Amara?

Amara glanced up and spotted Selene. Her eyes darted between Selene and Lord Damien, a scowl slowly spreading across her face.

Selene frowned, puzzled by her sister's reaction. Was the scowl aimed at Lord Damien or her? Or the fact that they were together?

Before she could think on it more, her mother appeared with Lord Ivulf near the window Lord Damien was heading toward. The blood drained from her face and her breath caught in her chest. *No, not there. Don't go there.*

As if sensing her alarm, Damien spun to the right and headed for an open balcony instead, but not before her mother caught sight of them. Selene cringed, waiting for the look of disapproval, or worse. Instead, her mother smiled.

Selene turned away, but her mother's look was imprinted on her mind. Her mother had smiled. Not an I'm-happy-for-you smile, but a sinister smile of approval. If her mother had fangs, they would have been gleaming in the candlelight.

She shuddered as Damien led her out onto one of the balconies that faced the eastern side of the mountains. The sky was dark, with only a crescent moon and handful of stars peeking out from behind scattered clouds. A cold wind blew, cooling her heated face.

The good feelings from earlier were now shattered by that one look from her mother. It was a reminder that her dance with Damien had been only a brief respite from reality. She was not a lady, not like the other ladies in the room behind her. She was a killer—or would be soon. And this . . . this was just playacting.

"The mountains are beautiful this time of night."

Selene glanced at Lord Damien from the corner of her eye. He was staring out over the balcony with a wistful smile on his face. She took in his physique, the pleasing lines of his face, his short hair almost as dark as her own, and the smooth muscles beneath his blue tunic.

"Is it just as beautiful as your shores?" she asked.

He looked at her. "Yes, in a different way." His dark blue eyes were almost black in the dim light. His face changed, and he cleared his throat. "Are you doing all right this evening? I couldn't help but witness the conversation between you and Lord Raoul." His eyes narrowed. "He didn't say anything ill-mannered toward you, did he?"

Selene tensed at Damien's bluntness. He saw their exchange? She clenched her hands across the railing and stared over the edge. The burning rage and hurt from Raoul's words came rushing back, overcoming any embarrassment she might have felt at realizing he had witnessed their conversation. The lords and ladies of their families were lovers, had always been lovers, he'd claimed. And that conceited, cruel man thought she would come to him like every other Ravenwood woman.

"Nothing I couldn't handle," she said through bared teeth. Damien's kind words drifted back, loosening the sudden tension inside of her. She relaxed and looked at him. "But thank you for asking."

He gave her a hard smile. "House Friere can be . . . a bit off-putting."

Selene laughed. "Yes, they can. I grew up visiting Lord Raoul as a child. I am not unfamiliar with his more nasty side."

"That is the first time I've seen you laugh. Or smile."

Selene lifted a hand to her cheek. Was it? Her brow furrowed. When was the last time she'd smiled? Before her gifting came? She couldn't remember.

"It becomes you," Damien said softly. "I'm glad Lord Raoul didn't get under your skin."

Selene felt like she was teetering on the edge of a cliff. Somehow during the last few minutes, she had let her guard down and her heart had emerged from that cold, dark pit where she kept it hidden. It beat with rapid, lively beats, and brought with it her smile.

She mentally grasped for her cold mask, shoving it down across her features with such force that her smile disappeared completely and her face paled. "I'm sorry," she said as she lifted the sides of her gown. "I-I'm not feeling well." She turned back toward the main hall. "I need to leav—"

Damien's hand grabbed hold of her upper arm. "Wait, did I say something that hurt you?"

She shook her head. "No." Her mask was slipping again. She needed to leave—now.

"Then can I escort you back? Perhaps take you back to your room? Or to a healer?"

Selene glanced back. The sincerity of his concern struck a chord inside of her. Did Lord Damien really care?

No! This needed to stop. If she let him further into her heart, then she would not be able to fulfill her mission tomorrow night. Already she could tell she would need to spend all of tomorrow mentally burying this past half hour. She didn't want to add more.

She turned back and lifted her chin, her mask firmly in place. "Thank you, Lord Damien, but I have no need of an escort. Please enjoy the evening, and do not let any thought of my welfare taint the rest of your time here."

His eyes roved across her face, as if searching for the truth behind her words. Her heart beat faster. *Don't let him see.*

His hand dropped from her arm and before Selene could react, he grasped her hand and brought it up to his lips. Her mind went blank while every nerve in her body centered on the point where his lips brushed her knuckles. "It was a pleasure dancing with you, Lady Selene. I hope you feel better." Then he let go and stepped back, his gaze still fixed on her.

Selene blinked dumbly. What just happened? Her body tingled and her mind refused to work. A voice inside her head, soft at first, then shouted louder at her to move. *Move, Selene!*

"I will. Feel better, that is." Even her mouth refused to work properly. Better to leave before she said something foolish. She turned and headed back into the room. A blast of heat, the loud music, and overwhelming smells assaulted her the moment she stepped inside, compounding her disorientation.

Selene spotted the main doors to her left, halfway across the room. Without another thought, she headed toward them, making her way through the crowd. She didn't care if leaving angered her mother, or if the houses talked about her sudden departure. She was done with the gala. She was done with people. What she needed right now was a quiet place where she could lock away her heart again.

O nce inside her bedchambers, Selene pulled the silver circlet from the top of her head and let it drop on the nearby table, then stripped off her gown and tossed it over the changing screen. After blowing out the candle, she crossed the room and fell across her bed. Pulling her knees up to her chest, she stared at the wall, waiting for the usual numbness to steal over her body.

But it would not come. And her mind would not stop replaying the night over and over again. She turned and curled tighter into a ball. Night moved slowly across the sky outside the window. The gala was still going; she could tell by the barest hint of music wafting through the castle.

After more tossing and turning, she finally rose from her bed. It was no good. All she could think about was Lord Damien. At this rate, she would fail in her mission tomorrow. She needed to do something about it, find a way to purge all thoughts of him from her mind. And there was one place where she could do that.

She moved across her room toward the changing screens and pulled on a dark dress. Then she grabbed her black cloak, clasped it around her neck, and pulled the hood over her head. It wasn't unheard of for disciples to visit the sanctuary at night, but she still wished to remain anonymous as much as possible.

A handful of people were still awake, making their way through the castle corridors on unstable legs. Selene bypassed them without a word, gliding like a spirit in the night along the walls where the shadows were darkest. No one seemed to notice her, and that's how she wanted it.

After weaving her way through the castle, she reached the corridor that led to the Dark Lady's sanctuary. The air felt chillier here, and the shadows darker. Selene stopped and hugged her arms around her body. Should she be doing this? She hadn't visited the Dark Lady since the morning when the priest spoke over her and marked her with an invisible sign.

Would the Dark Lady be angered that she never came back?

Selene clutched the front of her cloak. *But I don't know where else to turn.*

That thought propelled her forward. She needed strength right now. Willpower. Determination. Anything that would help her take these last few steps in accomplishing her mission. Because she was wavering, and she was afraid she would turn back.

She entered the sanctuary. The air was still and quiet, almost eerily so, and smelled of dust and stone. The chandeliers above were devoid of candlelight, and the platform at the front of the room was empty. She carefully made her way to the front, her gaze darting back and forth between the pillars, searching for any living thing. Nothing. Not even the priest, although given how late it was, she wasn't surprised but she was relieved.

She stopped slightly to the left of the platform and stood there. The silence grew heavy the longer she stayed, like a thick wool blanket across the sanctuary. Most of the room was hidden in darkness, with only a trickle of light from the night sky.

Selene gripped the front of her cloak, her throat tight.

I can't do this.

She sank to her knees and curled forward, extending her right hand until her fingertips touched the edge of the platform, her head bowed. "I can't do this," she whispered. "I don't have the strength to carry through." She thought again of Lord Damien, of his dark blue eyes and the way he gently led her on the dance floor. His kind words and inner strength. So young—as young as she was—and yet a leader amongst the Great Houses.

The light of his soul.

Her fingers gripped the platform while she curled her other hand and held it to her chest. Why did she have to kill someone so beautiful? To save her house? A house filled with hatred and corruption? To save herself? Was she worth saving? Her soul was as dark as his was light, and it was darkening even more each day.

And yet . . . her people were counting on her. Each mission provided the means to take care of them. A place to live in peace. A place to work. Food to eat. Without House Ravenwood, the mountain nation would have no leader and be vulnerable to bandits and outlaws, much how it was during the razing. Her family brought stability and income to their people.

A sob broke inside her chest, forcing its way to her lips. Hot tears flooded her cheeks. "Please, Dark Lady, help me! I can't do this on my own."

Selene withdrew her hand from the platform and rocked back and forth on her knees, crying out. But only silence met her prayers. Silence and darkness. Her soul fell deeper into despair.

"Where are you?" Selene whispered as she raised her head and looked at the retable filled with unlit candles. Her voice echoed across the sanctuary. "You said you would be with me that night when my gifting came. But you were never there. And now, when I need your strength to fulfill my mission, you're absent. Are you even real?"

Her eyes went wide and Selene sucked in a breath, horrified by her sudden display of irreverence. She glanced around, expecting to see a woman cloaked in darkness appear and chastise her—or worse. But nothing moved in the dark sanctuary. Not even the air.

Selene dropped her head. A hollow feeling expanded inside of her chest, spreading across her body until she felt like an empty shell. Her face was flushed and swollen from her tears. She wiped her cheeks and let out a forced laugh. Even if the Dark Lady did exist, it appeared Selene was not worth her time.

She stood up on shaky legs. The next day would be dawning soon, and with it her mission. She swallowed and turned. With each step, with each breath, she slowly began to lock away her feelings, trapping them deep inside of her heart behind doors of iron. She would fulfill her mission—not for her house, but for her people. If killing Lord Damien helped her people, then she would do it.

Even if doing so destroyed her in the end.

32

Damien stared at the ceiling, unable to close his eyes. Cohen snored in the room nearby and somewhere beyond the first door he knew Sten was on guard duty while Taegis and Karl slept. Damien's body was exhausted, and his mind was full from that evening. He knew he needed to sleep because tomorrow would require all of his strength, but he could not get Lady Selene out of his mind. The moment she smiled, it was like the sun had broken through the storm clouds and spread warm light across the land. It changed her. It removed the cold, hard mask from her face, revealing the living, breathing woman inside.

That one moment changed something inside of him. Did it alter his response to Caiaphas? No. It would take a lot for him to decide to align himself with House Ravenwood. He would need to know more about Lady Selene. Why did she hide behind a persona of coldness? Who was she really? And what made her run from the room?

That puzzled him most of all. She went from smiling to pallid—almost sickly—in moments. As if she had realized she had let her guard down and it frightened her.

Damien ran a hand through his hair and sighed. Taegis would tell him not to entangle himself with the Ravenwood family. And he would be right. There were so many things going on—his investigations into the murders, the coalition, trying to unite the houses, the Dominia Empire—that he didn't have time to spend on one woman. It would be better not to get involved. After all, House Ravenwood no longer possessed their gift and were the smallest of the nations. There was no advantage in aligning their houses together—

Damien sat up. *What am I thinking?* Since when did it matter what another house had to offer? Where was the advice he had given Lady Selene earlier tonight about a true leader leading by sacrifice and love?

He fell back down across the mattress. Perhaps the houses around him were subtly influencing him. Their own safety and security were all they cared about. He needed to be better. Just because Lady Selene did not possess her house gift didn't mean she was less than him.

He took a deep breath and closed his eyes. The Light could use anyone. Weakness could turn into strength. And he had a feeling there was a hidden strength within Lady Selene waiting to be unlocked.

Damien splashed the tepid water from the bowl across his face and wiped the moisture off with the nearby towel. He tossed the towel on the table and stared into the opaque water within the bowl, his hands spread out on either side. Bright morning sunshine streamed through the nearby window with a cheerfulness that countered how he felt.

His dreams last night had been dark and foreboding, a reflection on how he felt about the treaty agreement today. Something was going to happen, a catalyst of sorts that would set in motion the future of the seven Great Houses. The question was, would it bring them together or would it divide them, inviting Commander Orion and the Dominia Empire to take over their lands?

After dressing, he headed for the meeting hall with Karl on duty that day as his bodyguard. By now Rook Castle had become a familiar place, and he made his way with ease to the double doors that led inside the spacious circular room. Most of the houses were already present and seated around the enormous wooden table in the middle of the hall. The only houses not yet present were House Ravenwood and House Friere.

Damien took a seat beside Lord Leo Luceras. There were dark circles beneath the young lord's eyes. It appeared his sleep had also been compromised, but whether by dreams or something else, Damien didn't know.

Lord Haruk Rafel sat across the table, his long silver hair pulled back, his wizened face looking even more aged as he gazed at the tabletop, almost as if he were avoiding looking at anyone else. Damien's stomach churned. If Lord Haruk's look was any indication, it would seem that he would not be voting in favor of the treaty. Damien hoped his suspicions were wrong.

Lord Rune Vivek and his sister Runa talked quietly across from him. He wondered how they were feeling this morning, since their land and people were most at risk from an attack by the Dominia Empire.

Next to them sat Lady Bryren. She leaned back in her chair with her arms crossed and a faraway look on her fiercely painted face. Damien wondered what she was thinking about at that moment.

The double doors opened a second later, and Lady Ragna marched into the meeting hall with Lord Ivulf at her side. She wore a long dark dress cut to accentuate her body, her equally dark hair flowing down to her waist. Lord Ivulf appeared almost wolfish beside her, his myriad golden jewelry twinkling from his neck, earlobes, and fingers.

As Damien watched Lady Ragna cross the room and take a seat to the right of the table, he couldn't help but compare her with Lady Selene. There was a regal haughtiness to Lady Ragna as she surveyed the table like a queen on her throne. Her cold dark eyes roved across the room in a calculating manner, causing a shiver to go down his spine.

Lady Selene was nothing like that. Yes, she was cold, almost chilly in her appearance, but nothing like the darkness exuding from Lady Ragna. He would not say Lady Selene was gentle, like Lady Adalyn Luceras, nor quiet like Lady Ayaka. Lady Selene possessed something like a hidden strength, a flower that only blooms at twilight, between the night and the day.

Lord Ivulf sat down beside Lady Ragna. The room grew quiet as faces turned toward Lady Ragna in expectation.

"Thank you once again for answering the summons for the Assembly of the Great Houses. As you know, we have come together during this time to discuss the alleged encroachment of the Dominia Empire."

Alleged encroachment? Damien bristled at Lady Ragna's choice of wording. He noticed Lord Rune's face darken as well.

"Even though it was such words that brought us here, it was still good for us to come together. It has been almost four hundred years since all seven Great Houses have met, and during this time, many alliances have formed and friendships made. But we are not here today to converse on the benefits of this assembly. Instead, we are here to talk about a unified treaty between the seven Great Houses, a treaty against the Dominia Empire."

She looked around the room. "I will not waste your time. We have spoken much over the last few days and each of us has come to a decision about what is best for our people and best for our house."

Damien clenched his hand beneath the table. She was wrong. If each house only thought of what was best for themselves, then there would never be any unity. But he had already spoken on the subject and to bring it up now would only open up the room to more debate. So he held his tongue.

"With that said," Lady Ragna continued, "House Ravenwood chooses not to sign the treaty."

The already silent room became even more deathly so. Heat flashed across Damien's body. He'd had a feeling House Ravenwood would go that direction, especially given his conversation with Caiaphas the other night. But to hear it spoken so boldly felt like a shot straight to the heart.

"Such a treaty, when found out by the Dominia Empire, will only provoke the very thing we are trying to avoid: an invasion. We have lived in peace with the empire for the last four hundred years. There is no reason to assume the empire has any ill intentions toward our lands or our people. Yes, there are skirmishes along the border, but there will always be tension along the border. That is the nature of things."

"And what of the new commander?" Lord Rune Vivek asked, his dark face tight. "He has already reached beyond the Dominia border to the east."

"We have no desire to go to war with the Dominia Empire. House Ravenwood will not sign the treaty. It is not in our best interest."

Damien could tell Lord Vivek wanted to say more, but he clamped his mouth shut. If the last few days had not changed people's minds, it would not happen now.

Lord Ivulf nodded. "I agree with Grand Lady Ragna. We must look out for our people first. House Friere will not be signing the treaty either."

Lady Ragna and Lord Ivulf's words seemed to have stirred Lady

Bryren. She sat up stiffly and looked to her left at the two heads of house. Her nostrils flared and a glint entered her eyes. "Let it not be said that House Merek lost their courage in the face of adversity. If there is war, then both House Merek and her people will be there to fight." She glanced at Lord Rune and his sister Runa. "House Merek will sign the treaty."

A smile tugged on Damien's lips. Count on Lady Bryren to come out fighting, even if it was only to show her support for the treaty.

Lord Haruk Rafel finally looked up, and Damien's good feelings from moments ago evaporated. Lord Haruk's appearance was even more haggard and aged, and there were great bags under his eyes. He avoided looking to his right where Lord Rune and Lady Runa sat as he gave his answer. "I'm afraid at this time House Rafel will not be signing the treaty." Then he folded his hands and looked back down at the table.

Damien wanted to ask why, so much so that the question burned behind his lips, but he stopped. The talks were done and now was the time for decision. But there was a part of him that wondered what was going on in the back of Lord Haruk's mind. Was he being coerced in some way?

Lord Rune straightened and looked around the room. Unlike Lady Ragna, Lord Rune Vivek appeared as a leader of nobility. His deep purple clothing accented his rich, dark skin, and the gold bands around his muscular arms stood out. His deep voice rumbled as he started to talk. "Lady Ragna, you are right in the fact that we should do what is best for our people and for our houses. But perhaps you should consider that sometimes means looking beyond our boundaries to the people and houses that border our own. One house, though powerful, will never withstand the might of the empire. But two or more houses, like entwined strands, will not snap. Their strength is in their unity. For too long

House Vivek has stood alone. It is time for my house to join the others. Therefore, House Vivek will sign the treaty."

There were murmurs around the table as Lady Runa squeezed her brother's arm in agreement.

Lord Leo cleared his throat beside Damien. The room grew silent again. "I have consulted with my father, Grand Lord Warin, about the matter of this treaty. It is my father's wish that House Luceras sign the treaty."

Damien narrowed his eyes as he stared at Lord Leo. It almost seemed like Leo did not agree with his father's decision, but as the heir and not the grand lord, it was not his decision to make.

All eyes turned toward Damien. Damien sat up and placed his hands on the table. "I originally called this assembly"—he glanced at Lady Ragna, who stared back with tight lips—"because of the growing threat of the Dominia Empire. But what many of you don't know is that it has been the wish of my father, and my father's father, to someday unite the seven Great Houses. A long time ago, although we were each different, with different gifts and as leaders of different people, we were one. Nothing could stand against us, even the empire. I had hoped that we could resurrect that unity once again. However, it seems this is not the time. Even so, House Maris will join those houses in signing the treaty."

Lord Rune bowed his head in Damien's direction while Lady Bryren grinned. Damien answered their looks with a small nod. He wanted to exude as much confidence and hope as he could muster, mainly for those houses signing the treaty, but inside, all he wanted to do was leave.

As Lady Ragna droned on with closing remarks, Damien sat back. He felt like a failure. He had failed to unite the seven houses. His heart thudded dully inside his chest as Lord Rune took his turn to thank the houses joining his in the treaty. A time was set for tomorrow for those houses to return, then the meeting was adjourned.

Damien glanced at one of the windows past the tall columns that surrounded the circular room as the others stood and talked quietly amongst themselves. It was only midday, which meant he still had half a day to fill, half a day to think about the conclusion to the assembly, half a day to finish up and pack. Then tomorrow, once the treaty was signed, he would head home.

The thought of Nor Esen and Northwind Castle stirred a longing inside his heart. He stood and headed for the double doors that led outside the meeting hall. He would spend the afternoon preparing for his journey home. But ten minutes later, when he stepped into his room, he walked over to the chair beside the unlit fireplace, sat down, and held his head inside his hands. His heart felt even heavier than it had inside the meeting hall. And with each passing minute, the weight increased.

"I failed," he whispered. "I failed, Father. I failed you. And I failed the coalition."

There would be no unity. Each heartbeat pounded that truth into his mind. There would be no help from those three houses if the empire chose to invade House Vivek's borders. Only House Luceras and House Merek were committed to helping if war broke out. And even Lord Leo seemed to have cooled in his enthusiasm to assist.

Damien ran his hands along his face. The problem was that House Merek was way down south and the farthest house away from the border, and Damien's own house had limited land military, since most of his forces were naval trained. If the empire moved on House Vivek, there would be no time to mobilize help, even from House Luceras.

It would be House Ravenwood all over again. Another house razed to oblivion by the empire.

He lifted his head up and stared at the empty fireplace grate. "Why don't they see? We need to help each other. None of us can protect ourselves on our own. We were never given these gifts just for our own benefit. I don't want to make the same mistake my ancestors made. But I'm not sure what I can do. I can't raise the water around all of the nations." Even now, he could feel the continual drain of the water-wall still in place where he had left it. He held his hands out, palm up. "I'm not strong enough. I don't know if any Maris lord ever was."

A deep ache settled inside his chest. Before he could think on it, Damien crawled from his chair and settled on his knees before the fireplace, his head bowed. "Light, please help us." That was all he could muster. The feelings inside of him were too deep and raw for words. He curled in on himself and held his hands up in supplication. Over and over he pleaded to the Light to save them. To save not just House Vivek or the other border nations, but to save all of them. To save them from the empire.

To save them from themselves.

The light from the nearby window moved along the stone floor, but Damien never moved. He knelt there, even when his legs began to ache and his knees felt like a fire had been lit inside of them. It wasn't until he felt a presence behind him that he looked up and over his shoulder.

Taegis stood in the doorway. "Karl hadn't seen you for hours, so I decided to check on you. I take it things did not go well today."

Damien slowly stood to his feet. "No." The deep ache continued to throb inside of his chest. "There was no agreement. There will be no help. Whether they believe the empire is a threat or not, half of the Great Houses will do nothing if the empire chooses to cross the wall."

Taegis scowled and crossed his arms. "How foolish," he muttered and looked away.

"Have the Great Houses ever really been united?" It was a question Damien had always wished he could ask his father.

"I don't know." Taegis continued to scowl. "Perhaps a long time ago, when the nations first formed, when all of the houses possessed their gifts."

Damien's throat tightened. "Do you think I was a fool to hope?"

Taegis dropped his arms and looked at him. "No. And neither was your father. This conflict with the empire should have compelled the houses to look beyond their borders, but apparently history runs too deep. It might take a war to finally wake them up."

"I had hoped it wouldn't come to that. Or at least that we would be unified if it does happen."

"And what do you plan on doing when it does?"

"I will assist House Vivek as much as I can. And hopefully House Luceras will come through with their promise. They plan on signing the treaty tomorrow, along with House Merek."

"But not House Rafel?"

Damien shook his head. "No. Lord Haruk decided to follow Ravenwood and Friere."

Taegis frowned. "If war does break out, we will need skilled healers. And the healers from Rafel are the best, even those from the lesser houses without the gift. Why did Lord Haruk agree with House Ravenwood and House Friere?"

Damien shrugged. "I don't know." But he had an idea. He was sure there was something going on. Perhaps Lord Haruk was being manipulated, or the elder lord was holding out on an alliance for his daughter.

"Well, at least you were able to bring four of the seven houses together. That's something."

But not enough. Not against the Dominia Empire. Last time it took six houses to push the empire back and build fortifications against another invasion. Four was not going to be enough. It would only delay the inevitable.

Damien ran a hand across his face. He had planned on packing, but he was exhausted. "I think I'm going to turn in early tonight after dinner."

"Good idea. Tomorrow you sign the treaty, then we can start back home."

Home. Just the thought made everything inside Damien relax. A window a few feet away overlooked the Magyr Mountains. High peaks and rock. That's all there was around here. It was beautiful, in a rugged, wild sort of way. But his heart longed for the water, for the seacoast and the call of the gulls, for the sound of crashing waves, and the scent of salt in the air.

He longed for home.

He let out his breath. "That'll be good."

Taegis bowed. "Good night, Lord Damien. I will be on guard if you need anything."

"Thank you, Taegis, for everything."

"I only wish I could do more." Taegis turned and quietly left the room.

Damien stood for a moment and stared at the door. Dinner would be served soon. But he wasn't ready, not yet. Instead, he headed back to the spot where he had been kneeling before Taegis entered the room and sunk down to his knees. Bowing his head, he started praying again.

elene skipped dinner that night, choosing instead to remain in her bedchambers and prepare for the evening. She stood in the middle of her room, one arm flung across her middle and gripping her other arm as she watched the sun sink beyond the Magyr Mountains.

Her secret excursion to the Dark Lady's sanctuary last night had done nothing for her. Instead, it left her feeling numb and lifeless. As if she were a husk, moving, doing, but feeling nothing.

But perhaps that was a good thing. If she couldn't feel her heart, then carrying out her mission would be that much easier. Maybe she had finally learned how to lock it away. Her black tunic, leggings, boots, and cloak were laid out behind her across her bed, along with her facial scarf, ready to be adorned and used in this evening's covert mission.

Minutes ticked by. She knew she should start preparing. But part of her was afraid to turn and begin dressing, fearing that by moving, her heart would emerge again.

So she stood there and watched the crimson light disappear beyond the craggy peaks until the last ray disappeared into the inky blackness. Then she stood in the darkness and closed her eyes. She would enter Lord Damien's dreams and head directly to the memory of that stormy day at sea. She would reenact that memory and build up the storm. She would take away his ship, leaving him alone in the midst of the crashing waves with the carnage and debris from the ships he had destroyed, building up his fear until she felt his heart thrashing inside of him.

Then she would let him drown.

Selene slowly opened her eyes and swallowed the lump inside her throat. It was a perfect plan. The fear was there—the fear of drowning and the fear of the devastation his power could cause. She would simply allow the memory to spread across his dream-scape and his body would take over.

And if that wasn't enough, there was also the death of his family. . . .

At the edge of her being, she could feel a storm brewing over what she was about to do, but she mentally shut the door on those feelings and locked them away. Then she took a slow, deep breath and sunk back into the numbing coldness of her soul.

She glanced at the window. Mother would soon be heading to the guest rooms given to Lord Rune Vivek and his sister Runa and accomplishing her own mission. She turned and headed for her bed. It was time she left as well.

Selene quickly pulled on the black clothing. With each garment, she felt herself slipping into another person . . . into the dreamkiller. She clasped her cloak around her neck, wrapped the scarf around her face until all that remained were her eyes, then pulled the hood up and over her head, taking care to tuck her long braid inside the head covering.

Her boots were silent as she made her way across the room to where her dual blades lay on the short table against the wall, next to the fireplace. She belted the double scabbard around her waist, then slipped the blades inside their sheaths. She had studied Lord Damien's guards enough to feel confident about entering Damien's room undetected, but she wanted to be prepared, just in case.

She took a deep breath and faced the door. There. She was ready.

Selene focused on her next step: making her way across Rook Castle to Lord Damien's bedchamber. She never let her mind slip, never allowed a lingering thought of Damien. Instead, she concentrated on the hallway as she slipped out of her room, on where the shadows were, and where any voices were coming from.

The corridors were empty as she entered the storage room. She bypassed the crates stacked against the wall, stopped in front of the back wall, and pushed down on the small lever near the corner. The wall slid to the side, opening the way to a narrow tunnel.

Selene stepped inside and shut the door behind her. She made her way in the darkness, following the same path she had followed before to the opening beneath Lord Damien's balcony. The air chilled her body. The smell of dust turned to pine as she reached the opening ahead.

Selene stopped outside and stood on the stone lip that jutted out from the cave entrance. Eight feet above stood the rounded balcony that connected to Lord Damien's bedchamber. She quietly listened but heard neither voices nor movement. Satisfied, she scurried up the rocky right side of the mountain where it connected to the castle, then twisted to her left when she reached the balcony, grabbed onto the railing, and gracefully swung onto the floor. She sidled up to the outside wall, just beside the doorway, and waited.

No sound.

She glanced around and found the glass inlaid doors shut. Made sense. It was cold this evening.

After making sure there was no light inside, she took a second look through the glass. Though it was dark, she could not detect any guards.

Selene straightened, her back flush with the stone wall. Ahead, stars were starting to come out, filling the night sky with their tiny but brilliant light. A timber wolf howled, its voice echoing through the narrow gorges. She took a deep breath, then turned and grabbed the door handle.

The metal lever sank down and the door opened without a sound. Selene crept inside and gently shut the door behind her. Another quick glance confirmed that there was no one in the room, save for the figure lying on top of the large four-poster bed.

If the guards followed their usual routine, then the older guard would be on duty tonight. She brushed the hilt of her right sword as assurance, just in case she was proven wrong.

Quietly, she made her way across the room to the space between the bed and the wall that was out of view of the other doors. As she moved along the bed, a tangle of knots began to form inside her middle, and her mouth grew dry. Selene licked her lips as her heart beat faster. This was it. Time to fulfill her destiny and become the next Lady Ravenwood.

Damien lay on his side, face toward her, arms spread out toward the edge of the bed, knees bent. The covers lay in a heap at his feet, as if he had kicked them off and left them there. He'd stripped down to a simple tunic and trousers, the top of his tunic undone, exposing his chest and neck.

The moonlight from the balcony highlighted his face, revealing sharp, chiseled features and the beginnings of a beard. His dark hair had grown longer during his stay here, covering the tips of his ears and reaching down to his eyebrows.

His eyes were tightly closed, almost as if his sleep were painful to him. Selene narrowed her eyes as she studied his face. What was he dreaming about right now? And could that work in her favor?

She was already beginning to think like her mother. And yet, wasn't that the point? The moment she killed Lord Maris she would take her place as a lady of Ravenwood and a dreamkiller. She knelt down beside the bed where his fingers trailed off the mattress, a feeling of shame and mortification bubbling up inside of her.

A vicious spell of nausea hit her, sending bile up her throat. Selene hunched over, willing her body to calm down as she stared down at the stone floor. *I don't have time for this*, she thought, clenching her hands.

Moments later, the sickness subsided, and she slowly straightened. There was movement in one of the rooms beyond. Selene froze, listening and watching. No one emerged.

She took a deep breath. The faster she carried out her mission, the quicker she could leave and put this all behind her.

She smiled sadly to herself as she reached for Damien and prepared to enter his dreamscape. She would never be able to put this behind her. This encounter would forever be etched on her soul, a dark blot she would never be able to wash away.

But . . . if this saved her people, if this saved her sisters from becoming dreamkillers, if doing this allowed her to control her house someday, then maybe it was worth it.

Until she found another way.

With that, Selene clamped her fingers down around Damien's wrist.

34

Like the other times before, Selene was pulled into the dreamscape as if Damien himself had grabbed ahold of her hand and hauled her into his mind. She'd never told her mother about that experience, so she still wasn't sure if this was normal or not. Her gut feeling was that this wasn't normal, that there was some kind of connection between herself and Damien that went beyond the usual emotional attachment formed during a dreamwalk. And if so, what would happen to her the moment she killed him?

Would it affect her too?

Those thoughts swirled inside her mind as her body transformed and she caught the wind inside the dreamscape with her newly formed wings. She hovered for a moment, adjusting to the form of a raven, and glanced around to get her bearings.

White sand stretched across the dreamscape, bordered by deep grey waves on one side, and rolling hills of grass and pine trees on the other. The sky around her was bright blue and full of sunlight. The air was crisp, cool, and smelled of salt and water.

Her heart soared at the beauty and peace of the dreamscape, only to crash moments later. She knew this place. Even as her mind registered that thought, her eyes caught sight of the glowing orb nestled between two sand dunes.

Damien's soulsphere.

At once, everything inside of her was drawn to the brilliant sphere, a longing so deep that it felt like it was physically pulling her. Her beak parted, and her body flashed with a sudden burst of heat. She angled her wings toward the sphere and began to descend toward the beach. There were no thoughts in her mind except one thing: Damien's brilliant soul.

Just as Selene swooped in toward the sphere, her senses came back and she took a hard right, passing the sphere and coming up on the other side only a couple of feet away.

The heat from moments before turned to a chill as she hovered above the sand. From here, she could see the swirls of light within the orb, almost like living strands moving and dancing.

She closed her eyes. She had almost touched his soul.

Another chill raced through her body, causing her to shudder. Selene opened her eyes and flapped her wings, lifting high into the sky. Once she was at least a hundred feet away, she looked back. The orb glistened amongst the white sand, and the desire for it enveloped her heart. But she held back. Instead, she turned around and flew as hard as she could in the other direction.

With each pump of her wings, she forced her emotions into the deepest part of her, ready to lock them away. At the same time, she searched for a way to escape this particular dreamscape and begin her exploration of Damien's memories of that stormy day.

On and on she flew, first up the coast, then along the ocean as far from the beach as she could, then down the other side of the coast. But no matter where she went, it seemed to bring her back to Damien's soulsphere.

After encountering it a third time, she took off for the hills of pine. Soft wisps of fog were forming between the tree trunks and rising toward the sky like steam off wet clothing on a hot day.

She flew until there was only fog and pine trees below her and kept on going. A moment later, the beach showed up in front of her as well as the orb of light, shining even more brilliantly than before.

Shaken, Selene landed on the branch of one of the pine trees that bordered the beach. Her heart dashed against her rib cage as she looked to her right, then her left. Her breath came in ragged rasps through her beak, and for a moment she felt light-headed.

She couldn't escape this dreamscape. It was almost as if something—or someone—wanted her here.

She blinked her eyes and steadied her breathing. She needed to think and not panic.

Another breath.

Something was going on, of that she was sure. Maybe she should head out and try reentering the dreamscape.

Selene pumped her wings and soared up away from the trees. Up and up she went. But when she reached the place where she had first entered Damien's dreamscape, she couldn't find the opening. In fact, it was as if she were flying in place.

Her heart jumped into her throat, followed by bile. She looked down. Hundreds of feet below her was the same beach, the same water, and Damien's soulsphere.

What is going on? Is Damien doing this? But how?

Terrified, she slowly circled back down to the ground until she reached the sand and landed. She curled her talons beneath her and refused to look at the orb, even as every fiber in her being screamed for her to turn.

There was only one other option: she would try and alter this dreamscape. Taking a deep breath, Selene closed her eyes and spread out her wings. She pictured the beach: the long stretch of sand, the gently rolling waves, the cool breeze, and the clear blue sky. She couldn't make Damien's soul disappear, but she could change everything else. She would create a great storm, one that would hide the soulsphere from her vision. If she could do that, then at least it meant she could still manipulate his dream.

She let out her breath with one great whoosh and brought her wings down. She felt her power surge inside, crackling along her spine and mark. But it never expanded.

She opened her eyes. The dreamscape remained as it was. Not even a cloud had appeared. She waved her wings again and again, exerting her power until the heat from the effort overtook her. Then she let her wings hover in place while she held her beak slightly open and breathed quickly to cool down.

Nothing had changed. Behind her, the waves moved in soothing monotony, the wind blew through the dune grass, and she could feel the pull of Damien's soulsphere.

Selene had no power here.

Her breath came out in short rasps and her body shook. She was not prepared for this, whatever it was. Mother never mentioned a dreamscape where she could not escape or change—or the powerful pull of certain soulspheres.

Maybe her mother had never experienced this.

What do I do? I can't leave. I-I can't do anything! Why is this happening?

No. She clicked her beak. *I can't panic. I cannot lose control of my emotions. Think, Selene, think. What else could be happening?*

She paused and swallowed, picturing every part of her body and forcing each muscle to relax. She couldn't change the dreamscape, but that didn't mean she was in danger. And even if she was, she could still fight, even within this place.

With that in mind, Selene slowly twisted her neck until she could see Damien's soulsphere from the corner of her eye. What if someone or something was keeping her here? It was possible it was Damien, but she felt like it was something more powerful. A god or some being?

The Dark Lady, perhaps?

Selene stood still. No, it did not feel like the Dark Lady. The sanctuary always felt cold and dark. This felt . . . warm. Welcoming, even though she was trapped.

She shuffled her claws across the sand and turned more fully toward the orb. But if it wasn't Damien or the Dark Lady, then who? The god of the old ways? The one the followers of the Light were devoted to?

Was he real?

And if so, maybe she *was* supposed to be here.

Her eyes widened. She stared at Damien's soul, her heart quickening at the sight. A tingle started inside her chest, spreading across her body, to her head, to her wings, to her claws.

She swallowed, her throat dry. She took one step, then another toward Damien's soul. What caused it to be so full of light? Petur's had been grey and cloudy, and Renata's—

She stopped, her insides clenching.

Renata.

Her servant girl's soul had been as dark as night and surrounded by chains.

Selene closed her eyes and breathed through the nostrils along her beak. Did that mean Damien had never experienced pain or heartache? No.

She opened her eyes and stared at the orb. She had seen his hurt, experienced his fear. His heart still grieved over the death of his parents and brother. He feared his gift and what it could do. He was just like everyone else whose dreams she had walked through. There was a hint of darkness within the light of his soul.

So what made him different?

"I want to know," Selene whispered and took another step toward his soulsphere. "I want what you have. I've experienced pain and grief and fear, same as you. Yet you live with a burning hope inside of you, and I . . ."

A tear formed in the corner of her eye as she continued toward the orb. "I live in darkness. And I can't find a way to escape."

Could he hear her inside the dreamscape? Did he know of the immense light he carried inside of him?

I would do anything to be free. To have what you have.

But maybe there was no escape for her. Darkness and hatred tainted House Ravenwood from as far back as she knew, all the way back to Rabanna.

Then why was she stuck here? She stopped and looked around. Why couldn't she escape Damien's dreamscape? Why was she drawn so strongly to his soul? Was there another purpose?

She sucked in a breath and looked ahead. The glowing orb stood twenty feet away, swirling with life and light.

What if she had it all wrong? Despite her fears and hesitations, she had come here tonight to fulfill her mission because she believed that in doing so, she would be helping her people and her sisters. She was willing to sacrifice herself for others.

But what if killing Damien was not the answer?

What if keeping him alive was?

Could he do more for her people than she could, since he had that light inside of him? Could he save her sisters, especially little Ophie?

Selene closed the gap between herself and the soulsphere until she was standing before it. Even now, her mother was carrying out her own mission on House Vivek. Tomorrow, the bodies of Lord Rune and his sister Runa would be found dead in their beds, as if they had passed away in their sleep. Selene should be doing the same to Lord Damien.

She stretched out one wing, letting it hover inches from the orb. She knew what Damien's fears were. All she had to do was have him relive his parents' death over and over. Or . . .

She spread out her other wing. She could let him drown and shatter his dream world. She could even search out that shadowy hole she had seen inside of him during her second excursion into his dreams.

She stood there, her wings spread. A cool wind came over her, and in that moment, she felt every current of his dreamscape, every thread that tied his memories, hopes, and wishes together. Her power had returned. Whatever had prevented her earlier was now gone. She could fulfill her mission.

Do it, an insidious voice whispered. *Do it now and claim your right as heir to Ravenwood. Your sister Amara would not hesitate. You're more powerful than her, are you not?*

But I do not want power. I want freedom and peace. I want the light.

The yearning returned in her heart, so powerful it took her breath away. All she could see was the light from Damien's soul. She wanted it. More than anything else. To cup it in her hands and place it where her own cold, dark soul lived.

The yearning turned into a deep ache, and her throat grew tight. If only this had been her destiny: to carry light instead of darkness. This world needed Lord Damien. It needed souls like his. It needed more light. There was too much darkness already.

She shook her head and lowered her wings.

I can't do it. I can't destroy something so beautiful.

If she couldn't carry the light herself, then she would make sure it lived on.

I will do anything—even give my life—to make sure the light carries on.

With that, Selene took a step back. It felt like a burden had fallen away from her shoulders. The vacillation was done. She no longer questioned what she should do. The weeks of agonizing over whether to dreamkill or not had ended. She had her answer.

She needed to save Lord Damien.

Her mind now feverishly searched for a new plan. She could help him escape. She knew the old tunnels below the castle better than anyone. One of the mines met up with an underground river that led north. It was dangerous, and it would take over a day to reach the opening, but it would leave him close to the border of his own country where he would be protected.

And then she would return home.

Selene smiled sadly. Yes, she would save him. And it would cost her. Mother would not face her in the dream world, as Selene was much too powerful. No. She would be marked as a traitor to House Ravenwood and executed.

Selene rose and transformed into her human body. Her unbound hair flowed with the sweet wind blowing across the dreamscape. A simple gown covered her form, and her dual swords were strapped to her middle. She no longer cared if Damien saw her here, in her human form. The time for secrets was over.

She watched Damien's soulsphere. It would end this way, with his life spared and hers lost. But strangely she found peace in the exchange. She wasn't a killer, she never had been. Ultimately, she wasn't like Rabanna or her mother. She would not be the savior of her people. But maybe, just maybe, by letting Damien live, he would find a way to share his light with others. Like her sister Ophie. Perhaps even Amara.

She held out her hand. The heat of his life flared, warming her fingers. Her smiled widened. What a beautiful soul.

Selene took a deep breath and brushed her fingers across the surface. The light rippled beneath her, then flared again. She felt his conscious awaken to her presence.

She leaned forward, almost as if to kiss the soulsphere. "Wake up, Damien," she whispered softly. "You are not safe here."

His soul grew brighter and brighter until it was a blinding light flashing across the dreamscape. Selene closed her eyes, feeling the warmth of his life and soul across her face and body. Energy surged around her, pulling her to her feet, then rushing through her like a river.

Well done, Dreamer.

That voice . . . Selene opened her eyes, then shut them against the bright light. She knew that voice. It wasn't the corrupt voice from minutes before. It was the one that spoke after she received her gifting so many months ago. The one that had declared a dreamer had been born.

She listened, waiting to hear more. But only a dull roar filled her ears. At the last moment, she let go of the dreamscape. Instead of flying upward, she remained in her human form and let herself be carried along with Damien's subconscious toward reality as his mind and body awoke.

35

Lord Damien!"

Damien blinked his eyes as the beach near Nor Esen and the dream voice faded from his mind. There had been a raven there too. Or had it been a woman? A woman with long dark hair . . .

He blinked again. There was a figure hovering over him, dressed in black.

What the—

Taegis yelled again and pulled the figure away. There was a thump against the floor and a low groan.

Damien sat up, his mind speeding to the present. A stranger. In his room. He swung his legs around, fully alert.

"My lord, are you all right?" Taegis asked, his sword out.

"Yes." He mentally checked his body as he spotted the intruder lying near the middle of the room close to the right wall. His face was swathed in black cloth and a hood, only leaving his eyes—which were presently closed—visible. "I'm fine." He stood, ready for a fight.

Wake up, Damien.

He frowned. The dream voice again.

You are not safe here.

Taegis turned his attention to the figure lying on the ground. "Who are you?" he said as he took a step closer, the tip of his sword pointed toward the intruder. "What are you doing in Lord Maris's room?"

"My lord?" Cohen stumbled out from the other room, rubbing sleep from his eyes. "I heard yelling."

Karl and Sten entered the room at the same moment. They both spotted the trespasser and pulled their swords. One of them lit a candle on the side table near the bed.

"Stay where you are, monk," Taegis said without glancing Cohen's way. "We have an intruder."

The figure used the nearby wall to stand. Damien narrowed his eyes. In the candlelight, he could see the intruder better. His physique was small, almost feminine—

The intruder wasn't a man.

It was a woman.

And she wore dual swords along her waist.

Wait. He recognized those swords—

Taegis brought his sword up and pointed it at the woman's heart as she turned. "Either reveal yourself and what is going on, or I will cut you down here and now."

Damien walked over to Taegis while Karl and Sten hovered behind him. Yes, he knew those swords. He would never forget watching her practice with them. He looked into her eyes. Dark and rich. No doubt about it. The intruder was Lady Selene.

Her eyes focused on him, and there was something in her gaze. A deep sadness. Her eyes crinkled. "I couldn't do it." Her voice came out muffled from behind her wrap. She lifted her hand, but Taegis brought his sword up, stopping her.

"Don't move," he said.

"You asked who I am. Well, I'm showing you."

Taegis grunted and pulled his sword back, but only far enough so she could reach her hood.

Damien stared at her as her hood fell back and a long black braid fell out from the dark folds. She undid the scarf around her face and let the black cloth drop to the floor, revealing her face. Cohen gasped, but Damien ignored him. The voice he had heard in his dream. The one warning him. It was Lady Selene's voice.

He placed his hand on Taegis's arm as his guardian raised his sword again. "Lady Selene. What's going on?"

Her eyes darted between Taegis and Damien. Damien kept his hand on Taegis's arm. He wanted to hear what she had to say first, before any action was taken.

Her shoulders dropped in resignation. "I was sent here to kill you."

His eyebrows shot up. "Kill me?"

"Yes." She looked away and visibly swallowed. "I couldn't do it."

Her words echoed again inside his head. *You are not safe here.*

Taegis's nostrils flared, and he brought his sword within an inch of her chest. "You were assigned to kill Lord Damien? Who sent you? And why?"

Damien detected deep anger in his voice. No doubt Taegis was remembering the death of Lord Remfrey Maris, a death he could not prevent. "Taegis, wait."

Taegis's gaze never left Selene's face. "This woman just admitted coming here to kill you. We cannot let her go. Give me permission and—"

"No."

"My lord?"

"Harming Lady Selene would create an international incident. I came here to broker peace, not start a war, no matter what the other houses' intentions were."

"We can't trust her." Taegis lifted his sword until it was just beneath her chin. Karl and Sten came to stand behind him, their swords drawn as well.

Selene glanced back. She never flinched, even with Taegis's blade near the pulse of life beneath her skin. Instead, she focused on Damien.

"If she had wanted to kill me, she would have done that already, isn't that right, Lady Selene?"

"Yes." There was no emotion in her voice. Only sadness reflected in her eyes.

"Instead, she chose not to." Damien pressed down on Taegis's arm. "I think that has at least earned her a little bit of trust. However, I still wish to know what is going on."

Lady Selene's eyes darted toward the door. "We don't have much time. She might be coming already to check."

"Who?"

"My mother. You were named a threat to our house. Because of that, I was sent to eliminate you."

"A threat?" Damien furrowed his brow. "How?"

"The Dark Lady said a threat would come from the north and destroy House Ravenwood."

"The Dark Lady . . ."

"So the rumors are true. She *is* the patroness of House Ravenwood," Cohen answered quietly. "A dark and formidable being."

Damien glanced back. "She's real?"

"She exists where she is given power."

"That's not all," Selene continued.

Damien turned back.

"There is an alliance between House Ravenwood, House Friere, and the—the—"

"The what?"

Lady Selene opened and closed her mouth again, then said

something under her breath. "I can't say. That information is bound to my house."

"An alliance? Between Ravenwood, Friere, and . . . the empire?" Damien had suspected something, but not that. Not something so bold. He took a step back, a ringing in his ears.

Caiaphas had been right. The skirmishes along the border, the unexplained deaths amongst some of the houses . . . it was all part of a much bigger plan. No wonder House Ravenwood and House Friere had voted against the treaty. A fire began to burn inside his chest, and his eyes grew hard. Was House Rafel also a part of it? He clenched his hand into a fist. "So what stopped you from killing me? Why did you betray your house?"

Selene turned away. "I'm not a killer. I won't be a part of this. My mother's plans—ambitions—they go too far. I can help you escape. I know a way out of here, a way back to your country. But we must hurry." She glanced back. "If we are caught, I can't help you."

"How can I trust you? And what about the other houses? If what you said is true, then they are all in danger. Shouldn't we help them?"

"We can't. If we leave this room, then we are all dead."

He noted how she included herself in the current danger. By saving his life, Lady Selene had forfeited her own. But why?

He glanced at the outer door, a part of him ready to dash out and warn the other houses. But deep down he knew it was foolhardy. If Caiaphas was right, and it appeared he was, this plan had been in the making for months, if not years. And it seemed Damien was the only one in danger at the moment.

"So the other houses are safe at the moment, yes? You said that you were sent here because of something the Dark Lady said, not because of the alliance between Ravenwood, Friere, and the empire." Saying those names left a bitter taste in his mouth.

Selene lifted her chin. "My mother wasn't sure who was the threat: House Maris or House Vivek. So you were both to be eliminated tonight."

Damien felt like he had been punched in the middle. "House Vivek? Are you saying that someone is killing Lord Rune and Lady Runa right now?"

"Yes. My mother." Selene straightened her shoulders as if gathering her courage back. "And she will soon be here to see that I fulfilled my mission as well. So we need to leave. Now."

"No." His muscles quivered. "I will not leave House Vivek. How could I leave behind the one house that needs our help the most at this time? If House Vivek falls, it will leave a void behind, ready to be filled by the empire."

"And what about your own house?" Selene's eyes flashed, the barest hint he had broken past her cold veneer. "What happens when both House Maris and House Vivek fall? I can't save you both. I can only save one." Her words hitched at the end.

Damien stared at her, his heart pounding, his blood whooshing inside his veins. "And what kind of man would I be to let someone else die?"

"It wouldn't matter if you left at this very moment. They are most likely already dead. My mother is fast and thorough. You would only be throwing away your life, and then there would be fewer houses left. Live, Lord Damien, and find a way to save the people House Vivek leaves behind."

Damien sucked in a breath and turned away. Everything he had done to help House Vivek had been for nothing. Nothing! But there was no way he could have predicted that one of the other houses would turn on them so fiercely. He held an arm across his middle, feeling as though he was going to retch.

"How do we escape?" he heard Taegis ask, his voice cold and controlled.

"There is a tunnel near this room that leads to some old mine shafts connected by an underground river. We will follow it north where the river exits the mountains and feeds into the Hyr River that follows the border between our two countries."

Damien barely listened as he struggled to bring his racing thoughts back together. Lord Rune had a son—a son he had sent off quietly to be raised as a scholar in the libraries of Vivek, but who could still rise up and lead House Vivek and her people. The nation of wisdom still had a chance. But Damien was the only member of House Maris left. If he died, he would leave his people leaderless. He needed to escape, he needed to live. For his people. For Lord Rune's son. For all the nations.

He turned back as Taegis spoke to Selene, his sword still out and ready, just in case. "The Hyr River? How long will it take to get there? And you know the way? We won't find ourselves trapped underground?"

Cohen paled as he watched the exchange. Karl and Sten stared at Selene with distrustful looks.

Selene focused on Damien. "About a day. And yes, I know the way. As a lady of Ravenwood, I know all of the secret passages and recently inspected the one we will be following."

"Then your mother knows the passage as well."

"Yes. That's why we need to leave now. It won't be long before my mother discovers that I—" She blanched and looked away.

Damien crossed his arms. "That you chose not to kill me."

She paused, then nodded.

"All right, then. Let's go." He turned around and reached for his jerkin and belt.

Taegis stepped back, his sword still trained on Lady Selene. "You believe her?" he whispered.

Damien tugged on the leather vest with more force than necessary. "I believe her enough to think we should escape."

"And how do you know she won't turn on you in the tunnels?"

"I don't." He started on the clasps. Perhaps Lady Selene might change her mind and decide that she would rather assassinate him than face the consequences of betraying her house. "That's why we will be taking her swords and you will be protecting me." He finished the last clasp and glanced at Taegis. "What choice do we have?" A painful lump filled his throat. "If what she said is true, and I believe it is, then we need to escape." His hand shook as he placed his belt around his middle, the faces of Lord Rune and Lady Runa hovering along the edges of his mind. He stopped and pressed his eyes shut.

Taegis let out a long breath beside him. "You're right. But I have one request."

"Yes?"

"I want not only her swords taken away, but her hands bound as well."

"I think that is wise. Proceed."

Damien let out a long breath, then cinched his belt tight, looping one end over the other. Cohen appeared moments later, dressed and ready. Taegis gave instructions to Sten and Karl, then proceeded to inform Lady Selene of their decision. Her face paled, but she nodded.

Damien glanced around the room. He needed to focus. There wasn't much time to gather supplies for their getaway, and who knew how long it would take for them to reach one of his villages on the other side of the border once they emerged. He spotted their saddlebags in an empty corner on the other side of the room and headed over to see if there was anything left from their trip here.

After rummaging around, he was able to procure hard biscuits, a sack of barley, and some dried meat. At least it was something. He also grabbed the waterskins and quickly filled them with the water from the washing pitcher. He stuffed the provisions in the smallest saddlebag and hoisted it onto his shoulder.

"All right." He turned around and found Taegis had already taken Lady Selene's weapons away and hidden them, but her hands were still loose. "I gathered a few things for our trip. I'm ready to go." He felt like his heart had been replaced by a bundle of bricks, but he had to keep going. His hand tightened around the saddlebag strap. He would see to it that House Vivek's people were taken care of.

"I'm ready as well." Cohen adjusted his maroon cloak over his clothing with one hand while he held the abbey's book of sacraments with the other. He spotted the saddlebag across Damien's shoulder. "Would you like me to carry the bag?"

Taegis glanced over. "Good thinking on the supplies, my lord. Let Karl or Sten carry the saddlebag."

Damien handed the bag to Karl, grabbed his own sword and sheathed it, then looked at his party. "Taegis, you are in charge of Lady Selene. Sten, Karl, you will assist him. We will each take turns carrying the supplies." He gave each man a firm look. The four men nodded back. "Now, let's go."

36

Damien's question as to why Lady Selene's hands were unbound was answered when Taegis led her to the balcony outside.

Selene headed to the railing and pointed down below. "There is a small cavern beneath this balcony that leads to the mine shafts." She spoke in crisp words, leaving no doubt she had pulled her cold mask back over the troubled woman from moments ago.

Damien was impressed with her ability to change her persona so quickly. No doubt she had trained hard to hide who she was and camouflage her true self. What else did he not know about her?

Taegis stepped up beside her, his sword still drawn. "We will go together." A threat hung in his words. He glanced back. "Then Karl, then you, my lord. Sten and Cohen will follow."

Damien nodded. He watched as Selene gracefully bounded over the railing near the rocky wall and disappeared below. Never had he seen a woman who could move like that. Then again, the women he knew did not sneak into rooms with the intent to murder. He shook his head and followed after Taegis.

Below the balcony was a narrow rocky ledge with a small opening that led into the base of Rook Castle. Taegis and Lady Selene stood just inside the opening. Taegis was currently binding Lady Selene's hands behind her with his belt. Damien stepped to the side as Karl jumped down from the balcony and landed on the ledge.

Cohen followed, his feet landing on the edge of the stone protrusion. He wobbled for a moment before regaining his balance. "No wonder we didn't know about this passage," he said, his voice cracking. "You can't see it from the balcony, and there is hardly a spot to land on." He gave a nervous laugh and stepped inside the cavern as Sten touched down nearby.

As the men and Lady Selene moved into the cavern, Damien glanced back. Moonlight bounced off the craggy Magyr peaks and patches of pale light mingled with the shadows in the valley far below. He turned around and headed into the dark tunnel. The next time he would see the sky, he would be near his own country.

After the first bend, Damien could hardly see and Cohen bumped into him from behind.

"Hold up," Selene said. "There are two torches here, hanging from brackets along the wall. And a flint rock in a tiny opening near one of them. We will want these for our journey."

Damien listened as Taegis felt along the wall. "Found a torch and the flint rock," Taegis said. Moments later, sparks flashed and the torch caught fire, lighting the small space with orange light. Taegis held up the torch and looked back. "Sten, grab the other torch."

"Yes, sir."

With the torch now lighting their way, the small group continued along the low, narrow passage, the crunch of gravel beneath their boots and soft, measured breaths the only sound.

Minutes later, the passage intersected with a wide-open area the size of the bedchamber they had left behind. From here, five passages emerged.

"Which one? Damien asked, his voice echoing inside the cavern.

"The first one on the right," Selene answered. "It will take us to an abandoned mine shaft, which will lead us to the underground river I told you about."

"Where do the others go?" Taegis asked.

Selene glanced back. "Other parts of the mine and castle." Then she turned around and continued toward the passage she had indicated. Taegis stayed next to her, Karl close by. Damien, Sten, and Cohen followed.

Unlike the tunnel they had recently exited, the mine shaft was wider—at least two persons—and tall enough that Taegis's hair barely brushed the top. The air was stale and cool with no smell to it.

Damien remembered his father saying that the mountain nation was once famous for the gems and precious metals that were mined from the caverns that dotted the Magyr Mountains, bringing wealth and prestige to the mountain people. Then the razing happened and the mines dried up, plummeting the mountain nation to near extinction. Even now, the mountain nation was the smallest of the nations, with no house gift, and few resources by which to fund itself. Truly, its only value was its central location to all the other Great Houses and nations.

Damien shook his head. House Ravenwood had used its strategic location to help the Dominia Empire by bringing all of the Great Houses together in one place to gather information and destroy any unity between them.

But in a twisted way, he could understand why. His chest tightened at the thought as their small company plodded along the dark mine shaft. The other Great Houses—including his own—had never bothered to help House Ravenwood. His father had even surmised that long ago the original House Ravenwood had been given over to placate the power-hungry empire, although there were no records of such an exchange.

Now the Great Houses were being handed over to the empire by the very house they had betrayed hundreds of years earlier.

And no one saw it coming.

Except . . .

Damien watched the back of Selene's head. Her dark hair hung in one long braid down the back of her head, reaching almost to her waist. He could barely make out her slender body, hidden by the dark clothing she wore and the shadows that filled the passageway.

Once again he wondered why Lady Selene had chosen to rescue him. Did she not hold the same bitterness the rest of her house did? And what would happen to her after he was in his own country? Would she go back?

He frowned. Back to what? What would Lady Ragna do to her daughter once she discovered Selene's defection? He had promised Caiaphas he would keep his daughter safe. How did he do that in this situation?

Hours later, Taegis called for a rest. The first torch was already halfway gone, and they still had farther to travel. They would need to conserve as much light as possible.

Karl placed the saddlebag on the ground and said something about relieving himself. As he disappeared around the corner, Damien walked over to the saddlebag and pulled out six hard biscuits the size of his palm. He gave one to Taegis and Cohen, then paused in front of Lady Selene. She looked up from where she sat against the wall, fatigue and sweat across her face. Dirt had mixed in with the sweat, causing her to look like she had shadows across her cheeks and below her eyes.

Sten came to his side. "My lord, I can watch Lady Selene so you can eat."

"No, my friend. Go ahead and rest. I will watch her first," Damien said without taking his eyes off Lady Selene. He held up a biscuit for the guard.

Sten paused, then took the biscuit and sat down nearby. Taegis watched from the shadows.

Damien crouched down. "I'm going to untie you so you can eat. Don't do anything rash."

"I won't," she said in a flat voice, then she twisted her body around so he could access her bound hands.

Damien frowned. Perhaps those dark circles were more than dirt and fatigue. He still did not have his answer as to why she was doing this, or what would happen to her afterward.

She can't go back, he thought as he undid the belt wound around her wrists. *She betrayed her house. Lady Ragna will not show mercy, not even to her own daughter. But can I really bring her to the Northern Shores? By her own words, she was originally sent to assassinate me. Can I trust her not to fulfill her mission?*

He stepped back as she brought her hands around and rubbed her wrists. "Here." He held out the hard biscuit. She took it without looking at him and began to nibble on the edges.

Damien watched her, waiting for . . . what? For her to suddenly run? For her to lunge toward him? Instead, she slowly ate the biscuit, pausing at one point when he swore he saw a tear in the corner of her eye.

She finished the rest, then wiped her hands on her thighs. "I, uh . . ." Her face darkened. "I need to relieve myself."

Oh. He hadn't thought about that. "I'll come with you."

Her head snapped up. "What?"

"My lord," Taegis said, taking a step forward.

"I'll have my back turned, but I'm not letting you go alone."

Her face darkened further, but she nodded and stood. Damien felt his own face flushing. He had never been around many women, just his mother and the servants, and the few times he'd visited Lady Adalyn and Lady Bryren. But this was different. He didn't even know . . .

Damien abruptly stood and motioned to Lady Selene. "There's a spot we passed a few minutes ago that should do."

Selene didn't bother to acknowledge his words. Instead, she walked hurriedly in the direction he had pointed. There was enough torchlight to see the small hollow, but also enough shadows to provide privacy.

Damien followed until he was a short distance away, then turned around and waited, hoping with all his might she would not do anything reckless.

A minute later, she emerged. "Thank you," she mumbled, then headed back toward the light.

Damien let out a sigh of relief as his shoulders sagged. Never had he thought about the difficulties of traveling with a woman.

After passing around the waterskins and securing Lady Selene's hands, Damien quickly ate his own biscuit. "All right," he said as he wiped the crumbs off his pants. "Let's keep going for a little longer."

Sten grabbed the saddlebag and gave the unlit torch to Karl.

"My lady," Karl said, a hint of sarcasm in his voice as he took a step back and waved for Lady Selene to lead the way with Taegis.

She made no indication that she had caught the guard's disrespectful tone. Damien frowned at Karl. Yes, Lady Selene was the enemy, but there was no reason to treat her in such a way. He would speak to Taegis about that.

Damien started after them, Cohen and Sten behind him. More

hours passed as they went deeper and deeper into the mountains. At times the passageway became jagged, and they had to carefully make their way along the broken path. Other times the tunnel narrowed to the point where they had to stoop down. Damien could hear Cohen breathing heavily during those periods and felt the same sense of panic inside his own chest.

"How much longer?" Cohen asked breathlessly as he ducked to avoid a particularly jagged point.

Lady Selene paused. "We are almost to the underground river."

"Thank the Light," Cohen muttered behind Damien. "I feel like the mountains are going to fall on us."

"How much farther after that?" Damien asked. Having already lost almost a night's sleep and walking for hours, he was exhausted and was sure he wasn't the only one.

"A couple more hours" was her reply.

"Only a couple of hours?" Taegis said in disbelief. "It took us nearly three full days to travel from the border of our country to Rook Castle."

"Yes, but you were traveling across the mountain roads. Here, underground, there aren't as many obstacles, and we follow almost a straight path."

"Can you travel this way to any of the other nations?" Damien asked.

She didn't answer for a moment, but Damien caught her mouth moving from the side of her face in the torchlight. Her shoulders sagged. "I-I can't say."

Interesting. That information was a house secret, one she was not permitted to speak of. What other secrets did Lady Selene have locked away? "Do you think they are pursuing us yet?"

"Yes." There was no hesitation in her voice.

"And which way are they coming? By tunnel or by mountain?"

"I'm not sure. It depends on who my mother sends and if they know these tunnels. She might even send a raven to one of the strongholds at the base of the mountain."

Damien grew quiet as he thought. Did they have time to rest? Or should they push on? Karl stumbled in front of him, barely catching himself before walking again. They needed at least a moment of reprieve. And they would probably make better time refreshed than they were making now.

The subtle sound of water drifted through the tunnel. "Do you think we have time to rest?" Damien asked.

Selene was quiet for a moment. "Perhaps. A few hours maybe."

"I think we need it."

"Good idea," Taegis replied, his voice muffled ahead. "Should our pursuers catch up we will need our strength to fight or outrun them."

Sten grunted in agreement behind him.

The sound of water grew louder. Ahead, the mine shaft opened up into a wide cavern. Upon exiting the tunnel, a blast of cool, misty air hit Damien's face. The ceiling rose at least two stories above them, dotted by jagged rocks. At the far end of the cavern, a narrow river rushed by. There was a platform near the water's edge with old barrels, carts, and a large wooden contraption the size of a wagon, all leftover equipment from when the mines were active.

The group approached the platform. Farther down, a thin stone ledge followed the river along one side. Yes, they would definitely want to rest before walking along that path.

"This looks like a good place to stop." Damien wiped the sweat from his face as Sten lowered the saddlebag onto the ground near the platform and rolled his shoulders.

Taegis came up beside him. "I'll take the first watch."

"I'll let you do that," Damien replied. He felt like he could fall asleep on his feet. He glanced at Lady Selene as she looked around, her hands bound behind her back. "I'm sorry," he said, catching her attention. "But I must insist on keeping your hands tied."

She lifted her chin. "I understand."

However, he could make it a bit more comfortable for her. He removed his jerkin, bundled it up, and laid it on the ground near the wall. "Here. Cohen, you sleep near the tunnel we just left. I'll lay down by the riverside. Sten, Karl, spread out."

"I'm going to stay right here," Taegis said, taking a seat across from Lady Selene and between Cohen and Damien. He braced his arm along his knee and held the newly lit torch.

Lady Selene struggled down onto her knees, then turned around and placed her head on the jerkin, keeping her back to the men. Damien lay on his back nearby, his arms behind his head, and closed his eyes. But no matter how tired he was, sleep did not come.

The top of Lady Selene's head was a few feet from his, the orange glow from the torch reflecting off her dark hair.

I couldn't do it.

Her words echoed again inside his head. She said House Ravenwood saw him as a threat and she had been sent to eliminate him. How was he a threat? His brow furrowed. His only desire had been to unite the houses against the empire. If House Ravenwood had indeed aligned itself with the Dominia Empire, then yes, he would be a threat. But he would have first tried to negotiate with them. This whole situation did not seem strong enough to warrant assassinating him or House Vivek. There seemed to be more going on—even more than some prophecy uttered by the Dark Lady.

Damien sighed and rolled over. He frowned as he stared at Lady Selene, now curled up in a ball. What made her stop? She had been in his room tonight with her swords, which meant she had come with the intention to fulfill her mission. But she didn't. So why? Every Great House he knew owed its allegiance first and foremost to itself, evident by the closing remarks of each house yesterday. Even his own house, by aligning with the others, benefited from that alliance. With her disobedience, Lady Selene had broken the fundamental rule of every Great House and thus had forfeited her life.

All to save him.

He couldn't help but be impressed at her courage, and he was reminded again of how little he knew about her.

Her breathing steadied into slow, even breaths. At least she could sleep.

He watched her a moment longer, then shifted onto his back and closed his eyes. What did she plan on doing next? Did she plan on going back? She would be most likely executed for treason against House Ravenwood. Or had she hoped to disappear into the mountains? But she had no supplies.

You could provide her sanctuary in the Northern Shores, a quiet voice whispered.

He opened his eyes and sat up. Yes, he could do that. It would not help his relationship with House Ravenwood, but there was no salvaging that relationship now that they had tried to kill him.

"My lord?" Taegis said quietly. "Are you all right?"

"Yes, Taegis. Just plagued by thoughts." Damien settled back down and closed his eyes again as sleep drifted toward him. He returned to his earlier musings. Yes, he would be happy to offer Lady Selene sanctuary in his country. After what she had done to save him, it was the least he could do. But they would have to cross the border quickly, before their pursuers showed up and he was forced to raise the water-wall to protect Selene. And his people.

There is a way to make her a part of your people, that same voice whispered from earlier.

He squeezed his eyes shut. No. He would find a way to save her. He would not let Selene drown by his power, even to save himself. But there had to be another way. Any way but that.

37

Selene woke up to someone shaking her by the shoulder in the darkness.

"Time to go," Damien said close by.

It took her a moment to remember where she was. She pushed herself up and blinked as the dull roar of the nearby river filled her ears and her senses acclimated to the dark mine. Her arms and wrists ached from the odd posture her bound hands put her in.

His hand moved from her shoulder to her upper arm. "Here, let me help you up."

She struggled to her feet and shook out her legs. Taegis, Damien's personal guard, seemed as though he had just woken up, as he sat up and ran a hand over his face. The guard with the dark curly hair stooped down and grabbed the saddlebag nearby, the last remaining torch in his other hand. The monk and the other, shorter guard were also waking up on the other side of the cavern.

"Did something happen while I was asleep?" Taegis asked, coming to full attention. Damien and Taegis must have switched duties while she slept because she remembered Damien falling asleep when she did.

"No, but . . ." Damien looked back toward the tunnel they had left. "I feel like we need to go, and the sooner the better."

"You've always had an instinct for danger." Taegis stood to his feet and Karl handed him the torch. "Probably due to your gift."

Gift? Selene looked up sharply. She knew very little of House Maris's gift, other than that it was connected to water. But if Damien could sense danger, why had he never sensed her those nights she visited his room? Or maybe he never sensed danger because he was never in danger. . . .

Damien glanced at her. "Which way?" he asked. "I'm assuming it's the path that follows the river over there."

"Yes." She carefully brought her face back to her normal impassive look.

Taegis lifted the torch and headed for the river. Selene followed, taking up her position from yesterday. Karl followed close behind her, along with Damien, the monk, and the other guard.

Only a few hours left before they reached the end of the tunnel and the edge of the Magyr Mountains. Then she would see Lord Damien safely across the river. No doubt her mother had already sent a contingent of guards after them, and the chances they would meet up with them once they exited the mountain grew with each passing hour, which meant her chances of escaping after she left Damien grew slim as well. Not that she ever really had a chance. Her last-minute choice to save him left her no time to plan or pack anything. In truth, it was a suicide mission. From the moment she was caught, it would only be a matter of time before her mother's swift and decisive wrath would end her life.

The very thought choked her. She knew deep down when she chose to help Lord Damien that it would most likely end her life, but as the reality of it all sank in, fear overtook the rational part of her mind.

She licked her lips and stared at the torchlight ahead. What was on the other side of death? The Dark Lady? Something else? The Light, like the one that illuminated Damien's soul?

She liked the last thought the best. But she also knew her soul was too dark to exist in such a place. No, most likely she would finally encounter the Dark Lady and be made to pay for her defection from her house and from her patroness.

She bit down on her lip to keep from crying while her body surged with cold adrenaline. *I'm stronger than this. I can do this.* She watched the flame from the torch, the way it moved, the way its light danced across the wall. Just like Damien's soulsphere.

Slowly, her body relaxed as she watched the light. She couldn't forget why she was doing this. Even if she did not carry light inside of her, she would protect it. For Ophie. For her people. Even for Amara.

Fear tinted the edges of her mind, but she held fast to her resolve and watched the torchlight.

The river roared to their right, rushing along toward the surface. The travelers hurried along the path. Selene did her best to keep up, but exhaustion, emotional whiplash from the last few days, and being unaccustomed to such long treks made her feet feel like lead. And she could sense the growing anxiety of her companions.

"How much farther?" Lord Damien asked behind her.

Selene mentally pictured one of the secret map vellums from the castle and her own knowledge of the mountain path. "We're almost to the exit. Once we leave the tunnel, it's less than a mile to the Hyr River and your country."

"I didn't realize we would be so close to the border once we left this place."

"Yes. This path was used to deliver our mining goods to the north back when our mines were still operational."

"I see. Good."

She heard the relief in his voice, and her stomach twisted. Soon Lord Damien and his companions would be across the border, safe in the country of the Northern Shores. And she . . .

She would buy the men as much time as they needed to cross. It was a small comfort, but not much, and even the torchlight could not stop the shaking of her limbs or the cold clamminess spreading across her palms.

What would Mother say of her now? Where was her boldness? Her courage? No, she had always possessed small, cowardly thoughts.

Just think of the light. Selene swallowed. *Remember what you're saving.* She breathed in and out and used her training to force her fear back until the tight invisible cords around her loosened.

A half hour later, light appeared at the far end of the tunnel. The brightness seemed to inspire the men. Taegis walked faster, and Selene could feel the others pressing in behind her.

"Thank the Light." Cohen panted behind her. "We're almost to the surface."

"Yes," the other guard—Sten?— replied. She heard relief and an almost happy note in his voice.

Selene's stomach whooshed, as if she had missed a step on her way down a staircase. *I can do this.* She clenched her hands behind her. *I can finish what I started. I will see Lord Damien to his country. I only ask one thing, please save my people, especially Ophie. I won't be around to help her anymore. And Renata.*

She blinked, startled by the change in her thoughts. Who was she praying to? Lord Damien? The Light? Whatever deity was listening? Whoever it was, whoever heard her petition, all she asked was for the people she cared about most to be protected when she was gone.

At the cave's entrance, a forest of conifer and brightly colored deciduous trees spread out along the base of the Magyr Mountains as far as the eye could see, like a patchwork quilt of many fabrics. Colorful leaves of red, orange, and yellow littered the forest floor, while up above the sky was a deep blue. Beyond the trees and below the cave's exit, the Hyr River flowed, marking the boundary between the mountain and sea nations.

The air was cool and held a woodsy smell. Birds chirruped nearby, unaware of the strangers who had just left the underground. And the sun . . . She sighed. The autumn sun felt so good against her face.

Selene stopped and looked over the valley. So beautiful. So achingly beautiful. She caught sight of Damien nearby taking in a deep breath, a satisfied look on his face. For the first time, a sad smile spread across her lips. Did he feel it too? The beauty of this place?

Selene closed her eyes. She wanted to soak in this moment, let it fill her and carry her.

She felt someone watching her. She opened her eyes to find Damien's gaze on her, an understanding look on his face.

"Feels good, doesn't it?" he said quietly. "To be outside."

"Yes," Selene said, withdrawing back into herself.

He stepped closer toward her. The others were gathering outside the cave. Taegis was studying the landscape below, while Karl dug around in the saddlebag. "Listen, I need to ask you something. What did you plan on doing when we—"

A horn blasted through the forest.

Damien whipped around, his words forgotten.

Selene's heart flew up into her throat as the warm feelings vanished, leaving behind that familiar deep chill. She looked up toward the mountains, her face grim. Their time was up. Given where the horn had come from, her mother had sent word to the nearest garrison, and the guards were on their way.

A horn blew again, the sound bouncing across the hills.

"Dart'an," Selene said under her breath. They would be able to reach the border, but barely. "It looks like they found us." She glanced at Damien. "You don't have much time. You need to make a run for it."

"And what about you?"

"What about me?" she answered carefully. Did he not know?

"What were you planning to do once we reached the end of the cave?"

"My goal was to get you as far as I could. Now I have."

"And then what?"

Her nostrils flared. "We don't have time for this. You need to go! Now!"

"Then come with us."

Selene glared at him. "What do you mean?"

"If you stay, you'll be captured. But if you go with me, I can provide sanctuary for you in my country."

Sanctuary? He would provide sanctuary for her?

"Lord Damien, we must go," Taegis said, pointing toward the Hyr River.

Damien stepped behind her and began to undo the leather belt that held her wrists together. "I won't leave Lady Selene."

"My lord!" Karl exclaimed as he looked their way. "You cannot free her. She poses a threat to you, and our pursuers—"

"I won't leave her here to die," he said to Karl. Damien finished untying the belt and stood in front of Selene. "All you have to do is come with me."

Safety from her mother. A chance at a new life.

"What if she tries to stop us?" Karl said, his voice rising in pitch.

"Come with us," Cohen said, coming around her right side. "Lord Maris is a very kind man and takes good care of his people. He will protect you."

The horn sounded again, making Selene's heart thrash inside her chest. "I—" She glanced back. "I—"

If she lived, she would always be in danger. Her mother would hunt her down to the ends of the world. But . . . She looked back and found Lord Damien staring intently at her. With all her heart she wanted that light he carried within his soul. She would do anything to have it. But she would never have that chance if she didn't go with him.

Death lay behind her. And life lay before her.

She knew her answer, and it carried her through. "Yes."

He nodded and grabbed her hand. "Good. Let's go."

Before she could say anything more, he turned and started running downhill in the direction of the river. His hand was warm and strong, and he guided her as they crashed through the leaves and branches and dodged fallen logs. Distant shouts joined the horn blaring across the valley. Taegis and Karl ran on either side of them, Cohen and Sten behind.

"Once we reach the river, I will put up the water boundary," Damien said.

"Water boundary?" Selene said and sucked in another lungful of air.

"Yes. There's only one problem. . . ."

She glanced over at him. There was a pensive look on his face, tightening his features. Whatever the problem was, it seemed to be weighing more on him than their pursuers.

Selene breathed heavily and glanced back. She couldn't see them yet, but they couldn't be far behind.

She ran faster, keeping up with Damien. The two sped across the forest, her actions just a second behind his own. When he jumped over a log, she followed. When he ducked to avoid a tree or a low-hanging branch, she went with him.

And he never let go.

With each step, she felt like she was leaving hopelessness behind. Each step lighter than the one before. Instead of heading toward death, she was running toward life. Toward sanctuary. Toward haven. Toward . . .

The light.

Such a torrent of relief flooded through her that laughter threatened to burst from her lips. And tears. Lots of tears. She could feel them streaming down her face, mingling with the sweat as she panted and ran.

Is this what Damien felt in his soul? Is this what the Light felt like? If so, she would grab on to it with both hands and never let go.

They reached the edge of the water where the underground river and the Hyr River converged. Water rushed over rocks in a spray of white waves, crashing across the land as it made its way to the sea. Washed-up debris, logs, and boulders lined the riverbank. Damien paused and stared at the river as if he were studying it.

"Is there a way across?" Taegis asked.

Damien nodded and pointed toward a sandbar to the left. "We can cross there, away from the tributary. The water isn't too deep, and there aren't any boulders."

The travelers hurried toward the sandbar. Selene's heart thudded inside her chest. She could almost hear their pursuers crashing through the forest behind them.

Damien dashed across the sand and into the water. Selene followed, her hand still in his. She gasped at the cold intensity. Moments later, her feet and legs grew numb as she trudged across the river. Damien seemed to know where every foothold was beneath the water as he guided her across. She only slipped once but caught herself before going down.

At the halfway point, the water reached her waist, and Damien let go of her hand. Holding out both arms, she slogged through the icy waters. Her teeth began to chatter and every wave made her flinch.

The waterline receded on the other side of the river. Damien scrambled up the rocky bank first, then turned and held out his hand. Selene grabbed hold and scuttled up behind him. Taegis followed with Cohen and the other two guards panting behind him. They climbed onto a wide, flat rock, dripping wet and teeth chattering.

Selene wrapped her arms around her middle, hugging as much warmth as she could to herself. Cohen did the same, his maroon robes clinging to his thin body. Damien stood still, his eyes narrowed as he searched the far bank and forest.

The horn sounded again, much closer.

Taegis swore under his breath. "What do we do?" he asked, glancing at Damien. "We don't have time to get Lady Selene far enough away from the riverbank."

"I know." Damien closed his eyes and sucked in a long breath through his nose.

"We should have left her behind," Karl said under his breath.

"Not another word, Karl," Taegis barked.

Damien didn't answer.

Selene watched their exchange, the familiar tendrils of ice wrapping around her heart. What did Taegis mean about getting her far enough away from the riverbank? Did it have to do with Lord Damien's power—

His dream of that stormy day came back to her in vivid clarity: a wall of seawater, the Dominia ships rising in the air, dead men floating on the surface. And his fear that he would kill again with his power.

If he raised the water here and now, he would not only take out the men following them.

His power would kill her too.

Damien opened his eyes and stared at Selene with a severe, serious look on his face. Like he had a hard decision to make.

The invisible tendrils inside her grew stronger, gripping her from within, squeezing her chest until she couldn't breathe. It felt like the trees were closing in on her and the rushing of the river was deafening. Karl was right. He should have left her at the cave. Instead, she had foolishly given in to hope.

Her face blanched, and everything began to spin around her. It had all been just a dream. For a brief moment she had believed she would live. What a fool she had been.

"I promised your father I would protect you."

Selene blinked. "Protect me?"

Damien ran a hand along the back of his neck. "But there is no time to get you far enough from the river. Once I raise the river boundary, the water will sweep you away along with our pursuers."

"I see." The gift of House Maris was one of protection. Damien could protect his people with water. But she wasn't a part of his people. She wasn't a part of any people now. She swallowed. "I understand." She looked across the river. She had a small amount of time to cross back and hopefully slow down the men chasing them.

"But if you marry me, the waters will see you as part of me."

Her head jerked back. "What? What did you say?" Did she hear him right?

The tendons stuck out along his neck as he glanced back across the river. "It's the only way I can save all of us. I need to raise the boundary now, but I can't with you here."

"But we're both heirs of our houses. It's not done." And he would know of House Ravenwood's secrets.

He would know she was a dreamer.

Taegis stepped forward. "Wait, Lord Damien, are you sure about this?"

He held up his hand toward his guardian, his gaze on her. She could see it in his eyes. He was not asking her out of love. He did not want this. But he was offering himself to her.

To save her.

"Cohen, do you know the rites of matrimony?" Damien asked without looking at the priest.

"Matrimony?" Cohen said.

"I'm taking Lady Selene as my wife. Unless you object?" he asked, his question directed to her.

"Lord Maris," Taegis said again. "*Damien!*"

Karl and Sten looked on in shock.

Selene couldn't speak. This wasn't happening. Things were moving fast, so fast she couldn't seem to catch her own thoughts.

Damien grabbed her hands and pulled her closer to him. "Yes . . . or no."

Something rose inside of her. One desperate gasp for hope. It roared inside her chest, bringing life and warmth back to her limbs. She would do anything—*anything*—to live and take hold of the Light. Even marry a man she did not love. After all, none of the women of Ravenwood ever married for love. She would be no exception. She would even risk the fact that Lord Damien would find out about her gift.

It was worth it.

Heart racing and throat dry, she looked into his eyes and nodded.

38

Damien's heart pounded inside his ears. Lady Selene said yes. Or at least she nodded. He would take that as a yes. "Perform the rites, Cohen."

Cohen stepped forward, his eyes wide as he stared at Damien. "My lord, are you sure?"

"Yes, and we haven't much time." Already he felt panic bubbling up his throat, and every nerve in his body screamed for him to stop. But deep down, he knew this was the only way. He couldn't leave Lady Selene behind, and he certainly would not drown her with his own power. He might not love her, but he would not be her executioner. Many other houses married for reasons other than love. Saving her was his reason.

Cohen took his place in front of the couple. Damien positioned Lady Selene in front of him, then clasped her hands between his own and lifted them between their bodies.

Taegis stood nearby, worry etched across his face. Sten appeared stoic, and Karl sported a terrible scowl. At least they had the three witnesses required for a marriage, even if some of them were unwilling.

Damien focused on Lady Selene as Cohen began to chant the

rites. Her face was pale and her fingers chilled. When he had imagined his wedding day, this was not what he thought it would be. Nor the woman who he thought would be in front of him. But here he was, and this bond would be for the rest of his life. *Well, Caiaphas, you got what you wanted. I'm marrying your daughter.*

The words Cohen spoke were simple. A pledge between himself and Selene to honor and love each other, to serve the Light, and seek no others. Then Cohen switched over to the ancient tongue as warmth began to spread between their palms.

At the sensation, Selene's eyes widened. Damien frowned. Didn't she know what would happen during the bonding? That their souls would soon be connected?

His heart beat faster, and he closed his eyes. The moment they joined, he would know her, and she would know him.

I have a duty to my people, and to the people of this land. By marrying Lady Selene, I will know Ravenwood's secrets, which might help us against the empir—

Damien barely heard the last words of the rite. His eyes flew open, and he stared at the young woman in front of him. The moment the last word was spoken, a flame flew up between their joined hands. In that instant, he knew her—all of her. The very essence of who she was.

And he knew her power.

"You . . ." Damien took a step back, his mind barely comprehending the truth the bonding had just bestowed on him. "You can't be . . ."

Selene was deathly pale, her pupils large and dark.

At Taegis's shout, Damien shook his head and let go of Lady Selene's hands. He tried to clear his mind, but all he could feel was the impression of her power.

She was a—but she couldn't be! They were all dead!

Focus, Damien!

A hundred feet from the river, their pursuers appeared between the trees. At least twenty men in all, dressed in the black and purple colors of House Ravenwood and approaching fast.

For a split second, Damien thought of yelling out to them, to warn them to stop and turn back. But that would bring them too close, and if some were carrying bows, they would most likely start shooting.

He had no choice. He needed to raise the barrier now.

Drawing on the ancient power inside of him, Damien held out his hands toward the river. He curled his fingers and readied his arms to raise the boundary.

One . . . two . . . three.

He gave a great shout and brought his hands up. A massive weight pulled down on his arms as the river steadily rose into the air, foot by foot. Every tendon bulged, every muscle was tight as he brought the river up. Blood rushed through his body, and his face grew hot. Sweat began to trickle down the sides of his cheeks and forehead.

Through the stream of running water, he could see their pursuers caught by the raging tidal wave on the other side. Like an enraged monster, the water tore through the men, whipping them into the air in a frenzy of white waves and foam, and dragged them to the left and down the riverbank. Their screams were barely audible above the roaring water as the river marked them as enemies to House Maris and wiped them out.

Damien swallowed, his muscles quivering under the weight of the river. Spray from the water washed over his face. It didn't matter that the rational side of him knew those men had come for either him or Lady Selene—or both. He could only feel regret. His power had once again taken lives.

Was this what it meant to have a protective gift? That in order for some to live others had to die?

Why, Light, why?

The moment the water-wall reached thirty feet, Damien thrust out his hands and twisted his wrists. The boundary was now set, a barrier that extended along the entire Hyr River and could only be brought down by him. He and his people were safe from House Ravenwood, or any other house for that matter for as long as the river barrier remained locked.

Selene was safe.

He stumbled and fell to his knees, breathing in deep draughts of air. The pull of both the sea-wall and the river-wall were hitting him hard. Taegis came to stand beside him, sword drawn, ready to protect his lord. Sten and Karl also took a defensive stance. But there was no need. There was no one left on the other side of the riverbank.

Damien held a fist to his mouth as bile rose up his throat. His eye caught a shadow on his right, and he glanced over to find Lady Selene staring down at him.

He slowly rose to his feet and let his arm drop. His body felt like it would collapse beneath him, but he kept his back rigid.

"You . . . the river . . . those men." Selene glanced at the river-wall, her fingers brushing her parted lips. "I had no idea your gift was that powerful." She looked back at him, her face a strange array of emotions. "Thank you." She visibly swallowed. "Thank you for not letting the river take me."

Damien nodded, too tired to do much else. He wiped his face with the back of his hand and sat down on a slab of stone.

Slowly, his heart rate returned to normal, and his body cooled. His mind also returned. He glanced up to find Selene's back to him, her arms wrapped around her body, staring at the river-wall while Taegis hovered close by her with a concerned look on his face.

Now he knew why Caiaphas had been so adamant about an

arranged marriage between Damien and his daughter, why he believed Lady Selene Ravenwood was the person who could unite the Great Houses. It was the one secret Caiaphas could not reveal about the Ravenwood family.

Lady Selene was a dreamer.

"It will take a couple of hours on foot for us to reach the small village of Riveram," Taegis said to Damien five minutes later. "We will most likely find lodging and provisions there. Do you need to rest or should we push on? If you are still exhausted from raising the barrier—"

"No. I'm fine." Damien stood up. His strength would not fully return until he took one of the barriers down, but he could certainly walk for a little longer. He could see the exhaustion on the faces of his men—as well as Lady Selene's—and knew something more than the cold, hard earth would go a long way toward helping them regain their strength for the long trek home.

"All right, then." Taegis turned to Sten, Karl, and Cohen. "Time to go." He turned toward Selene. "My lady, are you ready?"

Damien frowned as he spotted Selene standing away from the others. Her cold mask was back in place. "Yes," she said, lifting her chin, her arms still tight across her middle.

Taegis seemed taken aback by her cold, abrupt answer. Karl scowled and looked away.

Damien opened his mouth to say something, then stopped. Beneath the mask, he could see it. She was afraid. The way her chin quivered slightly, the way she refused to look at anyone, the way her fingers dug into her arms. She had just left her home and bonded with a man she hardly knew. Her coldness was understandable.

His own fear kept him rooted as well. He wanted to speak to her. So many questions filled his mind as he tried to sort through what he had learned the moment they bonded. But this was not the place to speak, not with others around.

Cohen walked up to her side and gave her a soft smile. "Welcome to the Northern Shores, my lady. If there is anything I can do to make you feel more at ease, or if you have any questions, please let me know."

She gave him a firm nod, but Damien noted the glistening in her eyes as she looked back toward the river, back toward her homeland. As her gaze swept forward, her eyes stopped on him, and they stared at each other for a moment. Once again, he felt her heart, her mind, her power. Impressions imprinted on his soul. He didn't understand how her dream power worked, but he knew it existed inside of her, just as he knew she had been forced to keep it a secret. Just as she knew of the power that existed inside of him.

Two souls, now one.

The moment was broken when Taegis came to stand beside him.

"Sten, Karl, lead the way," Taegis said as he stopped beside Damien. "Cohen, you and Lady Selene will follow. Lord Damien and I will bring up the rear. Trader's Road should be a little beyond these trees. We'll follow it to Riveram."

The two guards headed for the forest opposite the riverbank after Sten grabbed the saddlebag. The river-wall roared behind them as it kept its vigil over the land of House Maris. Damien could feel the wall siphoning his power to feed itself. Same with the ocean barrier that still circled the coast. He could live with both—barely—but erecting another water barrier would take its toll on him. Hopefully these two were enough for the time being.

The sun sparkled through the colorful forest, and every few minutes a bird sang. Damien watched Lady Selene as she walked alongside Cohen. Her braided dark hair dangled down her back, swishing across her cloak with every step.

A dreamer.

He shook his head, still unable to believe it. Had a true member of Ravenwood survived the razing? How else could the gift still exist? If so, why did they hide it all of these years?

What did this mean for the other Great Houses? Could she really unite them?

What did this mean for him? For Lady Selene?

No, not lady anymore. Not to him.

Wife.

The word brought on a whole new array of feelings, making his stomach clench and his heart beat faster. When he came into the title of grand lord, he knew a little of how to rule a country, but at least he knew something. But marriage? He swallowed. This was something of which he had no knowledge or experience.

Not in his wildest dreams did he think he would be coming home from the assembly with a wife at his side. The same woman who two nights ago had been sent to assassinate him. The woman who would one day be the mother of his children. Their children. Both House Maris and House Ravenwood.

Selene turned her head and spoke to Cohen. He smiled back and answered her.

Something shifted inside of Damien and his breath quickened. Selene was an enigma. She possessed a hidden strength that he'd witnessed when she chose to spare him at the expense of her own life and at the moment of their bonding. He couldn't help but admire her for it. And she was beautiful in a dark, secretive sort of way. And cold, but the more he watched her, the more he knew that wasn't her true self.

These thoughts and feelings weren't enough on which to build a solid marriage. But maybe Caiaphas was right. Perhaps it was possible that Selene could become more than a marriage partner. They might also become allies in the upcoming conflict. The Light knew he would need allies, especially with the treaty unsigned and the chaos that undoubtedly ensued once he failed to show up for the treaty signing and they found House Vivek dead.

Damien would have to start all over again in building alliances with the other houses. He would need help. He would need a partner. And his new wife might be the one to help him—and all of the Great Houses.

And perhaps through the process he might even learn to love her.

39

Lady Ragna paced the length of her bedchambers, waiting for the messenger from the Vanguard Garrison at the northern base of the Magyr Mountains. Sunshine streamed through the windows, spilling light across the ornate rugs and stone floor. She couldn't linger here long. The other houses were convening today to discuss the absence of House Maris and the sudden deaths of Lord Rune and Lady Runa Vivek.

She had an answer for House Vivek's deaths, but she wanted more information before she fabricated a tale about Lord Maris. Or perhaps she wouldn't even need to, depending on what she found out.

She turned and paced the other direction, one hand against her forehead. She rubbed her temple where the tension was strongest. Did she go wrong somewhere? Had she underestimated Selene's talent? Did Lord Damien abduct her daughter? But how? Captain Stanton had found Selene's swords underneath Lord Damien's bed, but no sign of a struggle, nothing to indicate Selene had been attacked.

Did they find and grab her while she was dreamwalking?

Lady Ragna turned the other way. She herself had come close

once to being caught. But Selene would have fought. And there would have been evidence of such—a rug shoved across the floor, or perhaps blood. But there was nothing, not one piece of evidence to support that idea. Which then begged the question, did Selene defect?

Ragna stopped. Was that a possibility?

She clenched her hands and stared out the window.

Although powerful, Selene appeared to have a hard time disconnecting herself from her dream victims. Lady Ragna thought her daughter was improving, but what if Lord Damien had been more than Selene could handle as a new dreamkiller? The young lord was a notable follower of the old ways, of the Light. Had she underestimated Lord Damien? Had his dreamscape proven to be too much, like his father before him?

"Maybe I should have left House Vivek to Selene and done away with Lord Maris myself," Lady Ragna murmured. Not that Lord Rune or his sister had been easy victims. Their minds and gifts of wisdom had made navigating their dreamscapes difficult.

Knock. Knock.

Lady Ragna looked up. Had the messenger finally arrived?

The door cracked open, and the guard looked in. "I'm sorry, my lady, but the priest—"

The door flung all the way open and the young guard was thrust aside. In the doorway stood the priest of the Dark Lady, clad in a long black robe, his cowl pulled low over his head, shadowing his eyes.

"Wise one." Lady Ragna bowed before the old priest.

"Lady Ragna," he said in a raspy voice. "We must speak. Alone."

Lady Ragna waved dismissively toward the guard. "Leave us."

"My lady?" he said. "Captain Stanton ordered—"

"I am ordering you to leave this room now and close the door behind you."

With an exasperated look, the guard bowed and left, making sure to shut the door behind him. She knew Captain Stanton feared for her safety, hence the added security. It was an annoyance, but one she could not dismiss. The captain had no idea that she could take care of herself, so she went along with his overbearing caution.

"The Dark Lady has brought another message." The priest made his way along the floor toward the center of the room. A chill seemed to follow him.

"Another message?"

"Yes. It seems the threat from the north has grown more certain."

Lady Ragna sucked in a breath. "How? I took care of House Vivek. Is it because House Maris escaped?"

The priest lifted his head, revealing his watery blue eyes. A slip of white hair hung down across his wrinkled forehead. "The hope from the north has survived. The same hope that will unite the Great Houses, but also be the downfall of House Ravenwood."

Lady Ragna's body tightened. She knew it! She should have been the one to take out House Maris. "It's House Maris, isn't it? I chose the wrong house. I should have taken care of both of them myself."

"And there is more. Lady Selene is no longer part of House Ravenwood."

She looked up. "What do you mean? I have yet to receive word back from the Vanguard Garrison about Lord Maris or my daughter. Is Selene dead?"

"No. She has joined House Maris."

"Joined . . . House Maris?" The words sank in, leaving a hollow feeling inside her belly. "My daughter . . . joined House Maris?" The room began to spin. Not only had her daughter failed to destroy the threat to their house, she had aligned with the enemy.

Lady Ragna ground her teeth and glared at the priest. "What do you mean *joined*? Tell me plainly what the Dark Lady said."

The chill in the room grew stronger, and the hairs along Lady Ragna's arms stood on end.

The priest seemed even taller as he stood before Lady Ragna. "A union has formed between Lady Selene and Lord Damien. The hope of the Great Houses still burns brightly. And if not stopped, the downfall of House Ravenwood is certain."

"Selene married Lord Damien?" Lady Ragna stumbled back toward the chair near the empty fireplace. "But why?" she whispered. What had transpired between the two of them that her daughter went from killing him to marrying him? Was there something she had missed? Her heart sank even further.

"If they have indeed bonded, then Lord Damien knows . . ." She covered her lips with her hand. Her whole body tingled with adrenaline. Her mind felt like it had crashed into a stone wall.

Lord Damien knew their secrets. He knew their gift.

The tingling turned to a fiery burn. Her hands began to shake as she turned back toward the priest. "Why did the Dark Lady keep this hidden from me? Why didn't she tell me it would be House Maris? If I had known, I could have gone after Lord Damien myself." Fire burst inside of her, sending her to her feet. She stared at the priest, her hands clenched at her sides. "Why?"

"The ways of the Dark Lady are a mystery." The priest folded his hands in front of his robes.

"Or could it be she didn't know?" Lady Ragna said before she could stop herself.

His eyes flared. "The Dark Lady does as she pleases."

"At the expense of losing the prestige she has gained here? If House Ravenwood falls, then the Dark Lady falls with us."

The priest glared at her for a moment. "I do not know," he

conceded. "Perhaps she is bound as well by a higher power. Perhaps her vision was clouded."

A higher power? Did he mean the Light? Lady Ragna crossed her arms and shivered. Up until now, the Dark Lady had brought secrets and power to House Ravenwood. And in payment, the women of Ravenwood were devoted to her. Lady Ragna didn't think of the Dark Lady as inferior to the Light. But what if she was? Where did that leave House Ravenwood?

She turned around and shook her head. She needed to correct this. She *would* correct this. "It's not too late. The rest of the houses are not united, not yet. And I will be sure to keep it that way today when I meet with them. And I will begin training a new dreamkiller. Amara will be coming into her power any day now."

The priest nodded. "Time is still on your side, Lady Ragna. You can stop the threat to your house. But it will cost you the life of your firstborn daughter."

Lady Ragna clenched her jaw. "That house traitor is no daughter of mine. Selene is dead to me now. I will train Amara to take over for her sister, then I will send her after House Maris." She looked at the mountains outside her window and raised her fist. "Mark my words: House Ravenwood will not fall. We will fight, and in the end, we will win."

Morgan L. Busse is a writer by day and a mother by night. She is the author of the FOLLOWER OF THE WORD series and the steampunk series THE SOUL CHRONICLES. She is a Christy and INSPY Award finalist and won the Carol Award in 2018 for best in Christian speculative fiction. During her spare time she enjoys playing games, taking long walks, and dreaming about her next novel. Visit her online at www.morganlbusse.com.

Sign Up for Morgan's Newsletter!

Keep up to date with Morgan's news on book releases, signings, and other events by signing up for her email list at morganlbusse.com.

You May Also Enjoy ...

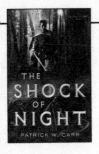

Reeve Willet Dura is called to investigate when a brutal attack leaves one man dead and a priest mortally wounded. As he begins questioning the priest, the man pulls him close, cries out in a foreign tongue—and dies. This strange encounter sets off a series of events that pull Willet into an epic conflict that threatens his entire world.

THE DARKWATER SAGA: *The Shock of Night, The Shattered Vigil, The Wounded Shadow* by Patrick W. Carr, patrickwcarr.com

You May Also Like. . .

Lady Shona, the newly crowned queen of the realm, is a leader without a throne. Pursued relentlessly by a dark force, she must make a difficult choice—flee or fight. But there is one shred of hope for Lady Shona and the realm, and it comes in the most unlikely of forms. A young orphan, untested and untrained, could well mean the difference between victory and total defeat.

The Golden Vial by Thomas Locke
LEGENDS OF THE REALM
tlocke.com

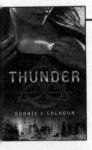

After she captures a Lander on the eve of her 18th Born Remembrance, Selah Chavez is forced to leave her family as she changes from bounty hunter to the one everyone is hunting.

Thunder by Bonnie S. Calhoun
STONE BRAIDE CHRONICLES #1
bonniescalhoun.com

King Echad believes the disasters plaguing their land signal impending doom, but Prince Wilek thinks this is superstitious nonsense—until he is sent to investigate a fresh calamity. What he discovers is more cataclysmic than he could've imagined. Wilek sets out on a desperate quest to save his people, but can he succeed before the entire land crumbles?

King's Folly by Jill Williamson
THE KINSMAN CHRONICLES #1
jillwilliamson.com

BETHANYHOUSE

You May Also Like ...